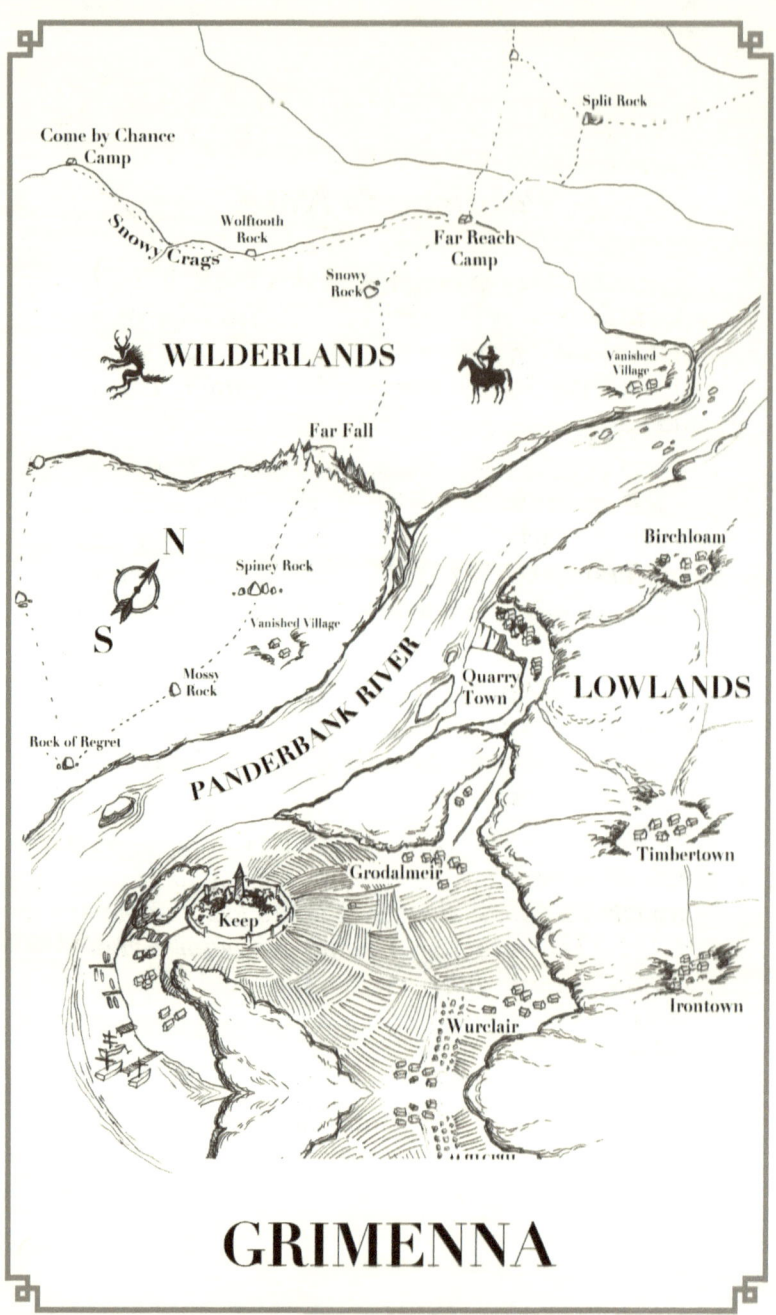

GRIMENNA

Grimenna

N. K. Blazevic

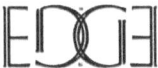

EDGE SCIENCE FICTION AND FANTASY PUBLISHING
An Imprint of HADES PUBLICATIONS, INC.
CALGARY

Grimenna

Copyright © 2018 by N. K. Blazevic

EDGE SCIENCE FICTION AND FANTASY PUBLISHING
An Imprint of HADES PUBLICATIONS, INC.
P.O. Box 1714, Calgary, Alberta, T2P 2L7, Canada

The EDGE Team:
Producer: Brian Hades
Acquisitions Editor: Ella Beaumont
Edited by: Leigha A. Smith
Cover Design: Ella Beaumont
Book Design: Mark Steele
Publicist: Janice Shoults

ISBN: 978-1-77053-170-3

EDGE Science Fiction and Fantasy Publishing and Hades Publications, Inc. acknowledges the ongoing support of the Alberta Foundation for the Arts and the Canada Council for the Arts for our publishing programme.

Library and Archives Canada Cataloguing in Publication
CIP Data on file with the National Library of Canada
ISBN: 978-1-77053-170-3
(e-Book ISBN: 978-1-77053-169-7)

FIRST EDITION
(20180321)
Printed in USA
www.edgewebsite.com

Dedication

For Tatiana

Prologue

There was once a virgin forest to the north, shrouding the ragged peaks of mountain ridges and misty hollows in endless miles of trees. It had lain in stillness, untouched by man, since the first flux of life began on this earth. Slowly men did come creeping, exploring its fertile bounties, claiming land, charting and mapping its depths. They found it empty of inhabitants except for its wild and naive creatures who had never before seen men. Man was quick to claim it, quick to plunder the trees and build homes for himself and give names to the rivers that flowed with clean water and schools of fish. The King of the southern lands set his crown upon it and because the forest had the whims and the mood of a woman, he named it Grimenna. He sent pilgrims to settle it and they brought with them their tools, their strong backs, and their horses to cleave a path for themselves and begin a new life.

When their tools and their backs were broken, when the King became distant to their suffering, the only things the settlers had left were their own prayers to guide them. When even their God did not hear their prayers and the great forest threatened to consume their lives, they turned their prayers to the forest itself. Through starvation, disease, wolves and the bitterness of cold winter, they prayed to the forest to relent. As the years passed, it became common for men to offer their thanks to the forest instead of their God. For when man had no control beyond his own means, what was there left but to hope and to pray to the forest on which his life depended?

That was how the first spirits were created. Man gave each of his prayers its own personhood, made them beings as elemental and primal as the forest itself. Man gave a face to fear, a face to hope. There were age-old stories of a man in the woods, a spirit, who would watch over those that were lost and suffering. There were myths and legends of a hideous woman who lived in the trees and swooped on the wings of an owl, the bringer of ill luck and death and ruin for the wicked, used to scare children and warn men who were cruel to others. It happened somehow through collective thought that the spirits made by man settled into the likenesses of these myths. The great forest mysteriously conjured them into physical forms, and through the spirits was channeled all that was good and evil of the human heart.

Over time, the forest changed. Mountains crumbled stone by stone, trees were felled and hills were cleared. Man became comfortable in the forest as his numbers grew and it came to pass that he forgot the old stories that had guided him. The spirits he made were shunned and forgotten as man's beliefs turned back to a God that promised heaven on earth. He neglected to give his thanks to the forest and the spirits lost their hold in the hearts of their believers, losing their purpose, their identities. Yet they did not vanish and disappear as memories do. They did not cease to exist. Only those who came from the old blood of the first people of Grimenna remembered, but even they were ignored when they cried out their warnings. Nobody listened. Nobody cared. Man thought he had tamed Grimenna at last.

But villages began vanishing. Hellish creatures rose from the earth and drove men from their homes. Some called them demons, while others called them the Folka, angry creatures of the old spirits. Fear restored itself in the hearts of man — fear of the unknown, fear of forces greater than himself against which he was helpless.

Instead of being humbled, man became hateful.

Chapter 1

Ramsi Lier was the most handsome young man Paiva had
ever seen. His hair was perfectly curled, deep brown with
auburn highlights, and it framed his youthful and spectacu-
larly carved face. Every rise and fall of knitted bone beneath
his soft skin gave him the perfectly molded look of what
might be pictured in the mind's eye of a hero in any fable.
It was his eyes above all that caught her — a hazel coloring
that reflected only warmth and steadiness. Wearing the deep
wine-red tunic of a ranger, he dressed in finer clothes than
most young men because he was the Warden's son. He rode
a roan charger, the same deep russet brown as his own hair,
marked by a spray of flea-bit white on its rump. The horse
was a stunning beast, with heavy iron hooves and polished
mane. Yes, Ramsi was the most handsome man Paiva had
ever seen.

She watched him ride down the laneway of her little
village, Birchloam, named so for the thick cropping of birch
that surrounded the pastures. He sat in his seat, absorbing
the momentum of each striking hoof, as if he were but an
extension of the horse itself. Behind him followed the other
rangers, each dressed in their own red tunics clasped in
brass brooches over their shoulders. Some had bows across
their backs, others held spears, while Ramsi carried a gilded
sword at his hip. He led the procession down the laneway to
the Wardens Quarters in the heart of the village, next to the
market, trades guilds, and lawyers. Paiva stepped aside to let
them pass, hoping he would look her way.

He did, turning his tousled head towards her and smiling
winsomely. She smiled in return as he called her name.

"Will you be out for Mummers-eve?" he called, his white teeth flashing.

"I will," she replied. "And is the forest safe for gathering tonight?"

"It is," he said. "It is time for us to set aside our horses and our swords and find a dancing partner." She felt her face grow hot, felt her toes curl in her shoes.

"I will be in the square as soon as my chores are done," she called.

"Then I will see you there. If you can recognize me."

The next step she took seemed jolted full of energy. She felt like skipping the rest of the way home but restrained herself, for in the crook of her arm she carried a basket wherein a precious item was safely stowed in a scrap of wool cloth. She had spent all afternoon in the market square sorting through the wares in the apothecary shop run by an old woman named Mama Hexava. She offered an array of intriguing clay masks to wear for Mummers-eve, each finely made and painted by the dark haired and quiet woman who was Hexava's apprentice. The shop had been full for nearly two days as people prepared for the festival, searching for an unusual face to hide behind on the coming night. Paiva had chosen hers through careful deliberation, placing it in her basket with the utmost care, then had gone out to help other young maids braid garlands of fresh spring flowers to string with ribbons across every post in the village square. She was filled with excitement, and as the sun waned in the sky she knew it was time for her to be getting home to prepare her own costume. She was only too happy to have encountered Ramsi coming back from the woods along the way.

She hurried along the dirt road to the farm nestled in a pasture at the edge of the village and hurried inside the timber house that was her home. Her mother, Kess Ibbie, stood over the fire simmering a stew of fresh spring herbs and mutton. Her father was nowhere to be seen and she presumed he was out in the fields yet tending to the last of his lambs. She placed the baskets atop the table before the hearth where they ate and did most of their work, and then threw her wool cloak over the wood pile to warm.

"Warden Lier's son says he'll see me at the dance tonight," she said to Kess cheekily. She was expecting her mother to say something smart, perhaps rebound with a comment or two, but she said nothing. She stirred the soup and simply acknowledged Paiva with a nod.

"He said it in front of all the rangers when they came riding back from the woods, I saw them in the laneway," Paiva said. She felt her exhilaration drain. Her mother was distant, lost in a worried thought over her soup.

"Mother?" she asked, frustrated her zeal was not shared.

"Yes, Warden Lier's son is very fetching," Kess replied. "Did you finally decide on your costume? You've been gone for some time."

"I have, and what is the matter with you?"

"Nothing, nothing." She smoothed her graying hair back and dusted off her apron, then turned to Paiva and her basket. "Perhaps you should stay in tonight."

"Not a chance. Did you not just hear me?"

"Yes, I suppose." She turned back to her soup, not caring to look at the mask in the basket. "Did you help with the decorations?"

"Yes. Where is Father?" she asked, thinking to find him instead to restore her spirits. It was Kess' yearly routine to be unnerved on Mummers-eve — the rest of the year floated by with ease until spring came and her mother began muttering things about spirits and the coming season under her breath.

"He went up to the woods — brought the last of the offerings up to the altar," Kess replied. That was how it was in the far-off village of Birchloam: Where peasants in any other village gave thanks to the holy God of the new era, those of Birchloam suffered a double faith, giving thanks both to the God they swore their lives to, and to the spirits they feared in the forest that surrounded them for miles. They belonged to the most remote, most northern settlement of the land, the lower villages more easily connected to the Keep of Lord Pratermora, who oversaw them all. When men were afraid of wild spirits in the lower villages, Pratemora sent armed men. When the people of Birchloam were afraid, they gave bread, wine, and other offerings into the trees to try and appease the whims of these beings. Lying in the shadows of the hills of the great forest Grimenna left most men humble and afraid of the powers that be, of the powers that were ungodly and misunderstood.

Paiva's father, Viviel, was the greatest believer in the mysteries of the forest. Some in the village supported his beliefs, joining him in laying out offerings and listening to his peculiar wisdom. People who didn't know him could have easily accused him of witchcraft, but everyone who was familiar with him loved him for his warmth of character and kind disposition. He was easily the unspoken village chief, the one they turned to for hope and direction when there were problems within the village. He had more than once helped a neighbor pay his tiff, more than once settled an argument between friends, and always offered food and drinks to anyone who walked in through his door.

"Pray the good spirits are watching over me tonight," Paiva remarked, ignoring her mother's somber mood. She was about to race out into the yard to fetch her father when he came through the back door, almost blundering into her.

"Father!" she exclaimed. "Warden Lier's son said he'd see me tonight."

Her father smiled, spreading deep lines in his weathered face about his eyes. His brown beard was littered with hay and his hat was damp around the brow despite the chill of late spring. His eyes, a strange golden brown, lifted to hers.

"You're not still going on about him, are you?" he asked, brushing passed her into the house.

"He is the singularly most beautiful and brave man I have ever laid eyes on."

"I'd always hoped you'd fall for a sheepherder or a field boy. The dowry would have been much more manageable," Viviel teased.

"Don't set your hopes too high," Kess warned with pursed lips. "Often when one expects something so greatly the disappointment of not having it is very bitter."

"Go on, get dressed," Viviel said. "Your mother's worrying again. That is what mothers do." He brushed his hand across Kess' back soothingly and smiled.

"It is Mummers-eve, Viviel," she said, looking worriedly into his eyes.

"And she'll be in disguise. She'll be with the warden's son." He kissed her temple. "And in a circle of friends. She'll be fine."

Paiva laughed and dashed up to the loft where she slept and kept her assortment of things.

"Will you not go with her?" she asked.

"No, I will stay in," said Viviel. "I've an ewe that won't take her lamb and the poor thing's half dead. I'll see if I can find a bottle and get her milk into the wee beast before the sun comes tomorrow, or the poor creature will be lost. The woods are quiet, my love, they stir only with the life of a new spring. The altar has never been so full with offerings. I fear not for our future."

Kess smiled wanly, soothed by his presence. "I will not try to change your mind then," she conceded. "Of all people you know these things better then I."

— «» —

"Do not take your mask off," Kess warned. "You may let them guess who you are but do not reveal yourself. That is the trick to Mummers-eve. Not even if Warden Lier's son wants to kiss you all over your face, he can wait until the next day when he's not half as drunk."

"What is the point of even going then?" Paiva complained.

"To trick and confuse evil spirits who may wish to find out who you are."

Paiva rolled her eyes and put her mask to her face, tying it securely behind her head. She was pleased with her costume, having made it herself with any available material she could get her hands on. She wore her wool cloak, over which she laid a pattern of young aspen leaves she had woven into a shawl. They were wilted now, giving her the air of a green lion with a tired mane. Atop her head was an intricately woven laurel of feathers and leaves she had stolen from her mother's garden. She had been collecting feathers for some time — most scavenged from the chickens in the barn — and had taken her time in placing them. Most others in the village would do the same, only the more well off would buy materials and have more intricate costumes made.

"Promise me!" Kess hissed.

"I promise I will not remove my mask, even if the Lord himself or a Prince from the South should arrive in Birchloam and wish to kiss me."

"The Lord is an old man." Her mother's nose turned up in disgust. "There are other old men in disguise tonight, and spirits, and possibly men from beyond the Panderbank. If you dance with anyone, make sure their right hand doesn't have a brand on it. If they do, make sure you alert the Warden at once."

"Really, Mother, you might as well come with me."

"I never have and I never will. I trust you, just heed my warnings. Your father will come to fetch you at midnight. Don't leave before, and don't leave the crowd."

"I won't."

"Remember the old stories, of the Strix in the woods who punishes children for misbehaving. Tonight is the night she is out and looking for wicked children to take for herself."

"I am not a child," she groaned. "Good night."

Viviel was leaning on his shepherd's staff by the front door, waiting for her. A warm smile spread across her face as she skipped towards him.

"You make a very fine Mummer Paiva. Who are you supposed to be?" He swung the door open before her. Her mother followed close behind and handed Viviel a lantern.

"I am a spirit of the meadows," said Paiva. "One who watches over stray lambs and keeps wolves at bay."

"That indeed you are," he chuckled. They headed out into the yard as her mother bid her good luck. Paiva hoped it was given in regard to the warden's son.

Her father's brown dog slunk out of the yard and trotted close on their heels, following them down the laneway to the heart of the village. As they passed the neighboring farms and drew closer, Paiva saw the spark-filled column of smoke rising from the bonfire in the village square. Her heart leapt as she saw figures dance and heard music lift high above the slanted rooftops.

"Look at all the Mummers," she exclaimed at the disguised revelers. "Look at the costumes!"

"How are you sure some of them are costumes?" he teased. "I'll be waiting for you at the baker's shop by midnight. You had better not have too much wine and forget." As they joined the Mummers, Paiva gazed around in awe. There were faces flickering through the bonfire light about her — shaggy shapes covered in furs and feathers and leaves. She thought it could very well be that there were spirits walking amongst them that night, unnoticed in the multitude of creature costumes, laughing and dancing and drinking about her.

"Mr. Ibbie!" a tall man in a beaked mask called out. The man was dressed in a brown linen cloak, and when he raised a tankard of ale in greeting, long strands of cloth mimicking feathers fell from his elbows to the ground. She recognized the voice and the costume as those belonging to Wernard Weeler, the miller who her father was great friends with. He wore the same disguise every year, and his red beard stuck out defiantly from below his mask.

He offered Viviel a drink and they fell into talk, laughing and enjoying the spectacle before them. There were musicians gathered on a stage piled with sprigs of flowers and ribbons: a wolf with antlers played the fiddle, a goat with wings kept rhythm on a heavy skin drum, and an ox with a crown of woven barley wailed on a set of pipes. There were figures about the fire dancing in pairs and by themselves. Wine and ale ran freely from barrels propped against the musician's stage and there were lanterns and lights glowing from every post and hanging from the garlands of flowers.

There were candles behind the windows of houses that invited Mummers in for drinks and jokes; those that were unwelcoming were dark. There were packs of Mummers that gathered and went from house to house, drinking freely until their identities were uncovered and they were thrown out to move on to the next house or return to the fire for dancing. The air was rich with laughter and music, and shrill delighted screams rang out when someone was spooked or tricked.

Paiva's father finished his drink and saw Paiva off with the miller's daughter, Rorna. Rorna simply had an old sack of flour stuck over her head with slits cut out for eye holes and hay stuffed out the bottom of it and from her coat sleeves. She had on her father's old straw hat and wore his britches which were too long for her and held up by lengths of rope over her shoulders. Paiva laughed at her costume, and Rorna explained the delights of wearing men's clothes.

The first house they visited belonged to Mr. and Mrs. Switch who brewed ale and were both muscular and strapping from hauling barrels. Mrs. Switch was middle-aged, her forearms the same size as her bearded husband's. They both called each other Switch because they were inseparable and often when they drank too much ale they couldn't remember the others real name anyways. Mrs. Switch studied the two visitors as she poured them each a mug of their own spiced brew.

"The only thing I can see of who's hiding under them costumes is a pair of green eyes and a pair of brown," she

mused. "Must be a pair of sweethearts eh, Switch?" She laughed to her husband. Rorna thrust out her straw stuffed chest and swaggered over to Mrs. Switch where she promptly sat on her knee and began trailing a finger over the woman's whiskered chin. Mrs. Switch threw back her head and bellowed a hearty laugh while her husband watched worriedly.

"Been a long time since I had a young lad sit on my knee," she laughed, then with a thick hand reached up and pulled off the flour sack, revealing Rorna's smiling face and the tumble of her curling russet hair. Both Mr. and Mrs. Switch boomed in laughter.

"Why it's Rorna Weeler!' Mr. Switch thumped his fist on the table. Paiva lifted the bottom of her mask to take a swig of the delicious ale, and Mr. Switch narrowed his eyes and tilted his head to try and glimpse the shape of her face.

"By my soul, that one is none other than Paiva Ibbie!" he bellowed. Paiva nodded happily and watched as Mrs. Switch levered Rorna over her shoulder and carried her out the house. She set her on the front steps, then grabbed her broom and chased them both off with it.

"Ha!' she bellowed, "Haven't been fooled by a Mummer yet." Paiva and Rorna laughed as they ran on to the next house. In each house they visited they were given a drink of wine while the patron studied them and either laughed or marveled at their costumes.

— «» —

Mrs. Switch headed back indoors, shaking her head in mirth, to sit back down at their table to await the next visitors. She left the door wide open and readied another brew to serve. Mr. Switch heartily threw back his head and downed the rest of his drink. Upon lowering his mug he startled at a figure that appeared suddenly in the doorway and nearly spat out his swallow of ale.

He wiped the spittle from his mouth and offered the stranger a seat at the table. "Halloo Mummer," Mrs. Switch regaled and came to sit down again. She peered at the Mummer and tried to discern who might be hiding beneath the costume. It was a man, she knew, for he was tall and broad in the shoulder. He remained for a moment, unmoving in the doorway, staring at them from beneath his strange mask. Mrs. Switch beckoned him to sit down again and silently he stepped closer.

Without warning a chill swept over her. He was dressed in pale white robes and beneath he wore fine clothes, finer than any peasant could ever afford. The mask he wore resembled a ghoulish creature that might have been half-cat and half-owl, and it was covered in such perfectly placed tiny feathers and hairs that Mrs. Switch had to blink again and marvel at its craftsmanship. There was a mane of white hair about it, covering his neck and running down his back where it began to mix with pale feathers. It was the eyes that chilled her, for they were dark as coals. The Mummer sat but didn't touch his drink, staring at them while they silently absorbed him and tried to discern his identity.

"Show us your hands," Mr. Switch said testily. The Mummer cocked his head curiously at them, then raised both his pale hands palm up. Both his palms were smooth and unmarked and Mrs. Switch smiled to know he was not branded. She began listing names quickly to distract him from being offended, thinking only of the rich merchants she knew, for no one else would be able to afford such a costume. The Mummer shook his head at each one, his eyes never wavering.

Their session was cut short when more Mummers appeared at the door. The white Mummer rose and Mrs. Switch was almost sure his mask was smiling at them.

"I don't have a clue," she said, readily hoping he would soon be gone. The other Mummers stepped out of his way as he passed and left the dwelling to head out into the square.

Mrs. Switch looked to Mr. Switch, who absently touched his forehead to ward off ill luck. She broke into another wild cackle and poured ale for the new visitors, ushering them in to rid the room of the chill the stranger had left behind him.

— ⟨⟩ —

A few houses in and both Paiva and Rorna were tipsy and flushed from the wine. Paiva did not care for Mummering; she wanted to search the crowd by the fire for Ramsi. She excused herself, saying she wanted to dance, and returned to the bonfire while Rorna careened off with other Mummers to visit the next house.

She knew it was him by his boots. She had memorized every facet of his person, down to the polished fine leather and silver spurs on his heels. He strode towards her from across the fire and she saw his dark eyes glitter beneath his fox faced mask. When he was before her, he tilted his head curiously.

"Is it you?" he asked, his breath sweet with wine. She bent her head back up to him and let him study her. He lifted his hands and pushed his fingers into her hair, gently searching for the string to undo her disguise. She stiffened as she felt the ribbon let go, only for a second remembering she had promised her mother not to take her mask off. But then the warmth of him so near sent her heart beating deafeningly into her ears, drowning out all distant echoes of her mother's warning.

"Is it you?" he asked again. He lifted the mask from her face.

"Oh, Paiva!" she heard him laugh behind his fox face. He looked down at the mask in his hands. "And who are you supposed to be?"

"A spirit of the meadows," she said. Her voice seemed small in her throat, for she realized then that he had been hoping it was someone else. She took her mask back from him and tied it back around her head.

Someone came up to him and slid their hand in his. It was a woman clearly, for she wore a pale dress fitted tightly with a bodice stitched with feathers. Her face was disguised behind that of a feminine cat mask, sequins caught the firelight and glowed beneath the eye hollows. Paiva felt herself sneering behind her own mask, recognizing the flow of darkly curled hair that tumbled down to the woman's waist. It was Miriel, a lawyer's daughter who lived in a stone house in the middle of the village. She looked at Paiva through the eyeholes of her expensive mask, gave out a sharp laugh, and pulled Ramsi away to the fire where he took her in his arms and led her into a dance.

Paiva swallowed a bitter taste in her mouth and watched, suddenly realizing how pitiful her hopes had been. She watched them circle the fire, watched how perfectly they molded to each other, the way she clung so close to him. When the music waned and the song finished, she hoped they would separate, that he would return for her. She waited; she did not move from her spot.

He did not once glance her way.

Chapter 2

Paiva had seen enough. Her heart felt low and aching in her chest. She turned into the laneway and headed home, not minding the music and laughter that echoed behind her. She drew the mask from her face and let it fall to the ground where it shattered, echoing the effect of the wasted pains she had taken to prepare for the night. She had had enough wine to encourage her temper and she let it sear through her veins heatedly. Angrily she headed home, marching as fast as she could.

She had made a good distance down the lane when a laughing voice called out her name behind her. She froze, then spun around. Ramsi's slim figure trotted up after her. His fox mask grinned at her in the lamp light.

"Are you off so early?" he called.

"I am tired. I had too much sweet wine," she said. "Good night, Ramsi. Miriel would not like for you to keep her waiting."

"Miriel can wait," he said catching up to her. "I have to admit, that was a rather cruel trick of mine. But it is Mummers-eve. It is a night for tricks."

"What trick?"

"May I walk you home? I do think your father will be upset for you walking alone in the dark on Mummers-eve," he said. She stared at him, at his eyes black behind his mask. She could not help the small smile that crept over her face. She turned back up the lane and he followed, reaching out a hand to grasp hers. She felt a thrill race through her, even though his hands were as freezing cold as the night air away from the bonfire.

"What trick?" she asked again.

"I wanted to see if I could make you jealous," he said. "I think I did." She felt her cheeks burn.

"I wasn't jealous," she spluttered.

"I think you are."

She blushed further and looked at her feet to keep from stumbling. They walked on until the little lights in her house grew brighter at the edge of the pasture. There were candles lit in the windows to invite in costumed visitors. Her house was well out of everyone's way; they hardly ever received any visits, Mummers-eve or not. There was no reason to visit the Ibbie farm at the edge of town.

His silver spurs clicked against stones in the road. Her breath came out in white clouds before her in the chilled spring air. The moon hung low and swollen in the sky, casting the land in a ghostly glow. She could hear the music and roar of laughter fading behind her.

She saw Ramsi lift his hand to his face and remove his mask, tucking it inside his tunic. His skin was pale in the moonlight, his handsome face otherworldly. He stopped all of a sudden, and she stopped alongside him while he canted his head back to look at the sky.

"What an eerie night," he said. She hoped there was only one reason he had taken his mask off. She imagined in that moment his head bending to hers and his lips softly moving against her own. He stared at the sky a moment longer, his cold hand making hers just as cold, then he faced forward and continued on walking.

"How mad would your father be if perhaps we went to walk a little bit longer, say up past the pasture, perhaps to the altar?" he asked.

"He would be mad," she said, "if he found out. But he won't." She saw his lips curve in a smile.

"Would be great fun to spook some spirits stealing bread, no?" he said, smiling back at her. His eyes were very dark, the hazel brown obscured in shadow.

"They don't eat bread," she said. "It's the gesture, the power of our thoughts and our prayers they eat."

"Is that what your father says?"

"Yes, it is."

They skirted a stone fence and went out through the pasture, keeping well away from her father's dog that was always quick to raise an alarm. He pulled her along after him, his long fingers clasped against her own while her heart thrummed in sweet contentment. She was afraid, but she put her trust in Ramsi, who she knew had gone deep into the forest before. She would have followed him anywhere in that moment. He was a ranger, so he was used to the creatures that lurked in the shadows and he had more than once defended himself. At least he had in the stories he told.

They slid into the woods as quiet as wraiths. The moonbeams filtered through the trees as she followed him up to the stone altar. She heard footfalls break through the forest: an animal startled off by their presence. She jumped and he chuckled, wrapping his hand tighter over hers.

"A wolf perhaps," he murmured.

"I hope you have a dagger."

"I have no dagger."

"You should not go into the woods unarmed. It is foolish."

"You do not trust me?" he asked.

"It is not you I do not trust, it is the woods."

Again he chuckled. His freezing hand remained on hers. She looked at him in the dim light, wondering if her eyes were deceiving her. His skin seemed so pale, his hair too gray. She drew a little away from him, suddenly overcome by a sense of unease.

"Why are we here?" she asked. He looked at her for a long moment, his face expressionless. Even in that moment her vision seemed to again play tricks on her. His eyes seemed hollowed, overcome with sinister shadows.

"Ramsi?" she asked again. "Why are we here?"

"Because I tricked you." His strange face drooped. She took a step back, pulling her hand away as a gasp caught in her throat. His features seemed to distort, like a ripple in molten glass. The color of his hair and his clothes drained and became as bleached and as cold as the moonlight. He turned away as this change occurred, and she gazed in numb horror.

"Who are you?" she demanded, her voice quavering with fear and with cold. He ignored her; he seemed intent on peering into the trees and cocking his deformed head as if listening for a faraway noise.

"There is someone else here," he said curiously. He swiveled his head as he listened, and in the slanted moonbeam she saw a face that could not have possibly been human. The mouth was stretched across a glitter of fangs, the eyes were deep pits of black. Its hair had changed into a mane of white bristles and feathers. It should have been a man, for it wore pale robes that floated to the ground like a shroud, but it wasn't. It stepped forward, its footstep landing with a dull click. She realized with horror there were no longer silver spurs, but jagged talons on birdlike feet. In her memory a face stood out to her that had floated across the pages of her father's books. She sucked in her breath as the horrible realization dawned on her, and from the bottom of her lungs, she let loose a scream that shattered the night.

She stumbled back, shock turning her blood to ice that froze her limbs. She hit the ground hard and then scrambled for her feet as the instinct to run overtook any other thought. She heard from behind her a rustle of feather and dead leaves. She felt claws pierce through her cloak dangerously close to her skin and the creature dragged her back. She screamed again, this time in lament for her utter foolishness. The breath was crushed from her, changing her scream into a strangled sob. Her hands sought purchase in the earth and in roots, desperately fighting to pull herself away. She felt coarse feathers brush her cheeks and then she heard a strange sound.

A swift hiss, followed by a wet thud. The creature tumbled to its side, releasing her from its grip. It writhed on the ground in a tangle of feathers and its shroud-like robe. She struggled to regain her feet, too weakened from the blow to stand. She managed to haul herself to a sheltering tree where she hid from her assailant and strained for breath. The creature tore at its throat; its features twisted in a strange silent pain, an arrow protruding from its neck. Her first thought was that the rangers had heard her scream, but then it would have been impossible for them to arrive so fast. She darted a look through the shadowed woods, searching for some sign of help. Another arrow hissed from the depths of the trees and thudded into the white monster's back. This time the beast let go a low wail, a mixture of pain and of anger. Whatever it was she saw before her, she had the satisfaction of knowing it felt pain.

It staggered to its feet and heaved itself wretchedly towards the tree she hid behind. Before she could react, a black shape hurtled out of the trees. There was a flash of a silver blade before it collided into the creature, and the two figures rolled to the ground in a blend of black and white. The immediate hope that surfaced in Paiva's heart was that the black shape was one of the good spirits her father prayed to, and that somehow before her there was a convening of both good and evil here on the forest floor. However she realized it wasn't so; the figure was no more than a man, quickly succumbing to his opponent's strength.

The white spirit sunk its claws into the man's back and, with a howl, threw him away as if he were no more than a ragged scarecrow. The spirit regained its feet and reached a claw to pull the arrow from its neck with a sickening wrench. It tossed the shaft to the ground as its black eyes landed on the shadowed man, and it started forward, claws curling. The man shakily raised himself on all fours. Paiva heard him gasp for winded breath. He scrambled away but the creature descended on him and Paiva cried out to him foolishly, alerting them both to her presence.

The creature snapped his eyes up and perceived her in the shadows, then started towards her. Suddenly another man appeared. Smaller and not quite as wiry as the first, he leapt into the path of the white spirit, distracting it as the first figure crawled into the shelter of the trees. Then there was yet another man, and in the cold moonlight she realized he was garbed in thick furs, a bow raised before him, carefully aiming at the white creature that snarled and fought to rid itself of the second attacker. The spirit tossed its opponent aside yet again, its wisps of robes molting into feathers, changing and taking shape into arched wings.

Another arrow flew, tearing feathers loose and sending them spinning into the air. As the spirit turned to Paiva again she bolted from her hiding spot, making for the meadow below on unsteady legs. The spirit launched itself after her on the span of its white wings. The man who had crawled away appeared out of nowhere and threw himself over her, tumbling them inches out of reach of the spirit's claws. The beast narrowly missed them, thrown off course as arrow after arrow struck it, ripping through its wings and back. It crashed into the underbrush with a grating howl and thrashed violently to regain its feet. Finally it hissed wetly and raised its head to the sky, lurching upwards with a billow of air, searching for escape; then it careened overhead and soared away, resembling no more than an owl on its evening hunt.

Paiva stared up at the empty sky with her heart in her throat, waiting for the creature to return, but it never did. The man who had shielded her gently released his hold and staggered to his feet with a pained grunt. She heard his footsteps move away, back to the others, and for a long moment she lay still, her mind reeling. She heard muffled voices and the snort of a horse. Delicately she sat up, still staring up to the sky in fear of a white shape returning.

When she lowered her eyes to the forest there was a black figure standing in the shadows not far across from her. It was the bowman, and though his face was hidden beneath a cowl, she knew he was studying her. Not far behind him were the other two. One was crouched to the ground while the other leaned over him and touched at his shoulders.

She rose shakily to her feet.

"Who are you?" came the rumbling voice of the bowman.

Her knees shook beneath her, her hands trembled at her sides. "Paiva Ibbie," she said hoarsely, swallowing the residual acid taste of fear. "I'm from the farm down below. Who are you?"

He was silent, studying her. He cocked his head back to the other two questioningly and she saw that he had a great beard beneath his cowl.

"Go get the horse, Jorn," the one leaning over the stooped man said wearily. The bowman moved away, padding silently into the trees.

"What was that thing?" Paiva asked in shock.

"A dark spirit," the first man said. "We call him Varloga."

The man on the ground groaned. Paiva realized he was wounded.

"I'm alright," he grunted. "I can stand now. Go see to the girl."

The first man moved towards her, coming to stand barely an arm's length away.

"Who are you?" she asked again, feeling herself shift away from him. His face was obscured in shadow beneath his hood, yet she felt his eyes on her and it made her nervous. There was an intensity to him, an edge. In the dark she could not tell his age, could not discern his intent towards her.

"Are you hurt?" he asked instead, avoiding her question. She took another step away from him, overwhelmed by his shadowy shape.

"I'm not hurt," she said defensively.

The bowman returned with a small pack horse and realization dawned on her when she saw the bulging satchels and packs strapped to its back. She noted the distinctive clinking of wine bottles and jugs.

"You were looting the altar," she said accusingly, turning her eyes on the man before her. She felt him bristle. "I'm sorry," she added, correcting her tone, realizing abruptly that they were in fact her saviors. "It is yours. Take what you need."

"Come along, we'll see you home," the man said, brushing roughly past her. Bewildered, she followed after as the others pressed in behind her.

They followed the stone fence down through the pasture to the back of the barn where a dim light glowed from within. As they drew close she heard the bay of her father's dog, and a second later its shadowy shape leapt from the barn door, followed by the silhouette of her father clutching a lamp and his shepherd's staff. He stared blindly out into the night as the dog bounded towards them.

The three men stopped in their tracks but Paiva broke away and ran as swiftly as she could towards her father's tense shape. As he saw her coming he let out a curse. He closed the ground between them and threw his arms around her as she thudded into his chest. She wept into the warmth of his deep chest, soaking his shirt with hot tears.

"What is the matter?" Viviel croaked, his voice shaking as she trembled in his arms. "What has happened?" The dog snarled and howled in the shadows and Viviel raised the lantern higher. "Who is there? What sort of trick is this?"

"There are three men back there," Paiva rambled. "They saw me safely home from the woods. I saw a most terrible creature, a white monster, half-man and half-owl."

"We'll find out in the morning who it is that put up this wretched trick. Go on in now and see your mother."

"No, he was real. They said it was Varloga."

Her father froze, his body going rigid. His eyes glowed with golden lantern light as they roved across her face with urgency. He blinked, then he pushed her behind him and strode forwards into the night towards the barking dog.

"Who goes there?" he called. As the glow of the lamp crept towards the three figures they shied back and her father clutched his staff all the firmer. "I said who goes there?" he called again, coming to a stop and planting his feet firmly in the ground. The dog raced back to him and stood between his master and the strangers, baring his fangs defensively. "If you are good souls and mean us no harm you are welcome here. Come forward, let me see you. It is unnerving talking to shadows."

The man who had led them down from the woods took a hesitant step forward into the ring of light. He was a young man, tall, with a dirty mess of black hair hanging about his hooded face. He stood stooped beneath his tattered cloak and drew his eyes up to Viviel's.

"We mean no harm," he said solemnly.

Her father tucked his staff beneath his arm and boldly strode up to the man and extended his hand in greeting. The stranger dropped his eyes to it and hesitated. Slowly, he extended his own hand. Viviel shook it, and then didn't let it go. He peered closely into the man's face.

"Ah," he said. He took the man's hand and turned it over to reveal his palm to the lantern light where he found a brand of riddled, burnt skin in the meat of the thumb.

"So," Viviel said. "You are a Wilderman."

Chapter 3

Wildermen were convicted criminals who had chosen to die in the woods instead of rotting in a prison or having their necks stretched in the gallows. They were branded, which made shaking hands, exchanging money, or even waving hello impossible and dangerous for them to do if they were ever to venture into the lowlands. They were called Wildermen because they were thrown into the Wilderlands beyond the great Panderbank River that separated the highlands from the lowlands of Grimenna. The Wilderlands are dangerous, consisting of untamed, undefiled forest. The advantage of choosing to die in the woods is that a man could have a chance at earning a pardon — a pardon that could be earned by severing the head of a creature like Varloga and bringing it back to the Lord Pratermora who ruled the land. The Lord was said to highly prize these heads; he mounted them in his trophy room at the top of his keep.

Paiva remembered well the day the Warden of Birchloam had caught a Wilderman trespassing. He had been caught stealing eggs, and to look at him you'd have seen why, for he was no more than skin and bones beneath layers of rotting animal hides and dirt. The rangers tied him in the village square while the Warden found his ledger and read it aloud for all to hear. Cowardice had been his crime, and for cowardice they had burned his hand and thrown him into the Wilderlands. Sometimes outcasts came back, searching for food or loved ones. If they were not drowned by the River they were caught by the rangers, as this man was, for it was his hunger that made him desperate. He simply hung his head in shame when caught and did not even try to avoid the stones the mob began to throw at him. It didn't take more than a few glancing blows — he was dead before the Warden had time to finish reading his ledger.

— «» —

Viviel boldly faced the three strangers, seemingly unalarmed. His voice when he spoke to them was even and strong, neither threatening nor friendly. The black-haired stranger took his hand away and stepped back towards the others. Paiva felt her nerves snapping as she watched her father for a reaction.

"I must give thanks then," Viviel said, "to the great forest for sending you our way this night. I cannot fault you for trespassing in the lowlands if it saved my daughter's soul. You must tell me what came to pass."

"There is a dark spirit loose in the lowlands tonight," the bowman named Jorn said. "Best to tell the Warden and have him send his rangers to guard your house tonight. We must be going." With that he made to turn the horse back up to the woods, but Viviel's firm voice spoke out.

"There are two of you who are hurt," he said, for he had noticed the stoop in the black-haired stranger, and the third man that held his arm close to his chest.

They said nothing and moved on.

"Wait," Viviel called after them. They did not stop, treading onwards silently towards the trees. Her father cast Paiva a backwards glance and then trotted off after them.

Paiva followed, close on his heels, the dog darting ahead of them. She did not know why her father would not just let them leave. She wanted more than anything to be back in their house with every door and window barred.

"Wait, my good men, please. I must talk with you," Viviel said. "Please, tell me what came to pass."

The bowman slowed, his wide shoulders tense with unease. He turned back and looked at Viviel, then lifted his head to look beyond at Paiva.

"Your daughter, good sir, should not be out alone in the woods," he said.

"No," Viviel said shakily. "Please explain to me what has come to pass. Tell me your names, so I may pray for you and give you thanks."

Paiva felt the return of heat to her cheeks and looked down at her feet. The bowman's voice grew deep and threatening.

"Tell you our names? So you may go and tell the Warden? If he marks my ledger because of you, be sure that I will be back for you."

Viviel shook his head vehemently. "I certainly shall not. If he'd done his job half-right he would have found you lot in the first place. I have no reason to help Warden Lier catch rogue Wildermen."

The bowman studied him in silence.

"Come, out of the dark," Viviel said sincerely.

"It's not a light punishment, getting caught giving sanctuary to Wildermen," the younger man said. "You could lose your home, your status. You could even be sent to the woods yourself."

Viviel gently reached out and took hold of the packhorse's bridle. Then, without a word he urged it alongside him, down to the barn.

"What are you doing?" the bowman growled. "Are you mad?"

"He's kind," said the black-haired one.

"Come along, there's no argument here. The entire village is drunk and oblivious. Come, out of the dark of the night. One old man and a dog won't keep a dark spirit at bay, but if I have you three by my fire tonight I'll sleep soundly. I am sure you would all be glad for some hot food and sweet cider."

"It would be wiser to fetch the Warden," said Jorn.

"I have little faith in our Warden."

Viviel drew the horse into the barn as Kess' worried voice rang out from the back of the house, calling for Viviel and asking what the dog had been barking at. Viviel turned to Paiva and ordered her up to the house.

She hesitated, nervous of leaving her father alone in the barn with three strangers, and even more anxious to face her mother.

"Tell your mother to be calm. Go on," Viviel said firmly.

Paiva turned and ran through the dark yard up to the house.

"By my soul, Paiva, did Viviel fetch you without telling me? What has happened?" Kess asked her at once. Then she saw the look on Paiva's face and the stains of tears on her cheeks, and an icy horror washed over her face.

"What is the matter? Where is your mask? Where is your Father?" she cried, hurrying Paiva into the house.

"Father has brought Wildermen back from the woods... they are hurt." Paiva couldn't find the right word to describe the creature she had seen. The very thought of it still left her trembling and weak.

Her mother didn't need to ask any more questions to realize that something was terribly wrong. She simply clasped her hand to Paiva's face and kissed the tears from her cheeks. "Mummers-eve," Kess complained. "Best we turn out the candles in the window so nobody visits."

"We need to lock the doors and windows," Paiva said. She moved to the front door where she latched it firmly. Kess watched her with pained wide eyes, then she nodded silently and they both went about the house, securing it and closing the curtains over their windows.

By the time they were done Viviel had entered the back door, followed by the three dirty, unkempt men. Paiva looked to her mother worriedly, who touched her forehead in the familiar gesture of warding off bad luck.

"It is Mummers-eve. This must still be a trick," Jorn muttered.

"No more tricks tonight," Viviel promised.

"I haven't been in a real house in so long," Jorn said, stunned, staring about. "A home. A real home."

"How long has it been since you lost yours?" Viviel asked.

"Four winters. I had a small farm, not as fine as yours, but it was mine and it was my home, filled with fleas and children. I'll get back there one day, I hope."

"Don't ever stop hoping, good man. You can lose your happiness and you can lose your love and your courage, but a man must never lose hope." Viviel strode into the house and dragged a bench towards the fire, inviting them to warm themselves.

"This is my wife Kess Ibbie," Viviel said, "and you've already met my whimsical daughter Paiva, and the dog, Elki." Kess nodded curtly to the strangers as they took their seats before the fire, shedding dirt and leaves on her freshly swept floor. Her nerves seemed to snap then.

"Will you please tell me what has happened?" she asked Viviel. "Why are there three Wildermen sitting in my house?"

Everyone turned to look at her. Even Viviel had a touch of worry in his eyes.

"It was my fault," Paiva said. She faced her mother. "I broke my promise to you."

She recounted the whole story to her wide-eyed mother. When she was done a long silence stretched through the room. Kess slowly drew her eyes from Paiva to the three men.

"Varloga?" she breathed, and again she touched her forehead. "By my soul, you three are lucky to still be breathing. Come then, you are very welcome here. Let me warm you some cider."

— «» —

Paiva had thrown away her ripped cloak and discarded what was left of her trampled costume, replacing it with a warm woolen shawl. She sat on the stairs as she descended from the loft, and quietly watched and listened to the Wildermen from there. She took the opportunity to study them, and wonder at them. The one with the sore arm had a great beard that rivaled her father's, though it was streaked with gray below his chin and tangled with burrs. He looked to also be about her father's age, with sunken gray eyes, gaunt cheeks, and deep lines in his forehead creased with dirt. He wore animal skins beneath a tattered leather vest and an oilskin cloak, and his boots were worn through at the toes and patched with hide.

The bowman, Jorn, was the biggest of the three, with a shorter beard and a balding head greased over with straggly wisps of hair. His eyes were as dark and brown as the dirt smeared on his face and hands. His britches were thin and worn through at the knees and thighs, patched again with scraps of different cloth. He looked fearsome in his tattered furs and cloak, more of a bear than a man, but she sensed there was a softness in him. About his eyes were the same deep lines like her father's — lines that had been made from years of smiling and laughing.

The youngest one, who looked a few years older than Ramsi, had hair as black as soot, as if a crow had made a nest of its own feathers atop his head and forgotten it there. He had broad shoulders, though the rest of his frame was narrow and sinewy, like a scarecrow that needed a few good meals. He had a nose that had suffered a break at one time and a grim mouth. He was the blackest and the dirtiest of the three, his boots caked in mud, his crow's nest of hair knotted with neglect.

They all had deep rings beneath their eyes and smelled of male sweat, leather, horse, woodsmoke and mossy earth. Her imagination spun with scenarios for how each one had gotten their brand, but she did not dare ask aloud. They seemed to be trustworthy-enough men — in her father's eyes, at least, if he was willing to open his door to these strangers. Yet there was something dangerous about them. There was a tension in their bodies, like a coil of uneasy muscle ready to spring. It was as if they were wolves sneaking around a trapped chicken coop.

Viviel poured them warm cider, filled bowls of Kess' soup and broke bread for them. He spoke to them like they were old friends, not outcasts who had spent the past years of their lives living in the wild.

"Varloga." Her father echoed the name, and she watched as his golden eyes seemed to dim as a shadow passed over his face. "Are you certain?"

"Yes," the bowman said. Viviel's eyes sought his daughter's shadowy form crouching on the stairs. His eyes were filled with worry, something that rarely reflected in them. It gave Paiva an uneasy sense of foreboding. She knew, sure as the sun would rise in the morning, that this night would haunt her the rest of her life.

"Then I am doubly glad I have asked you to stay in for the night. What may I call you all?" Viviel asked.

They looked uneasily amongst each other, then the bowman shrugged in resignation.

"In the woods I am called Bear Jorn." He motioned to the one with the bad arm. "That one's Trapper Terg, and the other is Black Renn."

"I suppose those are all names you earned," Viviel chuckled, though his eyes remained dim. "Tell me then, how you came to be in Birchloam for Mummers-eve. It makes me wonder now if it is the wolves that steal my sheep, or you lot." He procured his pouch of tar weed and handed it to Jorn, who took it with a look of surprise and fumbled for his own pipe beneath his greasy furs.

"It was Ulrig's idea," Jorn said. "We had a hard winter up at Far Reach camp. We're the only ones left asides from old Ulrig, and he's but a bag of bones himself. The Wardens never sent up any rations at all, and for most of the winter we were buried in snow and couldn't leave the camp. When spring came there were still no rations. The geese came back late, the streams stayed frozen over, we ate roots and bark and strange tubers. So we made our way down to the lowlands — Renn had come the last year and done the same, stealing bread and wine from the altar in the woods."

"I know of Ulrig," Viviel said, a curious look on his face. "He's a pardoned man, he is. He comes down to Birchloam and trades furs and wild meat for grain and tools. He comes less and less. Haven't seen him in Birchloam since last summer. I didn't know he was still living amongst the Wildermen. I thought him to be but a stray."

"He is but a stray, that one. He's the only reason we've been kept alive as long as we have. He can't afford to make the journey in the best of times. If it's not for fear of Folka, it's the Warden who has many times taken it upon himself to take a tax of Ulrig's goods. It doesn't matter if you're a free man or not, a brand or a double brand, you're still a Wilderman."

"How is it you do not care for our trespassing?" Renn asked. "How is it you offer kindness to branded strangers?" He took the tarweed. Terg and Jorn had their pipes lit and were puffing contentedly. They seemed resigned now, the tension released from their haggard frames, perhaps with the help of the warm cider.

"As I said," Viviel smiled, the sunburnt creases in the corners of his eyes widening, "if it hadn't been for you lot, I may as well have lost my daughter. To share a meal and give you a warm, dry place to sleep is but a small price to pay. Any man who faces Varloga deserves more than that." Not one of them dared lift their eyes to Paiva, sitting still and listening raptly. Not while Viviel sat before them.

"It is in our own interest to hunt spirits and their Folka," Renn said.

"The Forest stirs," Jorn said, dismissing Renn's comment. "The highlands are filled with nightmares. We are only too glad for your kindness. There are not many who would risk sharing their homes with outcasts."

"You're not bad men. I know it."

Jorn opened his hand slowly and revealed the red scarring on the meat of his thumb.

"You do not care to learn our pasts?"

"I do not. I wish to hear no dreary talk of wounded pasts that steals the light from our souls. I do not want to know what you did to earn your sentence in the woods," Viviel said. His eyes brightened again, his voice lifting as he made the effort to be positive. "I want to hear of the reasons you would want to return from it. I want to hear the tales of your old lives, of the good things you hope for when you are wondering why it is you hope. You sit before me as men, as equals, so tell me your tales so that in the morning when you depart I may call you friends."

Paiva watched a transformation on Jorn's face. She watched the haggardness lift for only a moment as a tender sentiment washed over it. His dark eyes seemed to glisten, his shoulders sagged in surrender. Viviel rose and clapped a strong hand over his shoulder. Then he raised his eyes and searched for Kess.

"Have you found your medicines?" he asked her. Paiva adored her father with all her heart in that moment. He was of a strong and rare character wherein he could feel sympathy for the most wretched of souls. His ruggedly carved face and work-worn body belied his capability of softer kindness.

Her mother must have shared her sentiments in that moment, for she returned from the back room with the color returned to her face and a warmth in her eye. She carried a small wooden box filled with ointments, salves and clean strips of linen. She went up to Renn and asked him where his hurts were, but he assured her he was not bleeding and refused her attentions, diverting them to Terg. Viviel went and fetched more food while Jorn helped Terg shrug out of his ripped cloak. Kess inspected him, her face again becoming taught when her eyes fell on his back.

"He got me," Terg said. "But not bad enough to get rid of me yet."

"I can see every last rib in your back," Kess said. "I don't blame you for stealing sweetbreads from the altar." The brunt of Varloga's claws had been taken by thick leather plates both men wore under their stained shirts and furs. Renn's shoulders were badly bruised and swelling, and had suffered only a shallow rake of claws. Terg's situation was more severe; there were lacerations beneath his right shoulder that had become clotted through the pressure of his vest. Kess soaked them, and he made not a sound as she cleaned them and urged them to bleed again.

"Tell me of your lives," Viviel continued.

"I was a farmer, from the lowlands outside the Keep," Jorn said. "About this time of year is when I'd go out to the fields with my boys and till the good earth. We had a horse I named King, a great monster of a beast. He was foaled off my old mare and sired by a stud a couple of farms over. I had wanted a team for hitching the plow, but that foal turned into a giant and I had no need of a partner for him. Clumsy as an ox but strong as ten of them. He took to the field like a duck to a puddle. My eldest son would guide the plow, and my youngest would sit on King's back. My daughter, by my soul, was the one carting stones out of the field and stacking new fences.

"My wife was always the one to tell us when to start planting. Women have a knack for these things; she always knew when the last frost had passed. There was nothing like the feel of a good day's work when you're hot despite the chill of the spring wind coming down from the hills and your throat's as dry as an old grain bag." Jorn's voice broke and he took a deep swallow of his cider. He swallowed it bitterly and continued. "We never were actually married. We just spoke promises to each other because I knew too well the uncertainty of life. When they branded me they had no right to touch her. When things started getting bad we put the farm in the eldest boys' name, and they couldn't take it from him because by law he was a bastard. Only me. Only I was sent away. But by all the shining stars, I will get back there one day." Paiva heard the twinge of remorse in his voice. She pulled her shawl up closer, imaging the pain of losing her home.

"I shoed horses," Terg said as Kess bandaged his torn shoulder. "All day and sometimes all night. I loved the smell of iron in the forge, the spark of my hammer against my anvil. Every horse I shoed, I met a new person. That's what I liked the best. I shoed the heavy horses from the farm fields, from peddlars' cart horses, to noblemen's and Knights' chargers. I always complained about the ones who tried to blame me for a lame horse. I thought of quitting it one time and smithing mail and armor. But it's not the same as putting iron on a horse's hooves and imagining where that horse might walk — whether it be up and down a field before a plow, or whether that horse might carry a lady in her carriage. I apprenticed for five years with Master Orif at the Keep. He said we smithies were spokes in the wheel that kept this land rolling. Without us the horses would be lame, the farmers would have no plows, and the guards would have no hunters."

"Our own horses are barefoot," Renn said. "The whole world does not walk on iron shoes."

"We ride Berg Horses," Jorn growled. "No one but Wildermen ride Berg horses. They're the scrap of horse flesh. Instead of bothering to cull them they let them loose in the hills. Just like us."

"The Bergs don't carry brands," Renn said tersely.

Viviel lifted his golden eyes to the young man. He had his head bent, sucking at the smoldering pit of his pipe.

"Tell me then of your life," Viviel said curiously. The young man lifted his brow and turned to his patron, revealing silver eyes that flashed in the firelight beneath his black brow. He seemed to be the most reserved, the most solemn of the three.

"I was highborn. I was spoiled and overprivileged. It was an empty life — not something I would return to, not for all the freedom in the world." Paiva took the chance to study him again as he lifted his head into the firelight. Beneath the batter that scarred him she could faintly see the remnants of good breeding. His nose must have once been perfectly sculpted, his cheekbones high and refined despite their gauntness. He must have been handsome once, or could be still, if he had been kept. Indeed, with his strange pale eyes, he was now more alarming than anything.

"What is it you hope for then?" Viviel asked, studying him much the same as Paiva was.

Renn stared back into the fire for a long moment. A crook of a smile tugged at the corner of his lips. "A pardon, of course," he said. "But I am content to have a warm fire, with real friends by my side, a pipe in my mouth and a Berg horse waiting for me in the barn. As long as I'm not bleeding, I'm quite sure I am content."

Viviel laughed and poured out more cider.

"He's special, that one." Jorn chuckled and took a pull of his drink. "It's true it doesn't take much to entertain him. He sometimes carves figures out of sticks and plays with them well into the night."

"Talismans," Renn corrected, "and they are better to play with then wild horses or knives."

Jorn laughed and turned to Viviel. "Renn and I were out in the woods once, on a chase, and we were waiting for the others in our band to catch up. I was sweating like a mad horse, scared to my wit's end of the spirit beast we were after and Renn was sitting there all quiet-like, staring at a tree. I thought maybe he was touched in some way, fear or shock perhaps. I asked him what the matter was. He said he was pretty sure he saw my wife in that tree. I looked, and all there was was but a tree with a lump growing out the side of it. He's never seen my wife, he only knows the stories I tell him so I thought he was mad. But he went up to that tree and knocked that lump off, and he spent the whole night by the fire whittling it away while I was too scared to go to sleep because I thought I had a madman on watch. Finally he handed the lump of wood over to me, and I tell you... it was no lump of a tree. It was a woman. Somehow that lump, with the bark peeled off and a few cuts made here and there ... turned into my wife."

"Didn't matter that one breast was half the size of the other," Renn said sincerely, then darted a quick look to Kess and bit his lip. Viviel laughed at Renn's insolent sense of humor, his golden eyes dancing in the firelight.

"It's not a talisman if you can't stuff it in your pocket or wear it around your neck," Terg protested. "The damned thing was too big to fit in a saddlebag, even. Jorn carried it under his arm the whole way back to Ulrig's, like he thought it would come to life."

"When I get my pardon," Jorn waved a finger at Terg, "that is the only thing I will bring back from the woods with me. My wooden lump of a woman, and I will give it to my wife and tell her it is the only thing that gave me courage in the dark of the woods. Everything else I will leave behind. Everything."

"If she's still waiting," Terg said sourly, taking another swig of cider as Kess finished bandaging his side.

"She is," Jorn blared. "There's no reason to get a pardon if she isn't."

The laughter died suddenly as the dog howled in alarm outside. Paiva bolted from her seat and came to stand nervously beside her mother. There came an excited yelp, and then the dog fell quiet. Everyone else fell silent, listening.

Claws scraped across the door. Something jiggled the latch. The Wildermen and Viviel rose, facing the door and pushing Paiva and her mother behind them. Kess touched her forehead absently, as if the gesture could ward off whatever ill luck was lurking at their front door. Through thin curtains of the window by the door, a pale shape floated by. Paiva seized her mother's arm in fear.

"Do something Viviel," she heard her mother whisper urgently. "Please."

Before Viviel could react, Renn crept forward towards the window. He pressed his back against the wall and peered out through a slit in the curtain.

"Mr. Ibbie," he whispered, his eyes flashing back to the fire. "It is no spirit. You have a throng of Mummers in your yard."

"What? There are no candles in the windows," he said, panic worrying his voice. He joined Renn at the window and peered out. A white masked face appeared at the window and Renn leapt back into the shadow. The visitor raised their hands and tapped wooden claws against the glass. The sound of muffled laughter rang out as the figure moved away to the door and rapped loudly. Viviel saw more coming down the yard and he whirled around to face the Wildermen in a panic.

"Hide, all of you," was all he said. There was a clatter of boots as the men disappeared into the far corners of the house. Kess quickly threw the bloody linens into the fire.

"Go upstairs," she hissed to Paiva. "Hurry."

She bolted up into the loft just as her father opened the door and a cheery voice rang out.

"Mr. Ibbie!" it cried in delight. "You look like you have seen a ghost!" There was a commotion as people pushed their way into the house. Paiva peeked down and saw five costumed people burst in on her startled parents. They were all dressed in long robes with masks, and to her horror she recognized both Miriel and Ramsi Lier, who was missing his fox mask. Paiva found this detail very alarming.

"It is too late for Mummering," Paiva heard her mother say. "I was just about to go to bed."

"No one else has any drinks left, in all the village, but look! I see you have cider there! Are we not allowed a drink until our identities can be guessed?"

"Ramsi, Miriel, Clare, Benvin, Piter, and Ernvig," her father listed smoothly. "And I don't suppose any of you paid any attention as to where Paiva went off to tonight?"

They teetered drunkenly as they looked about to each other.

"No, actually, we thought she was safe at home."

"She is, but not thanks to you lot," her father said heatedly. There was a chorus of drunken giggles and sniggers.

"Come let her have a drink with us then," Paiva heard Ramsi say. She felt her cheeks burn and angry tears whelm in her eyes. She turned away and thudded into a solid shape behind her. She nearly gave out a cry of alarm before she realized it was Renn, standing with his tall head stooped against the low ceiling.

"Miserable friends you have," he whispered.

"Not friends at all," she replied dismally. He leaned over her to look.

"That's the fellow you thought you were following up to the altar, Warden Lier's son." He motioned to Ramsi.

"Yes," she whispered back.

"Why on earth would you follow that fool into the woods?" he asked incredulously.

"What do you mean?" she replied in surprise.

"He's a sot. Shake a bush at him and he'll run off like a mad hare."

"I wouldn't have followed him if I didn't trust him," she said defensively. "He's very brave."

"He's scared of getting his boots dirty."

She listened to her parents quarrel with the drunken revelers below. She swallowed dryly, unable to stop her mind from wandering into Renn's past and pondering what it was he did to earn his banishment. Was he a thief? A liar? Or maybe worst of all, a murderer?

She was thankful to see her parents had given away the last of the cider, though the Mummers continued speaking in airs of the merrymaking in the square that night. Her father's responses were clipped and her mother was curt. The Mummers laughed obliviously amongst each other and didn't care. She felt a longing to be a part of them, as she had longed for Ramsi to offer her even one dance before he had swooped away with Miriel. In her longing she had made a stupid mistake, and it was only because of this shadow of a man beside her she was still standing.

"I suppose I should thank you," Paiva said. "You did save me."

"As I said. It is in our own interest to hunt spirits," he answered.

"He can't come back now, can he?" she asked. "He was stuck full of arrows."

"Alas, he is not yet headless. I doubt very much you will ever be safe in your own home again," he replied.

His words sent a chill through her. She looked to Ramsi again and felt her confidence in him drain. "Good thing young Lier is piss drunk," Renn murmured. "If he knew there were Wildermen watching him in this house right now he'd throw your father in chains."

"No. My father's a good man, they cannot punish good men. Ramsi would understand that."

"There have been many good men who end up in the woods, many innocents."

She looked back up to him then, studying his haggard profile. He was almost all shadow, except for a glimmer of silver where his eyes stared out.

"My father might think you're a good man," she said. "But you're not innocent, are you?"

He turned his bent head to her. She could smell horse sweat and earthy leathers. His silver eyes pierced into hers, and then her loft seemed to shrink. The air grew stuffy and hard to breathe, and she wanted desperately to find more distance between them.

A crook of a smile tugged at his half-obscured features.

"No," he whispered. — «» —

The Mummers left a short while later, after the pitcher of cider was found to be dry. Viviel watched them stagger across the yard, then turn down the laneway.

"Be careful," he called worriedly. "Safe home, straight away." They laughed and made screeching calls, mimicking what they thought an angry spirit would sound like. The sounds sent chills up Paiva's spine.

When they were a safe distance down the road, Viviel shut and latched the door. Renn quietly descended back to the main floor, Jorn burst out of a cupboard he had jammed himself into, and Terg crawled out from behind the wood pile with a slew of curses.

"I thought they were going to stay all night," he spat, rubbing his aching shoulder.

"We will leave," Renn said, but Viviel shook his head resolutely. He gathered blankets and handed them to the Wildermen.

"Rest here until the light comes. Please. I'm sure every last ranger in Birchloam is as drunk as Ramsi right now."

Renn took the blanket reluctantly. The three men lay down before the fire while her father laid back in a chair with his own blanket over his lap. He had his shepherd's staff beside him and he tilted his head back to close his eyes wearily.

Kess came up to the loft and they huddled together on Paiva's small bed. Paiva had a slew of questions for her mother but she sighed wearily and closed her eyes. Paiva lay awake for most of the night, listening for any noise that came in the dark. All she heard were snores from the men downstairs, the crackle of the fire, and the scurry of mice through the rafters. Slowly sleep crept over her and she closed her eyes, nestling into her mother's back.

— «» —

In the early morning she followed her parents and the three men out to the barn with a sack filled with foods. Jorn gathered up the horse and scratched his head shyly when he caught Kess staring at the haversacks overstuffed with bread from the altar. Viviel shook each of their hands, their branded hands, and wished them well and gave them his thanks again. Renn seemed troubled, and Viviel asked him what the matter was.

"Our tracks," he said. "The ground is wet from the spring rains yet. The Warden's twit of a son would be sure to follow them back here if he caught on to them. Best you gather a small flock of sheep and run them over."

"I will," Viviel said. "Do not worry about us. Best you hide your own tracks on the way out. If the Warden and his rangers caught wind of you, you would be in for it."

"Don't worry about us."

"They have hounds."

"Doesn't matter much if they have dogs," Jorn scowled. "Some rangers you have, if that's the lot you expect to keep you safe from the woods."

"It is," Viviel mused worriedly.

"If I were you I'd send word to Master Warden Yulin from the Keep," Renn said. "He'll send you good men, and we'll be sure not to cross the river while they are here. Tell him Varloga is here, he'll be sure to come."

"Now that's a Warden you don't want to meet in the woods," Jorn laughed. "And neither does any Folka."

Viviel nodded in thanks again and Renn turned to lead the men out. Paiva ran out a ways after them, leaping onto the stone fence to watch them pass. She called her thanks to them, and Renn kept his eyes on the ground. Jorn threw her a crooked smile and Terg a mischievous wink. She watched them disappear into the trees as the sun blushed the sky.

Viviel looked about for his wife, and came back into the house where she hid with her hands to her face, stifling sobs. He laid his arms around her and buried her into his deep chest.

"I knew she shouldn't have gone out, it was my fault. I knew better," she said.

"It didn't happen. Do not despair. It did not happen."

Chapter 4

A few hours later Paiva sat before Warden Lier in his quarters beside her father. The Warden stared across his tidy desk with the same hazel eyes he had given to his son, ringed with weariness from the festivities of the night before. Behind him on the walls hung a large map, showing the village and the huge expanse of forest beyond it separated by the Panderbank River. There were marks throughout the woods, showing Wilderman camps and trails. His entire office dripped in finery: there were red silk curtains in his window, ornately carved furniture and a tall crystal decanter filled with wine. He had a servant who tended to him and his dogs and horses, and Paiva began to believe what Renn had said about how he was not one to get his boots dirty. Despite this, his face was hard and his manners cool and calculated. He gave every impression of a capable and dangerous protector, though there was not a trace of dirt beneath his perfectly shaped fingernails.

Warden Lier dipped a quill in ink and marked the date on a piece of parchment, ready to record and note the statement they had come to give. He waited patiently while Viviel found his first words.

"She was walking home from the bonfire and Ramsi came after her," he began.

Warden Lier's brow lifted in surprise and looked to Paiva. "Ramsi was with you?"

"No Sir, it was not Ramsi," Viviel said. "She thought it was but she was deceived. She had thought Ramsi had gone off with another girl and decided to go home. She was surprised, and glad, to see he had come after her."

Warden Lier frowned and began scratching into his parchment. Viviel procured a small pouch and from it he drew pieces of clay, arranging them together atop Warden Lier's desk in the shape of a fox's face. It was Ramsi's own mask — Viviel had found it by the altar when he had gone to hide the Wildermen's tracks. The feathers he had found he burned, for there had been traces of black blood on them.

The mask was compelling enough evidence for Warden Lier, who scrutinized it. Viviel recounted the rest of the story simply. He had been very firm with Paiva to agree it had all happened in the front of the Ibbies' house in hopes of keeping the Rangers away from the pastures, where they might uncover evidence of the Wildermen.

"You're not hurt?" Warden Lier asked Paiva. "He did not touch you? There are no marks on your body?"

"Only bruises," Paiva said. "I was in a terrible shock and didn't speak with my parents about it until this morning." In fact, her entire body was covered in bruises and she smelled strongly of the healing liniment her mother had rubbed her with before she left the house that morning.

"Yes, I would imagine," Warden Lier said.

"It was Varloga," her father confirmed. "I am sure of it. She said he was all white, half-owl, half-man." Warden Lier scrutinized his parchment, his eyes deep and thoughtful. When they looked at Paiva there was no suspicion in them, only concern.

"I think it best I had rangers on sentry at your farm for the next little while. I'll send the rest into the woods and have them overturn every leaf until they are sure there is nothing hiding in there."

"I thought perhaps you could notify Warden Yulin from the Keep," her father said.

"What for?"

"Perhaps it would do well to have more manpower, is all," Viviel said.

Lier dismissed the subject carelessly. "I will leave Ramsi in charge of guarding your farm, and I will myself go into the woods in search of this creature. Rest assured the beast will be dealt with." He finished recording the statement on parchment, then slid it over to her father with his quill to sign.

Hesitantly, Viviel took the quill and made his mark.

They left the Warden's quarters and headed back up the laneway. Her father was quiet and thoughtful, sucking smoke from his pipe.

"What is wrong? What are you thinking about?" she asked him.

"I was thinking about your mother's sister who lives at the Keep." Paiva had only met her aunt Bessil a handful of times in her younger years. She knew she had spent the past years slaving away as a cook in the kitchens of the Keep and had very little interest in ever returning to Birchloam.

"I don't want to go to the Keep," she said as she followed her father's train of thought.

"I was thinking you would be safe there until this Varloga is contended with."

"I don't want to go to the Keep."

Viviel puffed on his pipe thoughtfully. They went on homewards in silence.

— «» —

Paiva's mother was in a terrible mood the rest of the day. It did not matter what Viviel said to her; she could not help but to be irritated by him. Paiva could not go anywhere without her mother coming to look for her and so Paiva could assure her she was well. Paiva ended up spending the rest of the day in the kitchens, for Kess was too afraid to send her outside unsupervised.

Viviel went up to the pastures and into the woods, checking again that there were no signs of Wildermen left behind. He stopped to kneel at his altar and send a prayer out into the forest. By midday the rangers had been assembled and led up the road to the Ibbies' homestead where they scoured the woods and the pastures. Alarming talk had started in town and Mr. and Mrs. Switch had come forward about the strange white Mummer they had encountered the night before. It was found that their description matched Paiva's perfectly. Kess was like a kettle on the verge of boiling over, but Viviel soothed her with gentle assurances.

Ordered to stay indoors and with nothing to do until the rangers concluded their investigation, Paiva joined her father by the hearth as he scribbled his writings into his journal. She did not ask him but she was sure he was recording what had come to pass with the Wildermen the night before.

Not wanting to interrupt him, she procured one of his older journals from his shelf at the back of the house and flipped through it, searching through his scribbles for the Old Stories of Grimenna. As she looked at his inky illustrations of creatures, she came across his work on Varloga. Below the name written in bold letters was an eerie drawing of owl. There were other drawings as well — shapes of men and other half-creatures Varloga was said to take, but it was the owl she returned to and studied. She read his slanted writing of the many stories of the spirit, and records of sightings and places he was said to haunt. There was one paragraph that caught her eye, and as she read it she felt as cold as ice.

"Spirit of the Dark Humors," it read, "Born of the Humor of Fear. The First People claimed this spirit to be the cause and reason of nightmares, ailments, accidents and misfortune. He was said to take the shape of a giant white owl and was evoked to curse enemies. He was warded off through generous sacrifices of livestock and precious objects. He was greatly feared for his dark powers of shapeshifting and conjuring, and later he became known as the White Magician, preferring the form of a man over that of an owl. He is ruled by the Strix, under whom he is commanded and compelled. To her he brings the gifts of the simple people, and if she is displeased it is he she sends back to torment them.

"It is through him the Folka beasts are conjured. The Folka are soulless, empty beasts manifested from nightmares, and often when they are killed, they return to trouble the dreams of their killers. It is not known if Varloga was ever an Incarnate, though there is a belief the guardian of the old temple of Morinvere sold his soul to the Strix who in turn granted him magic so he might become a sorcerer. Varloga is said to have taken this guardian's body, and thus he was able to leave the Forest and trouble mankind."

Paiva continued to flip through the pages, perusing her father's inky illustrations. Any one of them could have been a design for a costume on Mummers-eve. Paiva closed the book and weighed it in her hands. Within held all her father's secrets, myths and stories that were being forgotten by a sweeping belief in a mightier God. This book was precious and at the same time dangerous. Those that were Goddish would easily believe them to be a source of witchcraft and ill-doing.

She returned the book to its place on the shelf alongside the many others containing old songs, old remedies, old families and old places, mixed in with records of the farm and animal husbandry.

"Father," she said. "Why are you forever recording things and gathering stories?"

He looked up to her from his journal, his eyes soft and kind.

"I have old blood, Paiva," he said. "My collecting started when I wanted to find my origins. They are your origins as well." He smiled then, a lingering smile that touched into his eyes and made them glow. Then he dropped his head back to his writings, his interest becoming focused elsewhere.

— «» —

"I hear you had a good fright the other night," Ramsi said as he leaned against a post in the barn and watched Paiva muck the stalls. He had his arms folded across his wide chest and his sword hung at his hip in a prominent display of manliness. He had brought with him a small group of men that were standing idle at all corners of their property. They did not do much but sit and twiddle grass stalks between their teeth or throw stones at birds. Ramsi had been out with his father and a score of rangers for almost two days, tracking and searching, uncovering nothing. He was bored now, looking for something more exciting to do.

"I did have a fright," she said.

"I heard the spirit appeared to you in my likeness." She felt her cheeks burn with exertion and humiliation and stabbed the pitchfork hard into the muck of hay and manure as he chuckled quietly. "That's the best trick I heard of on Mummers-Eve yet." He smiled.

"It's not funny," she said.

"It sounds ridiculous to me. Why would a spirit like Varloga even want you? What could be so special about a sheep herder's daughter? To me it sounds like a very tall tale, told by someone in want of attention. I even came to your house on that night, and you did nothing but hide in your bed."

"My father found your mask in the front of the house," she scolded him.

"I could have dropped it there," he shrugged. "You could have stolen it."

"Just do your job Ramsi," she said as she tossed muck into a wheelbarrow. "If it isn't too much trouble."

"Not at all." He walked out of the barn, his hand on the hilt of his sword, his shoulders squared. She glared at him as he paced the yard, kicking at pebbles in the dirt. If he had not been so terribly handsome she probably would have thrown a forkful of muck at him.

She sighed to herself as a great realization occurred to her. Ramsi Lier wasn't worth getting upset over. He wasn't worth another wasted thought. She could wish it was him who had come to her rescue; she could wish it was him who had struck Varloga in the neck with an arrow. The simple truth was that it hadn't been him — he had been off courting a prettier, wealthier girl who probably wasn't standing up to her ankles in horse and sheep muck at this very moment. It had been a dirty, black-haired outlaw who had saved her, not Ramsi.

She didn't let herself feel disappointed, and she didn't lament over his loss in her heart. As her father always said, it was his loss, not hers.

— «» —

Viviel had sent two letters to the Keep, one to the Warden Yulin that Renn spoke of, and one to Paiva's aunt Bessil. They received a letter in the following week, written in a hand that clearly didn't care for writing. Paiva recognized it as Aunt Bessil's and waited for her mother to read it. There was only one small sentence.

"Send the girl then."

Her mother frowned. It did not sound very inviting.

"I think I should stay here," Paiva protested. "Ramsi says he's very sure Varloga won't come back and the last I did see of him he had an arrow in his neck."

"The only thing to stop a creature like him is an arrow in his heart and his head cut off. You'll go. There will be hundreds of soldiers and towering walls all around you, you will be a thousand times safer than here. Here you are like a mouse in the middle of a field trying to hide from a hawk."

"But I have never left Birchloam before."

"And you'll come home to it again." Kess smiled. "In the meantime you shall have an adventure and steal all of Bessil's recipes for me."

Close on the heels of the messenger came a score of men on dusty horses. At the lead was a stony-faced man with a cropped gray beard. He wore the same deep red garments as Warden Lier, only he carried himself differently. Warden Lier resembled very much an esteemed man of high rank, but Yulin looked like a warlord. The men that flanked him were twice the size of any of Warden Lier's rangers, and they had iron mail beneath their tunics and studded shoulders.

People came out of their homes and gawked as they passed, riding through the village and up the lane way to stop at the Ibbies' front door. Viviel came down from the fields to greet him, followed by Ramsi who looked concerned.

"Warden Yulin," Viviel greeted the man who swung from his horse and removed his leather gloves to shake Viviel's hand.

"Warden Yulin? From the Keep?" Ramsi blurted. "Why are you here?"

"I was sent word that Varloga was sighted here," Warden Yulin said briskly, sizing up the youth.

"Is my father aware of this?" Ramsi asked heatedly.

"If your father is Warden Lier, then no. I have only just arrived."

"He is the Warden in charge here," Ramsi said. "He is the Warden of Birchloam. Unless there has been a complaint that our services are lacking, then you should not be here." He looked accusingly at Viviel. Warden Yulin looked over the young man and sighed.

"Ranger, you may not jump to conclusions. I did not come to displace your father. I came simply for the interest of Varloga."

"With a score of men? Why can you not use our Rangers?"

Warden Yulin's patience seemed to fray. He spoke with a sharper tone then. "How about you run and tell Father I am here, boy? I will talk with this gentle farmer now. Off you go, at once," he snapped.

Ramsi looked taken aback. There was a murmur of a chuckle from Yulin's men that made Ramsi's ears turn as red as his tunic. He turned angrily and marched away to find his horse. Yulin watched him go with a smug smile.

"Pompous little twit, isn't he? I'll be sure to bring him out with us when we take to the woods. See if his back is as strong as his pride. Come now, Mr. Ibbie. We will have a chance to talk at last."

"Come inside and have a drink to wash down the dust of the road," said Viviel. "I will send food and drink for your men."

— «» —

Warden Yulin was a different man than Warden Lier indeed. Paiva had assumed all Wardens were the same, but Yulin scratched no notes into parchment. He kept his eyes level on Paiva's face as she spoke, studying every muscle that moved and every emotion she tried to convey or hide. She sat at the table across from him, her hands folded nervously in her lap. Her father sat at the head of the table smoking his pipe while Kess went outside with a tray of food and drinks for the rangers.

"So you say he revealed himself to you before the house, in the middle of the laneway," Yulin asked when she had finished her story. His eyes skirted over the yellowing bruises on her arms.

Paiva nodded and looked nervously to her father. Yulin stroked the dust from his beard thoughtfully. "Were there no more words that passed between you two before it happened? Did he give you no inclination as to why he was interested in you?" Yulin asked. His dark green eyes searched hers, his brow knitted together.

"No," she answered quietly. She felt her father's eyes on her face but she did not dare look into them. "Mother had warned me not take my mask off, but I did. I was foolish."

Yulin smiled.

"The only thing I can scold you for is walking home alone in the dark on Mummers-eve," he said. "I know Varloga. Whoever he chooses for whatever reasons, he vanishes them. If they are ever seen again, they are changed."

"I am not changed," she said. "Perhaps wiser now, but that is all."

"She has not been touched by him," her father said.

"It is a mystery to me why he is after you," Yulin said. "And you have right to be concerned and fearful. If a Wilderman were ever to capture Varloga's head, he would indeed be granted a pardon and perhaps even an estate. The bounty for Varloga is steep. I understand why Warden Lier would rather have kept it secret from me."

"Will I have caused problems by calling you here?" Viviel asked with a twinge of concern.

"You did the right thing. Lier will have to accept it. If anything he should be reprimanded for not informing me at once, as I am his overseeing official. Varloga is of crucial matter to me." He played with the handle of his mug for a moment as thoughts whirled through his head. His eyes were still and focused on the swilling cider, but Paiva knew he was coming to his conclusions about things.

"There is only one hitch to the story," Yulin said. Paiva felt her spine stiffen as he looked up to her. "I find it hard to believe that only one man with a dog and a shepherd's staff managed to frighten off Varloga." He tapped his finger to the rim of the mug thoughtfully.

"I lost near a score of good rangers one night to him," Yulin continued. "And they were all better armed than you were. I did not come all this way to be led on a merry chase. I want answers; I want the truth. How did you survive the night alone in your house with only a dog to defend you, all the way at the edge of town where no one can hear your screams?"

Paiva looked to her father, who sighed a great cloud of blue smoke. With resignation he drew the pitcher of cider to his cup and topped it.

"Very well Warden Yulin," he said. "I will tell you. I had help."

"I think so," Yulin replied.

"But if Warden Lier were to hear I may as well forfeit my lands to him at once."

"I see." Yulin was sharp, clever, undeceived. "There were Wildermen loose in the lowlands that night."

Viviel nodded and took a long swig of his drink. Paiva could not feel her fingers for clutching them so tight. "Varloga took Paiva up to the altar we leave filled with breads and wine," Viviel said. "An offering to the good spirits on Mummers-eve, so they may watch over us in the coming season. It was there he changed, it was there he revealed himself and would have struck her down, if the Wildermen had not been about pilfering the altar." She saw the look of dismay on her father's face and hastily inserted her own thoughts into the conversation.

"But one Wilderman said if we told the Warden, he knew where we lived and he would be back," she said, hoping to blame the Wildermen for why they had not told the truth. Her father shook his head at her.

"No, that's not why I didn't turn them in. They saved your life," Viviel said. "They weren't bad men, not at all. They were the ones who told me to notify you, Warden."

"Can I have their names?" Yulin asked, his voice and face expressionless.

"They didn't give their real names. There was one called Bear Jorn, another called Trapper Terg, and a third called Black Renn."

Yulin tapped his finger again on his mug, this time with an air of irritation. Paiva held her breath while she waited for him to speak.

"I suppose it was Renn or Terg who told you about me then," he said. "I do believe Terg Ramber was a smithy at the Keep."

Viviel nodded. "You know them, then. Will you mark their ledgers?"

Viviel watched as the Warden sipped his cider in a suspended moment. He smacked his lips and set the cup down.

"Ledgers? What ledgers? I thought we were talking about Varloga, what do Wildermen have to do with this?" The corners of his eyes crinkled into a kind smile. "Don't let Warden Lier hear any whispers of Wildermen in his woods. He's far too busy a man to be worrying about that right now. You'd only cause trouble for yourself."

"Rightly so, that's what I thought." Viviel returned his smile. Paiva blew out her breath in a sigh of relief.

"But what about this girl? What is it about her that marks her aside from the others in this village?" Yulin mused. "Is it truly because she unmasked herself? It is because she was all alone, vulnerable, or is there something more to it than meets the eye?"

"I don't know. The rangers won't guard this house forever. I thought it best she should go to her Aunt Bessil at the Keep, and stay there awhile and hope that Varloga is contended with."

"Ah Bessil, yes, your wife's sister. Interesting. Well, if you're willing, she can ride back to the Keep with us when we leave."

"How long will you stay?"

"A few days, perhaps."

"That would sit very well with me. I would be hard pressed to leave my wife alone here while I travel down through the lowlands. Thank you, good sir."

"Now, if you'll excuse me, I shall go to see Warden Lier and see what he has made of his investigation so far. Pleasure to meet you Mr. Ibbie, Paiva."

Paiva sat still at the table and watched her father escort the Warden to the door. When he came back he sagged into his chair and poured himself another drink. He looked at Paiva with utter bewilderment.

"I thought my heart was about to come out of my throat for a minute there," he said.

"Mine too," she replied. "But he seems to be a good man."

"By my soul, I give my thanks again to those Wildermen. Warden Yulin does indeed seem like a fellow who knows how to go about his business."

— ‹›—

Master Warden Yulin proved to be a man of his word. The following day he ordered Ramsi up on his horse behind a troop of men he sent into the woods. The Master Warden himself took a handful of his own men and headed up into the pasture towards the altar. He wasn't seen again for another three days.

Paiva spent the time that passed sitting on a boulder out in the pasture watching the sheep, waiting for him to return while Warden Lier's rangers paced the perimeters of her father's land. Ramsi returned with a squad of rangers first. He was filthy, his clothes torn and ripped. She had never seen him reappear from the woods in such a state. He was tired and had an edgy look in his eyes that he cast accusingly on the other rangers who were not nearly as dirty or tired looking as he. She could only imagine what they had done to him.

Yulin returned with the rest of the rangers during the night. The dog howled an alarm at his arrival and both the Ibbies and the rangers went out into the yard to greet him.

"Where have you been? What have you found?" Viviel asked. Yulin was dirty, his boots brown with mud and his neatly cropped beard was in disarray. He smelled of horse, woodsmoke and swamp. He was calm, his face unreadable.

"Nothing," he said. "No trace of any spirit. I will leave for the Keep tomorrow. If you wish for your daughter to accompany me, you had best prepare."

— ‹›—

To Ramsi's utter discontent, Warden Yulin seized his horse.

"That is my horse," he protested.

"See that brand on its neck? That means it is property of the Keep. And it was given to you under commission of the Master Warden of the Keep. And I am the Master Warden of the Keep," Yulin replied firmly. He led it out of the stables into the square where his men and Paiva were waiting.

"You can't just take a man's horse," Ramsi nearly yelled.

"The young lady certainly cannot walk behind us all the way to the Keep."

"She can't ride my horse, she can't ride a ranger's horse," he protested loudly. "She'll kill herself." But even as he complained Paiva swung up in his saddle without any trouble at all. Her father adjusted her stirrups and handed her the reins, then tucked a small bundle of her belongings behind her, securing it for the journey.

"Safe home," he whispered to her.

Yulin swung up in his own saddle, then delicately slipped on his leather gloves, eyeing Ramsi disapprovingly.

"If you would prefer to contest my actions I invite you to send a complaint to the Lord himself. I am sure the Lord will be quick to respond."

"You chose my horse on purpose," Ramsi spat.

"I did," Yulin frowned. "I like it. I'm sure you will find another."

Yulin turned his horse away, his men ranking behind him, Paiva in the midst of them. She looked back to wave to her parents, her heart tight in her chest. She had never left her home before; she had never even journeyed so far as the next town. She felt a mixture of anger and sadness towards her parents who were making her leave it.

Her father held his arm tightly around her mother whose eyes were filled with tears. Then Paiva's eyes raked across Ramsi, and for a fiery moment he held her gaze. He lifted his hand to his lips and blew her a kiss. She knew in that instant, his eyes she had once thought were so becoming, held a vindictive promise. She looked away quickly and didn't dare turn back for a final glimpse of her home.

— ‹› —

They stopped in the neighboring Quarrytown, a good day's journey from Birchloam. Quarrytown was a large and prominent township. There was a huge, dusty limestone pit that employed a good number of trades people from about the land; mostly masons, builders and laborers. The Quarry was also the place outcast women were sent to work, cutting and shaping the limestone that would be loaded onto oxcarts or sent down the river on barges to various destinations where stone was needed for building. Men were sent to the woods, and women to Quarrytown where they were treated like slaves. Just as the brand on a Wilderman's hand marked him as a pariah, a woman who had spent years toiling in the pit had hands as calcified and hard as the stone she cut and she too would hide her hands in shame. The orphanages of the God- dish monks were overwhelmed with children whose mothers had been sent to the pit. Sometimes children were rescued by relatives or friends, the unfortunate ones by the monks.

They passed through the dusty town, winding down long streets that were rutted and pitted from ox carts. The streets were filled with dirty, wild-eyed children and stray dogs that ran amok. They passed a beautiful stone Bethel House, a place for Goddish worship, and Paiva stared at it with naive eyes. She did not understand the symbols carved into the stone above the door, she did not understand how people could give their love and thanks to a god who had no face. The forest was all around them; the forest she could see and feel and understand. It was to the forest she offered her own thanks and love.

They rested at the Quarters of the resident Warden where the men's horses were taken into the barns. They were given rooms in which to sleep. They went to eat in a room called the Ranger's Mess where on the walls hung with hunting trophies and paintings of famous Wardens and rangers of the past. There were wooden tables with pews to sit in and Paiva stuck close to Yulin, who invited her to eat with him. Paiva found many curious eyes on her from the resident rangers who ate and drank together in the mess. Yulin seemed very uninterested in the curiosity he had aroused.

They were served hot suppers from a small kitchen and though Paiva was very hungry and weary from their travels, she found the food to be very bland. Potatoes and bread with a lean, unidentifiable meat were covered in a greasy, tasteless gravy.

"Master Yulin?" she asked. He lifted his brow in question, chewing a bite of gravy-soaked bread. "Those three Wildermen," she said in a low tone. "You know them."

"Yes," he said simply, taking a sip from his mug of ale.

"How?"

"I was the very one that branded them. It is hard to forget a man you cast a brand upon."

"How did they cross the river?" she asked curiously.

Yulin shrugged. "There are a few possibilities," he mused. "Usually we begin to comb the lowlands in midsummer for trespassers because the waters run low and the Wildermen begin to plot ways of crossing it. All the ones that I have caught have either swum or built coracles or rafts or other floating things. Many drown, but then there are the ones that appear in spring or in fall, when the waters are too cold or too swollen for crossing with such primitive equipment. I used to think there were hidden tunnels running beneath the river, until I realized that some Wildermen tamed these wild horses called Bergs that can tow a bloody war ship across the river. Luckily there aren't many Wildermen who can tame Bergs and the ones that do are too smart to be caught in the lowlands. Usually they cross for food, which is why they are sent rations, and don't often prove to be dangerous."

"I've never heard of Warden Lier going across the Panderbank."

"He has. He's supposed to bring the Wildermen in his domain rations, and tally them."

She frowned, remembering how the Wildermen had complained of not having rations since last autumn. She did not tell Yulin this.

"Did you mark their ledgers?" she asked.

He shrugged again. "If I marked their ledgers it would only come back to haunt your father. There was no point. They did no harm. Their ledgers are long enough."

She frowned, stirring her eating knife through the gravy on her plate. "What did they do to get sent to the woods?" she asked quietly. It was a question that had been burning in her.

"I think Jorn skimped on taxes. He was a farmer, if I recall correctly. He's harmless. About as smart as a sack of nails." Yulin frowned as he recollected. She was in awe of Yulin's sharp memory. She assumed he probably did know every man and his ledger that was ever sent to the woods, for he would have been the man that branded them. "Tergis Ramber, he worked for Master Orif at the Keep. He's a thief, a liar, and there was some sort of indiscretion towards Orif's daughter."

"And Black Renn?" she asked.

Yulin cleaned his trencher with the last of his bread. "Murderer," he said, stuffing the last bite in his mouth. "Terrible supper this. You'll find Bessil knows how to make real gravy."

Chapter 5

They left the dust of Quarrytown behind them the next day and headed into the foothills, following the slope of the land southwards where eventually it became flat and filled with pastures and farm ranges. They took the high road that cut from Quarrytown to the next village, a small place called Grodalweir. They passed peasants and carts en route to various business and errands and all stepped clear of the road when Yulin marched his men past. The peasants kept their eyes lowered and their heads bowed, not even curious enough to look at the strange girl riding on a ranger's horse.

When they came to Grodalweir, they stopped only for one short hour while Yulin went to visit with the resident Warden. Yulin's rangers tended to the horses while they waited in the muddy village square and ate stale bread from the dirty kitchens. For all they cared she was but an extra saddle bag to tow along. None ventured to speak a word to her, and even amongst themselves they were quiet and solemn.

The rangers of Birchloam were different from this lot of men. There was a camaraderie and a carefree brotherliness amongst Birchloam's ranks. When they left for the woods, usually headed off by Ramsi, they often went to it in a race through the village — their cloaks flying, their horse's heels kicking up dirt and dust. Yulin's rangers were entirely different. They were seasoned men, soldiers, not village boys who had earned a red cloak.

When one ranger handed her a bite to eat she smiled her thanks, expecting a kinder response than an icy silence. That ranger had a scarred claw mark streaked down the side of his chin to his neck, where it disappeared under the folds of his cloak. His eyes were a slate gray, almost colorless and empty of kindness. They did not look like they could truly hold thoughts, they looked like the lifeless eyes of a man who had been commanded all his life and whose only duty was to obey. These rangers were not village boys, they were hunting dogs, trained to the master's whip and the call of the hunt.

Grodalweir itself was a dismal place. The people who passed them in the streets kept their eyes lowered and their backs stooped, as if trying to ward off a chill that might catch them. None offered acknowledgment to the other, no one called their 'hello's or 'good-day's. It was as if each thought the other a thief or a scoundrel of some sort, for any looks that were exchanged were mistrustful and guarded. It was entirely unlike Birchloam and it made her heart pang with whimsy for her home.

Here the streets were dirty and the houses showed signs of neglect and poverty. The only work available, it seemed, were for oxcarters carrying stone from Quarrytown to the Keep, a chandlery that filled the streets with an awful stink of tainted animal fats, and a chapel house whose steps were filled with sleeping dirty urchins and drunks. The farms that encompassed the village were scraggly and unkempt. Some fields were so far gone with weeds and rabbit bushes that there was no use for them but to graze cattle and oxen. The cattle were thin and dirty, their eyes filled with flies.

Paiva was disconcerted by this town, for it seemed the closer she travelled to the Keep the dirtier and more hostile people became towards each other. She thought of how sad her father would be to see people live in such a way, for clearly, they had no love for each other or even for themselves, and certainly none for the great Forest.

Yulin pressed them onwards from Grodalweir and by the time the sun waned low in the sky the trees had given way to a great expanse of greening moors, and on the horizon, rose the steepled form of the Keep. They slept in a verderer's hut that night, and by full sun the next day they had passed through the moors and into the farm fields that encompassed the Keep.

Paiva was in awe of it when they arrived. She tilted her head back to take in the great expanse of stone walls that stood guard around the Keep. There were men at arms that paced the ramparts above her, banners that flapped in the breeze from the turrets, a cacophony of noises and smells. She felt so very small and out of place and wished for all the world to return home, where stone walls were not the size of mountains and there were not so many people that they did not all know each other by name.

Yulin led them through the gate and into the bailey square where there were so many things happening at once it made Paiva's head spin. There were people in bright clothes in colors she had not known could be woven into garments. There were sounds and smells that confused her, wood smoke and hot iron, horse and sweat and refuse and sometimes a wafting cloud of baking bread and the strange spices of roasting meat. There was the din of voices, striking metal, heavy hooves. There were was a dirty man tied to a pillar in the middle of the square, his hands chained and his body covered in the stains of refuse that had been flung at him. He sat dejected, his head bent forwards into his lap while he awaited an unknown sentence.

Above it all was the Keep itself, rising so tall into the sky it cast all beneath it in its long shadow. Around it wound streets lined with houses and shops, trade guilds and smithies. It was like a beehive. She had not known so many people could all live on top of each other. Yulin sensed her shock at this new world and gave her an understanding smile.

— «» —

"The kitchens are a rumor mill, it would be best if you kept to yourself," Yulin said as he led her from the stables. She nodded absently, too busy reconciling with her new environment. He led her through long stone corridors and up through a series of heavy doors, out into a hall with vaulted ceilings.

"This is the great hall," he said. His voice seemed to float away and echo through the large room. There were ornate tapestries hanging on the walls, tall arched windows that were flooded with beams of moted light, a massive fireplace that glowed with dying coals. In here it was quiet, the world outside muted by the thick walls.

He led her across the hall and into another passage, down into the kitchens where she heard the clamor of cook pots and the babble of voices. He came to a door at the bottom of the stairs and rapped sharply, then let himself in. The door gave way to a blast of hot air that smelled of roasting meats and breads, the commotion of noises within amplified.

"The Master Warden's here," a voice bellowed. Paiva entered the kitchen behind Yulin and blinked about. There was a column of steam rising from a simmering pot over an iron stove, a series of bread ovens lined a stone wall, each heated by the inner working of flues from the great fireplace over which spitted chickens were being turned by a freckled girl in a dirty apron. There was a long wooden working table over which many young maids bent their backs while kneading and mixing dough. From the rafters hung bushels of herbs and salted meats. One wall was dedicated to crockery and cupboards, and at the far end of the kitchen were windows above doors to the cellars and storeroom and streets.

A large woman with graying hair emerged from a cloud of steam and pushed her way through the girls.

"Master Yulin," she huffed. Then her eyes landed on Paiva.

"Hello Aunt Bess," Paiva said.

The heavy woman's red face broke into a grin. "By my soul have you grown, you're the spitting image of your mother. The last time I saw you, you were still sitting on your father's knee." She came and hugged Paiva with damp arms. She smelled of flour and spices. Paiva felt at home once again. Aunt Bessil was but a bigger, louder version of her mother.

"Did you come with Master Yulin? I expected your father would bring you down in the cart. You must forgive me but I haven't found you a place to stay yet. No troubles though, I'll find somewhere for you."

"All is well then," Yulin said, he nodded to Bessil.

"Ah, Master Yulin, can I fetch you something? I suppose you've just come back from the road. Perhaps you'd like to refresh yourself with something?" Bessil asked.

"Though I have been waiting to taste your cooking again, I have duties to attend to that cannot wait. I will return later for my usual treat." He bent his head in a curt nod to the both of them and headed back to the stairwell. Paiva noticed then the kitchen had grown quiet and there were a dozen eyes staring at her. Bessil heaved her frame around, bearing her hands on her hips.

"This is my niece, young Paiva Ibbie. We've been expecting her," she said sweetly to the kitchen. "Now back to work the lot of you, we've a supper to prepare for tonight." She ushered Paiva along to the far side of the kitchen where she opened one of the doors that led down to the cellar. She kindly helped to stow Paiva's travelling bag atop a row of pickling barrels and then embraced Paiva once again.

"Your father sent me news of what came to pass," she said. "I'm only glad that none of you were hurt."

"Thank you for taking me on."

"Oh it will be a pleasure," she beamed happily. "Having my own blood in my own kitchen. There's only one condition."

"Yes Aunt Bess, of course."

"You don't steal none of my recipes and give them to your mother."

— «» —

It was late in the evening, after the supper had been served and taken away. Paiva was helping a quiet maid named Dorta to scrub pots in a barrel when Yulin reappeared at the kitchen door. Bessil went over to him and he nodded curtly.

"Excellent meal, Bessil," he said. "Finally I have rid myself of the taste of Grodalmeir gravy and dust from the road." Bessil's red face seemed to flush deeper and she grabbed hold of her apron and mopped at her face.

"Thank you, Master Yulin. It pleases me to hear it."

The quiet maid next to Paiva leaned in close and whispered to her, "The way to a man's heart is through his stomach." Paiva smiled shyly.

"I would like to speak with your niece again, if she is not too tired."

"No heavens, no," she said sweetly. She turned her head to the kitchen and barked, "Paiva!"

Paiva set aside her pots and went with Yulin up the stairwell and out into the great hall. There were low candles burning on the table, a few maids scurrying about to sweep the floor. She followed him out into the hall wherein lurked the shaggy frames of hunting hounds beneath the tables and men at arms standing still beneath the low light of flickering torches. They went into a labyrinth of corridors and then up into a stairwell that seemed to never end.

She realized they were mounting the tower, and by the time they reached the top she was breathing hard. He led her to a chamber door and rapped on it. A voice from within beckoned him, and he swung the door open. Paiva blinked in confusion, for when she glimpsed the interior of the chamber there seemed to be a hundred faces staring at her. She stepped inside after Yulin, a shiver of fear sneaking up her spine. There were candles burning in the room, casting eerie, flickering light into a hundred pairs of glass eyes in preserved heads of hideous beasts, mounted like trophies lining the walls — their horror frozen on display. The faces were each unique, each a horrible blend of man and animal and nightmare. She stared at them, too shocked to see the man at his writing desk before her.

"Ahem," Yulin said, drawing Paiva's eyes back down. He looked at her and bowed, suggesting she follow suit. Immediately she bent her knees and bowed her head, pulling her dirty apron into a curtsy.

"My Lord," Yulin said, and Paiva realized with a shock who it was she was standing before. "I have brought you the sheep herder's daughter."

Sitting before her dressed in the finest coat of silk and brocade, with chains of gold and silver splashed across his chest and an ornately stitched cap, was Lord Pratermora himself. He was older than Paiva's father, his perfectly groomed blonde beard heavily streaked with gray. There were deep lines in his brow and about his mouth, but where her father had plenty of lines that crinkled in the corner of his eyes, the Lord had none. His eyes were a pale blue, startling against the deep purple of his robes and coat. They narrowed as they looked at her, as if he saw her very bones through her flesh.

"She looks afraid. I assume she has only ever imagined what you look like." A woman's voice floated out from behind the Lord. She moved from the window and stepped closer to the light. Paiva had to blink again, not believing what she saw.

A milky face with deep, pooling eyes came closer, belonging to a woman much younger than the Lord — beautiful, exquisite, as if made of clay. Her hair was the burnt red of the setting sun, strung up with a glitter of pearl pins. Her gown was the same deep and expensive purple of the Lord's, silken and flowing with intricate designs. Looped through her arms was a throw made of orange fox fur to keep off the chill of the tower. When Paiva met the lady's eyes, the chill deepened.

"I am Lady Ceitra," she said. "Please sit, and speak with us. We talked about you over our supper tonight and we were curious to meet you." Lady Ceitra's eyes followed Paiva as Yulin offered her a chair before the Lord's writing desk. There was a small smile that pulled at Ceitra's perfectly shaped lips. It was not unfriendly, but neither was it warm.

"Yulin tells me of what came to pass with Varloga," the Lord began, and Paiva felt a rush of relief for not having to tell a curbed tale to the imposing man before her. "We are all curious as to the reasons why Varloga chooses the people he does. He is like a hawk, forever circling in the light of the sun that blinds the hares below him. He is always there, always watching and waiting. Of a sudden he will strike, leaving the warren of hares ruined with terror and grief."

"I do not know, Milord. I wish I did. But I am safe now, behind your great walls."

Paiva saw the corner of Pratermora's lips lift in a smile. It was a sad smile that did not reach his eyes. "So you are. You see these faces about you, lining my walls?" He lifted his pale eyes to the flickering walls. Paiva followed them, fear turning her blood cold.

"What are they?"

"Demons, nightmares let loose from hell," he said. "Or what someone from Birchloam would call a Folka. This is a collection of preserved heads that began with my forefathers.

Every time a Wilderman culls a Folka he brings me its head back and asks for his pardon. Only the finest are mounted on my wall; only the finest are worthy of a pardon." Paiva looked away and found that Ceitra's dark eyes were on her, studying her with that curious little smile.

"One day Varloga's head will be on that wall," Pratermora said. "But I must know why it is he hunts the people he does. I must find some weakness to cripple him."

"I cannot tell you, Milord."

"No, I didn't expect you to give me any answers. I just wanted to look at you. I wanted to see if there was something about you that was different. But you are just another girl, like many others."

"Her eyes," Ceitra said. Yulin and Pratermora both looked at her curiously. Ceitra's strange smile grew, though it did not touch her eyes. Her eyes remained secret, liquid pools.

"She does have peculiar eyes, does she not, My Lord?" Ceitra said.

"Green maybe," Pratermora said indifferently. "Yulin's eyes are green as well."

"But there is a gold in them. Very peculiar, very stunning."

"Varloga does not go about collecting eyes," the Lord returned.

"No not eyes, My Lord, but souls. Those pretty eyes are linked to her soul. Every thought, every feeling that she has, you can see it in the light that passes through them, as anyone's soul can be seen. Perhaps that is something to think about."

"What would be different from her soul than any other girls?" Pratermora asked. "There is no pattern to the people Varloga takes. Some are poor, some are highborn. Some are children, some are old. Even when we researched their lineage, there was nothing that linked them. No great ancestor, no old blood that connected them from times past. There is no rhyme or reason to it."

"There is always a reason," Ceitra said. She went and fetched a decanter of wine from the far end of the room, her skirts gliding behind her, her footsteps echoing with sharp clicks of her heels. The sightless, soulless glass eyes stared down at Ceitra as she took a sip from her drink. "There is a reason why the woods are filled with nightmares. There is a reason why Varloga has risen again."

Paiva felt like a specimen in a glass case hanging on the wall of the apothecary shop in Birchloam. People were forever eyeing them, trying to identify the creatures so neatly pinned on display.

"Of course there is a reason, my dear," Pratermora said. "I just can't fathom it. I am so tired of being afraid of what I do not understand."

"Who else has been taken?" Paiva asked timidly. She saw a shadow slip across Pratermora's face.

"Perhaps we shall call it an evening then," Yulin said. "My weary back is aching for its bed. As you can see, I have discovered nothing new."

"No," Pratermora said. "Good night Yulin."

"Good night, Paiva Ibbie," Ceitra called from the window. "I am ever so glad Yulin was kind enough to bring you all this way."

"Yes, Milady. Goodnight." She rose from her seat and gave another wobbly curtsy, then followed Yulin back down the stairs. Yulin grabbed a torch from the wall and quietly escorted her back to the kitchens.

Bessil commented on the weary rings beneath his eyes and ushered him off to bed with a small sweet tart she tucked in a napkin for him. Then the kitchen was tidy and empty but for her and Paiva. A low fire crackled in the great oven and there was a lamp lit on the work table beside a mug of ale Bessil had been drinking.

"Well like I said, I didn't know you were coming so soon and I didn't have a chance to find room in the maid's quarters," said Bessil. "You'll have to sleep here in the kitchens, and if you ask me it's the coziest place in all the Keep, especially in winter, right by the oven. You wake up smelling like a loaf of fresh baked bread." On the wall alongside the oven was a frame of wood hanging on the wall. Bessil unlatched a hook and the boards fell away on a hinge, catching on two chains to make a very long collapsible shelf. There was a thin mattress on it that puffed a cloud of dust and flour when Bessil beat it clean. Paiva realized this was her bed.

"I never thought I would end up here," Paiva said, staring at the flimsy bed. She sat on it and tested her weight while Bessil fetched blankets and a flour sack stuffed with hay for a pillow. "I never thought I would meet the Lord and Lady of the land."

"Ah, how did that go? What did you think of them lot upstairs?"

"Lady Ceitra is so beautiful. Pratermora must have picked her from some faraway place."

Bessil heaved a laugh. "You think Ceitra is Pratermora's wife?" She cackled. "My goodness, what do they teach you up in Birchloam? Everyone in all the land knows that Ceitra is the widow of Pratermora's son. Pratermora's own wife died long ago. The Dark Spirits got her in the end."

Paiva recalled the shadow that had fallen over Pratermora's face. "I never knew. I suppose I was really never interested. Father's always talking of old families and lineages, it's hard to keep track. All I knew was there was some old man in a tower at the other end of the land that we had to make sure we paid our taxes to. I know all the local gossip, though. I know almost everything that happens in Birchloam the moment it happens."

"Yes, it's a small village," Bessil said, tossing her blankets to her. "I bet you are the talk of it, riding away with Master Yulin."

Bessil helped tuck her in by the fire, showing her where there was a broom and a bucket of water in case there should ever be a fire started in the middle of the night. She then went to the back door that lead onto the street and let in a black stray cat that jumped up on the table and looked at Paiva with wide, blinking eyes. Bessil locked and bolted the door behind it.

"This is Horrigs," Bessil said. "He chases the rats."

Bessil bid her goodnight then and trundled out of the kitchen with a sigh, weary of her day's work. Paiva watched the cat saunter his way to the fire where he sat on his haunches and blinked at her with wide yellow eyes. His tail twitched, then he threw himself into a long stretch, clearly more interested in the luxuries of the kitchen than in eating rats.

Paiva considered the course her life was taking. After the initial shock of the upheaval in finding herself far from home and alone aside from Bessil, she settled on not being unhappy about it. She focused on the good things that were all about her — she thought of her parents asleep in the little house beneath the pasture, of the stories she would tell them when she would be united with them again. Her father's happy smile, her mother's proud eyes. She would be the only girl in Birchloam who ever helped to cook the Lord his supper. She imagined her friends begging to hear of the things she had seen; she imagined how for weeks they would have visitors come to their farm to hear her tales. With that happy thought she succumbed to sleep, too tired to think any longer.

Chapter 6

She woke to Bessil blundering into the kitchen, the door swinging open and straining against its hinges. Bessil stomped down the stairs, rubbing sleep from her eyes and mumbling incoherently beneath her breath. The first thing she did was find Horrigs and chase him outside, then she swung her bulk towards the hearth and began throwing wood on the fire to get the ovens hot for the day.

"Come on girlie," she said to Paiva, who blinked disconcertingly into the gray light that filtered into the kitchen. Paiva woke with a sense of confusion, taking a moment to settle her wits and assure herself she was meant to be where she was and there was no mistake. Then she rose and began to help Bessil sort out the fire. Seeing that Paiva understood the concept of making fire hot, Bessil fetched herself a cup of watery ale and sat for a moment at the work table to drink it and liven herself.

"I'll expect you to get the fires hot before I come in from now on," she grumbled and then shoved a finger in her ear to clean it out. "I like efficiency in my kitchen, and seeing as you'll be sleeping here for a while yet we might as well find a use for you. Get the fire hot then open the flues on the ovens, boil some water, and there you have it." She then inspected her finger and frowned at it, and Paiva wondered what it was she had dislodged from the innards of her own ear. Bessil wiped it away on her apron, swallowed her ale and then went about preparing for the day. Paiva changed from her nightshift into her homespun dress and received a battered apron from Bessil on her return from the storeroom.

Soon the maids began arriving, each rubbing sleep from their eyes and yawning. Half-asleep, they went about their chores, eating their own hurried bowls of gruel before preparing the morning's meal for the rest of the Keep.

Paiva found the maids to have the same edge to them as everyone else she had encountered in the lowlands. They scrutinized her and threw her dirty looks, unwelcoming and mistrustful. They did not offer her any help and avoided speaking to her. She grew tired of their cool manners and opted not to talk to any one of them regardless of whether they showed interest in her or not. The only maid that was glad of her company was Dorta, a small freckled girl with mousy hair and a wiry frame. She was younger than Paiva, who would see her nineteenth year that coming summer. Dorta was shy and impressionable, terrified of Bessil, and in desperate want of a friend. Whether or not Bessil was aware of this Paiva did not know, but they found themselves paired together in scrubbing pots, peeling vegetables and most other chores.

As they worked together, Dorta eagerly divulged her life story, telling Paiva she came from a large family. Her father was a smithy and lived in a little shop in the working quarters, while her brothers were field boys and went to work in the farmlands beyond the walls. Her one sister she adored was the youngest and still no higher than her mother's apron strings. Paiva in turn told her about Birchloam and her own home. Dorta listened raptly, never before having met someone from the most far-off village. Paiva felt a pang of longing for her home as she described the pastures and the thick birch tree forests. She felt entirely out of place here, enclosed within this beehive of a castle where everyone was walking and talking over each other. She made no mention of Varloga or the reasons why she left it, for Yulin had warned her not to.

In the days that followed, she and Dorta became inseparable. They were sent into the market with a wooden cart to gather produce and ingredients from the local vendors. Dorta took her under her wing and taught her how to be a serving maid, teaching her how to curtsy properly and what and what not to say when talking to a Highborn. Paiva was sent up into the Great Hall under Dorta's supervision where she helped to serve and clear the meals they prepared. The first meal she attended to was a supper.

The Lord Pratermora, Lady Ceitra and Yulin sat at the high table at the far end of the Great Hall, their backs warming in the light of one of the hearths built into every one of the four walls. Joining them at the trestle tables were knights, highborns and other officials. They were all dressed in splendid finery, knights with golden sigils stitched across their chests and long swords at their hips. The highborns sat in tunics and robes that glittered with pendants and sequins, the officials in their designated uniforms. A notary was there with a cap on his head and a long swan feather stuck in it, with a lawyer dressed all in black but for a red cravat about his throat. Dorta had warned her not to gawk, for a serving maid was supposed to have a small presence, moving unnoticed and without bother as the guests went about their business and supper. Paiva could not help but to stare at the ladies accompanying the knights and highborns. She could not imagine how they could support their own dresses, so thick with layers of shimmering silk and blooming veils. Their bodies looked small and trapped within. She gaped at their hair, stacked and curled in towering masses, shimmering with opulent jewels and pins. Their faces had strange colors as well, their cheeks rouged with powder, their eyelids blushed the same color as their dresses. Some even had a small shining jewel pasted to the corners of their eyes or on the peak of their cheeks. Dorta rescued her a few times from her staring, giving her a sharp elbow or a startling whisper as she passed.

Lady Ceitra was always the finest of the ladies. There was something about her that made her outshine the others, something in her commanding presence that drew all eyes to her. Paiva found it disconcerting when she served her wine or cleared her plates, for Ceitra's eyes always had a way of looking at her that left her slightly chilled.

This supper was arranged for a hearing of wrongdoing. After the nobles had eaten guards presented the man whom Paiva had seen tied to the pillar for days in the bailey. His accuser came forward as well: a prominent landowner dressed in a fine tunic with a felt cap on his head. Between clearing dishes and serving wine Paiva was able to hear and see most of the trial.

The accused man stood hunched and listless before the tables, covered in filth and half-starved. His beard had grown in, hiding his dirty face. The lawyer, who was a relatively young and handsome man, addressed the case: the accused man owed rent and had been evicted from his land. This was not the worst of it, for in a cold vengeance the accused man had burned down the homestead.

He pleaded not guilty to the arson, though he did admit to being unable to pay his rent. The rent was not as serious an issue; that would only earn the man a small term in prison. The premeditated burning of a landlord's property was more serious.

"Why would I burn it?" the ragged man said. "Everything I owned was in it. All my tools, my horses…. Why would I burn it?"

"To spite me," the landowner spat.

"If I wanted to spite you Master Girt I'd have burned your own house down before I burned mine."

"Do you hear the threats he utters?!" cried the landowner to the Lord. The Lord looked to Yulin as if he was suffering a jogging headache. The lawyer handed Lord the ledger he had written up during the course of the hearing and he read it through thoughtfully. He then raised his eyes to the accused man and uttered the words no man would ever want to hear.

"I find you guilty," the Lord said. He lowered his head and muttered with Yulin before rising from his seat to depart back to his chambers atop the tower.

"To the woods then," Yulin said and went to throw a long iron in the hearth behind him. The accused man straightened then and a wave of fear spread over his face.

"No… please!" he shouted as guards came forward and seized him. He began to scream as Yulin turned the iron in the coals, watching it grow red hot. He drew it from the flames and strode towards the man, the glowing brand smoking. The man writhed as he had his hand pressed flat in a wooden press, a guard holding him still by a wrenching handful of hair. Paiva and Dorta both fled into the refuge of the kitchen before they could witness the horrible scorching of flesh.

Bessil was at the work table kneading a mound of dough, humming to herself as the man screamed. The other maids went about their chores as if there was nothing amiss and they were not all listening to the sound of a man's life being thrown away.

"Why can't he go to prison, why was he not given a choice?" she asked Dorta as they brought dishes to the sink.

"I suppose the prisons are full," Dorta shrugged. "There are enough mouths to feed around here."

— «» —

Paiva began writing to her parents shortly after, telling them of everything she had seen and describing the meals that Bessil cooked without divulging any secret recipes. She gave them to Bessil to post, who in turn brought Paiva the letters her parents sent in return. Each one she waited for eagerly always disappointed her in some way, for none of them were an invitation to come back home. So she bided her time in the kitchens, working hard during the day and spending long hours in the night trying to befriend Horrigs who remained too aloof for any want of real companionship.

The only other friends she made were the urchins that sat huddled outside the kitchen in the filthy streets waiting for scraps of food. She was under strict orders from Bessil to keep the door to the streets firmly locked at night for fear they would invade her kitchens. They changed from day to day — sometimes there were more, sometimes less, all huddled in a row along the street across from the kitchen door beneath their rags of clothes. They opened their hands to passersby and waited anxiously for the moment the kitchen doors would open and scraps would be tossed to them.

There was an old blind woman who could not work and had no one to take care of her. There was a toothless widow who had spent many hard years in the Quarrytown pit before her Wilderman husband had died and set her free. She was then left without a station and without work, but she said she would rather beg than to go back to the pit. Paiva was kind to them and even Bessil, who cursed them up and down, didn't mind Paiva leaving extra scraps out for them. But Paiva was diligent to never upset Bessil. She always made sure by the time the maids began filing in bleary-eyed in the morning that the fires were hot and roaring, the floor swept and hot tea and gruel ready for their breakfast. The days began to warm as spring blossomed into early summer and the kitchens became hotter and stuffier. Bessil seemed to like Paiva's sleeping arrangement and never bothered to find her other quarters.

One morning, Paiva rose in the first blush of dawn to chase Horrigs out onto the street with the broom when she was startled by the blasting call of a horn. She stepped out into the street curiously, wondering what the noise was all about. She asked the urchins what was going on and the toothless widow gave her a gummy smile.

"Wildermen," she said. Paiva's heart lurched.

"Coming back with a trophy," another urchin said. As the horn continued to blast Paiva hurried back inside, her heart surging with hope, for perhaps the head they were bringing back was that of Varloga's. Perhaps then she could leave this place and return to her home.

— «» —

Bessil trundled in with an exasperated look, knocking her maids out of the way as she muttered to herself and went to the cellars. Dorta came to sit next to Paiva with her breakfast and Paiva asked her about the horns.

"Wildermen," Dorta said. "There are Wildermen coming down the river."

"Down the river?" Paiva asked.

"That's how they come when they have a Folka head. It's the only way they have to cross the Panderbank, on a stonecutter's barge." Paiva felt it on the tip of her tongue to tell her otherwise but thought better of it. "Bessil's all upset about it. It means the great hall will be packed tonight."

"Why?"

"For the Pardoning. The Lord will be presented with the Wilderman's trophy, and if he deems it worthy of being mounted on his wall in the chamber atop the Keep, the

Wilderman will be granted his pardon. If not, he will be sent back to the woods to try again — or die, whichever comes first. But tonight they will eat and drink among civilized men again and the Lord will be happy to see a dead Folka. It is the best of entertainment, hearing the Wildermen tell the tale of their hunt and stories from the woods, where no one goes but them."

— «» —

Bessil came back from the cellars and started yelling orders, very much the captain of her ship. The maids hurried to finish their meals and gather their dishes to be washed, then hustled about gathering ingredients and preparing utensils. There was a light lunch of boiled ham and salted cabbage that the servants came and fetched to bring to their appropriate wards. The maids ate the scraps of their cooking's, too busy to sit and eat, while Bessil tallied orders. There was lamb stewed in a wine sauce, four cauldrons over the fires simmering with boiling potatoes, and the ovens were stuffed full of breads and pastries. Four geese were plucked and stuck on a spit, while three rows of chickens roasted below them over the same fire. A great bowl of pudding was baked, requiring two maids to each grab a side of the huge dish to stuff in the oven. Bessil sweated like a high-strung horse as she stomped around the kitchen. She could not read or write very well and had committed a hundred recipes to memory, and somehow, she managed them all at the same time. When she was not supervising her maids she went back down in the cellar and returned while single-handedly carrying a barrel of wine or cider on her shoulder. When she lowered it down into the service racks she would help herself to a mug of it, making her cheeks flush very rosy and her voice become all the louder.

"This is all for the Wildermen?" Paiva flustered to Dorta as they mashed butter into flour for pie crusts.

"No!" Dorta exclaimed with a light laugh, "For all the highborns and rich men who will come to see them. It's sport for them, like watching a dog fight or a horse race."

"Dorta! Paiva!" Bessil shouted from the ovens. "Go into the bailey and fetch me four dozen eggs, a tankard of vinegar, a roll of cheesecloth, and ginger if there's any to be found. Then go to the butcher and get him to bring over that pork flank he promised me."

Dorta struggled to remember the list but Paiva had an easy time cataloguing it. They headed out to the bailey with their little wooden cart, relishing the cool air that brought relief from the hot, stuffy kitchens.

They had no trouble fetching all the ingredients but they could not find the butcher. His wife, with her bloody apron and hands, said her husband was out looking at the Folka head in the bailey. She said when he was back she would send him over with Bessil's pork flank.

When they returned to the kitchens and carted the goods in Bessil was screaming at a crying maid who had scorched a meat pie. Bessil looked like a war chief in the fray of a battle. After scolding her soundly Bessil sent the maid with Paiva and Dorta to dress the great hall table.

— «» —

By the time the windows had darkened with dusk, Bessil was content that her supper was in order. She cracked open a barrel of cider and let each maid have a mug to drink and some bread to eat. They all fanned themselves exhaustedly and mopped at their necks with their aprons, most finding a place to seat themselves and rest their aching feet before the long ordeal of supper began.

When it did, every last maid carried a steaming platter of food up into the hall and set it before their assigned places on the table before the noblemen. There was the murmur of exchanged talk and a bard on a lute that strummed a dreary song. Purebred hounds the rich men brought searched the floor with wet noses for scraps, and a juggler juggled anything he could, discarding his colored balls to collect goblets and plates as he made his way along the table. No one minded him very much, for he was not the best of the entertainment to come.

The Lord Pratermora and the Lady Ceitra were seated at the head of the table. Paiva and Dorta were given the task of standing at the ready, each with a pitcher of wine to refill empty cups and to inform Bessil if platters needed to be restocked. Dorta smirked at Paiva's wide eyes again as she stared about the colorful array of people.

"Fancy marrying a nobleman one day, do you?" Dorta whispered discreetly to her.

"That one in the red vest is very handsome," Paiva replied. Dorta searched him out and giggled.

"He's a knight," she said. "Be careful if you serve him too much wine, he likes to hide his hands in our skirts. That's his wife beside him, and she's quick to catch him."

Paiva muffled a burst of laughter.

"Which one would you pick?" she asked. Dorta smiled ruefully.

"None of them stuffed pigs," she said. "I like hard-working men, field boys or smithies." But even as she said it her eyes trailed over to a man in a yellow tunic with rusty brown hair. He was tall and gangly, the young hair sprouting on his face teased into a fashionable beard.

— «» —

Warden Yulin came into the hall then and went to stand before the High Table. Everyone fell hushed as all eyes were turned to him.

"My Lord and My Lady," he said, "it is time to present to you the Wilderman's kill and see if a pardon is in order."

Pratermora raised his goblet of wine to the Warden. "It is. Let us see this beast and hear tale of the hunt."

Yulin bowed gracefully with a flourish of his red robes. Paiva was sure that Bessil would swoon if she saw him just then. He raised an arm and motioned for the head to be brought forth. A clatter of men at arms came forward carrying an ornately carved wooden stretcher with a shape covered by a purple silk cloth atop it. Yulin followed the men to the High Table who turned the stretcher lengthwise before the Lord. Yulin grasped the silk and threw it off.

The crowd gasped.

A black, furred head with empty eyes stared back at the Lord. Its twisted mouth was propped open to reveal a row of fangs the size of tusks. Its head was crowned with mossy horns, its ears sharp and pointed like a hound's.

The Lord gazed at it and then took a drink of his wine, a contented smile touching the corner of his lips. Paiva's disgust at the sight of the head was mixed with disappointment. It was not the ghoulish head of the white spirit that had upheaved her life.

"Very fine," the Lord said. There was a low murmur and the shaking of heads from the rest of the tables. Black liquid dripped from the stretcher, staining the floor. Paiva felt her stomach roll and she looked at Dorta who had grown very pale. She pursed her lips and then darted back into the kitchen, leaving Paiva standing alone.

"Is it worthy of a pardon do you think, My Lord?" Yulin's voice questioned.

"Bring in the Wilderman!" Pratermora cheered. "Bring forward the man who killed the beast and let me hear the story of his hunt."

The noblemen all cheered at this, banging their goblets and knives on the table. Yulin bowed and went to fetch the Wildermen while the men holding the stretcher began a slow walk down the length of the tables to display it to everyone there. Paiva saw a woman swoon, and another man looked as if he was about to lose his supper as the head passed them. Pratermora leaned back in his grand chair and tipped his goblet to his contented lips. Ceitra's face was a mask, her dark eyes glittering.

Yulin reappeared, trailed by four dirty, disarmed figures in mud-stained clothes.

"Come forward Wilderman who has slain this prized beast, like the Wildermen of old before you, so you may ask for your pardon," the Lord said.

Paiva felt her heart leap into her throat as the dirtiest of the four stepped forward. Yulin strode back to his Lord with his hands clasped tightly behind his back, but the dirty man did not approach any closer.

"Why, he appears to be a young one," the Lord laughed to Yulin. "Tell me of his ledger."

"His ledger is rather full, My Lord," Yulin said briskly.

"Come forward boy, and tell me your name."

The dirty figure took but one more step closer. "They call me Black Renn," he said. Paiva did not take her eyes from him.

"Speak up. Hold your head high when you address your Lord." A flash of irritation passed over Pratermora's face.

"They call me Black Renn," he repeated more clearly.

"I can see why," came the drunken slur of the man in the red vest. No one laughed and the man looked about in contempt.

Pratermora's face had suddenly become very rigid. Paiva noticed now how Yulin clasped and unclasped his hands nervously behind his back. "Your proper name, the name you wish to be restored to you," the Lord said slowly. "Please."

"Rennik... Pratermora," he said and bowed his head.

The air in the room seemed to freeze. The Lord looked as if he had suddenly been dealt a physical blow, for he sat back in his chair and looked to be sick to his stomach.

"Pratermora?" the Lord breathed after a long-suspended moment. Then his shocked tone strengthened into anger. "That is my own name, and I am the only Pratermora of these lands. It is an old and honorable name. Come forward, boy, so I may see who dares mock me."

Renn took another step.

"Closer!" The Lord's voice ripped through the hall, echoing up through the vaulted ceiling. Renn flinched, but obeyed. He came within a few paces of the Lord and lifted his head, his black hair tumbling back and his silver eyes flashing.

"I am Rennik Pratermora," he said again, his voice somehow broken. "Your youngest son, come to ask for your forgiveness."

Paiva felt her pulse stop. She heard someone whisper her name from behind her but she paid no attention to it. She was riveted in her place by the twisted look on Pratermora's face.

"You look like him," the Lord breathed. "Your face, your eyes. They could be my own. But my son was fair and golden, you are black as the dirty liar you are. Black as the thief that stole him from me."

Renn bowed his head shamefully. The Folka head dripped rancid blood behind him and a hound came to lick it.

"Odrik was my son," Pratermora said. "And he is dead." He rose, the feet of his chair screeching across the stone floor as he pushed it back. He threw his goblet of wine on the table where it clattered against a plate and spilled. He hurtled himself away from the staring eyes of all his nobles, up into the tower where he disappeared.

Yulin looked worriedly to Lady Ceitra, who delicately drank from her wine. Her fingers glittered with shining rings, her red hair laced with the sparkle of pearls. She swallowed bitterly, then looked at Renn, her beauty tragic.

"There will be no pardon," she said in a low voice, and excused herself. Renn watched her go, listening to the click of her footsteps vanish into silence. His face was bereft of emotion.

The Folka head was placed on the table where the Lord had sat. Excited murmurs rang out from the crowd, as did nasty whispers and accusing stares. "The Wildermen shall remain to eat and drink their fill, as is custom, unless they should wish to leave," Yulin called out to the crowd. He looked to Renn, who in turn looked at his hungry companions.

"We will stay," he said.

The Knight in his red vest and his roaming hands picked up a piece of bread and threw it at one of the Wildermen. "Eat blessed convicts, eat and drink and tell us your tales of this wretched beast."

The Wilderman scooped up the bread before the hounds got to it and without hesitation stuffed it in his mouth. The crowd laughed.

"Paiva!" a voice hissed from behind her. Paiva turned around, wide-eyed. "Come here girlie," Bessil hissed. Jolted out of her daze, Paiva went at once. Bessil pulled her down into the kitchen where three maids, including Dorta, had swooned and were being fed cold water by the others to revive them.

"Limp daisies, all of them," Bessil muttered. She shoved a tray at Paiva filled with trenchers and grabbed her own, then headed back out into the hall. Paiva followed, listening to Bessil muttering angrily to herself. They went towards the Wildermen warming themselves by the fire and Paiva felt a sudden stabbing fear.

Renn sat staring into the fire, his face taught, his eyes smoldering. Bessil gave them wine while Paiva let them take their trenchers off her tray. When she came to Renn he tore his eyes away from the fire and his angry glare landed on her. She froze and so did he. The anger melted from his eyes as recognition dawned on him and was replaced by helplessness and shame. He lowered his eyes from her and took his trencher.

Without a word Paiva turned and followed Bessil back to the kitchen.

— «» —

Paiva was acutely aware of Renn's eyes on her every time she stepped into the hall. She did not look at him as she went about gathering plates and sopping up messes. The nobles had risen from their seats and gathered about the Folka head, spilling wine on it as they toasted each other and made crude jokes. A bold lady had taken her fork and stuck it in the creature's eye to a loud cheer from the onlookers. They reminded Paiva of brightly colored crows, cawing over a corpse, leaving a litter of waste and scraps in their wake. The tables were spilled with wine, and there were bones and scraps of bread strewn about and dogs that leapt up on the tables to scavenge them. One of the maids received the sharp side of a lady's tongue for pushing a dog to the floor where it yelped.

Yulin had picked a Wilderman to stand before them all and tell the tale of the hunt. The nobles asked him his name and his ledger, then listened to his tale.

"They call me Millfire Mikal," the man said in a loud voice. "I was a miner from Irontown." He was middle-aged and bow-legged with a strapping chest. Either side of his beard was braided, his face was wide and hollowed, his eyes deeply set and stony.

"In my ledger you will find I was condemned for arson," he began. "I burned a mill down because the miller tried to steal my wife. I have killed two Folka that were not good enough for Pratermora's trophy room, and helped in the hunt of many more that were felled by greater men than I."

"Why on earth have you not got your pardon then, good man?" a fat noble called out in surprise.

"The mill fire burned both the miller and my wife. I'll let you lot imagine what they were doing atop his sacks of flour when I set light to it." For some reason the drunk nobles found this delightful and they erupted into laughter. Paiva and a few other maids had been sent to clear the tables, and she filled her tray slowly so she could listen. She imagined Renn from years ago, standing with them dressed in their bright colors, laughing at these heinous crimes. He was not like them; he had fallen from grace where his bright colors were trampled in the mud and became as black as the sin he had committed.

"What a way to go!" cried another. "Imagine dying making love to a woman? What better way could there be?"

"Burning is a horrible death," Mikal said. His voice was cold. "Whether you're making love or not." They did not hear the contempt in his voice; they laughed all the more. Yulin paced the contours of the hall in the far shadows while the men at arms stood still and rigid at their posts, ready to react should there be trouble between the Wildermen and the nobles or amongst the nobles themselves.

"I am from a hunting camp we call Come by Chance up northwest of the Panderbank. These other two are also." Mikal motioned back to the fire to the two men who curtly nodded their heads. "Renn comes from a camp down lower than us. We do not hunt alone for it requires the skill and the firmness of a group of men to track and chase a Folka to its death. Renn and another fellow came up to trade Berg horses, but they ended up in the middle of a chase with us." The nobles grew quiet, listening raptly. Mikal took a deep breath and continued.

"The beastie felled Renn's gangman and killed the horses, and that's how Renn ended up after it with us. We chased it for days, baited it, waited for it. We thought whoever the lucky man who felled it would surely get a pardon, for it was a fearsome creature. Renn struck an arrow through its heart on the last day of the chase, and the beastie ran and ran and ran, screaming the whole way. We followed the blood trail through the trees and heard its low howls. By the time we found it, it was lying dead in the slash." Paiva looked back to the hearth where Renn sat with his back to her, his black head wreathed in a cloud of smoke from his pipe.

"And that be the tall tale of the hunt. It is a shame the Lord shall not mount the beastie's head on his wall. It is a fine trophy worthy of such a thing."

"Oh, it will be hung on my wall then," said the fat man. "We cannot let such a trophy go to waste."

"I will have it," another quipped. An argument broke out, glasses crashed to the ground and hounds barked. Now it was Mikal's turn to laugh, and laugh he did. He shook his head and walked back to the fire, slapping Renn's shoulder as he sat.

"Gentlemen, Ladies." Yulin came forward. "The head will be sold to the highest bidder, no doubt, and it shall not be settled now." Discourse rang out, snarky voices and cheeky comments were exchanged.

"Let us end this night on a good note," Yulin admonished, and snapped his fingers for the Folka head to be taken away. That seemed to end the evening for the nobles, who began to leave shortly after. The hall emptied one noble by one and the maids slowly tidied up after them and threw the scraps out into the streets for the urchins to scavenge. Whatever had been left in the kitchens was eaten amongst the maids and extra breads were given to the Wildermen for their journey back. They would not leave until the next morning when the barge runner would head upstream. They would be allowed one night to sleep before a fire under shelter.

— «» —

The kitchen was tidied, though the multitude of dishes would be dealt with the next day and the maids went off to their quarters to rest. Dorta bid Paiva goodnight, Horrigs was let in and the door to the street was locked tight behind him. Bessil was the last one in the kitchen with Paiva who sat exhaustedly on a stool and drank a deep mug of wine. She looked thoughtful and reflective.

"It was an accident," Bessil said aloud.

"What was?"

"Rennik and his brother." She took a deep haul of her drink. "I've been here since the boys were little, since before you were ever born. I used to chase them with a switch for stealing my biscuits. I knew them. I knew how the Lord loved Odrik, his heir, and I knew how he disapproved of Renn. You saw those noblemen and ladies tonight. Odrik was like anyone of them. Proud, handsome, arrogant. Rennik was more sympathetic to us simpler people and I know it was because we were the ones who looked after him while Odrik got all the attention of his father and his peers. His trial was unfair, his nose was broken and his mouth bloody so he could not speak his own truth. For all the rest of the world he was guilty, but I know better. I know Rennik, though I hardly recognize him now. When he left he was a boy of seventeen winters. Now he is a young man and his face is so haggard you'd never know he was born genteel. He speaks differently, he swears and cusses, and he tries to hide how well he knows his words and his softer accent of the upper class. He eats and drinks with the manner of a dog, and you'd never know he was taught proper manners or that he ate from silver plates. But he's still Renn. He's still just a boy to me."

"What happened with his brother?" Paiva's curiosity was aroused, and she sat forward to listen attentively.

"They had a fight up on the ramparts of the tower. It was not unusual for them to fight; it seemed they were always at odds with each other. Rennik was accused of throwing Odrik over the ramparts, where he fell to his death on the ground below." Bessil touched her forehead at the memory. "But Renn was very well near lifeless from the beating he had taken. No one knew what prompted them to fight so bloodily, but there were many rumors about it after. Pratermora was quite broken by the death of Odrik, and it is only because it is his own law that a condemned man may choose the woods instead of the gallows that Rennik was not killed. He tried to have him hung, but he could not break his own laws so readily. It was a sad day when Rennik was shackled and put on the barge upriver. I didn't know if he had it in him to survive out there.... Pratermora has been insufferable ever since, and his precious daughter-in-law does not help. The two of them together is agony. All they care about is Odrik, even if he is dead." Bessil downed her wine and smacked her lips.

"What were the rumors?"

"There were many. Some say Rennik and Lady Ceitra were having a tryst, which started the fight. Some say Odrik was cursed by a dark spirit, some say Renn wanted to be heir ... then there were some that said it was simply an accident. No one is allowed to speak of it, lest the Lord should overhear. No one dares breathe the name of the Lord's outcast son. He is meant to be forgotten, he is meant to be a ghost.

"I do not blame Rennik coming back time and again with a Folka head seeking redemption from his father, but I also know what will happen in the morning. Rennik will be gone and his father will have locked himself in his tower for days. He'll grieve, for both his sons. What you saw tonight was a scared, sad old man trying to protect himself from grief. When he comes out of his tower at last he will be frail and miserable, and we will all pretend that nothing ever happened so as not to agitate him again."

Bessil looked sorrowfully into her empty mug, her cheeks shining rosy red.

"Be a good girl and get your aunt another drink," she said ruefully. Paiva filled both their mugs and returned to her Aunt's side again, hoping to coax more forbidden talk from her.

"Now, I have a curious question for you," Bessil said as she took another pull of her drink.

"What's that?"

"How do you know Rennik?"

Paiva lowered her eyes quickly into her drink. Her aunt was acutely observant. She knew when a spoonful of sugar was missing from her kitchens. She also had a tendency for assuming the worst of people.

"I don't know Renn," she said quietly.

"By my soul, you're a liar," Bessil chuckled. "I saw you standing there gaping, and I saw how he recognized you when you gave him his food."

"Aunt Bess…" she complained. "You're crazy."

"I am!" she growled happily. "Tell me. I am right, aren't I?"

"I met him in the woods, on Mummers-eve. He saved me from Varloga. He was looting Father's altar."

"Is that so?"

"It is. Warden Yulin told me to say nothing about it when I got here." She continued to tell Bessil the whole story, feeling relieved to finally share the burden of her secret with someone else.

She had just finished speaking when suddenly her aunt lifted her head towards the stairwell, like a hound sensing something amiss. Paiva followed her gaze and heard the echo of loud voices from up above. Bessil looked back at her and frowned, swallowing the last of her wine, and rose to her feet to investigate. Paiva followed her up the winding stairwell, curious of the commotion sounding out in the great hall.

There were guards and rangers surrounding the Wildermen before the fire, who were on their feet shouting at Warden Yulin. Renn stood quietly staring into the fire.

"What is the matter here?" Bessil cried as she rushed protectively to Yulin's side.

"The Lord has disappeared," Yulin muttered irritably. Bessil gaped at him.

"Disappeared? Are there dark spirits loose in the Keep?"

"No, on his own accord. He has taken a turn for the worse. I am afraid he has left a letter informing us to leave his legacy to the Lady Ceitra, and that he would be buried next to his son and wife in the Tomb of the Forefathers."

"By my soul," Bessil whispered. She touched her forehead nervously.

"Have you searched the Keep? Are you certain he hasn't flung himself from the tower?" Renn asked bitterly.

"He's not in the Keep." Yulin turned back to Renn. "He took his horse. Where would he go?"

"Wherever he is I hope he rots," spat Mikal. "Let him die. When an animal's sick, it goes off into the woods to die."

"Renn, you're not an animal, you have a conscience," Yulin said, ignoring Mikal.

"Let him die," Mikal protested. "You don't owe him anything. He won't forgive you whether you keep him from his peace or let him have it."

"It's a sin," another Wilderman said. "It is a sin to take your own life. There are men branded for such attempts."

"He is not well," Yulin said loyally defending his Lord. "Rennik, please, come help me search for him. You are not an animal. It will haunt you for the rest of your days."

"Have you checked the Tomb?" Renn asked.

"Yes. Empty."

"Don't do it Renn," Mikal said warningly. "He doesn't deserve it."

Paiva watched as Renn lifted his eyes from the fire and sighed. She could feel the hatred radiating from the Wildermen towards their Lord who had thrown away their lives. She understood Renn's silence — how he did not at once jump to help Yulin, who grew impatient.

"Damn you then," Yulin hissed and turned on his heel. "I haven't time to waste on you." He stormed off, leaving his guards to surround the Wildermen and threaten them into silence with the points of their spears.

Bessil clutched Paiva firmly by the elbow and began to haul her back to the kitchens, cursing under her breath, but Paiva pulled away. "Renn," she called out.

He looked up from the fire, his pale eyes flicking to hers curiously. Bessil reached again and clutched her elbow firmer.

"Go, Renn," Paiva said. "If you have the power to save someone, you must try. Otherwise it is as bad as murder."

The word 'murder' seemed to startle him. Shame swept across his face as he hurriedly returned his eyes to the fire.

"Leave him be," Bessil sneered. "You have no right to meddle."

"Yulin." Renn's voice echoed out into the hall, stopping the Warden in his tracks. "Get me a horse."

Chapter 7

Renn sat atop the finest horse he had ridden in years. When Yulin had stormed into the stables the startled grooms had gawked as the Master Warden ordered a Knight's charger saddled and readied. Yulin's own horse was already prepared, nervous and alert. Renn lost patience with the grooms who tripped over their own feet and argued about which saddle belonged to the charger. He grabbed the bit and bridle from the nearest groom and threw it into the horse's mouth, who tossed its head in protest. The grooms fell silent as Renn swung the stall open and led the horse out, shrinking back from a slew of bitter curses that flew at them from the unkempt Wilderman. Yulin cocked an eyebrow at Renn, then grabbed his own horse and led them out into the streets where he had three mounted rangers waiting for him, each with a tall, thin hunting hound at his side and a torch in hand.

Renn grabbed a fistful of the horse's mane and swung himself up on its bare back, not minding that it tossed its head and stamped its feet. It was a fine horse, its mane and coat slippery with grooming oils and its body coiled with well-conditioned muscles. Yet as fine and as tall as it was, Renn felt a pang of longing for his Berg horse.

"What do you think?" Yulin asked him, watching the dirty young man before him stroke a calming hand down the black horse's neck. Renn was silent a moment, his face lost in the obscurity of shadow.

"I remember a place," he murmured. He then urged the horse forwards and began a trot towards the bailey where there were men at arms, guards and rangers flooding through the gates with torches and hounds to search the woods. He called over his shoulder to Yulin, "There is a place off in the woods, towards the river. He met my mother there."

— «» —

The gatekeeper nodded to Yulin as they passed, but gave Renn a dirty, hateful look. They trotted out into the farmlands where the sky was wide and open above them, with a ghostly moon that hung shrouded in wisps of pale clouds. Renn circled his horse, who was excited from the noise of thundering hooves and the bay of hounds scattering across the farmlands. Yulin and the rangers sat on their still mounts, watching him. He searched through the fog of memory, back to a boyhood that seemed to have unfolded a century ago.

He felt the glance of pain as the memory flooded back to him. He remembered his father mounting his finest charger, Odrik atop a palfrey and himself on his pony. His father had been happy then, his beard golden and untouched by the gray of age, his eyes not so lost. He rode them down through the farm fields, surveying his land with pride. He talked to them of forefathers, of times past, of histories that Renn had not paid attention to. Odrik had ridden alongside father, his golden head tilted up, listening raptly to every word.

Behind them followed their escorts, a small score of men at arms and a knight with a falcon on his wrist. Renn remembered being more interested in the falcon, waiting anxiously for the moment when the tall knight would strip off its blind and send it on a hunt.

Pratermora had lead them into the forest where he had continued his talk with Odrik, telling him of trees that were older than the blood of man and stones that were filled with memories. They went onwards to the river along a small woodcutters' road, and there he decided to rest the horses and called for wine and a small meal of figs and bread.

Renn remembered how happy he was to sit in the dirt of the riverbank alongside his father. The jewels in his rings glittered like the water as he lifted food to his mouth, his mouth that was filled with laughter that day. When they were done eating he left the men at arms and took his two boys for a walk through the trees. Renn had been overjoyed, for he had never spent a moment with his father where there had not been the presence of some other person, whether a maid, a servant, a guard, or a knight.

It was a long walk. They wound their ways through the mossy trees and the senior Pratermora seemed to have lost all pretense. He was no longer a lord, but a simple man, a father. He spoke with carefree ease, telling tales of his own boyhood and its adventures, forgetting any lessons he meant to impart on heritage and history.

The sun-warmed trees filled the air with fresh, invigorating scents. The moss was soft beneath their feet, their laughter rang out and shivered through the beams of light that flooded through the cathedral of trees.

Of a sudden his father broke into a run, his long legs pounding the earth, leaving his boys shrieking in delight as they scrabbled to catch up to him. He came to a stop at a huge slab of granite rock that protruded from the earth, thickly intertwined with mossy roots and creeping things. There he caught his breath and went to sit beneath it and told them how once long ago he had been on a hunt, chasing a stag through the trees, when he had stumbled across this rock. It had been twilight, he said. The trees were growing dark with a red sun. The stag vanished, bounding over the rock and away, startling a figure that had been lying asleep in the moss beneath it.

He spoke of a beautiful woman, her hair as black as crow feathers, her eyes silver like a fish's belly. In her hair was a tangle of moss and crushed flowers, and her clothes were no more than tattered homespun wool. His heart had been lost to him right there. She was no more than a peasant, hiding from wolves and running from nightmares. He had leapt from his horse to throw his cloak about her.

Odrik had looked disappointed when his father told them this.

"You found mother under a rock?" he asked indignantly.

Pratermora laughed and tousled his golden curls. "Not just any rock. This rock," he chuckled.

Renn had thought it to be the most beautiful story he had ever heard. He remembered it long after his mother had been taken from them and his father's eyes had begun to grow sad.

The knight with the falcon had come in search of them by then, and when he arrived his father became a Lord again, shedding his happy memories and returning to the poise of duty and command. They trailed back to the horses and the other men while Renn had wished to have stolen only one minute more in the sheltering peace of his mother's rock.

— ‹‹›› —

Renn lifted his head towards the river, pulling himself out of the memory and swallowing a bitter taste in his mouth. Yulin waited, the black charger pawing the ground nervously.

"Well?" Yulin asked. "Do you remember?"

"Vaguely," Renn answered, then swung the horse around and gave him his heading. He grabbed a fistful of mane and lurched forward into a gallop, streaking across the meadows and farm fields like a black arrow. The others flew after him, the hounds howling on the heels of their masters.

— ‹‹›› —

It was hard in the dark to recollect the place. The trees had grown since he had been a boy and the forest floor was twisted and narrow with the overgrowth of roots and slash. Guided only by his distant memory he swung down from the horse when he thought he had reached the place where his father had stopped to eat figs and wine by the riverbank some twenty years ago. He could not say for sure, but he hoped he was headed in the right direction.

Yulin and his rangers dismounted their horses and the hounds began their search through the trees, circling and sniffing and panting hard from the exertion of running behind the horses. Renn could only smell the oily wick of the torches burning and the dampness of trees and river.

He grabbed a torch from a ranger without a word. The man's face twisted into a sneer. Yulin ordered them all to take a different course and they began their search. Renn darted ahead, slinking into the shadows and swinging the torch low over the ground, searching for signs of trespassing.

"You can't let a Wilderman like him off loose like that," he heard the ranger grunt to Yulin. "He can't be trusted. We might all get our throats cut."

Yulin cursed the man out, then their flickering torches disappeared into the trees and Renn was alone.

He cleared his mind, pushed aside all thoughts that would impair his search. He would remain calm, for being desperate or excited would cause mistakes. He searched, as if he was hunting a Folka and not a sick old man.

He soon came across a soft print in the flickering light, so faint he almost missed it. He stooped low and inspected it, finding it to be the stamped imprint of a shoed hoof. There was no mistaking the bars in the heel of the shoe: a mark of a Keep smithy. With a quick intake of breath he picked up the trail, raking through the slash until he came across signs of a struggle. In the soft loam and crushed, rotten leaf litter of the forest floor was the tale of a horse spooking, its hoof prints staggered and confused. Branches were broken and snapped overhead, and he followed the jolted direction the horse took, its stride lengthened into a panicked run.

He stopped when a muffled sound reached him in the dark. A deep, fast breathing. The hair on his nape stood on end and he felt uselessly for his dagger that had been taken from him. He crept forwards, pushing the torchlight ahead of him.

An eye reflected at him from the shadows of the slash, wide and white with fear. There was a pale horse lying on its side, panting hard, its legs tangled beneath it, torn and twisted in spiky brambles. Its reins were caught in a tree branch, pulling its head at an awful cant sideways. When it caught sight of Renn's scraggly shape moving towards it, it blew a hot breath through its nose and tried to lever itself up, but only managed to further twist itself into a tangle.

Renn swung his head around and roared for Yulin at the top of his lungs. The dogs howled in response, and then Yulin's distant voice shouted back.

Renn skirted around the horse and found a man's bare foot prints. His heart lurched in his chest as he followed them deeper into the trees. Then the shape of the great rock loomed ahead of him like a menacing, sleeping giant that ate men and spat out their bones.

Crumpled in the loam beneath it, like a bird that had fallen from the sky into a disjointed, broken death lay his father. His silk robes were splayed open, ripped and tattered from his struggle through the forest. He wore no more than his nightshift beneath, his legs and feet bare and muddied. One arm was twisted under him, his head thrown back and his mouth slacked open. His eyes were closed. Renn did not know if he breathed.

For a moment Renn could not move. He simply stared at his father, unsure he had not stumbled into a terrible dream he could not wake from. Then the hounds howled, coming closer, tearing through the bush. He staggered forward and dropped to his knees beside his father, casting the torchlight over him.

"Father..." he croaked, feeling his bowels turn to water as acid rose in his mouth. A strange smell wafted up to him: sour and rancid, like meat covered in spices to hide its decay. Something glinted in the torchlight and Renn retrieved a broken vial that protruded from the leaves. He sniffed it and with a curse tossed it away. The pungent, herbal aroma evoked unbidden memories.

After his mother had vanished and his father's eyes had begun to grow sad it was not uncommon for Renn to catch a whiff of that smell on his breath. His beard and his sleeping chambers smelled of it. Renn had never known what it was, but whatever was in the drinks he took washed the sadness from his eyes. A blank, empty look would replace it. A numbness of sorts, something that made him so tired no sadness or unhappiness could keep him from his sleep.

Carefully, Renn lifted his father's head into his lap. The old man moaned and sent relief spiraling down Renn's spine. It was his breath that was so fowl, for it smelled like death.

"Father," Renn said loudly, shaking the old man gently. The Lord Pratermora's eyes flew open, blindly circling and darting through the shadowy trees.

"Odrik?" he croaked, as if he had heard the voice of his dead son.

Renn felt tears sting at his eyes. "No father, it is Rennik," he answered tightly.

"Go away." His eyes clamped shut and his mouth clacked in a nervous twitch. Then he moaned and tossed his head, clawing at his face with limp, crooked hands.

"It hurts," he slurred. "I cannot... bear you near."

Neither could Renn, yet he clung to his father until Yulin broke through the trees, slashing at branches with his sword. He surveyed the tableau quickly, then lurched to his knees beside Renn and grabbed hold of the Lord.

"Evrik," Yulin shook him. "Evrik my good man, what have you done to yourself?"

The Lord remained unresponsive and limp.

"What is it?" Yulin breathed, pulling back one of his eyelids to shine light into a foggy eye. "What has he done to himself?" Yulin threw Renn a hounded look.

"There was a vial of that tonic. That sleeping tonic... he used to drink."

Yulin nodded, then shoved Renn out of the way and took the Lord's head in his own lap. Without a moment's hesitation he tilted the Lord's head sideways and shoved his fingers deep inside his throat. Renn looked away as his father gagged and spewed the sickening contents of his stomach over the forest floor. The stench made him weak and he crawled away, staggering to his feet where he went to stare at the shadowy rock and listen to the gurgles of his father's purge, fighting to keep his own stomach from spilling.

Yulin was quick about his work. After voiding Lord Pratermora's guts he wrapped his chilled body in his own red cloak, then ordered the rangers to carry him out to the horses. After wiping his hands in the dirt, he rose to face Renn.

"Come, Rennik," he said strongly. "The sooner we get him back to the Keep the sooner we can help him. You did well. He will remember when he wakes."

"No, he won't," Renn returned bitterly.

Yulin sighed. "Come, Rennik."

"I didn't kill Odrik," Renn said.

A long silence lapsed between them as Yulin registered what he had said. He blinked, shocked to hear such a confession after all these years. "What?" he asked, unable to keep the surprise from his voice.

Renn turned to Yulin slowly, his face grim and taught with the sickness he felt. "We fought up on the ramparts, over Ceitra," Renn said quietly. "Odrik had become hateful and cruel and Ceitra was suffering for it. I confronted her about it, I tried to console her, defend her, because I was completely besotted by her. When Odrik came upon us he flew into a rage. He warned me to get away from her, but with foolish valor I stood my ground boldly to defend her, fearing that his rage would turn on her. Then we fought as we never had. Odrik beat me within an inch of my life. I fought him back, but I was going to lose. Ceitra simply stood there watching us, but she had this funny little smile on her lips. As if she enjoyed the spectacle. My nose broke under Odrik's fist and I fell to the floor, hardly able to see. But what I did see I will never forget.

"Odrik's eyes were all changed. I did not recognize him. He bore down on me and rose his fist for the final blow, but then he suddenly stopped. He had me by the cuff of my shirt and I was calling out his name, begging him for mercy. Something strange passed over his face, like a battle of wills. His eyes seemed to clear for a moment, though his face was contorted with some inner struggle. He threw me away and staggered back towards the ramparts, as if fighting the impulses of his own body. He said he was sorry, over and over, he muttered warnings to me I did not understand. Then he crawled over the crenelation while Ceitra began to scream and I realized what he was doing. I tried to stop him, I grabbed hold of his cloak but I was blinded by blood and weak from pain. The cloak was merciful, and tore away before I could drop him. Because I would have."

Yulin breathed into the heavy silence between them, gazing into Renn's shadowy eyes with disbelief.

"Yet you said nothing at your trial," Yulin answered.

Renn stared at him blankly. "The last thing I saw was the horrible fear in his eyes as he began his fall towards earth. The last things I heard were his horrible screams. I tried to spare my father, I tried to save Odrik's honor. He took his life over mine. So much pain would have been saved if I had been the one to die instead."

"Rennik," Yulin began to protest, not sure what he could say to salve the guilt and self hate of this tortured soul. Unable to find any words that could repair, he simply let out a hot breath in a weary sigh.

"We need to bring your father back," he said. "Come."

— «» —

"What is he still doing here?" Ceitra snarled when she saw Renn sitting before the fire in the Great Hall the following day. Yulin sat with a handful of his rangers at a table eating a small meal of bread and cheese, all with weary rings beneath their eyes. He rose as the Lady approached him, his face growing taught.

"My Lady, I thought it would be best if he stayed. It was under my orders he was not sent back upriver with the others," Yulin protested.

"On what grounds? Do you not realize it is him who causes the Lord to take such fits?"

"My Lady, I do gravely apologize. I thought only to spare him the anguish of not knowing if his father should wake or not. He will leave when we know the outcome of last night's ordeal."

"It is because of Rennik this has happened to begin with!" she cried.

"He will be sent away again. I am just waiting, and hoping, that if the Lord should wake perhaps he will see things differently. Perhaps he will forgive him. Surely you must give him some acknowledgment. Without Rennik we might never have found the Lord in time."

"You... hope," Ceitra said slowly.

"I do, my Lady. I hope and I pray. Perhaps the fog of his madness will lift. Perhaps he will be able to come to terms with his son."

"There is no medicine, there is no hope that can cure the Lord!" Ceitra screamed. "There is nothing that can bring him back from his madness. There is nothing that can bring Odrik back. The only thing we can do is avoid upsetting him." Her eyes narrowed accusingly on Yulin.

"He must stay," Yulin said strongly.

"If he stays behind the walls of the Keep, he will stay as a prisoner. Throw him in chains, for he is not a free man."

"He's harmless," Yulin protested again.

"He is not a free man," she snarled. Her eyes fell on Renn's hunched shape before the fire. He did not lift his head to her, but simply sat and stared quietly into the flames. Ceitra called forward her men at arms and ordered them to seize him. Yulin looked despairingly to his Lady again but was met by a hateful fury.

"My Lady, this is not necessary. He has a truth he must speak, that has long been silenced. It must be heard," Yulin snapped.

Ceitra's eyes opened wide. "What truth?"

"Of Odrik's death." Yulin eyed her levelly.

"Rennik is a liar," she said coldly. "He has had long enough to think of a way to free himself of the woods. Take him away, chain him in the bailey like the criminal he is."

Renn stood stiffly as the men approached him and, with a solemn nod to Yulin, was escorted away. Despairingly, Yulin sat down again and threw his meal to the floor, where the hounds leapt on it.

Ceitra pivoted on her heel and stalked briskly from the room, her head held high, her red hair shining in the splendor of her command.

— «» —

A cold pit formed in Renn's stomach as he approached the bailey square, remembering from years ago when he had stood on trial for his brother's death and every last person in all the keep had come to stare accusingly at him. He remembered the feeling of the chains that locked over his wrists, and gritted his teeth at the memory of how his hand had been flatted under a wooden press and a red-hot iron pressed into it, scorching his flesh forever with the mark of shame. He remembered the only sound he had been able to make throughout the whole trial was his angered, bewildered scream when they marked him. He had looked in disbelief to his father whose accusing eyes burned into him like the brand on his hand.

Renn felt his heart beat wildly as the shackles closed over his wrists again. The guards grunted and chuckled to each other and then returned indoors.

"I'm sorry," he said to himself as he tugged futilely against his restraints. He canted his head up to the tower to where he knew his father lay in his sickbed. With a surge of anger and frustration he roared it again, hoping his voice would carry into his father's deafened ears and into Ceitra's angry heart.

The peasants, who would have normally thrown waste and scraps at a man tied to the pillar, shied away from him and touched their foreheads. He spat and snarled at them, lunging at them on the length of his chains. They called names at him over their shoulders, whispered "murderer" and "criminal" to each other.

"I am not!" he roared at them, and snarled all the more. Then a voice floated out to him calling his name, breaking through his blinding rage. He swiveled his head and saw a pale-haired girl facing him — Paiva.

"Get away from him," someone shouted. "He's a mad dog."

Paiva didn't move. She stood before him, quietly watching him with her strange green eyes.

"Go away," he growled, staring her down warningly. There was something about this girl that unsettled him. If there had been one person in all the world he could have kept his past, his identity hidden from, it would have been her. He remembered how she had looked at him in Birchloam after having saved her from Varloga. She had stood atop her father's stone fence as he had departed into the woods and looked to him as if he had been a hero. Now in her eyes he was nothing more than a scoundrel, a murderer. It infuriated him to be so shamefully exposed.

He turned away from her. When he looked back, she was gone.

— «» —

Lord Pratermora lay in his bed, still as death, his beard seeming to have turned white overnight. His face grew sunken and haggard, his lips bluish and withered as a corpse. An assortment of physics attended to him, dripping restoring fluids into his mouth and pasting his skin with clay to draw out the poisons in his body. Slowly he began to tremble, then he shook with violent shivers. His mind surfaced and he began to let loose loud yells. The physics, afraid his mind would be broken if he woke, tied him to his bed. A Goddish priest stayed vigilant at his side, murmuring chants and dispersing burning oils into the air about the chamber to ward off the ills of dark spirits.

He thrashed in his bed with nightmares, and in a semi-wakefulness would open his eyes and stare blindly about the room, moaning broken words and crying out for help. He'd try to fight the physics and the nurse maids who came to soothe him, twisting against his restraints. He'd speak of shadows, of Odrik, of Rennik lost in the woods, of his wife calling to him, until suddenly he seemed to surrender and went still and listless.

Days passed and he remained the same, sleeping as if enchanted, oblivious to the world he had tried to leave behind. Ceitra assumed his duties as his steward in his absence, sitting at the head of the table in the great hall and attending to his business. She grew irritable and spiteful, the noblemen and knights that joined her at her table for supper thinned, leaving only those that supported her dark moods.

The trials for wrongdoing that were held in the great halls had unjust outcomes. Men were stripped of their names and homes, branded and thrown across the river into the Wilderlands. She found blame in every man, whether it was far-fetched or not. There was no compassion, no understanding. She gazed on each person with hate, and each person who felt her hate shook with fear.

Paiva found even the kitchen maids grew fearful, for Ceitra was quick to displease and often found pleasure in choosing one maid during meals to taunt and belittle for shortcomings Ceitra always found unnecessarily. It seemed the more unhappiness Ceitra caused, the more beautiful she became. While the maids began to look haggard and worn, Ceitra shone as if her very skin were made from some precious luster. Her eyes glittered darker, her hair seeming to burn more red.

Bessil seemed to have lost her joy of cooking. She worried excessively over her recipes. The sweetness of sugar seemed to have lost its taste to her, and the love and the care she poured into serving meals seemed to fade. The bread never seemed to leaven quite right — pots scalded under distracted watch, and maids ended up crying as they suffered a curt lashing of her sharp tongue. Paiva herself wished more than ever to be back home, but it seemed that in such uncertain times she had a duty to help those around her for whom she had come to love and care.

It was exhausting to try and deflect the unhappiness around her. It was exhausting consoling Bessil over a spoiled batch of tarts, and trying to coax small smiles from her friends. She waited anxiously for Yulin to come to the kitchens, but he never did. Now more than ever, she prayed her family would come to retrieve her, to take her back to the sanctuary of the little pastures in Birchloam. She was left hoping, for there were not even any letters.

She could hardly bear going out to the market on Bessil's errands, for it involved passing by the bedraggled form of Renn chained to his pillar. Most times she saw him he was hunched down, head bowed beneath his hood. He did not react to anything, even bold little boys who crept up to him to prod him with sticks before their mothers hollered at them. Wherever his mind was, it was a thousand miles away from here.

She wondered if he prayed. She wished she had the courage to call out a passing word of comfort, to tell him to have hope, to throw him a scrap of food. Instead she always passed by hurriedly, and only offered her own silent prayers to him, too afraid to attract the attention of the guards or the spiteful peasants.

The thought of Renn bothered her as the days passed. One evening when the kitchen was empty she stole a small loaf of bread from the pantry and went outside to the urchins, coaxing one to deliver it to Renn in exchange for extra scraps. One grabbed it eagerly, tucking it away under the folds of her ragged cloak and hurrying down the street into the bailey. She approached Renn but he did not look up from his pious hunch; he did not even notice the bent figure until the loaf of bread hit him in the chest. He stared at the bread for a moment before he realized it was food, then hurriedly swept it under his cloak. He looked up to the urchin who smiled at him with rotten teeth.

"From my little mistress in the kitchens," she said, then trundled away to collect her reward.

If Bessil had noticed the missing bread, she said not a word.

— «» —

Paiva attracted Ceitra's attentions one night as she served supper. The lady sat back in her great chair, toying her fingers around the rim of a golden goblet. Paiva felt the black stare from across the room and shuddered beneath it. She heard her name called out, for it seemed Ceitra had not forgotten it.

"Come here girl," the lady demanded. "I want more wine." Paiva brought forth a decanter and filled Ceitra's extended goblet. The wine rippled in, swirling into the gold like liquid ruby. Ceitra smiled her curious little smile and brought the wine to her lips, never taking her eyes off Paiva.

Paiva suddenly wondered if she knew that she was stealing bread for the accused murderer of her husband and her palms began to sweat in panic. She could not imagine the punishment she would endure for such an act. She tried to keep her face expressionless, washing it clean of worry.

"I hear times are troubled in Birchloam," Ceitra said. Paiva felt a prickle of anxiety run up her spine. She had not heard of trouble in Birchloam. Her thoughts raced out worriedly to her parents. Ceitra's smile deepened, her eyes pooling darkly.

"I have had no news from Birchloam, my Lady," Paiva replied quietly, "but I am sure there are still good spirits left in the world to watch over it. That is all I can pray for." Then she smiled and curtsied. The smile froze on Ceitra's face.

"How dare you speak of good spirits," came her cold voice. Paiva felt the dread of having made a horrible mistake. Ceitra delicately lowered her goblet onto the table and stared at Paiva as if she had grown two heads. Paiva watched a strange change occur: the smoothness of Ceitra's skin suddenly became strained, her hair seeming to grow coarse and dull as a rage began to build behind the masked eyes.

"How dare you speak of good things in a place like this," Ceitra said.

Paiva blinked, confused. "But my Lady," Paiva said, "surely you believe there is still good left in the world. Surely you still have hope."

The Great Hall fell into a deep silence. Not a breath was drawn; not a single person stirred. A brittle tremor rippled across Ceitra's face.

"Hope," Ceitra echoed, drawing in a low breath. "Are you mocking me, little one?" Her eyes suddenly darkened, dimming the room with their intensity.

"I will teach you about hope," she said. "Hope is belief, hope is faith. Hope is putting that faith in a person, or in a dream, or in a place. When that faith is taken from you, when hope is driven out, it leaves the believer in despair." She rose from her seat, towering over Paiva in her violent reds and oranges.

"I will teach you," she said again, and Paiva felt a hollow pit form in her stomach. In a rustle of bright silks, Ceitra sauntered away, leaving the Great Hall chilled in her wake.

Chapter 8

Paiva was busy with work in the kitchens one late, drizzly afternoon when a page arrived asking for her attendance in the Great Hall. Bessil threw her a concerned look, then asked the page what the matter was.

"Her Ladyship requests an audience with young Paiva Ibbie is all," the page replied, though there was something apologetic in his manner. Paiva followed him up the stairwell and into the Great Hall, Bessil curiously following on her heels.

There before the High Table was a proud figure in a red tunic. She recognized his tousled head instantly and she felt her heart drop. It was Ramsi Lier. Beside him stood two hunched figures under the vigilant guard of men at arms. Her parents.

Paiva felt Ceitra's black eyes on her and looked to the lady in shock and dismay.

"Please come forward," Ceitra gestured to her. Paiva stepped carefully towards her parents, though a man at arms moved to block her from touching them. She strained to look over at them, but each one had their heads bowed, and to her horror, their hands bound behind their backs.

"What is the meaning of this?" Paiva asked heatedly. Yulin stood beside Ramsi, a black frown on his face and his hands clenched to his sides. Ramsi had his head held high, a small, proud smirk pulling at his mouth that Paiva would have loved to rip off.

"As I remember telling you, Ms. Ibbie," Ceitra said, "there was trouble occurring in Birchloam." Paiva could not comprehend her meaning. She did not know how her parents could be the cause of any trouble. But even as her thoughts raced, her eyes landed on an assortment of books spread atop the High Table. Her father's books — his leather-bound journals and scraps of parchment. There was all sorts of trouble a vindictive, angry person like Ceitra could find scattered inside them.

Rain pelted the arched windows of the Great Hall, spilling a gloom that settled over Paiva as thick as a wool cloak.

"Young Ramsi Lier, Ranger of Birchloam, has brought to my attention a serious matter which has been long overlooked." She procured a parchment paper, neatly unrolling it and scanning her eyes over it.

"This is concerning the night of Mummers-eve, in the springtime of the year," Ceitra began. "Mummers-eve is a primitive festival wherein common people dress up in mock disguise of Folka. I find it most distasteful. No wonder the people of Birchloam provoke the attentions of malicious beings.

"Warden Lier of Birchloam's statement collected from Viviel Ibbie the following day states that the dark spirit Varloga attacked Paiva Ibbie in the front of the house on the night of Mummers-eve, after she began her walk home alone from the festivities in the village square. The dark spirit was said to have appeared in the likeness of Ramsi Lier, who is standing before me now. An investigation was initiated by Warden Lier, providing no further proof as to the presence or whereabouts of any evil spirits or malicious entities.

"Shortly after Warden Lier's investigation began, Master Warden Yulin received a missive from Viviel Ibbie with the concern of Varloga loose in the lowlands." She procured this letter as evidence. "It states simply that there was an occurrence with the dark spirit and if men could be mustered from the Keep for further protection it would be of great significance. Master Warden Yulin dutifully obeyed and took his own troop of rangers to Birchloam where he uncovered nothing Warden Lier had not already."

She set aside the letter and statement, then rifled through Viviel's books and procured his worn leather journal.

"I have surveyed Mr. Ibbie's collection of books. Among them were documents found but to be but innocent recordings of farming, animal husbandry, and an interest in herbs and plants. All this is not uncommon for a gentleman farmer and does not concern me. However on further perusing I came across a compilation of myths, folklore, and old wives' tales from across the land. This has led me to suspect that Mr. Ibbie is indeed fascinated in the beliefs of Old Grimenna. Clearly this shows that Mr. Ibbie does not worship the God, but instead worships the Forest."

She looked at Viviel.

"But this neither is of great concern to me. I understand the people in the far-off village of Birchloam are a little rustic." She flipped through more pages. "What does concern me is a passage the journal where is described the festival of Mummers-eve. On this night Mr. Viviel Ibbie made a recording of Wildermen he harbored in his own home. This is an offence to the Lord and to the King who has ordained these laws of the land. The law is that no branded man should ever be given hospitality, food, warmth or comfort until his sentence is served. Men like Mr. Ibbie threaten the whole system that has been so long ago established, and if more men like him persist in showing mercy to Wildermen then the system will have to be abolished for being futile. Condemned men will have to spend their lives rotting in prisons instead of being given the chance to redeem themselves and earn a pardon. Do you deny this, Mr. Ibbie?"

"No," Viviel said, his voice grating low. Paiva looked to him desperately. She remembered the words Ceitra had spoken to her but a few days ago when she had simply served her wine and spoke of having hope in dark times.

"I will teach you," Ceitra had said. The words echoed in Paiva's mind and made her sick with guilt. Ceitra continued with her interrogation.

"Above all, which I find most offensive, is that the names of these harbored Wildermen were recorded as well. Bear Jorn, Trapper Terg," and then a sneer pulled at her face, "and Black Renn. Viviel Ibbie has been proven to give sanctuary to a liar, a thief, and a murderer. And not just any murderer — the very man who took my husband, who took the heir to Prater-mora's legacy away from him. I find this to be unforgivable."

Yulin's face turned as red as his tunic then. Ceitra turned to him.

"This incident forces me to review Black Renn's ledger. Please bring him forth and also his ledger."

Paiva watched as Yulin ordered his men. A short while later the ledger was presented to Ceitra and Renn's scraggly shape was hauled towards the High Table. He was soaked from the rain and muddy, a pool of dirty water formed on the floor beneath his dripping, tattered cloak. His eyes alighted on the Ibbie's with a flicker of confusion, then they turned to Paiva's white face and filled with muted concern.

"Black Renn," Cietra said slowly and he turned his befuddled face to her. "Do you recognize these people? Do you recognize this girl?"

Renn looked back again, his eyes narrowing suspiciously. Paiva's heart racketed against her ribs as she waited for his response.

"No," he said, "not them. I recognize the girl as a serving maid, that's all."

"Are you sure?" Ceitra asked as her strange smile pulled at her lips.

Renn bristled at the tone in her voice. He turned his head back to her, his eyes steady on hers. "Yes," he said blankly, for he must well have known she already knew the truth. Yulin's face went tight. Ceitra's eyes fell back to the book before her.

"Then kindly explain to me this following passage recorded by the man who stands alongside you, Mr. Viviel Ibbie. '...There was one man named Black Renn. He is a cantankerous character, deeply bitter and angry at the world though I don't think the worst of him yet. I was glad to have them sleep by my fire, and did not mind that they had been pilfering my sheep and the sweetbreads of my altar.'" She raised her eyes to stare at him. "This passage is in reference to the night of Mummers-eve in Birchloam. Clearly you have proven yourself to be a liar. Another mark in your ledger, and another for your trespassing beyond the Panderbank."

Renn stared at her in silence, his face impassive. Yulin spoke up then.

"My Lady, you cannot punish a man for ignorance. He did not know who Black Renn was. I am sure it is written in his records of how it came to be that he harbored the Wildermen in the first place. That they saved the poor girl from Varloga."

"Ah Master Warden," Ceitra smiled, "that is all written — the true story of what came to pass that night. Ramsi Lier brought me the statement that Viviel signed, which records an entirely different story. Another lie.

"That does bring me to another topic I wish to address today. It seems I have suffered another loss of faith in you, Yulin. Mr. Ibbie kindly wrote of you as well in his journals, of how you dissuaded him from revealing the part the Wildermen had to play in this story to keep him safe from persecution. Mr. Ibbie spoke very highly of you, for your reserve and intellect and the confidence you instilled in him. I, however, do not share his sentiments. I therefore have decided to strip you of your title and replace you with someone in whom these sentiments I can instill." Her eyes trailed to the proud face of Ramsi. "I think Ranger Lier would be fitting for this title, for he has proven his loyalty and dedication to me."

Ramsi's chest swelled. He cast a sidelong glance at Paiva and smiled. Paiva remembered his outrage when she had left Birchloam on his horse that Yulin had taken from him. She remembered the cold promise of vengeance in his eyes and knew this was the moment he had been waiting for.

"By my soul," Yulin hissed, "this is preposterous. I have dedicated my entire life to being loyal to the Pratermoras. I have sacrificed everything. Sparing an ignorant farmer is a small slight."

"You have proven to be lacking. You may leave now on your own accord, or you may leave under force."

"I am loyal!" Yulin roared. Ceitra glowed with contentment.

"If you are loyal, then throw the brand in the fire and burn this man's hand. For he will be thrown into the Wilderlands," she said.

Yulin gaped at her. For a long moment they held each other's gaze.

"Won't you, Viviel?" she asked. "To the woods, is it not?"

"To the woods, Milady," Viviel whispered.

Yulin reached up and tore the cloak from his shoulder, throwing the silver brooch that marked him as Master Warden to the cold, hard ground.

"I am not your hound," he said and stormed from the Great Hall. Bessil sagged against the wall of the stairwell, a hand to her fluttering heart. Paiva turned her wide eyes back to Ceitra.

"Viviel Ibbie," she said, "I accuse you of breaking the laws of the land. You will be branded and thrown away."

Viviel gaped at her, his face shattering.

"Furthermore," Ceitra continued, "your land and your home will be forfeit to the Warden of Birchloam to do with as he pleases. Your wife, who is your conspirator, will be sent to Quarrytown where she will cut stone until you are either dead or pardoned."

Paiva heard her mother let loose a low sob. Ceitra's eyes found Viviel's and her strange smile returned to her perfect lips.

"Master Warden Lier," she said. "Throw the brand in the fire. He will go to the woods."

Ramsi bowed deeply and went to the great hearth where he set the long crook of iron into the flames and watched it grow hot. It was then that Renn gave a start, swinging his black head towards Ramsi with a snarl. He took a step forward, but a guard's sword-point leveled at his throat and stopped him. Paiva felt her heart begin to beat deafeningly in her ears. Her blood ran piercingly cold through her veins. As Ramsi lifted the glowing brand from the fire and strode towards Viviel, Paiva cried out and flung herself towards her father. She wrapped her arms about his broad chest and rasped her cheek into his coarse beard, as if her little body could shield him from the fate he was soon to meet.

"I love you, Paiva," he murmured, as tears trickled from his eyes. A man at arms pulled her roughly away and she screamed, fighting against him. Another man cut loose her father's bonds and tied a rope about his wrist, stretching his hand forwards and into the wooden press so that Ramsi could sink the burning iron into the meat of his palm.

Paiva heard the sizzle of flesh, smelled the vapors of melting skin and screamed all the louder. Her mother dropped to her knees, wrenching her head away from the sight, and sobbed bitterly.

Ramsi withdrew the smoldering iron, and there was a moment wherein he looked down into the blistered brand with satisfaction. Viviel's golden eyes glimmered with tears as he looked into the melted skin, then in a low voice he began to sing. His lilting voice echoed softly through the vaulted ceilings:

> "I'll travel far into the woods,
> When I am gone from here,
> I'll find the Vale of Spirits,
> Where hidden deep is Morinvere.
> For 'tis there all good things go,
> When they are pushed away,
> driven there by darkness,
> by creatures gone astray."

"You're nothing but an old heretic now," Ramsi murmured to Viviel.

"And you, Black Renn," Ceitra said, "your ledger is full, and you have proven yet again that you are a liar. You will not go back to the woods. The system has no merit for you, or any hope of redeeming you. You will be hung by the neck until you are dead."

Then the men at arms were hauling Viviel away from his daughter and wife, down to the river where he would be tossed on a stone cutter's barge or a fishing ketch and thrown into the Wilderlands. Kess cried out to him and to Paiva, but she too was seized and hauled away.

Paiva screamed until her throat was raw, until her lungs seemed to collapse under the weight of her despair. The guard that held her fast kept her from falling to the floor as she sobbed, her tears burning hotly down her face. She bowed her head and shook it, as if trying to dispel a nightmare.

Ceitra smiled, her eyes like black ink pots. Before Renn was hauled away, back to the pillar where he would await his execution, his eyes trailed over Paiva. His face was awash with sadness, his eyes turning a cold gray with shock. Paiva watched him disappear with the guards, and then it was only her and Ceitra. Somehow, she wished to hurt this woman to stifle her own anguish.

"I hate you," Paiva whispered hoarsely. That was a word her father had forbidden her ever to use but now it tasted like honey in her mouth. Sweet and satisfying.

Ceitra cocked her head and took a deep sighing breath, smiling in her peculiar way. She closed the books and ordered them brought up to the trophy room. Then in a rustle of skirts she disappeared from the hall.

— «◊» —

They sat alone in the storeroom, Paiva atop a pickling barrel and Bessil strewn over a crate. Bessil sobbed bitterly and gave herself another drink from the nearest keg. The maids worked on without her. There were no voices to be heard, only the clatter of pots and pans.

"Your family is ruined," Bessil said. "You'll stay here with me, by my soul, you will always have a job here in my kitchens. And Master Yulin…" Her voice broke into a pitiful wail and she hid her face in her hands. "How could she do that to Master Yulin! He's been loyal and honorable to his Lord since the very beginning. He never took a wife, he never had a family, all so he could serve his Lord. Fie on the Lady and her black soul."

Paiva had not taken one sip of her drink. She was numb and unbelieving. Ramsi Lier had taken her home from her, had taken her family from her. Her mind raced with questions. The one at the foremost of her mind was how Ramsi could have discovered what was in her father's books. None of it made sense.

Her father's song echoed in her head and she wondered what it had meant. Was he trying to send her a message?

"Morinvere…" she whispered. It pulled at her memory. She saw an inky shape form in her mind's eye, lifting from the pigment of her father's scribbles.

"Aunt Bess," she said aloud. The old cook looked up at her through red-rimmed eyes. "Have you ever heard of a place called Morinvere?"

"Morinvere?" Bessil echoed. "It was a temple that the believers of the Old Ways built in the deep of Grimenna long ago. But it was lost; the forest swallowed it up along with any other villages and towns they ever tried to build in the Wilderlands. But don't let the Goddish hear you talk about Morinvere. They say that is where all the Old Spirits come from. That is where the Folka were born."

"Father was singing of it."

"Your father!" Bess subdued a flash of rage. "Kess should have never married him. He's always had good intentions, always been so kind... but he has his ideas about things. I'm surprised it took until now for him to get in trouble. For all you know he is probably going to try and find Morinvere and raise the Old Spirits and try to save the world! He'll wind up dead, leaving you and your mother penniless and destitute."

That *was* where he was going.

She sat up straighter. Morinvere, the Vale of the Spirits. She had to find his books.

— «» —

Paiva stepped into the trophy room as silent as a wraith and froze at the glassy, sightless eyes that stared down at her. She had little trouble bypassing the men at arms and guards on her way up, for they were used to maids scurrying about the Keep. She raised her candle and peered back down the corridor to make sure it was empty and then slipped inside the room.

She saw her father's books lying scattered across the Lord's desk and rushed to them, setting the candle down and sifting through them. She searched furiously for his ruminations on the Old Temple. She did not want to steal the book in case someone should notice it missing, but there were many to sort through and they were all badly organized. Her hands shook as she sorted hurriedly through the pages, the Folka heads above her staring down accusingly, seeming to move in the dancing flame of the candle. She found the page she was looking for at long last, just as her courage began to fail her. She braced her hands on the book about to tear the page out when the door to the trophy room swung open.

Paiva's blood ran cold as Ceitra's face appeared in the doorway, white and ghostly, flickering in the low light. Her dark eyes were black, looking like Viviel's pools of ink on parchment.

A slow smile pulled at the corner of Ceitra's lips. "Whatever are you doing up here, in the Lord's own chambers?" she cooed.

Paiva felt ice run down her spine and she quickly closed the book and drew it to her chest protectively.

"I wanted to retrieve my father's property," she spluttered.

"Your father has no property. Your father has no name to hold anything to now."

"Please, I wanted but one token of him. You have taken everything from me. Please. Just let me keep one piece of him."

"No, his books have been confiscated. And even if they were due to you, you have no right to be intruding up here. You are a kitchen maid, and now you are a Wilderman's daughter as well."

Pure hatred boiled up through her throat and made her spit her words out angrily.

"He did not deserve to be cast away. You did it to spite me."

Ceitra smiled and tilted her head in a birdlike fashion. "Such sharp tones you take with your High Lady."

Paiva was almost blinded by the angry tears that suddenly welled in her eyes. "Why have you done this?" she asked, unable to help the words explode from her mouth. A cold silence hung in the air between them. Ceitra's smile vanished, her black eyes raking across Paiva's face.

"The air is growing stale between us," she said. Her footsteps clicked sharply as she walked across the stone floor. She unlatched the window and opened it, drawing in a swift current of cool air that fluttered the pages of the books and threatened to smother the candle. Shadows leapt across the wall in its flickering light, the Folka's glass eyes glowing eerily.

"Hmm..." Ceitra mused. "I suppose he never told you then."

"Told me what?"

Ceitra swiveled her head back to her slowly. "That he is an Incarnate."

Ceitra's words hung in the air before slicing into Paiva's heart. An Incarnate. A spirit who stepped from the woods and took human form.

"No..." Paiva breathed.

"It's all there in those books," Ceitra smiled. "Your father collected the Old Stories so that they would not be lost. I expect he would one day give them to you to pass on to your children. The Stories that guided lost men through the darkness of the woods, that guided them through the darkness of their own hearts.... Surely you know the Wolf Man of old, who flitted through pastures keeping watch over the gentle farmers. Wolves were greatly feared until one-day man learned not to cower, when he heard wolf-song in the hills he knew the Forest was alive and well. For Wolves are not naturally the hunters of men, they are the keepers of the Forest, the governors of natural balance. You would have thought that Hope would have been associated with pretty white winged things, but it was not. It was born from the bitter hearts of men who heard wolf-song in the hills and hoped and prayed the Great Wolf would keep order in the forest so the wolves would not starve and prey on men, that there would be enough game for all, that the forest would provide for all under his watch. With his fangs he ate those prayers, and with his great claws he protected the people from nightmares."

"He can't be."

"Yes. And you are his Virtue. Born both of myth and man."

Paiva rolled her eyes back to the books in disbelief, wondering if she should instead pity Ceitra for being mad. There seemed to be something about the Pratermora family and everyone attached to them that lent itself to madness.

Ceitra seemed to hear her very thoughts, for a knowing smile crept over her lips. "Don't pity me, for I am fulfilling the purpose for which I was created," she said as she turned back to stare out over the darkened woods. "It seems you have been born into the middle of an old battle, as old as mankind itself."

"My father is not an Incarnate. I am not a Virtue. I am a simple girl from Birchloam."

"Yes he is. And he is the last of his kind left in the human world, for all the others have been banished."

"You are mad."

Ceitra shook her head, "Do you know the name of the Eater of Hate?"

Feeling chilled to the bone, Paiva could force the name out in no more than a whisper. "The Strix."

"I am she. There was a time once when I was mad," she began, "when I had nothing to eat. I was mad with hunger for it was I who was banished, driven deep into the woods with starvation. I was malformed, misshapen, grotesque. I was kept at bay and hidden there by beings like your father. The Good Spirits — Hope and Love, Courage, Mercy, Patience and all the others. They were fat with the prayers they ate, feasting on the happy hearts of man. They used my name to instill Fear, to keep man from straying into darkness. It was their mistake, for Fear is the very thing that set me free."

Paiva stared at the silhouette in the window, feeling small and minuscule. She hugged her father's book closer. She felt then that she stood in the moonlit shadow of an old and ancient legend. Faces lifted from the memory of her father's pages — inky swirling forms of the ghoulish owl woman. The mother of darkness.

"That is the very thing the Good Spirits forgot," Ceitra continued. "You cannot live in light without casting a shadow. You cannot have Courage without Fear. You cannot have Healing without Hurt.

"When man began to believe he truly had dominion over Grimenna, he began to forget the Good Spirits and they were not remembered for their help. But I was remembered — how could something all men feared be forgotten? Fear grew deeply in their hearts, and from their fear grew the hate that drew me back into their world."

She looked to Paiva icily. "Your father took the form of a man as the others tried to do and walked amongst the people to remind them of the Old Stories so that they would not be lost. One by one they have been driven away as I was, and the children that were born of their earthly love ruined. As you are now."

"But why?" Paiva lamented.

"Your Father was born with fangs and claws as I was, but only Hope he ate. Hope is bitter to me, it tastes like cinders in my mouth. It makes my bones brittle, makes me restless with aches. But Despair is something sweet, almost as sweet as the hateful hearts of the Pratermora's..."

"What sort of existence is this?" Paiva whispered. "How can you stand to be such a thing?"

Ceitra's black eyes reflected back at her with a peculiar look, and for a split second Paiva thought she saw a moment of weakness. Perhaps to be the eater of hate, you must hate yourself the most.

"You cannot shine light without casting a shadow," she repeated coldly. "I was that shadow. There will be long shadows you will cast, little Virtue, and darkness you will find when I take the last of your light. When Hope dies it becomes Despair, and from Despair the most terrible of nightmares will be born. The most terrible Folka will rise from the earth and the Forest will once again have dominion over man."

"No!" Paiva nearly shouted. "I will not hate you, I will not despair."

"But you already do. I can feel it beginning. I can already taste your hatred, flavored with a most potent anger I find exhilarating. Almost as sweet as Odrik's, as Renn's. Sweeter still then their father's."

Paiva clutched her father's book, remembering her home in Birchloam, remembering her sheep and the meadow flowers and her parent's happy faces. She felt her heart calm and Ceitra gave her a stern look.

"I see your father has done his work well. But, oh, there are ways I can compel you." She reached her arm out into the night air and a white winged shape swooped down onto it. She drew it in, holding her arm high to reveal a strange creature.

"Hello my love," she cooed. The bird had a strange face, owlish, yet with a dwarfed human nose and peeled-back black lips like a cat's. Paiva stared at it in horror.

"I believe you two have already met," Ceitra said.

Paiva stumbled back. "Varloga," she breathed.

The bird blinked its wide black eyes, then opened its wings and swooped to the floor, its feathers lengthening into a billowing white cloak, its face changing into that of a man's. He alighted nimbly on his feet, then stood tall and brushed himself off. He canted his face to her with a peculiar, curious look.

When she had first encountered him in the woods his face had never become fully human, but now she suddenly recognized it, for it was nearly the same as the one stitched into the tapestry in the great hall. The only difference was that the color was drained from him: he appeared stark white, as a ghost would.

"Odrik..." she breathed.

"Only in shape," Ceitra murmured. "Odrik is dead. But his face pleases me so much Varloga took it as his own."

Paiva did not need to wonder now how Lord Pratermora had succumbed to madness. She imagined the vile tricks Varloga could play on him, haunting him with his dead son's face, appearing in his ghostly form and tormenting him. There were endless possibilities to his methods.

"Paiva Ibbie," Varloga greeted her. His voice sent waves of fear through her.

"You have already met my White Magician," Ceitra murmured contentedly. "Isn't he fine? You do not yet know all his talents, for he is a great manipulator of shape and also of fear. He is a great conjurer, for he can take your memories and the love that you have known and twist it into something else." She raised her head to the Folka creatures lining the walls.

Paiva was held transfixed by the cold smile that slithered across the white face before her. Ceitra nodded to Varloga, who stepped forward and reached a clawed hand for Paiva. She let loose a blood-curdling scream as he started forwards and reeled away from him, but he caught her by the throat and slammed her back into the writing desk. The book went flying from her hands as she fought and writhed against him, unable to look away from his dark eyes that drew hers in. His face pressed close to hers and she stared transfixed into his gaze, lost in its immeasurable black depths. She felt a rush begin behind her skull, her blood pounding smoothly and bringing to the surface a myriad of memories. She knew she was not the only one watching them — Varloga's presence overshadowed each one that flew by, tainting it with his poison, corrupting a happy memory into one laced with fear so that she would not ever want to look back on it.

She cried out, tears erupting down her cheeks at the realization of what was beginning, and she tried vainly to wrestle herself free. It was too late. Varloga would at last accomplish what he had set out to do. She sobbed as she tried desperately to cling to her mother's face, to the sound of her father's laughter, but they were pulled away from her.

A whiff of smoke wafted up to her. Varloga's face flickered with a bright light and something hot licked against her back. Varloga's smile faltered and his clutch slackened, his gaze breaking. She wrenched her head away from him and looked over her shoulder and saw that the candle had tipped over and spilled its hot wax over the pages of her father's books. Smoldering flames erupted and the pages began to curl and burn. She cried out in alarm, not meaning to have caused such ruin. In seconds the fire spread, erupting over the rest of the desk. Sparks flew and caught in the shaggy beard of a mounted Folka head on the wall. Paiva backed away from the fire, feeling a rush of tears behind her eyes as her father's life works dissolved into hot ash before her.

Ceitra stepped back, pulling her skirts out of the way of the spreading fire. She looked about in anger as tendrils of flame began to creep up to the mounted heads and singe their furs.

"No," she wailed as she watched them catch. "Do something!"

Varloga turned on Paiva again as sparks settled onto his robes and singed at his hair.

Then the door burst open, bringing with it a draft that fueled the fire and sent the flames higher. Guards rushed in brandishing swords and spears. Paiva saw Varloga and Ceitra freeze. Then the flames leapt higher up Varloga's cloak.

The guards paid no mind to Paiva trying to scramble away. They lunged at the white figure with their spears and swords, trampling into the flames in their haste.

"It's her!" she heard Ceitra yell as Paiva sprang for the open door. "It is her who commands and compels Varloga!"

The guards didn't react to her cries but fought to draw her out of the burning room while others faced the dark spirit that whirled through the black smoke, snarling and tearing through the flames. His cloak mottled back into wings, and with burning feathers, he dove out the window.

Paiva raced down the stairwell, straight into a troop of guards clambering up from below her. They pushed and shoved her out of the way, hurrying upwards to reach Ceitra's screams. Paiva saw Yulin pushing his way up from behind them. He caught sight of her instantly and made for her, blocking her from descending by stepping into her path. His eyes were hard and calculating, assessing her frightened face.

"What has happened?" he asked, stopping to catch his breath as the guards disappeared.

She trembled violently, her mind still unsettled with a swarm of shadows. She tried to gather her thoughts through the fog of it. Yulin noted her state and gripped her arm hard.

"What has happened?" he repeated.

"The tower's on fire," she said. Before he could recover from his shock she hurried on. "Master Yulin, Lady Ceitra summoned Varloga. I will be blamed." Ceitra's howls drew nearer and Paiva looked up nervously. "She's evil. You can't let her kill Renn. Save him somehow, however you can. Please." She turned to hurry on but he gripped her hard by her arm.

"Where are you going?" he asked.

"Master Yulin please, you have to believe me."

His eyes searched hers, his face registering neither accusation nor belief.

"The gates are closed at night, you'll have to pay off the gatekeeper," he said. With his other hand he reached to his belt and drew out his purse, handing it to her. "Take it, find yourself a fast horse if you can," he said, "or run like there's a demon on your back."

"And Renn?" she said. He released her and pushed her down the stairs.

"Go," he said.

She did not look back but stumbled down into the darkness of the stairwell as fast as she could.

— «» —

She ran into the kitchens and gathered her belongings in a basket, slipping into her cloak and heading out the back door into the streets. She took one last look in through the windows with longing, knowing she was going to miss the comforts of it. She wondered whether she should bother leaving a note for Bessil, but no sooner had she hesitated than did guards come bursting in through the door and crash down the stairs. She jumped back in surprise, then looked about for a quick escape.

Across the way from her huddled the urchins and she ran towards them, ducking down under her cloak and hiding her face beneath her hood. They said not a word, but clustered against her, concealing her. Above her in the black of the night sky, the top of the tower blazed like a torch, sending bright ribbons of sparks trailing into the air. Cinders and ashes fell to the ground and settled on her clothes.

The back door of the kitchen was flung open and guards flooded into the streets. They looked about and called to each other, formed pairs and went in search of her in different directions. Two came up to the urchins, surveying them under the glow of a torch.

"You lot seen anyone come out that door before us?"

"No Masters," they murmured and huddled together. The guard swooped the torch lower over their heads and peered at them with suspicion. The other guard grumbled and trudged away through the mud of the streets, calling his partner after him. Paiva let out her breath shakily as they moved on.

"Thank you," she said to the urchins.

"I suppose we won't get no more sweet breads now eh," said the old blind lady.

"I'm sorry," she said, keeping her eyes on the guards.

"What they want you for?"

"Lady Ceitra branded my father," Paiva muttered. The blind urchin cackled.

"I smell a great smoke," she said, her laugh breaking into a wet cough. Paiva looked up into the night air, at the blaze that was cascading ash onto their heads.

"I need to get away from here," she whispered.

"Go down to the south gate Miss," said the toothless widow. "They let women through in the night to go down to work camps by the river sometimes. You know, that sort of woman. The gatekeeper don't mind taking a few coins."

"The south gate?"

"In the working quarters. When you get out there's a foot trail along the river. No one will notice you, not with the tower burning. By the gods' own will, I hope it burns to the ground, and I hope the Lord's in it."

Paiva felt for Yulin's purse, which was full, and delved out a few coins. She placed them in the palms of the blind woman.

"Share this among you," she said, "for thanks."

As she rose and slunk away they muttered their own thanks and wished her well. She made her way into the working quarters, where the streets became uglier and the air was thick with smoke from kilns and smith fires. She felt as if she had crossed some invisible line, stepping into the same world the urchins lived in — the world of the outcasts and the wretched, wherein she would find no help from anyone but those like her. She felt tears burn down her cheeks as she mourned her losses. How was this going to end? How did all this even begin?

People had begun to mill onto the street to look up at the blazing tower. There was commotion as people began to gather pails of water and douse their roofs and scurry about with brooms to beat out red embers that fell from the sky. Paiva was able to slip through the cluster of people without notice, hiding between the stacked houses when guards trotted by.

She made it to the south gate without a hitch and found the iron bars slid shut and locked. Standing in the stone arch by a small fire was the gatekeeper, a stout man with a bent nose and a grisly chin. She approached him, and when she was all but a few yards from him he looked up with bleary eyes.

"What do you want?" he called. She came closer and could smell the drink on his breath.

"I'd like to be let out."

"Would you now? On what business?"

"I'm going down to the work camp."

"Are you?" His eyes roved over from her head to her feet as he appraised her. "A little fresh-looking thing like yourself? You sure?" He smiled toothily and procured from his chest pocket a silver flask. He bent his head back to take a drink, eyeing the burning tower without a care.

He nearly spewed his drink on her when she procured a handful of glittering coins.

"By my soul," he coughed, his eyes fixed on her money.

"I want to be let out," she said again. He nodded vigorously and went to open the side door for her. She was about to step through when he stopped her, his better judgement suddenly awakening.

"Wait a minute there," he said. "I ought to know who it is coming and going through my own gate."

She smelled his sour breath and wanted nothing more than to bolt out into the open. Instead she opened her hand and let the coins fall to the ground. He eagerly fell to his knees and gathered them, and only when they were all clasped firmly in his grubby hands did he look up and find she was gone.

— ‹› —

Paiva kept clear of the work camp with its smoky fires and searched for the foot trail by the riverbank. Drunk voices wafted up to her and bounced off the water and the stone walls. She stumbled through thickets and nearly lost her footing on the steep crags in her hurry, but her years of wandering the pastures and keeping watch over her sheep had made her quick of foot. Her eyes were sharp and her mind alert, helping her to deter through the shadows until she fell upon the foot trail.

The moon was risen over the river, sparkling its light over the wide expanse of choppy water. There were boats anchored offshore, lights from the decks twinkling and swaying. Beyond them was the dark shape of the Forest, the

Wilderlands of Grimenna, that rose into shadowy hills. Great plumes of sparks eddied out in currents above the Keep, though she could not see the tower from her position so low on the crags.

She hurried along, her heart beating wildly in her chest, fueling her with speed and necessity. The foot trail gave way to farmlands and she spread her gait into a run over the flat lands. She hopped fences, startled sleeping cows and scattered a flock of nervous sheep. She reached the safety of the trees on the far side of the farmlands, her lungs and her legs burning with exertion. There she collapsed in the shadowed nook of a tree and caught her breath, tilting her head back against the trunk. She stared out over the farmlands, out to the Keep where the tower was lit up like a beacon. She reconciled her mixture of emotions, trying to find calmness in the maelstrom of her whirling thoughts.

She would go to Quarrytown and find her mother. Together they could find somewhere safe, somewhere far away from this hellish place. Her heart lurched as she thought of her father somewhere out across the river, lost in the Wilderlands. She was beyond bewildered and confused, so she heaved herself up and began to follow the riverbank north to Quarrytown, towards her mother.

Chapter 9

She found herself on an old woodcutter's road along the
river the next day. She had stumbled onwards into the
woods by the cover of night, trespassing along the bank of
the gleaming moonlit river that lit her way. She stopped to
rest when clouds moved in and swallowed the moon, taking
with it any light she might have had to guide her way. She
became lost in the dark, and the fear of what she could not
see sent her scrambling into the crook of a tree. There she
huddled into herself and shut her eyes against the black
woods to wait out the rest of the night. She swallowed her
fear and murmured a prayer to the trees.

"Great Forest," she whispered into the shadows, "please
guide me. I am alone and I am afraid of you." Somewhere
on the other side of the river her father was just as alone as
she was. The thought of him, the want to have his warm,
unfaltering presence beside her to face this night with made
tears burn behind her eyes. She found no rest despite her
weariness. She stayed awake, listening as the midnight calls
of animals lifted across the black waters of the river, and
hummed her father's song to herself quietly to keep the
creeping shadows at bay.

By midmorning as she made her way along the road,
weary with exhaustion and fatigue, she stopped to point her
head at the sky and shake her head in dismay. The clouds
opened and spouted rain on her, making her journey all the
more dismal. She sighed as her face was sprayed with rain-
drops. She dropped her head back to the ground as the woods
became alive with the sound of falling rain. She continued
on nonetheless, though she allowed herself to expel her in-
gratitude towards the weather with a series of hushed curses.

Paiva was following the woodcutter's road north when she suddenly had the fleeting feeling she was being followed. It was the same feeling she had when she sat in her father's pastures and felt a wolf lurking nearby. She could not see it, but the presence was there nonetheless, prickling the hair on the nape of her neck. Quickly, she slid behind a tree. She listened for sound, then peeked an eye around the tree, waiting breathlessly.

Her heart leapt when a red cloaked figure on a tall horse rounded the bend in the road behind her. A ranger. He seemed to be alone and without dogs, but he was bent over the horn on his horse's saddle studying the ground, following her tracks. She looked about for an escape, eyeing the river and its swift current. She was not a strong swimmer; her facet was running. An image of being swept into the rapids and her cloak and skirts catching on rocks strangling her came to mind and she decided for a clean break through the trees. There was a rocky outcrop she spotted not far off. If she could make it there she might have a chance to evade him.

She darted silently towards the rocks, great boulders heaved together and fallen on their sides with streaks of hardened sediment. She cast a glance over her shoulder and crouched low, then saw the red cloak pass through the trees. She was suddenly thankful for the rain, thinking perhaps the great forest was lending itself to her cause, for it muted her trespass through the trees. She saw the ranger pass her trail and continue on down the road. With relief she skirted onwards to the rocks, then crouched and hid, not knowing what else to do.

To her horror Paiva saw him rein his horse to a halt. He doubled back, making tight circles until he picked up her trail again. He swung the horse's head in her direction, pointing it into the trees. The ranger's head lifted searchingly, and then he discerned her in the damp leaves.

For a moment they were both frozen. The horse snorted and she whirled and took to a mad run towards the stones. She heard the horse crash through the trees behind her, heard the ranger's voice yelling out. She ran with the feeling that any moment an arrow or a sword would pierce her back, and she tore through the trees with all abandon. She dropped her basket, its contents spilling across the forest floor.

She was nearly at the stones when her foot sunk through the dead leaves into a hollow of roots. She went flying forwards into a sprawl on the ground. The wind was knocked out of her, her elbows stinging. A sharp stick came dangerously close to her eye and raked across her cheek as she fell.

The ranger vaulted off his horse and darted forwards as she tried to scramble away. She cried out as she realized he was an immense person, his movements quick and steeled. Then she realized something else. His boots were worn through at a toe, the seams tearing and frayed. She tilted her head up to him as he bent over her and recognized the glimpse of his obscured, dirty face beneath his red hood.

"By all the shining stars," she cried. "Renn!" She sat on her knees and stared at him in disbelief, trying to catch her breath. He lowered his hands to her and pulled her upright. "Why are you wearing a red cloak," she asked, trembling.

"Yulin," he said simply, then she recognized the horse as well. "Wasn't hard to slip out with the Rangers when they went out looking for you. I even gave young Ramsi a good direction to go in."

"Where?"

"Up his arse." He drew his hood further over his eyes to keep the rain out of them.

"How did you find me?" she asked, still shaken, as he went to gather her basket.

"Well, to start, I figured if I was you my only exit was through the kitchen. I saw the urchins huddled across and asked them, but they were loyal to you. Didn't say a word until I showed them my brand. From there I went to the south gate." He returned with her basket and stood but a few paces away.

She stood unmoving and staring at him with wide eyes. "Why did you come after me?" she asked worriedly.

"Yulin says Ceitra summoned Varloga on you," he replied. "I wouldn't have believed it if it hadn't been for Mummerseve. I need to know what happened."

"She is not human," Paiva whispered. "She is the Strix, the Eater of Hate. She is evil."

Their eyes met through the rain falling steadily between them. She could not read his impassive face but his intent stare left her slightly breathless. She told him everything that had transpired in the tower; there was no reason not to. What more could she lose by telling him?

When she had finished she took her basket from him, dropping her eyes from his as she rearranged its contents nervously.

"Your father is a heretic, not an Incarnate," he responded, studying her. Again she met his eyes and held them until it was he who looked away. She shrugged.

"I don't know," she said. "But I sincerely doubt you are the cold-blooded murderer they make you out to be, and I don't know what you will do now. Ceitra will continue to ruin families and eat the hate that comes of it."

"But I don't hate her. I never have," he answered.

"Maybe that's why she wants you dead then. Regardless, there is no safe place for either of us now." She swallowed a lump of pain that rose in her throat.

"There is." His head swiveled and he looked out to the river and beyond to the rising hills of the Wilderlands. "I'll help you cross the river."

"I'm going to Quarrytown to find my mother," Paiva said. "She's the only one who can yet explain all this. I need to help her."

"You can't go to Quarrytown," he sighed.

"I'm not crossing the river. I'm not going into the Wilderlands."

"Every ranger and Warden in the whole country side will be out looking for you. The most obvious place that you would be headed is to your mother. I figured as much myself."

She felt her lips tremble and her eyes burn with tears. "Renn, I have to find my mother."

"I am willing to help you. I will keep you safe," he said. "But I cannot help you if you go to Quarrytown."

She shook her head, then turned away from him and headed back down to the road. "You go your way and I'll go mine. I am going to find my mother."

"Paiva," he growled angrily and started after her.

"I don't need your help, Renn. None of this would have happened if it hadn't been for you." She said it a little too strongly. She couldn't help the words from spilling out and she relished pinning the blame on him when in her heart she knew all this trouble had started the night of Mummers-eve when she had broken her simple promise to her mother. She couldn't look back; she offered no apologies, even though she knew her words had cut him. If there was anything that could hurt Renn, it was more blame.

She broke into a run and disappeared down the bend in the road.

— «» —

She pulled her hood up high over her head as she walked into Quarrytown. The road was churned into mud and as she travailed along her feet plunged into a rut and remained stuck, sucked down in the mire. An oxcarter came along then, huddled under his cloak in the rain, and cursed at her for blocking his path. Her shoe was sucked off, and as she bent to retrieve it he cracked his whip over her head. She hurried out of the way and the ox trod over her shoe, sinking it deep into the mud where it disappeared. Her other shoe soon met a similar fate as she pressed her way into the town, and she arrived barefoot with mud streaked up her legs to her knees and her skirt hems black with sludge.

Oxcarters hauled their stone-laden wagons by while laborers pushed by wheelbarrows filled with pit run and chaff. The clamor of chisels and striking hammers in stone rose up above the dismal sounds of grunting oxen and laborers. Rangers on tall horses with their hounds were milling through the town, but none looked her way, for she was not noticeable amongst the other dirty, muddy peasants milling about.

The town houses were crowded and built atop each other, standing all the way to the edge of cliffs that gave way to the quarry below. It was a huge pit, perhaps four times the size of the actual town — a great, naked hole in the ground that had been formed after years of men cleaving limestone. The Keep itself had been built from its stone. There were fires

smoldering where laborers were burning limestone to make
mortar, rigging and scaffolding built against the face of the
cliffs where workers toiled in the rain and the dirt, cutting
stone from the cliff face. People milled about below, like ants
busy in an anthill. At the edge of the Quarry was the river
where stone barges waited to be loaded and sent downstream
to the Keep. Oxen carted wagons up a treacherous, winding
road towards other areas where stone was needed. There was
a fine mason's lodge built on one side of the pit, and on the
other side were little scattered huts built from stone rubble.
They were big enough for one, maybe two people to lie down
in to sleep at night. Some had a canvas roof, some had no
more than branches or driftwood instead. In these little huts
lived the wives of the branded men. About these huts were
wooden platforms and tables on which these women were
carving stone in the rain.

Paiva followed the stream of workers down into the pit,
then dodged through the crowd of laborers and animals
towards the huts. She scanned the women with their backs
bent over their stones, chipping away with empty, defeated
eyes. Her feet stung as she walked over the sharp shards, and
she noticed many of the other women too had no shoes.

Suddenly she saw her mother. Her head bowed low
against the rain, an angry glint in her eye as she clumsily
struck her chisel. Paiva slowly approached and called out to
her. Her mother looked up as if she had heard a voice from a
daydream, then looked at Paiva standing in the driving rain
with bleak eyes.

Recognition dawned on Kess' face, then fear crept into it.
She dropped her chisel and mallet.

"Paiva?" she cried. The other women looked up towards
Paiva, each one with guarded, empty eyes.

"Mother," Paiva breathed and ran towards her, dropping
her basket in the mud as she threw her arms around her. Her
mother's arms encircled her and clung to her desperately.

"You should not be here," she wept. "You should not see
me like this."

"Mother, something horrible has happened," Paiva
cried into her arms. Kess pushed her away and then led

her into one of the huts. They huddled together inside, for it was hardly tall enough to stand in. On the ground were reed pallets to sleep on and a flimsy wool blanket, a pot for water and a small dish for eating. Her mother embraced her again and kissed her wet cheeks as they sat down together.

"Paiva," she crooned. "My child. You should not have come here. You should have stayed safe and warm in the kitchens with Bess."

"Mother..." Paiva felt her eyes explode with tears, and then in a spew of excited words she told Kess everything that had come to pass at the Keep.

"There are rangers after you?" she exclaimed with a worry-frayed voice. "Paiva, they will find you here."

"Mother, you have to tell me the truth. Who is Father, really? Why did Ceitra call me his Virtue?"

Her mother's green eyes clouded with worry, her lips pursed in silence.

"Who is he?" Paiva pled. "What is he?"

Kess looked at her with anguish, opened her mouth to speak, and froze. From outside came sounds of hurried footsteps, then the canvas door to the little rubble hut was swept aside and a man pressed his face inside.

Paiva's mother bolted to her feet, bent beneath the shallow roof. "Master Rojik," she said. "I am sorry, I am headed back to work now."

"Are you?" the man growled. His narrowed eyes fell on Paiva. He had a felt cap on his head, his beard glistening with rain. At his belt was a coiled whip.

"Outside, the two of you, now," he said gruffly. His head receded back outdoors. Paiva looked worriedly to her mother. Together they stepped out into the rain and Paiva felt her heart leap into her throat. There, standing in a semi-circle about the contours of the hut, was a party of men in red cloaks. Their hoods were drawn up against the rain, giving them a formidable air. Paiva swallowed hard as she faced them and her mother reached out and clutched her hand. Master Rojik unfurled his whip and let it drag through the mud as he came towards them. He was a short man with thick shoulders and a scowly face. His hands were like calloused mitts, his eyes dark with ill will.

"Mistress Ibbie," he said. "It seems we have ourselves a problem. Can you tell me — that girl there, is she your daughter?"

"No," said Kess. "She is my niece. She was just visiting. She only recently had news of my situation. She does not know she is trespassing."

"Trespassing," a voice laughed, and one of the red-hooded men strode forward. Paiva felt her blood run cold, for she knew the voice as she knew the silver brooch that gleamed wetly on his shoulder.

"Trespassing is the least of her problems," Ramsi said, "and I know on good account, this girl is in fact your daughter. Is she not Mrs. Ibbie?" He canted his head back and revealed his handsome, pompous face. His mouth twisted back in a contented grin.

Paiva felt her mother's grip tighten. "Ramsi Lier," Kess said, trying to repress a sneer.

He assessed them, from their dirty bare feet to their ripped and stained clothes. "Well, well," he said. "There we have it. Seize them both." His men stepped forward at his order, but before anyone could be seized Kess pulled Paiva into a run and together they fled towards the river. There was truly nowhere for them to go, for they could not scale the cliffs or wind their way through the mass of workers and if they tried to cross the river they would surely drown in the swift current.

Master Rojik's whip cracked out and Paiva heard her mother fall behind her with a muffled scream. Paiva slid to a halt, her feet slicing over the wet shards of stone littering the quarry floor. She looked back to her mother who lay stricken from the lash of the whip across her shoulders. She struggled to her feet and screamed for Paiva to run, but Paiva could not stand to see her mother in such pain. She darted back and tried to haul Kess to her feet, but she was too late. A ranger hurled himself atop of her; the whip cracked again, and her mother screamed her name. Paiva felt herself crushed to the ground under the weight of the ranger, a knee in her back, while her hands were twisted behind her. She tasted blood in her mouth, heard Ramsi's laughing voice, and then she and her mother were dragged to their feet to face him.

She saw it again in Ramsi's eye then — that same look as when Yulin had taken his horse from him in Birchloam and she had ridden away on it. That cold, vindictive look filled her with dread. She wondered how she could have ever once fancied him.

"My Lady will be most pleased that I have collected you," he said. His eyes gleamed darkly in the wet daylight and Paiva had the feeling that he was somehow changed. She wondered if that darkness looking back at her was put there by his new mistress, or if it had been born naturally. He tipped his hood lower and turned away, smiling to himself.

— «» —

Paiva and Kess were thrown in a cramped cell in the Warden of Quarrytown's quarters. It was a foul little room below street level. The tiny, grated window let in runoff and rainwater from the street that dripped down the stone wall and onto the filthy floor covered in moldy straw. There was a heavy iron barred door that held them trapped. The cell was cold and damp and smelled of horrible excrements and rotting things. Ramsi had thrown them in and barred the door, then disappeared with his rangers back upstairs where he promised to keep watch over them for the night until they departed back for the Keep in the morning.

Paiva worried over her mother's back, but there was nothing that could be done but to wash it with the little water they had been given. She put her hands over the wounds, much like her father would have done, and willed them to heal. They remained bloody, but Kess was comforted by her touch. Eventually daylight wore out and they huddled together in the dark cell in the farthest corner. The streets outside grew quiet but for the sound of distant brawls and drunken slurs.

"What do we do?" Paiva whimpered to her mother in the dark.

"We can't do anything right now. Just pray to the good spirits. Pray they send someone to save us." Then Kess leaned her head back against the cold stone wall and sighed.

"When I was a girl I fell in love with a wolf," she said. "I would tend to the sheep at the top of the pasture, just as you did. Times were hard. Winters were starving. I lost my brother to sickness, Aunt Bess left Birchloam to find work. Father was cruel, and mother was blamed for all his shortcomings. Yet she was true to him until the end of her days.

"Father soon died — an inflammation of his blood he got from cutting himself on a rusted blade. Mother became feeble after that and I was alone to tend to the farm which was our only means of survival. The only thing that kept me going was my friend the wolf, who lurked in the shadows of the woods at the edge of the pastures. At first, I had thrown stones at him, thinking he was after my meagre flock. But my stones did little to thwart him, and I soon realized he was more interested in listening to me talk to him. He did not bother the sheep; nothing bothered the sheep while he was near. I'd find him in the gloaming, slunk down in the tall grasses, his fur mottled and brown, his eyes glowing gold like something old and wild. He never fully revealed himself to me, but he was always there, watching over me." Kess sighed and Paiva felt the weight of her words, the revelation of a great, secret truth.

"Mother found me a husband," Kess continued. "Mother knew the farm needed a man to run it. I refused this man, but mother insisted and tormented me over it until I decided I really had no other choice. I could not forever spend my years alone on a farm talking to a wolf. People had already begun to think me a little odd. I reconciled myself, and I went up into the pastures and found him. I told this wolf I was going to become a wife. He looked at me with his golden eyes, so deep and sad I felt my heart fall from my chest. I thanked him for watching over me, and told him I was growing old and soon no one would want me.

"But then one evening in the twilight a man appeared from the woods. His face was handsome and young, his eyes as golden as my wolf's had been." Tears spilt down her mother's face and she looked to Paiva with her sad smile. "He said he had never grown old before, but he wanted to grow old with me.... You know the rest of the story after that."

She reached out her hand and touched Paiva's face. "He loves you more than anything in the world. You are his child, and you were born from his love, as you were born from mine."

"Why have neither of you told me anything of this?"

"How could I tell you? How could you believe it? It is hard enough for me to believe. Viviel never speaks of his life before he became a man. What he was before lost its purpose. That is why he collected the stories — searching and wanting to find a reason for his existence. But he became committed to being a man, just a simple man, and a father and husband — things he had never known before and which he earnestly tried to be."

"I think he is going to Morinvere," said Paiva. "He sang that song after he was branded. I think he was trying to tell us."

"Yes," her mother said. "Yes, that is where he says the other spirits are kept hidden. That is why he prays so hard, trying to provoke them to return to the world. He will go to summon them, but I do not know if he will ever return. For the Vale is guarded by Varloga and his conjuring's of nightmares, the Folka. Even your father is afraid of Varloga."

No sooner had she uttered those words then they heard the door to the floor above them open. They froze as they listened to padded footsteps descend the stone stairs. A moment later the form of a ranger appeared before their cell door and peered in.

"Mrs. Ibbie?" he asked. Then there was the shout of voices, the clatter of boots and the clang of metal. The ranger looked up hurriedly as lantern light flickered from above. He fumbled for a ring of keys. Angry voices shouted out and rushed towards them. The ranger threw the keys into the cell and then his shape vanished before them.

Red cloaks swarmed passed the cell door. A man carrying a lantern set it in a rung on the wall as they peered about into the shadows. Kess sprang for the keys while commotion sounded out. Suddenly bodies slammed into each other, swords scraped, men grunted and cursed. Hurriedly Kess sought to thrust each key into the lock, her hands shaking with excitement as she tried to force it open. Paiva peered through the bars of the cell to try and discern the shadowy shapes battling before them.

The lock sprung open and Kess threw the door wide, slamming it into the shape of a man lunging towards her. He howled as his teeth broke against the iron and he staggered back, then was felled to his knees by a blow to his head from behind. Kess grabbed Paiva and they bolted out into the corridor. A body hurtled through the air and crashed into their empty cell, then the door was slammed behind it with a vibrating clang of metal.

Kess and Paiva halted halfway up the stairs as a voice called out to them. They blinked into the dim light, their eyes focusing on the tall shadow of the ranger that had tossed them the keys. He was resting his hands on his knees, back hunched as he sucked in pained breaths. With a curse he straightened and flexed a sore arm. At his feet were several bodies in red cloaks, none seeming to move or breathe. He stepped over them neatly into the lantern light.

"Renn!" Paiva exclaimed in a hoarse whisper.

"I told you not to go to Quarrytown," he snapped. His mouth trickled with blood, his eyes gleaming coldly. He nodded respectively to Kess, then spat out a bloody tooth chip.

"By my soul," her mother breathed. "The Wilderman."

"At your service," he said and wiped his mouth. "Come along, we haven't much time before the alarm is sounded. The last thing I want is the dogs on us." He brushed passed them and up the stairwell. They followed him swiftly, not daring to question where they were headed.

Paiva heard him muttering to himself under his breath as they headed up into the Warden's Quarters. They entered a storeroom and fled swiftly through, then out into the Ranger's Mess where reed lamps spilled their light over an unsettling scene. There were four red-robed men, their bodies slumped over with their drinks spilling across the table.

"Come along," Renn muttered to them, for they had both

stopped short and stared in horror at the limp men.

"Did you kill them?" Kess whispered. Renn gave her an exasperated look.

"No," he whispered angrily. "I slipped some Winkweed into their store of ale."

"Winkweed," her mother nodded. One man lifted his head from the table gingerly and blinked at her. He smiled pleasantly at the sight of a woman, was about to lower his head to go back to sleep, when a sudden thought jarred him back awake. His mouth flapped open in shock as he blinked at Kess again.

"By my soul," he breathed. "You're supposed to be downstairs." He then staggered to his feet with a teetering sway.

"Master Warden!" the man shouted at the top of his lungs and fumbled sleepily for his sword. "Get the dogs!" He sat down again seeming to have forgotten what he was doing, then fell forwards across the table in a faint. In half a second he was snoring.

Renn seized Kess by the throat of her dress and hauled her along. They fled through the Mess and then out into a corridor where Renn heaved his shoulder into a heavy wooden door. It burst open, spilling them out into the darkened, rainy streets. They ran hard through the mud, Renn ahead swinging his head back to check on them. From behind them rose a chorus of hounds and angry shouts. The noise terrified Paiva and made her run faster, though she could hardly keep pace with Renn.

When they rounded a street corner and dove into an alley, Paiva found her mother had lagged behind. She stopped and leaned against the corner of a brick house while her mother caught up. Renn barked for them to hurry on, but Kess sagged against the house in exhaustion. She was battered and weak, her body not as young or swift as either of theirs and lame from the lashing Master Rojik had given her. She placed trembling arms around Paiva and kissed her cheeks, then fumbled for the cords of Paiva's cloak and stripped it from her. She placed it over herself, then drew up the hood to hide her face.

"What are you doing?" Paiva gasped as the soft rain

chilled her.

"You won't be able to outrun them," her mother said. "The hounds will run you down. I'll lead them away."

"No, Mother. You come with us."

"No!" Kess shook her head. "You cannot let that evil woman have you. I love you. There is nothing worse that can be done to me than to lose you, anything else I can bear. Find your father, help him." Then she turned her face to Renn and pointed a stern finger at him. "You, Wilderman," she said heatedly. "Promise me you will keep her safe."

Renn tensed.

"Promise me, Wilderman!"

He gave a slow nod, then his eyes flickered up at the sound of howling dogs. Kess kissed Paiva again, then without a word darted back out into the street.

"No!" Paiva yelled and lunged after her, but Renn caught her and drew her back into the shadows of the alley. Paiva's cry was muffled by Renn's firm hand clamping over her mouth as she saw her mother's shape disappear down the street. Moments later a staggering ranger leading a pair of hounds on leashes appeared. The hounds swept their noses over the wet ground and Renn drew Paiva further into the crevices of the alley. The dogs moved closer to them, circling and pawing at the ground in confusion. But then her mother let go a low whistle from the other end of the street and the dogs pricked their ears up and threw their weight against their leashes, jerking the ranger forward and away from the alley. They howled and snapped their frothy jaws into the air as the ranger shouted out for others to join him.

Paiva struggled to free herself from Renn's grasp as she saw the ranger stagger forwards after the hounds. Renn dragged her down the alley out of earshot. "She might get away," he murmured, but Paiva found that did not ease her in the slightest.

"We can't leave her," she said as she tore his hand from her mouth.

"We already have," he replied coldly, then he was dragging her down the alley again, forcing her to shimmy in between houses and skip through yards. Her mind went numb, unable to understand why her body was still running forwards when it should have been running back to help her mother. Renn berated her, pushed her, shoved her and pulled her along until they were on the outskirts of the town, running through the trees along the riverbank.

She faltered behind, and when she found the conviction to stop and turn around he caught her swiftly by the hand and hauled her back. He found his horse hidden in a copse and swung up onto it, taking her with him.

"Where are we going now?" she asked uneasily as he trotted the horse down to the water.

"We'll lose them in the river."

The thought didn't even register. She was still absorbed in worrying over her mother. He urged the horse down to the bank of the river and scanned the current, then spurred the horse forward and they plummeted in with great plumes of water. She clung to his waist as the horse jolted and slipped, up to its flanks in the surging current. To her surprise they reached the other side safely.

"That wasn't so bad," she said, thinking she would be able to cross back herself if given the chance.

"You really are a simple girl from Birchloam," Renn remarked.

"I'm not simple."

"You are if you think that was the Panderbank."

She looked back at the wide divide behind them. "That is a river, is it not?"

"It's an outlet from the lime kilns. It joins with the Panderbank a little lower. The real river is through here."

He led the horse onwards into the dark trees and a short while later they came to an expanse of water that was triple the divide they had just crossed. Paiva muttered a bitter curse. It looked like a narrow lake: the water looked still out in the middle, but she noticed a log float by at an alarming speed.

"Can you swim?" he asked, noting the sound of hounds baying behind them.

"Not across that."

"Berg horses are powerful swimmers. They know how

to cut the current. I don't know how well Yulin's mount will like this, so hold fast to my cloak. Do not let go or you will be swept away."

He forced the horse into the water and soon they were floating out into the freezing current. She felt her lungs collapse with cold shock and she struggled to hold onto him. Renn clung to the horse's mane and stripped the saddle from its back, letting it sink to the bottom of the river. Paiva felt the powerful thrust of the horse's legs, heard its deep breaths. The falling rain splashed into the water and created a fog before them.

When they eddied out towards the middle of the river, the current swept them downstream. The horse began to panic as it saw the bank sweep by before its eyes. Renn spoke to it in a calm voice, pulling its reins hard to keep its head pointed to the far side of the river. The horse fought him, its mouth dipped into the river as it twisted its head. For a moment Paiva thought it would rather drown than continue onwards. It snorted a spray of water and lifted its head, its mouth bloodied from fighting the bit. Then, with the whites of its eyes rolling, it straightened its course. The water was black and deep, and she could not fathom what sort of creatures lurked below. There were stories that kept people fearful of the waters, stories of the quarry women who drowned trying to escape the pit, and whose ghosts lived in the water weeds waiting to drown anyone who ventured too far into the shallows. She forced these thoughts away and focused only on staying afloat.

As they neared the other side, panic rose in Paiva again. They had been swept far downstream. The shoreline looked to be tangled with driftwood and uprooted trees. The horse evaded the dark shape of a clawed mass of roots rising from the water, but as it drew closer to land its legs suddenly struck something below and became tangled. It began to thrash and sink.

Renn pushed Paiva free as the horse panicked and Paiva cried out as the current swept her away. The horse's head sank underwater as its tail end rose. Renn found a submerged log to stand on and he levered the horse's head up with the reins. Snorting and choking, the horse grappled with whatever it was tangled in, broke away from it and dragged Renn to shore.

Paiva's skirt caught on a spiky, bone-like piece of driftwood and her swift flight downriver was jolted to a halt. She clambered for grip on slimy underwater branches, choking on mouthfuls of freezing water. She pulled herself towards shore, shrieking when water weeds wrapped around her legs and sluiced against her skin. When her feet touched bottom she sunk to her knees in a soft, silty muck.

The horse had sunk almost up to its neck in the loose sediment. The water boiled with rotten leaves and silt that its hooves churned up from the river bottom. A foul smell bubbled up, escaped from the layers of rot. She thought her first impression on stepping foot on the far side of the Panderbank was likened to stepping foot into the gateway of hell itself. The wet air around her was thick with the sulphurous smell of rot, the horse's black body appearing nightmarish and grotesque in the muck.

The horse soon tired and looked resigned to die in the mud, its flanks heaving and its nostrils and mouth bleeding. Renn found a branch and slapped it across its hindquarters. The horse panicked again and then wrestled itself out of the mud with its last effort, finding mossy respite further up.

Renn patted it over as tremors ran down its legs and, finding it was still in good conformation, left it to recuperate while he went to fish Paiva out of the muddy shallows. She wrapped her arms around his neck as he scooped her up and dragged her to firmer ground.

She had never imagined in all her life to step foot on the other side of the Panderbank. When she felt its dirt beneath her feet she could not help to let loose a low sob. She clung to Renn, unable to find the strength to stand on her own. Gently he pried her arms from about his neck, then set his hands on her shoulders and gripped her firmly.

"You're alright," he said, giving her a small shake. "Your mother will be alright."

She nodded and wiped tears and muck from her face.

She shivered violently in the cold. He turned away, back to the horse while she looked up to the dark, rain-soaked trees looming above her.

"Welcome to the Wilderlands," he muttered. It sent a chilling rush through her and she had to stop herself from cowering back into the waters of the river. There was no sound but for the rain and the horse's labored breathing. She was filled with ominous uncertainty, but she reminded herself that her father was out there, even more alone than she was.

At least she had Renn. She dropped her eyes to him and perceived him in the shadows by the horse, waiting for her to gather herself. He seemed to be looking out over the river and she followed his gaze, drawing in a sharp breath when she spotted distant lights moving along the far shore, disappearing and then reappearing as they swung through trees. They had been swept farther down then she had expected.

"Are we safe here?" she whispered as panic surged inside her.

"Yes," he sighed with relief. "No one would think us mad enough to cross the river in the dark." With that he stepped into the trees, pulling the unwilling horse behind him. He was almost out of sight before Paiva sprang after him and she stumbled behind and kept her eyes on the ground, unwilling to look up to the trees she felt were about to swallow her.

Chapter 10

Paiva had not the faintest notion in which direction they were headed. The forest was tangled all around them, wet and black and filled with the calls of nightly animals and a deafening chorus of peepers. The lights and the river disappeared behind them as they stepped into the dark. For all she saw she might as well have been blindfolded. She could just barely make out Renn's shape ahead of her and struggled to keep up with him. Her feet were bare and were soon slashed and worn raw from the tangled undergrowth. She fell countless times and went most of the way with her arms outstretched before her to shield her face from raking branches. Despite her struggling she remained cold, and as the rain continued to fall she became much more so.

Renn was distant and quiet, trespassing through the woods without the sound of a single footfall. She began to grow nervous, for she remembered when she had followed Ramsi into the woods so trustingly only to be tricked. Her fear began to mount the deeper they went, and she thought that surely wherever Varloga was now he was relishing every moment of it.

Suddenly Renn seemed to have a notion, for he stopped and turned back to her. She stumbled to a stop and blinked at him in the dark, unable to keep her teeth from chattering as shooting panic swept over her. Even if he wasn't a spirit in disguise, she had the racing fear he could suddenly abandon her at his own whim.

"Forgive me. You must be freezing," he said flatly.

"I'm fine," she said through numb lips, thankful he did not have the intention to abandon her after all.

"No, you haven't shoes or a cloak. You won't make the night like this," he said.

"I'm fine," she said strongly as she hugged her arms around herself to ward off the chill of standing still. "Let's keep moving."

Suddenly he was standing before her, fumbling with Yulin's red cloak. "Lay down on the horse, share his heat. You will help keep him warm as well."

"Alright," she nodded, shaking with bitter cold. She clutched at the horse's mane with numb hands and he helped to lever her up. She lay down along the horse's back, looping her arms and pressing her face into its warm, wet neck. Renn tucked her under Yulins cloak, under which his lingering warmth and scent clung, immediately shielding her from the prickling rain.

It sent relief sweeping through her, for Varloga did not smell of horses and earth, nor was he warm. "What about you?" she asked.

"I can walk faster now without you blundering behind, I will keep warm."

Slightly stung by his comment, Paiva receded under Yulin's hood and buried herself into the rising warmth of the horse. Hidden beneath she let the tears come unrestrained, her heart crushed under the weight of longing for her home and her family. She reconciled her father's true identity, and knowing what he truly was made it that much harder to bear. He could have had any life he wanted but he had stayed to be her father, to be a husband, because he loved them.

They trudged on until the rain stopped and the clouds suddenly parted and filled the woods with cold moonlight. The sky opened up above and soon was glowing brightly with stars. She did not know how far they had gone before Renn decided to stop in a clearing beneath a great wounded tree that was barren of leaves, its naked branches twisted up into the sky like skeletal fingers.

He tethered the horse and helped her off, then wearily sat against the tree where she joined him. She did not ask him, but it seemed they would go no farther for the night, and she huddled beneath Yulin's cloak and canted her head up to the swollen moon. She was bone-weary, but she imagined Renn must have been beyond that. Not only had he been tied to the pillar without proper food, he must have received a few bruised ribs from his encounter with the rangers in Quarrytown.

That made her think of her mother. "I shouldn't have left her," she half-whispered, half-sobbed out loud without thinking.

"I forced you. I'm sorry," he said, his breath clouding in the chilled air between them. "I am sorry for it all."

"Don't be. I shouldn't have blamed you for anything. But I did. And that was wrong. This is the second time you have saved me now. So thank you, and don't be sorry."

He remained quiet for a moment, his face impassive, then he shook his head. "You helped me as well. You gave me bread when I was starved. You sent Yulin to free me."

"By all the shining stars," she said looking up to the celestial bodies above, "I want to go home."

"We will have to find your father."

"Thank you," she breathed with relief. "I can't do it alone. I'm afraid of these woods, and I'm a woman. I wouldn't be able to fend off raving Wildermen or hungry wolves or Folka. I mean, I'm probably the only woman whose ever crossed the Panderbank."

"No," he answered. "There are a few women out here. It's only a river. Many women have crossed it searching for their husbands or sons... or fathers. Sometimes lonely Wildermen cross the river and steal women, hiding them away in the mountains where no one can find them ever again. There are even children born out here. Wildermen have many tales of such things."

She blinked at him.

"I shouldn't be telling you tall tales," he apologized. "You're already very frightened."

"You will help me?" she asked, though she was ashamed at how her voice broke and became raw. She did not want to sound like she was begging.

"Go where you will, so long as it is in the Wilderlands. I promised your mother I would keep you safe," he said. "I assure you I still remember how to keep promises. I wasn't always a brute."

"You're not a brute," she said, not entirely sure how she found him. "A brute would have let me drown in the river or die of cold. A brute would certainly not have risked his neck to come to Quarrytown."

"I am simply trying to control the damage I have caused," he said incisively. Her mind spun to Ceitra.

"But you didn't cause it," she chided. Again he shook his head, then pursed his lips and leant his tired head back against the tree to close his eyes in resignation.

"But I did," his voice was bitter. "Ceitra used your family so that she could condemn me."

"No. No, it's not that at all. She isn't even human. She is an Incarnate of the Strix."

"The Eater of Hate," he murmured. His eyes opened and stared into the dark of the woods.

"What do you think of my father's stories? Do you really think he's a heretic?" she prodded, watching his brow furrow.

He considered this, and she could hear the strain of weariness in his voice when he answered. "I think people should be allowed to believe in anything they want, as long as they find some comfort in it and cause others no harm."

"But what do *you* believe, of the old stories, the old ways?"

He shrugged. "I don't care for them. I don't understand them either. I have never found any comfort or direction in spirits or gods. I just don't care."

"You have no faith, in anything?"

"I have faith in Berg horses because I know they can outrun a ranger's charger. I have faith that I will die if I do not eat. I have faith Folka will kill me if I do not kill them first. That's all I need to believe to keep me alive. I do not yearn for the protection of something greater than myself. My prayers are empty, my thoughts are small."

"I've never met anyone quite like you," she blinked. "Everyone believes in something, whether it's the Forest or the God."

"I believe in the Forest, just not the way you do. Whatever these spirits and gods are, they were made by man and are his own reflection, not the Forest's. Man should have known his place, and tread lightly over the roots and green things that gave him life. I believe in life and the struggle to live. It is the common ground on which we all stand."

Paiva found a deep truth in what he said. She had never before thought there was anything in between the divide of the two beliefs. But there was. There was Renn's reflection, and it stirred her.

"We have many leagues to go tomorrow," he said as his head slumped forwards in exhaustion. "All the newly branded pass through Crowbill's camp. It is a good place to begin searching for your father. I must rest, we can talk tomorrow."

She nodded and let him rest. The wool of Yulin's cloak was still damp but she curled beneath it into the hollow of the tree. She closed her eyes to the low breathing of the horse and the call of wild things in the woods and wondered if it would be sleep or Folka that came to claim her first.

— «» —

Renn half-woke to the gray light of dawn. His body was warm. There was someone curled against him — a comforting, warm presence. Slowly his mind drifted back to sleep until a jarring thought burst through. In a moment of confusion he thought he had woken in a Wilderman camp with one of his comrades tucked beside him. He lifted his head and looked down at Paiva, and to his relief found she did not have a beard.

She was yet asleep, her breathing slow. She had rolled over and curled against him in the night, searching for his warmth. He allowed the initial shock he had felt to wash away while he studied the morning light glistening on her eyelashes. He sat up quietly into the chilled morning air and drew away from her quickly, not allowing time to savor a delicate feeling that took shape.

He went and peered into the trees, still dripping from the night's rain. The air was fresh, damp and earthy. All about warblers twittered and small creatures and insects stirred. He went in search of food, leaving her to sleep off the last of her chills and wake in the peace of her own thoughts.

— «» —

They followed the river upstream while they ate handfuls of berries and chewed on the succulent roots of a sweet plant the Wildermen called Grompsin Grass. Paiva donned the red cloak for she had nothing to keep her warm besides her own thin dress, and he was quite comfortable in his ripped oilskin.

Renn led them deep into the woods where the trees became old and wide. There were few old trees in the lowlands, most of the forest having been coppiced and felled for timber through many generations and was young in its verdancy. Here the trees became tall as the very tower of the Keep and as wide as horse carts. They stretched endlessly up towards the sky where their great branches were woven overhead like a tapestry. Entwined and mossy, so strong and old a castle could have been built atop them that would have crowned the clouds. The forest floor became barren and easily passable, the sunlight low and muted giving no nourishment to low-growing things aside from rings of mushrooms and beds of moss.

Paiva felt as if she were in a cathedral and her very bones vibrated with the energy of such a deep and sacred place. The forest that surrounded her farm was thick with slash and rooting things, brambles and rabbit bushes. It made the forest thorny and prickly, and she realized it was through man's own hand that it had become so. This was old forest, virgin and untouched but for the Wildermen who passed through it and the many creatures that lived within. Undisturbed, primal, and wild. So quiet and hushed not even the horse's hooves disturbed it.

They passed through miles of these trees and she wondered how Renn could have found his way. But he knew where there were great upheavals of boulders that lay mossy and twined with ancient roots. One led to another; they were markers the seasoned Wildermen used for navigation. Each rock had a name, and in the four directions of the compass it pointed depending on the path you were going.

It was a path committed to memory, a web of trails and unseen meridians that was a creed for the Wildermen. The Rock of Regret, which was where the newly branded were disposed of, led straight to the Mossy Rock. The Mossy Rock would point you further north towards the Spiney Rock or west towards the Crumbled Rock. They went north towards the Spiney Rock, and from there it led to three more in different directions, or back towards the Mossy Rock.

Paiva did not know at first how Renn could commit this all to memory but she learned the Wildermen had formed songs and stories that helped to serve as a map when wandering the woods. She thought how her father would have filled a whole book in recording their folklore. Paiva sensed that Renn secretly delighted in sharing them with her. They were stories that only the Wildermen knew, and if they were ever pardoned and left the woods, stories that they would leave behind.

Each rock held true to its namesake. Spiny Rock was a line of jagged slabs that were heaved onto their sides into the ground, so they resembled the spine of a giant, decaying, monstrous creature. From there they went uphill and northwest to Far Fall Rock, that sat atop a cliff so high and steep it made the trees below look like rabbit bushes. It was a huge mass suspended over all the land, its weathered face peaked into the wind. Renn decided to make camp there and left Paiva with the horse while he went in search of food.

Paiva crouched on all fours and peered over the rock, feeling her senses spin as her mind tried to register and understand the depths into which she looked. At first it felt her own weight on the rock would somehow displace it, making it tumble from the cliff face where it would send her crashing to the trees below. It held fast, her own presence unfelt in the magnitude of its existence. There was a high wind that ripped through her hair, and it drew her eyes upwards from the gorge below to the sky where great billows of clouds roiled and churned in pinky oranges and subtle purples. She felt as if she was among them, eye-level with heaven. Slowly her senses calmed, a great feeling of wildness and of being alive and set free overtook her. The Forest was a majesty, a kingdom unto its own. When she had first seen the Keep she was in awe of man's abilities to construct such a place, to carve stone from the hills and lock it into a structure so tall and magnificent. Gazing down on the forest from the rock she was beyond awe. She was taken apart, she was no longer human. She felt a part of it all, welcomed back to the place where all life seemed to flow from. There were no walls to guard her from it, to keep out its dangers and unpredictable powers. She was raw and exposed and dismantled, her soul awakening to its beauty.

The smell of woodsmoke made her turn back to Renn at the edge of the trees behind her. He was busy ripping the meat off a grouse and spitting it over a small fire, his pipe dangling between his teeth though he had no tarweed to light it with. When he caught her looking at him he gave her a wary glance.

"I see why it is called Far Fall," she said.

"Many Folka have been driven off this rock, falling to their deaths below. A few Wildermen too, some willingly who have leapt. Used to be called the Tall Rock." He bent his head back to the fire and sucked on his pipe before continuing. "There's a story that tells if a Wilderman does not touch the Rock of Regret upon coming to the woods, he will forever be haunted by it. He will surely be led to Far Fall, and when he stands before the Forest at its peak all his regrets will come back to him and make him jump. Wildermen have a high regard for stones and rocks, mountains and hills. They seem to think they all talk to one another. Ulrig is especially keen on talking to the rocks, he's always muttering at them. He seems to think they're the only ones who remember anything."

"Did you touch the rock?"

"I have, I slept under it my first night cast off. I didn't know these stories until later. I also know they are only stories, stories passed down from the old Wildermen to the youngest ones. It's a warning. It tells to leave behind regret or you will not survive the woods. That's what I make of it."

"But there is truth to it."

"Surely. There's truth in all their stories."

"As there is in my father's."

He fell quiet and sucked on his empty pipe while he roasted the grouse, seeming to have forgotten their conversation. She looked back over the Forest and found that in the moments she had looked away the sky had darkened and the first stars had begun to glimmer above the pillars of clouds.

"I didn't know what this place was like," she said.

"Oh it changes you," Renn replied. "The pardoned often have a hard time going back to the lowlands. Ulrig, who runs the camp I settled with, he was granted a pardon and he came back. He just didn't know how to live amongst civilized men anymore."

"I didn't know you were allowed."

"Of course you're allowed. It's no man's land out here. There are no rules except to not cross the Panderbank. If it's not the Folka and the wild beasts trying to kill you, it's the other Wildermen. They're like wolves, they form packs, they claim territories and drive off others from hunting it. It is man returned to the wild, and wild he becomes again. There are even those that camp up by the Highpeaks. They've abandoned all hope of ever returning to the lowlands."

She rose then and came down to the fire, sitting across from him and smelling the roasting meat with hunger.

"Who claims this part of the woods then?"

"No one really, there's just the River Runners run by Crowbill that flit through here. They don't have horses usually so they're not hard to get away from if they prove to be any trouble."

"How did you survive? Who did you meet?" she asked curiously.

"There is not much to tell," he shrugged. "I was a complete dolt. Went from having servants emptying my chamber pot to not having a pot for anything at all. I had to wise up very fast. Unfortunately anyone who recognized me tried to kill me, being the very son of the Lord who had damned them. Eventually young Lord Rennik did die; in fact he was thrown into a gully to be rid of. A Wilderman crawled out of it, covered in muck and filth. That man they called Black Renn.

"Crowbill and his band found me after that. We got on fairly well; I learned much about the woods from him. When I left his gang to hunt Folka there was a bet on my head that I wouldn't make it through the winter.

"The River Runners prefer the sanctuary of the riverbank to roaming the deep of the woods where the Folka lurk. I took my leave of them and headed out, following stones and valleys. I had my troubles with different bands. I was still unused to the rough customs of these men. Some ran me off, some tried to kill me, some tried to steal the boots off my feet. I wandered far and wide, and only in the autumn did I find Ulrig at Far Reach. I never would have made it the winter if it had not been for him."

His eyes shone in the firelight as he reflected. She was quiet as she absorbed his story.

"The truth is, I could not return to my old life. If I was ever granted a pardon and forgiven, I could no more shed this life that I have lived than I could my own skin. I am a Wilderman, and the forest is my home. Why would I want to return behind stone walls and shut all of this out?" He inclined his head towards the sweep of forest as a howl of wolves rose up, greeting the darkness that settled over the hills. It sent a chill up her spine. He pulled the meat from the fire and offered it to her. She did not move to take it.

"What happened with your brother?" she asked, swallowing dryly. She was profoundly curious and afraid of this question. The grouse dripped its grease over the ground between them. Another chorus of howls rose up chillingly and the wind spluttered sparks from the fire.

Renn looked like a chill had swept over him. Something strange passed over his face, a lifting of shadows and a revealing of something soft and helpless.

"Taking your own life is a sin," he said. "It is cowardice, and is punishable by the laws of the land." He recalled how they had had a terrible fight atop the ramparts and it was Odrik who ended up broken on the ground below.

"Odrik saved you," she breathed. "But you took the blame."

"I should have helped him. Instead I fought him."

He looked to the edge of Far Fall Rock, out to the sky wherein the swollen moon began to rise from the black silhouette of hills. He then put the skewered meat aside and went to stand at the precipice and look down into the chasm below. His tattered oilskin cloak flitted in the stiff wind, his hair as knotted and wild as a Berg horse's mane.

"The funny thing is I would never have had the courage to take my life," he breathed. "My brother was brave. He was no coward."

Paiva rose anxiously, watching him balance precariously at the edge of the rock. Renn swept his eyes up from the fathoms below, catching sight of a pillar of smoke rising from the tops of the trees in the moonlight. He pointed to it and looked back to her.

"That's Crowbill," he said.

She nodded, concerned for his footing on the rock. He stared out a moment longer over the forest.

When he returned to the fire to eat from the roasted grouse there was little evidence of the revelation that had occurred. He was quiet and taciturn, his eyes thoughtful, but there was no struggle in them.

They ate their meagre meal in silence and then he lay down wrapped in his oilskin and closed his eyes without a word. He seemingly fell into an exhausted sleep. Paiva sat and gazed over the daunting, dark forest, overwhelmed by the magnitude of open sky and endless trees. Then, with the chill of the high breeze at her back, she too lay down beneath the red cloak and tried to find her own rest.

Chapter 11

In the morning Renn took note of the smoke below them, then threw Paiva up on the horse and wound their way down Far Fall and into the woodlands below. He kept vigilant, his eyes and ears pricked for any movement in the trees.

They were travelling hard for some time before Renn suddenly halted the horse and began scanning the trees. Paiva saw nothing, but a moment later dark shadows gathered and took the form of men. They crept out of the trees and came to stand in a half circle around them. All were bearded and dirty, covered in furs and leathers, each brandishing a weapon of their own comportment.

The leader came forward, sporting a braided dark beard and a leather cap stuck with feathers. His face was peaked, with high cheek bones and a long, hooked nose. A smile lit up his birdlike face.

"By my beard, that was you atop Far Fall last night then," he cackled. "Where are you headed with a horse like that and a girl in a ranger's cloak?"

"Crowbill," Renn called and returned a small smile. "We've been looking for you."

"I'll trade you good swill and hot meat for your stories," Crowbill replied. "Sure looks like you could use it."

"Fair trade," Renn agreed, and then they were following Crowbill and his band into the trees. They came to a camp gathered in a copse of pines by a brook and there was the fire whose smoke had led them to Crowbill. Over it a wild boar was roasting in skewered pieces. There were little huts constructed from hides with pine boughs for roofs. Renn said they were called Thimblehuts and were easily collapsible and transportable for a roving band like Crowbill's.

Crowbill invited her to the fire where she seated herself on a mossy log. Renn went to water the horse and rub it down, then left it to graze through the underbrush. He returned and took a seat beside her, keeping a watchful eye on the other men who gawked at her. Renn's edge returned when he caught one man staring rudely at Paiva; he set his cold eyes on the man until he shrunk back and looked away. Crowbill caught the interaction and laughed, bringing them a clay tankard filled with swill to share. He then turned his attention to his roasting meat while he drank from his own. Other men gathered round, all eager to hear tell of Renn's stories.

"So Renn, tell us," Crowbill commanded cheerfully.

"Lady Ceitra passed a sentence for me to have my neck stretched in the gallows," he stated flatly.

"However did you manage that?" Crowbill asked.

"She replaced Warden Yulin with a ranger from Birchloam," Renn continued, "and Yulin in spite of her sprung me, gave me a horse and a cloak to escape with."

"Master Warden Yulin sprung you?" Crowbill gaped.

"Like a rabbit from a snare," Renn mused.

Crowbill then took a long haul of his drink. "What is she thinking to strip a man like Yulin of his rank?" Paiva noted that there seemed to be a certain amount of respect for Yulin, despite that she understood all Wildermen hated Wardens and rangers irrevocably.

"By my beard," Crowbill laughed. "And what did you do to catch your neck in a noose?"

"A good number of things."

"He lied to try and save my father," Paiva interjected. All the men looked at her as if she had grown two heads. She felt Renn bristle beside her and she reached for the tankard and lifted it for a drink, then choked on the volatile liquid within. It burned her throat and sprung tears to her eyes. It had the powerful taste of medicine, like pinecones and cedar bark. She coughed it up, wondering if it was some sort of horse liniment, and handed the tankard to Renn who took a swig without complaint.

"I call that Crowbill swill," Crowbill chuckled. "Put hair on your chest and make your beard shine."

"I'm looking for my father," Paiva said as she wiped her eyes, noting that she wanted neither chest hair or beard. "His name's Viviel. He was branded and sent to the woods not too long ago. Wrongfully branded."

Crowbill looked back to her from the fire, his face drained of color.

"Viviel you said?" he asked. "Tall fellow, big brown beard? A shepherd from Birchloam?"

Paiva nodded anxiously.

"Yes, he was here. And now he's gone," Crowbill said. "Slept by my fire for half a night. The woods began to stir with Folka. The trees shook, they howled and gnashed their teeth until we all thought we would perish. Never in all my years in the Wilderlands have I ever seen the likes of it. I was scared, so scared, as I never have been in all my years." He pointed to a gray streak in his beard. "Never had any white in my beard before that night. We tried to frighten them off, started a huge blaze of a fire and shot arrows into the trees. They kept coming, howling and scraping their claws against stones. Some men got dragged off and we heard their bones broken as they screamed. Viviel fought alongside us, until he told us to lay down our arms. He walked into the trees after that, and with him went the Folka."

Paiva looked to Renn, whose brow creased into another of his thoughtful frowns. He looked sideways at her, and she hoped he would believe her stories now.

"You know what I think," Crowbill continued. "I think he had spirit blood in him. That's why they wanted him. I don't much like spirits, good or bad. I don't like priests or sorcerers or magicians or soothsayers. Can't stand none of it, and I hate the Folka. More than I hate Rangers and Wardens and sore teeth." He looked back to Paiva and took a long swig of his drink, hissing out a hot breath. "You're welcome to my camp, but if there's trouble I want you gone."

Paiva nodded solemnly.

"And you, Renn. What are you going to do with her?" Crowbill asked.

"Well," Renn shrugged. "I'm not going to let the wolves or any Wildermen eat her just yet."

— «» —

Paiva ate and drank until she couldn't move. She had not known how hungry she was until she tasted Crowbill's finely roasted meal. There were chestnuts roasted in the hot embers, ash cakes made from acorn meal and wild eggs to top off the thick chunk of boar meat Crowbill sliced into a wooden trencher for her. The meat was spiced with a wild flavor of woodland herbs and even a little salt. The men fell on it and devoured it with relish.

"You see," Crowbill winked at her. "Men don't need to live in castles to eat like kings. I am a King, I am King Crowbill. King of the River Runners, Lord of all that is green and free."

His men jeered and laughed, raising their drinks of swill.

"Life is wasted for any man who could want more than what we have," Crowbill sang. "We have freedom, we have a river that feeds us with fish and a forest that gives us shelter and medicines. Here they think they're punishing us by sending us away."

Paiva felt her head swim from the swill she had managed to drink by watering down, and she laughed loudly and cheered along with the River Runners. They spent the remainder of the day eating and exchanging stories, until night crept in and the men began to trail off to their appropriate Thimblehuts and sleep. Crowbill offered them a hut to sleep in, and Paiva was overjoyed to discover inside there was an abundance of furs and pelts in which to keep warm. She sprang inside and curled into the furs, falling into a dreamless sleep in seconds.

— «» —

Renn tethered the horse by the hut and brushed it down with dry grass, then Crowbill motioned him back to the fire where they sat together and shared swill.

"What is happening at the Keep?" Crowbill asked. "Mikal and his fellows passed through here and told us what came to pass with the Lord." Crowbill stuffed a pipe and gave it to Renn, who lit it from a smoldering stick he pulled from the fire.

He breathed a long breath of smoke and shook his head. He began to reiterate the tale of his hunt for his father through the woods, he told of Ceitra and a guarded story of what had come to pass with the Keep tower burning. Renn related the whole tale, back from the beginning when he had first encountered Paiva on Mummers-eve. He explained how Viviel had been branded and outcast for harboring them that night, and though he knew it was unjust and cruel he felt entirely guilty about it all.

Crowbill listened raptly. "If you really think about it, all of this madness that has happened with your family started with Ceitra. I remember you telling me how you had fallen for her wiles as a boy. You were there on the ramparts that day to comfort her, maybe confess your love, I don't know, when Odrik came upon you... Ceitra enjoyed watching you fight over her." He took a swig of his drink. "I think you should believe the girl. You have nothing left to lose if you do."

Renn was silent, watching the folds of smoke spewing from the fire.

"I told you once long ago the only way to salve your conscience and rid yourself of guilt was to kill a Folka. But it never salved anything, did it?" Crowbill asked.

"No," Renn said. "Not at all."

"It's a stupid way to be forgiven. What mad man decided so long ago sending men into Grimenna would cure them of evil? What mad man had the idea that killing something would salve great wrongs?"

Renn shrugged, knowing very well it was some great forefather of his.

"You know what I think?" Crowbill mused as he sucked down another swig of his swill. "I think this girl's telling you the truth. I think these spirits that haunt these woods is all our own ill-doing. Your father might never pardon you; his pardon might not be worth it all in the end. But helping these Ibbies might be the cure of your evils."

"I don't care, Crowbill," he sighed.

"Sure you do. If you didn't you'd have let that girl drown in the river."

Renn's head swum with the swill. He tucked the pipe away beneath his cloak and thanked Crowbill for his hospitality and bid him goodnight. Crowbill chuckled and spat into the fire.

"Anything for Black Renn. I know I'll sleep safe tonight with you in camp."

Renn went back to the hut where Paiva was curled sound asleep. He bent and reached in, searching for a fur with which to sleep and found he ached for her warmth. Away from the fire the night was damp and chilled.

Instead he withdrew a fur from the hut and lay down on the cold hard ground at its door, guarding Paiva from the outside, and the unworthy wants inside him.

— «» —

Paiva woke late in the morning and when she pulled herself out of the Thimblehut she found that the camp was being dismantled by the busy Wildermen. She looked about for Renn and found him hunched over with Crowbill, rolling up the hides of a hut and securing them into a bundle.

"What's going on?" she asked worriedly, for in the air hung a palpable tension. The fire was doused, the forest floor swept clean.

"Milady," Crowbill inclined his head in a curt nod. "Scout came down from the hills this morn and said there was a patrol headed our way. Seems they picked up your trail. Poor Renn's losing his knack for evading rangers. Best we move out, I think. We'll fuddle the trail for you and lose the rangers."

Renn was quiet and went about his business of gathering up hides.

"That's... nice of you," Paiva said.

Crowbill grinned. "Anything for a pretty lady," he said.

"I'm not pretty," she stammered bashfully and hurriedly bent to help.

"You could look like the back end of a bull and he'd still think you're pretty," Renn murmured. Paiva gaped at him.

"That might be true but she sure don't look like no one's back end," Crowbill said cheerfully. "Might even call her beautiful, no, Renn?"

"I haven't bothered looking," he said tersely. She was sure Crowbill would erupt into flames with the look Renn threw him.

"You'd have to be blind not see that," Crowbill laughed.

Paiva went about helping to gather up the camp. By the time the Wildermen were ready to move out each was burdened under the trappings of their rolled-up huts and bundles of furs. They used their bows as staffs and cleaved off into the woods at a quick pace, moving silently as wraiths and quick as hares. Renn threw Paiva and a few bundles up on the horse's back, then with a bow and a quiver from Crowbill slung over his shoulder, he took the horse's reins in hand and followed the band into the trees on foot.

"Where are we going now?" she asked Renn as they dodged through the trees. The horse was pulled into a trot behind Renn's quick pace. She sensed his urgency and felt a lump of fear begin to knot her stomach.

"We'll head to my camp at Far Reach," Renn tossed over his shoulder.

Crowbill joined up with them, jogging beside the horse, huge bundles bouncing on his back. Crowbill didn't look the least encumbered by it. Between his teeth he clamped his pipe and he sucked on it thoughtfully as they moved along.

"I told the fellas we'll go as far as the Snowy Rock," Crowbill said to Renn. "Give me your horse and take what supplies you'll need to go on to Far Reach. The horse with its damned Keep smithy shoes will leave too clear a trail; the dogs will smell it out. You'll have an easier time evading them without it."

"They catch you with a ranger's horse they'll mark your ledger and give you a beating," Renn replied.

"Agh," Crowbill laughed. "Then I won't let them catch me. I'll send them on a good chase. You'll be well clear of them before they even realize it."

"Thank you Crowbill," Paiva said down to him from the horse. He winked up to her.

"It is you I must thank, for you have brought me good gossip and gossip is a prized currency in the woods."

The River Runners, aptly named for their ability to run long through the trees, winded themselves at the top of Snowy Rock by the midday sun. From atop the huge body of rock, which was covered in strange white moss and lichens, they looked down onto the Far Fall valley below. Paiva slipped from the horse and gave its neck a quick stroke before Renn handed it over to Crowbill.

Renn took a fair share of rations he wrapped in an oiled skin and threw it over his back with a quiver and bow. Crowbill also took her red cloak which was doused in a foul-smelling liniment he said would evade the ranger's hounds. Renn shook hands with Crowbill, then nodded towards the others who nodded back.

"You keep close to Renn, girlie. Don't go wandering off in these parts of the woods," Crowbill said. Then he pulled the horse into the trees and disappeared. The other River Runners each skipped away in different directions, slashing at branches and leaving their footprints rutted deep into the loam of the forest floor.

Paiva turned and followed Renn northwards, into the trees where he found a game trail over which he trod softly. He warned her of leaving no sign of her passing and she placed her bare feet on stones and roots, keeping clear of any dirt that would leave an impression.

They travelled hard, scaling a ridge and passing through thick copses, making their way steadily upwards. By the time evening fell they were at the edge of a mountain that blotted out the setting sun. Renn said that on the other side was Far Reach, and if she wasn't too tired they could press onward and reach it by morning.

Paiva looked up at the mountain and felt a tremor of exhaustion run through her aching legs. Renn's stride was twice as long as hers and she had spent the day stumbling to keep up with him. He seemed to sense her derision of scaling the mountain in the dark, so instead he led them beneath a ledge as darkness fell and decided to let her rest there.

She drank from the waterskin and ate from the wild meat Crowbill had given them. They sat in silence and darkness, looking out over the forest and star-soaked sky. Animals called through the dark; wolves bayed in the hills.

Suddenly a strangled wail rose up far off in the distance and the wolves fell silent. It sent shivers over Paiva's skin despite the sheen of sweat that clung to her body from her day of hard travelling.

"What was that?" she asked fearfully.

"Folka," he answered. "Don't fret, they're many miles away."

Renn sat still and calm, unbothered by the deep of the forest and their small presence in it. Paiva let herself relax, trusting the tranquil tones in his voice. For long moments the forest was silent, then the wolves began to sing again and Paiva felt relieved.

"How long have you been out here for?" she asked, studying his profile in the blue moonlight. He had not allowed them to have a fire, but the moon was bright enough.

"Seven years I think," he said as he chewed a minty sprig of a plant he had pocketed earlier that day.

"It seems different out here," she pondered. "I was not expecting the River Runners to help us the way they did."

"Along with gossip, favors are currency out here," he replied. "Some men have more credit than others. Besides, the horse will fetch them iron and salt with the Come by Chance gang."

She nibbled at more of her meat before setting the rest aside for a meal the next day.

"I think you believe me now," she said. "What with my father and the Folka."

"Never mind," he said. "Go to sleep."

She gathered the fur that Crowbill had given them and unbundled it, throwing it over her shoulders. She sidled towards Renn where he leaned against the rock wall of the ledge and curled up alongside him. Not close enough to touch, but close enough to be near. She tucked her head under the fur and closed her eyes, feeling safe beneath his watchful shadow.

Chapter 12

When Paiva woke in the morning she found that every bone and muscle attached to her ached. The first light of morning was creeping through the woods and Renn was already on foot waiting for her. Blearily she looked up at the daunting slope he meant for her to climb. With the fur tucked about her and rubbing the sleep from her eyes she followed after him, wincing on her raw feet.

"Just to the top and you can rest," he would call back to her, but it did little to ease the pain in her feet. They hadn't made it far before she sat down miserably to shake the exhaustion from her body. He waited for her silently, watching her gauge the steep ascent.

"Ulrig will make you some shoes," he noted. She responded by wearily getting back to her feet and hobbling after him. He took a few steps onwards before he turned around and came back. Deftly he grabbed hold of one of her hands and slung her up on his back as if she were no more than a haversack. At first, she was alarmed, but he seemed to hardly notice her weight and went up at a steady pace without breaking his breath. Resigned, she crooked her arms around his neck and held fast. His pace was much more steady and she might as well have been riding a horse for he was sure-footed and quick, hardly seeming to notice his burden.

He made quick work of scaling the mountain, cresting the summit by the time the sun was hot. There he set her down and stretched his back, searching for a drink from the waterskin. She would never have known the camp was there if not for the smoke that rose from a chimney made of stacked stones protruding from the earth. It was a cave on the top of the mountain, its opening concealed by the thick roots of a dead tree. From the top there was an endless view of Grimenna. Looking southwards the hills could be seen beginning to rise from the Lowlands, while looking northwards they could be seen rising into mountains that broke the skyline with jagged peaks.

The thin trees that grew above the cave were stretched with animal skins drying in the sun and wind. There was a figure standing amidst them, just as shaggy and leathery looking as the hides. It was a stooped old man leaning against a twisted staff.

"Ulrig," Renn smiled. The old man tilted his head curiously towards them. He had a cap on his head stitched together from different colors of tanned leather. From beneath it a set of bushy white eyebrows protruded like antenna. His cheekbones were high and pointed above a long, wispy white beard that was tangled with burrs. He looked every part the image of a wizened old hermit, or perhaps a deranged sheep herder.

"Renn," Ulrig said, and blinked at him with speckled green eyes. "Who's the girl?"

"Paiva... from Birchloam," he replied. On spindly legs Ulrig hopped down the rocks to come to a teetering halt on the roots of the tree above the cave entrance. He proved to be rather spry for such an old-looking being. He swung his head down and peered at Paiva with his strange eyes and she found his face to be scarce of wrinkles. It was only the white of his beard and his hunched frame that gave the impression of age. His eyes were clear, a pearly green with rusty flecks. They looked her over with bemused curiosity, and then his lips pulled back in a smile over long yellow teeth.

"From Birchloam?" Ulrig whistled a laugh through his teeth. "I know Birchloam, my daughter's from Birchloam. Quiet little place. But you're coming from the wrong direction if you were coming from Birchloam." Then he swung his arm out and pointed southeasterly, towards the gleam of the river winding through the hills many miles away. "Birchloam's far over there," Ulrig nattered.

"We've a long story to tell you," Renn interjected, "and we've come a long way to tell it."

Ulrig's eyes alighted on Paiva, and he reminded her of some sort of toad that would live under a ring of mushrooms.

"Paiva Ibbie," Ulrig muttered to himself, his brow crumpling into a frown as he searched his memory. "Are you the one who encountered a mishap on Mummers-eve?"

"The very one," Renn answered for her. "As I said, it is a long story."

"Yes, Renn. Last I heard of you was you asked your father for a pardon. Then silence after that. I'd begun to worry, just a wee bit. When the Wildermen and the Stones have no news I often think someone has died."

A smile touched Renn's lips. "Very nearly."

"Scared the beard off me," Ulrig said, then he hopped down from his perch and tapped Renn on the head with his staff. "Left me here with a pack of Wilder-whelps to contend with. Best you go make amends with Runa. She's been miserable since you left." He then bent and pushed the hide away to enter the cave.

"Wilder-whelps?" Paiva asked.

"New gang members," Renn answered.

"And Runa?" Paiva looked to Renn as Ulrig disappeared into the cavern. Renn smothered his smile.

"A sweetheart," he said mischievously. Paiva remembered how he had once told her how there were other women out here in the Wilderlands. He motioned for her to follow Ulrig and she ducked in hurriedly, swallowing a dry lump in her throat. She found herself wondering if Renn had a stolen woman waiting for him.

She walked into a smoky little cavern. The air was thick and hot from a choking fire in a crudely built fireplace with black scorch marks blazed into the front of it. The ceiling was half-root, half-rock, and she realized it was a man-made cave: a den of sorts, dug out and reinforced with stacked stone walls and timbers. There were openings for windows, covered with scraps of hide; there was a crude table on which were stacked earthen wares for eating, stone and iron tools of various sizes and shapes, and a clutter of furs and leathers. All about were frames on which smaller furs and pelts were stretched on sinew cords. There were pots and barrels in which soaked raw hides in fowl smelling liquids. There were wooden shelves against the walls containing bags, bottles and boxes, baskets woven from rushes filled with bunches of drying plants and tubers, and a string of pheasants and fowl hanging to soften on pegs from the ceiling. There were horns, antlers, bones tied to the wall and it vaguely reminded her of Lord Pratermora's trophy room. The rest of the cave was akin to a den of thieves, for there were trinkets and objects that surely must have been scavenged from the lowlands — there was no possible means a Wilderman could procure them without stealing. There were openings in the walls, crooked doors held up by sills of great slabs of stone that led to other rooms into which she could not see, for they were dark and obscured. She thought perhaps they were store rooms, but decided to keep her questions for later.

"Welcome to Far Reach," Ulrig said to her as he began to clear off a large stone slab that served as a cluttered table. "I am Ulrig Leathermaker the Tinker, Wisest Wilderman in all Grimenna." He let forth another of his whistling chuckles through his long teeth and procured a small wooden tankard.

He drew forth drinks for them from it. He handed Paiva a wooden mug and invited her to sit at the table with him on a stool that was made of a small wooden frame with leather stretched on sinew for a seat. Ulrig began to light tallow sticks to shed light into the room.

Paiva took her seat and peered warily into her cup, fearing it was a concoction similar to the one Crowbill brewed. Upon tasting it she found it to be sweet and only mildly medicinal.

"Drink," Ulrig urged. "It's wine, not swill. Made from berries and honey. I call it Cures All, for it cures all ills, from miserable moods to the pain of broken bones."

Renn took his own cup from Ulrig and downed it heartily, then scanned a glance about the empty cave. "Where are the fellows?" he asked.

"On a chase," Ulrig answered. "Been gone for two days."

Renn nodded and helped himself to another cup of the Cures All. "Well," Renn admonished, "I'll let Paiva tell you her tale. I will go to visit with Runa."

Ulrig nodded happily and watched him depart through one of the crooked doors and disappear.

"Who is Runa?" Paiva asked the hermit worriedly.

"A Berg mare," Ulrig replied, and chuckled at the relief that flooded her face.

"You said your daughter is from Birchloam," Paiva said, quickly changing the subject. "Perhaps I know her."

"I'm sure you do; Birchloam is a small village. Her name is Jekka. She works in the apothecary shop."

Paiva's eyes snapped open wide. "Of course I know Jekka!" Paiva cried. "I didn't know her father was a Wilderman."

"Yes," Ulrig replied, and then Paiva noted a distant look that entered his eyes. "Poor girl. After I was sent to the woods her mother died in the Quarry. It took many years before Jekka would ever talk to me again. Although, Jekka has never been one much for talking." He nodded his head against some inner pain and he took a deep swig of his Cures All to ease it. "I tell her to stay out of the woods," Ulrig continued. "But she's more often here at Far Reach than she is in Birchloam. Comes as she wills, like a wayward wanderer."

"Jekka crosses the Panderbank?" she asked in amazement. "All by herself?"

"It's only a river." Ulrig smiled, then he thumbed the double brand on his hand. "When I found my pardon I was determined to go back to the world and set things right between her and I. How the years had passed. I had not realized she had grown into a woman. It was difficult and painful, I couldn't bear it. I couldn't find my place again. Even if you're pardoned, people still see the brand and people still treat you like dirt. I ran away again, back to the woods like a coward. But Jekka followed me."

"Jekka loved my father," Paiva said, not meaning to cause the pain that rippled into Ulrig's strange eyes. "I mean, my father was a teacher. He revered the Old Ways of Grimenna. He believed in the Old Spirits. Jekka was always there to help, always there to give thanks to the forest and listen to my father's teachings. She believed in the old ways, even when everyone else in the village began to turn away from them."

"Your father is Viviel then," Ulrig said. "I have heard of his teachings. Jekka has shared them with me over the years. She recorded some of the Wildermen stories for Viviel, traded them for his knowledge of herbs and healing."

Paiva excitedly spilled the entire story to him then, starting at the very beginning with Mummers-eve and the mask she had bought off of Jekka for her disguise that she had failed to use. Ulrig listened intently, his speckled eyes wide and unblinking. She ended by telling him of what Crowbill had seen of the Folka chasing her father off into the woods in the dark of the night.

When she was done Ulrig was silent for long moments, digesting it all.

"So you say your father is an Incarnate, and you intend to find him in the Vale of the Old Spirits?" he asked at long last.

"I do," she said with conviction. "But I do not know where it is."

Ulrig regarded her another long moment, studying her with a furrowed brow. She did not know if he believed a word she said. But then he rose on his spindly legs and went to a far corner of his cave and rummaged through the contents of his crooked shelves. He withdrew a roll of leather and brought it back where he spread it across the table.

A map was burnt into the tanned leather. There was the river separating the great divides of Grimenna, the Lowlands from the Wilderlands. There was a rough marking for where the Keep, villages and towns lay scattered below the river. Above it there were more detailed markings. There were the Stones, starting at the Rock of Regret and spreading out in their navigational network to the farthest reaches of the mountains. There were trails and routes, the different Wildermen camps and territories.

What Paiva found most interesting were markings of vanished villages and towns, for once before the Wildermen, the forest had been tamed by common people. The map expanded all the way up to the north of a mountain range called the Highpeaks. Ulrig stabbed a finger at it.

"This map is all I know of Grimenna, all the places I have been and seen and mapped. I can promise you no Warden, not even the Lord himself, has a map so detailed. These here mountains — the Highpeaks — no one has ever crossed. Not since the First People of Grimenna. Not since the Folka were risen.

"Beyond the Highpeaks is a valley I have only ever heard tell of. It is in the Old Stories, a valley filled with babbling streams that run down into the great river. Beyond this valley is the Winterlands of Grimenna, that is where the mountains begin to rise so high above the earth they become covered in snow and barren of trees." He tapped his finger thoughtfully on the map.

"It is in the valley beyond the Highpeaks wherein the Old Stories tell tale of a place called Morinvere. Some say it was a castle, some say it was a shrine built around the heart of the Forest from which all life flowed — a pool that runs deep into the earth, filled with magical waters. They say there were pilgrimages to it, by the penitent and the worshippers of the Forest who cast their prayers into these waters. No one knows for sure, for it crumbled into ruin and was swallowed by the Forest as all the Old Stories have been swallowed and forgotten.

"It is said there was a sorcerer who guarded it who conjured the first Folka. He used the powers of these waters for his own self-gain, and then he was punished and turned into a cursed creature himself. Morinvere fell, its secrets forgotten, men driven out." He shook his head sadly. "It is said that this creature is Varloga himself. The cursed white magician, possessed by the Dark Humor of Fear. His mistress is the Strix, the very one who punished him for being so wicked."

He slid his hand away from the map as Paiva stared at it and sat heavily back in his seat. He began to pull at a burr stuck in his beard as his eyes filled with troubled thoughts.

"There are only a few places in the woods the Wildermen do not dare pass," Ulrig muttered. "We have respect for the ghosts who dwell in the old vanished villages, and we respect the Highpeaks, for it is there the Folka are thick and dangerous. The valley beyond those mountains is filled with nightmares. No man who wanders into it ever returns."

"That is where my father is going, for that is where all the Good Spirits have been banished."

"Banished," Ulrig exacted the words.

"Driven there by Folka, by creatures gone astray."

Ulrig nodded solemnly. "But how will you overcome the Folka?"

"The Folka will not kill me, I would already be dead if the Strix or Varloga wished it. They want to use me and ruin me, not kill me. From my broken thoughts they will reap more nightmares. As long as I hate her I am safe."

Ulrig blinked at her and a slow smile spread across his face. "Yes, they may let you enter the Vale. But how will you return? Varloga guards the Vale with his Folka creatures," he said.

"But I'd summon the others back somehow. Surely, they could rally against him," she said.

He sighed. "The Old Spirits are weak, they are trapped. What if you can't coax them back?"

"I will."

"You will have to cut off Varloga's head," Ulrig said. "You would need the help of a powerful Virtue. You would need the very son of Courage."

"Grand," she sighed. "And you wouldn't happen to know where he is?"

Ulrig smiled.

"Indeed. He is the very one who brought you here."

She blinked in astonishment.

Ulrig nodded his head eagerly and snatched up their mugs to fill with more Cures All. "I feel it in my bones, from the bottom of the good earth up to the top of my skull. This isn't coincidence. This is fateful synchronicity. This is the power of prayers that has coincided you two together, however unlikely it may be. At last, at last, Courage has found his Hope in the dark of the woods." His eyes glazed over as he spoke and a toothy smile spread across his face. "The Old Ones must have brought you together, they must have designed this. They are trapped there, of course, in the heart of the Forest. It must be so; it must be meant that you two were to find each other, so to set the Old Ones free."

"Ulrig." She drew him back sharply from his rambles. "Renn... is a Virtue?"

"Indeed, indeed. Long before I became a Wilderman I was a Knight and I had the Lord's favor. I hunted with him and I was the champion of many of his tournaments. But I fell from grace, on account of a woman." Ulrig handed her a drink and took a deep swig of his, as if steeling himself for a painful truth. "The Lord enjoyed his hunts in the lowlands. I was with him one day in the woods when we startled a most peculiar-looking stag. Its fur was black as coal, its eyes shining a strange silver like an alchemist's mercury. Its antlers had so many points we could hardly have counted them all. We took chase and set the hounds on it, firing arrows and lances after the poor creature, not knowing we were trying to kill an Old Legend. We chased it hard until it suddenly disappeared, bounding away over a great rock we could not pass with the horses. The dogs chased after it and came across a woman.

'I had never seen a more beautiful, magical woman in all my life. She was dressed in no more than rags — a peasant on the run from wolves, she said. But I knew better. She was a Spirit. Her hair was black as night, and her eyes as bright as star silver that struck me to my soul. It was a disguise, you see, so that we would not harm her." Ulrig shook his head discontentedly over the memory.

"I had a wife," he continued. "I had a good name. I was once called Ulrig the Lionheart, and now I am Ulrig the Leathermaker. I once held my Lord's banners proudly and carried his sigil on my chest. Now I'm stooped and old. I carry only regret... because I fell in love with this woman and shamed myself and my Lord, who loved her more than I. Her name was Lady Embril, and she was Renn's mother."

Paiva blinked at him again, too stunned to say a thing. Ulrig nodded into her silence.

"She was the Incarnate of Courage," he said. "She could fill a man's heart, raise his spirits, and soothe his fears. She was extraordinary, beautiful, strong... and the Land flourished under Pratermora's rule while she lived. Varloga found her in the end. They said when they found her body her eyes were empty, her hair white as snow.

"When Renn was thrown into the woods I could not help but see so much of her in him. At first I was angry, for half of him was made of the man who had thrown me away. But the other half of him was her. I took him under my wing. I made him my own son and have tried to guide him. I have tried to tell him, but he thinks I am just a mad old man."

"But he is a Virtue."

"Yes, his mother was an Incarnate."

"That means Odrik was a Virtue as well," Paiva exclaimed. "Ceitra did not want Odrik dead, she wanted him to suffer. She wanted Renn to suffer... to corrupt him and provide her with more power."

"The Pratermoras have a dark legacy," Ulrig said. "It is understandable the Strix was attracted to them. She was created to punish wicked men, to use fear to guide them from treachery, even if now she is beyond that. They come from a long line of corruption, of greed and fear mongering. I think to this day Embril came to them to teach them differently, to give them heart, to make them stronger. The Strix, I can only imagine how she feasted on them without her."

"But..." Paiva trailed off. "Why would she have Renn hanged then?"

"Who knows? There could be many reasons. Perhaps it was because of you." Ulrig gazed at her with speculative speckled eyes. "Perhaps it is because Courage found Hope. Let me tell you, it has been a few seasons Renn has not returned to the Keep with a trophy. The Folka heads he claimed he often gave to other men, for he had long ago given up asking his father for a pardon. Of a sudden he decided to try again, perhaps for no other reason than that he met the Ibbies of Birchloam."

"It was hardly an inspirational meeting," she said, stunned.

"You might be surprised to find that it was. Your father's kindness struck deep. The very thing is you can't have Courage without Fear, and facing his own father again took Courage. Rescuing his father from madness took Courage. Killing Folka is easy if they're not your own nightmares. Facing a world that hates you, and asking forgiveness for your own hated self is something else. But if you can face your Fears because you suddenly found Hope, well, that is a powerful thing." Paiva absorbed what he said, both fascinated and overwhelmed.

"What I wouldn't give to be a hundred miles away from here, back in the pasture tending sheep and watching the grass grow," Paiva sighed. She cast her eyes back to the map. "How do we get to Morinvere?" she asked. "How do I find my father?"

"It would entail a long journey," Ulrig resolved. "We would have to cross other Wilderman territories. Mad Maggra runs the Painted Camp in the Northwoods below the Highpeaks. Not a good lot — they're the worst of the Wilderman. Down here it's just oath breakers, heretics, thieves and tax evaders. Up north is where the worst of murderers and tormentors flock. There are even children born up there, off women the Wildermen have stolen for themselves. They are the ones that suffer from the worst humors of the human heart. But, they're always up for barter. I'll offer them a good trade for their help."

Then he smiled at her kindly, his speckled eyes twinkling with the shine of his Cures All. "Don't you fret, you'll not go alone. I'm completely dedicated to this adventure now. What a great joy it would be! How the world would change if the spirits of the good humors were set free, if they could restore good will in the world of men! Perhaps Lady Embril would rise again...." Then he sprang to his feet and loped to the wall where he retrieved the curled horn of a mountain ram.

"Come along, Paiva Ibbie of Birchloam," he said and scurried out the main entrance of the cave.

"Where are we going?" she asked worriedly as she followed him out. She found the Cures All had eased her aches immensely and she was able to walk without complaint.

"To gather the others back to camp." He loped up to the top of his cave and inhaled a deep lungful of air. He pointed the horn to his lips and let loose a deep, howling call that reverberated out over the land. He blew for some time, with short breaths and then long. Then he stuck the tip of the horn in his ear and pointed the flared end out towards the hills, trying to catch any distant sounds.

Paiva stared at him, finding him to be a wonderful oddity. She tried to imagine him thirty years ago, dressed in a knight's armor, serving his Lord with pride, and found her imagination lacking. He did not look like a man who had come from, or ever belonged, in the higher crust of society.

From out over the hills a returning horn sounded and Ulrig's bushy eyebrows shot up in delight. The call came from the south and Ulrig eagerly swung his horn in that direction, listening to his answering calls and gauging the distance between them. He pulled the horn from his ear and wiped clean its tip with a handful of beard.

"They went southwards then," Urlig noted to her. "Down into Far Fall. I'd say by evening tomorrow they'll reach camp if they have no problems. I'm sure you'll like the gang. One of them has a certain compulsion towards women but I'm sure the others will keep him in his place."

Paiva smiled feebly and turned to look northwards, out over the sweep of mountains. "There," Ulrig said and pointed to the jagged seam of a mountain range. "That's the Highpeaks. Below it is Maggra's camp."

"That looks like a long ways away."

"Oh, it is." Ulrig smiled happily. "Full of bogs and fissures and back-breaking hills. Even the rangers don't make it that far. Well… I think Yulin might have, once."

"I don't know if I could walk that far."

"You don't have to," Ulrig scoffed. "We're the Far Reach Gang. We ride Bergs. I've been catching and breeding them since I came to these hills."

He then brought her down the north slope of the mountain on a steep, rocky path that winded through some thinning trees. At the bottom of it was a ridge ledge that dropped into a cliff and was not passable. On this ledge, trapped there by a little wooden gate were a few straggly looking Bergs grazing on mountain grass. Renn looked up from a rock on which he sat smoking his pipe amidst them.

"You ever ridden a Berg?" Ulrig asked her as they came up to the gate.

"No," Paiva said. "Though I've heard much about them."

"A Wilderman's best friend — a scrappy little beast that can carry a man over the tallest mountain and across the widest river. Their only downfall is that they have rather boney withers and can make a man sore real fast if he loses his seat."

Paiva chuckled and leaned onto the gate to watch the animals shake flies and tear at the grass. From the rocks ran a stream of water that pooled into a stone trough. There was a small wooden lean-to constructed against the rock face and beneath it stood a black-eyed mare that was busy tearing strips of wood from it with her teeth.

"Is that Runa?" Paiva asked.

Ulrig chuckled as the mare pinned her ears back at him and snorted with ill temper. "Berg mares are a special sort," Ulrig smiled. "Harder to gentle than any wild stud. Perhaps you should go to talk with Renn."

Paiva nodded and slipped through the rungs of the gate while Ulrig departed back up the path.

She went to sit beside Renn on his rock who was staring intently at the mare with a bemused expression.

"Why did Ulrig call the gang back?" Renn asked. "Can't have been because he's decided we're all going on a journey to this mythical Morinvere?"

"Yes," she said. "I was hoping you would come with me."

"Agh," he sighed dismally. "Why can't you just let me be? My life was much simpler before I stumbled upon you."

"I'm sorry," she said.

She turned away from the mare and gazed at his profile. She watched his black hair flutter in the low breeze of the mountain top and studied the scar that ran across the bridge of his bent nose. His jaw was hairless and a question suddenly came to mind, pushing through the sadness she felt for his own dejection.

"Why do you have no beard?" she asked. He swung his head to look at her in surprise, then he uttered a warm, genuine laugh that sent a thrill of pleasure through her. He rubbed his chin wistfully and felt for a scar beneath his jaw.

"I had a beard," he said. "Ulrig stole it."

She gaped at him.

"I got it caught in a bow string and ripped half of it off," he began. "I tried to grow it again and it came in all funny, and I kept getting scraped in the face or cut in the mouth. It got tangled in a branch once and I stayed stuck in the tree while my horse ran away. Wounds are very hard to heal when they are covered in bristles. Ulrig decided it was best if I just kept a clean face. He said my beard was bad luck and made me get rid of it. He rubbed a salve he concocted over it and it hasn't grown back since."

Paiva laughed heartily and he smiled, rubbing his naked chin. She noticed his teeth were almost perfect, if not for a few chips. Another sign of his higher breeding. She had almost forgotten he was a Lord's son, and the realization that he was a Virtue as well made her smile falter. There they were together, a Wilderman and a shepherd's daughter, both sharing origins as concrete as mist.

"They were starting to call me Badluck Blackbeard," he continued thoughtfully. "I prefer Black Renn."

Paiva shook her head at the Wildermen's superstitions and swung her head and looked out towards the far off Highpeaks, her laughter dying in her throat as she caught sight of them.

"Renn," she said. "Ulrig says we're to go to the Northwoods."

"Did he?" he mused and followed her gaze out to the north. "I haven't been there in a long time. Not since Mad Maggra chased me off."

"What happened? Would you be in danger if you returned there?"

"No, not really," he said. Then a troubled thought drew his brow down. She wondered at his curious reaction, but before she could ask him any more questions he had sprung to his feet.

"You'll have to learn how to ride a Berg if that's where we're headed."

"I can ride a horse fine," she said. "I grew up on a farm."

"With a hitching horse, no doubt," he said as he went towards the black-eyed mare. "I grew up riding stallions and war chargers. But they were nothing compared to these wild little ponies."

Runa pinned her ears back at him and swung her head through the air, shaking flies from her scraggly brown mane. He stuck a finger through her halter, which was a loose scrap of leather twisted into a rope, and pulled her head down. She swung her body into him and struck out her foot, but he was wise enough to keep his feet well placed and out of harm's way.

"They were domesticated once," Renn said. "The Wildermen say they were either the horses that remained after the forest swallowed the Old Settlements or that they were pests in the lowlands that they herded into the river to drown. No one really knows. They weren't meant to survive either way, and when they did, they became quite wild again." The mare eyed him, the white of her eye rolling. "Funny enough, it's the mares that make better mounts for a Wilderman. The studs are rather lazy." He stroked Runa's neck. He seemed to think better of asking Runa to teach Paiva, and opted instead for a barrel-bodied male with long whiskers about his nose and eyes.

"Here," he said as he drew the shaggy, brown horse up to the rock. "You can try Felder. He's Ulrig's old stud."

Paiva went and pet the Berg, scratching flies from his ears and loosening burrs from his mane. He appeared to be calm and harmless, his eyes half-closed in a doze from the late morning sun. Paiva grabbed a fistful of his mane and launched herself up onto his back to Renn's surprise.

He scrabbled under her weight, but Renn held him fast. She felt Felder's body coil with nerves under her, and as Renn led him forward into a walk she felt her own tension mounting.

"You'll have to relax," Renn said. "You're making him nervous." He led her in a tight circle, then along the ridge. Felder trod unbothered along the precipice while Paiva clung to his mane with terror and gazed down into the fathoms below. Renn laughed at her taut face, then circled and passed her by the precipice again until she grew accustomed to the dizzying height.

"I've never seen a Berg horse fall off a mountain," he said. "I've seen Wildermen fall but never a Berg. Ulrig thinks they talk to rocks as well. They seem to know when a ledge is safe or not. Always listen to your Berg when you're not sure if the way is clear."

Renn tied a thong of leather to Felder's halter and passed them to her, giving her control of the horse. He stepped back and watched as she urged Felder forwards with a sharp kick. Felder hardly moved. So much for reacting to the slightest touch.

"Kick him harder," he ordered. Paiva did and Felder responded by throwing out his back legs with a twist and bucking her off. She rolled into the grass as Felder trotted away to join the other Bergs and continue his grazing.

Renn helped her to her feet, suppressing a smile.

"Berg studs are lazy," he said. "Not nearly as wild as the mares though." Paiva got to her feet and brushed herself off, then went to retrieve Felder and try again. He allowed her a short walk around the ridge before he grew tired of her and bucked her off again, leaving her to nurse her bruises while he sauntered back to his grass. Runa watched with pricked ears and Paiva was sure she was enjoying the spectacle.

She got back on her feet and tried again, this time managing to keep her seat through Felder's bucking. Renn narrowed his eyes suspiciously at the old stud and went to stand at the edge of the ridge.

Paiva had him in a neat little trot until she circled him back towards the other horses, then he broke into a jolted canter and made a dash for his escape. Paiva tried to counter him, pulling on his reins and swinging his head away from his friends. He was stubborn and sure-footed. He threw his shoulders and she tumbled off, rolling to a stop on Renn's feet at the edge of the cliff.

He shook his head piteously and bent to help her up. "Oh, it will be a long ride to Maggra's," he sighed. He looked back up to the Bergs grazing and flicking their tails with a thoughtful frown.

"Ulrig says Bergs bond with their riders, and Ulrig's the only one who's ever ridden Felder, just as I'm the only one who's ever ridden Runa. Perhaps you need a young horse, one without the imprint of a rider."

"I don't like the thought of that," she said as she nursed her scraped elbows. But Renn had already headed towards a lanky colt and snatched him up. Paiva looked dismally at the horse. He was longer, leaner and younger than Felder.

"He's never had a rider?" she asked as she went and patted his neck.

Renn shrugged. "Well, he's broke, more or less. We've used him as a pack horse. He can be ridden. But no one's claimed him yet."

"What's his name?"

"Jakbur."

She patted his neck thoughtfully, looking up into his deep eyes. His nostrils flared and took in her scent. His tail swished and whisked flies away from his belly. She grabbed his mane and levered herself up stiffly, sitting on his back while Renn held him fast.

"I like this horse," she said, sitting for a moment longer to get a feel for him. She stroked his neck and ruffled his mane. Runa gave a low nicker and the colt responded in kind.

"Is he Runa's colt?" she asked.

"Yes," he said. "And Felder's."

"He's nice," she said, then wearily she slid off. "But I think I'd like to take a break from being thrown off Bergs for a while."

Renn smiled and released the colt, watching him trot off with the others.

"You should smile more," she said. His pale eyes looked to her in surprise and she immediately felt her cheeks burn. "You look less terrible," she blurted, then turned on her heel and headed back up to the cave, wincing on sore feet and happy to leave the unruly horses behind her.

Renn jogged to catch up to her and they began the walk back up to the cave while he chuckled at her under his breath. Of a sudden a shaggy shape appeared in their path, stumbling out of the trees. She gasped and took a step back at the shape before her. It was an immense man covered in furs with a great beard, and under the crook of his arm was a twisted crutch made of carved wood he leaned on heavily to support a dragging leg.

"Jorn!" she cried.

"By my beard!" he exclaimed and a smile broke across his dirty face. "If it isn't the little shepherdess from Birchloam. What in the name of all the shining stars are you doing here? I thought Renn was going to fetch a pardon, not a sheep herder's daughter!" Over his shoulder was a string of fish that gleamed like oblong pearls against the dark of his matted furs.

"What happened to your leg?" she asked in alarm as he hobbled towards them.

"Got torn off my horse by a Folka beast," he said. "I'll be lame for a while yet."

"The Folka whose head Renn brought back to the Keep?"

"The very one," he smiled painfully. "But what are you doing here? Where is your father, where is your mother?"

Tears whelmed in her eyes at Jorn's compassionate tone, and she furiously blinked them back as she explained what had come to pass. Jorn shifted his weight painfully on his crutch as he listened, his brow furrowing with troubled thoughts.

"Ceitra branded your father?" he hissed angrily. "Your mother's been sent to the Quarry?" He reached out and laid a firm hand on her shoulder. "I'm sorry girl," he said. "With whatever is left in me I will help to right this."

"Where is Terg?"

"I think he might be dead. He left to find a bigger hunting party a while back and we haven't heard of him since." His eyes lifted to Renn's. "This is utter madness."

They made their way back up into the cave through a slanted hole of a door that led into a storeroom of sorts and out into the main room of the cave. Ulrig was hunched over the fire busy sorting through a small wooden box and drinking freely from his cup of Cures All. He looked up to them and shook his head at Renn.

"What did you do to the poor girl?" he asked with alarm. "Did she fall off a cliff?"

"Very nearly," Paiva griped and went to find her own drink to cure the aches in her bones. Ulrig chided Renn and went back to his box while Jorn hung his fish alongside the string of pheasants.

"Ulrig," Renn nodded. "Can you make her some shoes? I can't stand watching her walk around like a drunken Wilderman any longer."

"Already at it," Ulrig nodded, smiling at Paiva's further reddening cheeks.

— «» —

They ate the fish for supper and drank copious amounts of Cures All as daylight waned to dusk. Ulrig had pulled a needle out of his box and began sewing together a pair of shoes out of leather and felt scraps.

"The needle," he said, drawing it through the hole he had punched. "I came from a world built of iron and stone. When I arrived out here I could not tell you how much I learned a needle was worth. More than a castle. It can sew your clothes, sew your wounds shut, pry out splinters, tell you which way is north.... I cannot name you all its uses for there are too many. A man who owns a needle in the Wilderlands might well call himself a king." Paiva watched his gnarled hands work in the firelight, suddenly aware of just how precious such a small tool was.

The shoes were a rustic implement with heavy stitches, but they did well to protect and warm her battered feet. Afterwards Ulrig bundled her up with furs to sleep in and she went to lay down exhaustedly before the fire while he and Renn had a conversation in low murmurs. For the first time since her arrival on the far side of the river, she felt truly safe.

The next morning Renn had disappeared again down to the horses with Jorn and Ulrig let her bathe in a spring on the other side of the cave while he washed her clothes and hung them up to dry in the sun. She was filthy and stayed in the cold water until she was numb. She garbed herself in an old shirt and breeches from Ulrig until her own dress was dry. When she fetched it, hanging in the trees, she noticed Ulrig had put his needle to work again and patched the holes she had torn in the hem. She then helped Ulrig with stretching hides between trees to dry in the sun and wind. They had been stewed in fowl liquid made from the brains of the killed animal, and once dried in the sun they would be worked supple. She had many questions for Ulrig and a voracious curiosity about the Wildermen's ways.

Ulrig was only too happy to share his wisdom with her, which was much. He told her how Jekka procured for him the things he could not acquire in the woods, like yeast and linens and iron tools. Sometimes, he said, he made the trek to Birchloam himself and traded wild meats and his leathers for salt and grain in great quantities Jekka could not carry up by herself. Tools were essential to survival, and the newly branded had to make do with crude weapons to defend and hunt with. Metal was a precious commodity. Ulrig spoke of a band up north that had learned to smelt ore from the mountains. He had traded his first Berg horse for his first knife. When he had acquired a knife he had acquired the ability to carve wood.

Now it was much easier — he could go freely into the lowlands when he so chose, and Jekka was keen to collect things for him in exchange for herbs and plants he gathered for her that she could not find in the lowlands. He named a great number of plants he collected for her, including a flower he called Bettledrops that Paiva could not recall from her father's books, which only grew on a certain rocky crag at a certain time of the year. To Jekka it was a precious commodity, for supposedly Hexava used it to cure the pain in her joints, which made her much more amiable. Paiva realized that half of the medicines in Hexava's shop were bootlegged from across the river.

Along with outfitting the apothecary shop with precious botanicals, Ulrig also outfitted all men who came to him with weapons, for he remembered well the feeling of being unarmed and helpless. Just like a long beard, a Wilderman with a metal weapon was considered well-seasoned, for he had earned it through many years of tribulations.

"It is amazing," Ulrig said, "how metal things can define a man. Metal is one of the strongest of all elements. Cleaved from the earth, able to break both stone and wood... but each element has a weakness, just as it has its strength. Metal is not completely impervious, but how useful it is."

"What is the strongest?"

"A man's will, of course." He smiled. "To his will he bends both iron, stone, and wood, and uses them against those greater then himself."

When they were done with the hides, they went down to a spring in the rocks and washed their hands, then gathered buckets of the water to bring to Ulrig's patch of Tarweed growing on the south side of his mountain. These they tended to while Ulrig continued his talking. She realized that despite his shabby appearance he was remarkably resourceful and inventive. He told her how there was enough out here for a man to live a contented, simple life. He was able to provide plenty for himself and those that were in need. In exchange, he was granted the protection and help of younger, stronger hands than his.

"But what about thieves?" Paiva asked. "Surely there are those that would take from you without asking."

"Oh indeed. As you can see, I am but one old man. When I was younger I was swift enough and able enough to deter any threats, but in my winter years I have been raided many times. Most times I had sent word out to the older Wildermen, for we are loyal to each other. It was only when Renn arrived that I haven't been bothered. He has a formidable way about him. No one gets too far with any stolen items. I don't often let people into my camp if I can't find a use for them, and I have no use for thieves."

"Who do you allow to camp then?"

"Oh, the common liar, the heretics, the wrongly accused, the insane. They come and go. Some find other gangs to join, some find pardons, some die."

"You're pardoned yourself, no? Why wouldn't you try to find somewhere safer to live?"

"You mean in the lowlands? No, never go back there. The forest is my lady. Sometimes she's hard to bear, sometimes she's cold and empty, but other times she's so full of life she leaves me enchanted. I wake up every morning and tell her how beautiful she is."

A call from below drew their attention to Renn looking up at them with Runa and Jakbur in tow. Ulrig gave Paiva a worried look and shrugged.

"I suppose you don't really have a choice if you want to come to Maggra's with us," he said. "Might as well."

Paiva hopped down to the trail and Renn swung her up on Jakbur's bare back. He mounted Runa swiftly and led them together up and over the west side of the mountain. She clung to Jakbur's mane as the horses took to the slope, their bodies arching and dipping as they found footing along the narrow decline of rock and root. When Renn was sure Jakbur was content to follow his mother without trouble, he tossed Paiva the reins and led the way ahead.

Paiva began to relax and come to grips with the Berg, allowing him free range of motion and never pulling on his reins so hard to cause him to throw his head. Jakbur was content to follow Runa and this seemed to please Renn.

They came to a plateau where the land became even again and the trees, a mixture of birch and pines, filled the air with a fresh, invigorating scent. She began to have a lonely feeling, as if the world around her were too large and her own being too small. She was humbled by the great expanse of forest, and it made her feel like a desolate speck of dust in an infinite cosmos. Her presence felt suddenly small and meaningless, her plight to save something greater than herself overwhelming.

"What are you thinking about?" Renn's voice broke through her thoughts. She found him looking back at her with narrowed eyes. A shaft of sunlight fell into them and she noticed for the first time his eyes were truly blue — a metallic, shimmering blue that in the absence of light made them look like liquid silver.

"Ulrig told me you are a Virtue," she said.

A grim smile pulled at his mouth.

"He has told me that as well," he said. "I thought it was another of his stories to help guide me through the woods. Face your fears with firmness, don't let the Folka fill your heart with the shadows of their terror.... That kind of nonsense a foolish boy needs to hear to help him go to sleep in the dark of the woods."

"He said your mother was a Spirit."

"Ulrig says many things." He turned back round to face the woods. They lapsed into silence for a long while after that and Paiva felt it weigh on her heavily. She heard him sigh, then he halted Runa and swung her around to face them.

"What is a Virtue?" he asked. "I mean, yes, I understand the whole part about a Virtue being the child of a spirit and a man, but what is their purpose? I mean... I have no unnatural powers that I am aware of. Neither did my mother. As far as I know I am just a man, nothing more and nothing less."

"You are a man," Paiva said. "Just as I am a simple girl from Birchloam. A Virtue has powers over the humors of the human heart. Our hearts are the compass of our souls and the soul is that strange thing that connects us to the spirit world beyond this physical one. Whatever magic is in our souls can be used for the greater good or for the worse. Like how Varloga can conjure nightmares. He has no magic, unless we give it to him. With us it is more powerful. And there is no reason I cannot use it to help raise the Good Spirits."

A sad smile spread over Renn's lips. His eyes fell away from hers as he shook his head.

"You could just be blind," he said. "You could just be a fool." Then he turned Runa around and spurred her into a trot back up the mountain slope.

Jakbur nickered and cantered after her, in a panic of being abandoned.

— «» —

That evening Ulrig tittered about plucking pheasants and preparing an enormous amount of food. Renn sat before the fire, whittling a piece of wood and smoking his pipe. Jorn dozed by his side, his lame leg propped on an upright length of firewood with his head nestled into his chest where it mostly disappeared into his beard. She amused herself by looking over Ulrig's shelves of wares, inspecting their odd contents.

She wasn't at it long when of a sudden Ulrig dropped his head to the stone floor, looking at his feet as if they were trying to tell him something.

"What is it?" she asked, wondering if he was suffering from an odd bout of achy bones.

"The stones are rumbling," he said. Renn rose and followed him outdoors, leaving Jorn asleep by the fire. Paiva hurriedly followed after. They went to stand atop the cave and look down the southern side of the slope. There was a thick fog shrouding the twilit hills and Ulrig peered down into it eagerly.

"What is it?" she asked him.

"That would be my pack of Wilder-whelps."

There was a rumbling that came. It started far below them and rose into a clamor of stampeding hooves and tearing branches. She stepped back towards Renn, alarmed and nervous.

"What *is* it?" she whispered fiercely.

He smiled. A moment later dark shapes burst through the thinning trees, heaving bodies lurched up the steep slope — Berg horses, running madly up the incline, their hooves striking rock and their bodies tearing through the thickets. On their backs were the figures of furry men, their bearded faces obscured in the low light. They came in from the fog like hounds out of hell.

The horses galloped wildly towards the camp and came to a sliding halt before the cave. She heard laughter and jeering, saw the gleams of grins in bearded faces and heard the deep breathing of frenzied horses. She thought perhaps there were ten of them in all and they swarmed together in a mass of fur and hide.

"Ulrig!" called a great bearded man who dwarfed the horse he swung down from. Paiva caught the unmistakable odor of Crowbill's swill from him. The man nodded to Renn and Paiva, seemingly unsurprised to find a girl in his camp.

"I brought you a trophy," the Wilderman boomed to Ulrig. Ulrig's bushy eyebrows shot up in delight and he scampered down to get a closer look at the other men. He stopped of a sudden, teetering on a rock as he stared at a man that was sitting on a Berg with a gag in his mouth and his hands bound behind his back. Ulrig swung his head back angrily to berate the Wilderman.

"Ennig!" he roared. "Warden Yulin is not a trophy!"

Paiva started in surprise and peered down at the disheveled figure strapped to the Berg. Ennig roared with a drunken laughter and slapped his knee. "We found him slinking outside of Crowbill's camp," Ennig called down. "That was after us being chased by a pack of hounds. Said he wanted to talk with you and demanded we bring him back to Far Reach. Pretty high and mighty for a lone warden."

Ulrig ordered Yulin to be brought down off the horse and his bonds removed. Two Wildermen quickly sprung from their horses and moved to obey Ulrig's furious demands.

When Yulin's hands were free he tore the gag from his mouth and spat loudly.

"Blasted, cursed, filthy Wildermen," he fumed. He righted his tunic and brushed the spit from his beard. Ennig laughed and swung his head to Renn, his dark eyes dropping to Paiva. She heard his sharp intake of breath as his eyes roved over her rudely. Renn stepped between them and sucked on his pipe, the embers making his eyes glow red. Ennig chuckled.

"Crowbill said you was headed up here with a wench," he said.

"Ennig Strapback," Renn replied coldly. "Careful where you trod round here."

"She's yours, then, is she? Never did like to share, did you? Unless it was your troubles."

They stared at each other a long moment, Ennig with a leering smile on his face. Paiva could feel the tension in the air between them. There was something murderous in the way Ennig gazed into Renn's eyes.

"Everyone," Ulrig said in a raised voice. "Go tend to your horses and then come inside and have something to eat and drink. I've called you all back on important business. I expect you'd all like to know what it is and I'd also like to know what the lot of you have been up to."

Ennig turned away then, jumping down the rocks and back to his horse. He slapped Yulin on the back as he passed and laughed.

"Welcome to Far Reach, Yulin."

Chapter 13

Yulin sat at the table with Ulrig, Renn, and Paiva. The other Wildermen began crowding into the cave, finding various spots to sit before the fire where they emitted rude noises and shoved into each other. Paiva likened the whole environment to a den of wild dogs. They lit their pipes and soon the air was thick with blue smoke. There were seven of them in all. Half of them had not been in the Wilderlands for very long and were still trying to find a place for themselves. There was an obvious pecking order, with Ennig demanding the most respect under Ulrig and Renn.

Ulrig introduced his Wilder-whelps to her one by one. There was Mervig, who was so covered in hair and dirt the only feature that made him recognizably human were his beady eyes. There was a weasel-faced man with a patchy beard named Jerrik; another who was tall and bald named Gartri; then a duo with red beards who were father and son. They were Lorik and Lotri, though she learned the father was not branded. He had crossed the river to find his son and keep him safe in the Wilderlands. The only one who had earned a nickname was a young man they called Ginver Grapple, who was supposedly very good at climbing rocks when he wasn't busy singing. He had a soft, youthful face covered in freckles with a sprouting, goatish beard and a mane of dirty blond curls. There was something distinctly effeminate about his mannerisms and he was the only one who, with his cornflower blue eyes, didn't look at her with male curiosity. She wondered if he had not been thrown into the woods for loving another man.

Yulin was haggard, with deep rings of weariness beneath his clever eyes. He was the very man who had laid the brand on each one of these men, and they stared at him with a hostility he blatantly ignored. Paiva found it strange to see him amongst this scraggly crowd, for she was so used to him being surrounded by finery and elegance. He retained a dignified air, and sat as if he was still in the great hall dining on the finest of meals Bessil could procure and conversing amongst the highest of society.

"I can't go back to the Keep," Yulin stated and took a long swig of Ulrig's Cure All. "Seems there was trouble in Quarrytown. Apparently a tall, black-haired Wilderman slipped into the Warden's Quarters and did a good deal of damage to the premise and the rangers on duty. Master Warden Lier was locked into the holding cell, though he swears up and down he ran this Wilderman through with his sword. He identified this intruder as none other than Black Renn. When they began to interrogate Mrs. Ibbie, I pretty well knew I would have my neck stretched once Ceitra found out it was I who set this raging criminal loose." Yulin sized Renn, his eyes skirting over his unharmed torso, then downed the rest of his drink. Renn raised his eyebrows and shook his head in mild disbelief.

"Run through with a sword did you say?" Renn scoffed. "Liar Lier."

"I'd love to see that little brat branded and thrown into the woods. I would love to see that right bastard Ennig Strapback get a hold of him one day," Yulin scowled.

"Is she harmed?" Paiva broke in. "Has my mother been harmed?"

"She'll live," Yulin said, his eyes growing soft. Ulrig gave him another drink.

"And what plans did you have now that you're in the woods? You're not branded, but you might as well be," Ulrig questioned. "Why did you want to come to Far Reach?"

"He should be branded," Ennig interjected. "I'll do it myself."

"That is not necessary," Ulrig replied firmly. "Yulin?"

"I swore an oath to protect the Pratermoras and serve the land. I cannot do that with Ceitra in the way and the Lord succumbed to his dreamless sleep. I will serve Rennik instead — as a Wilderman if I must. I believe Rennik is innocent of his brother's death and I believe Ceitra is a dark and malicious creature that must be destroyed. I don't know what she is and I don't know what she has done, but I know my Lord's madness, Odrik's death, and Rennik's exile have been caused by her manipulations and exacted by her ill will. I know Paiva Ibbie is not a summoner of dark spirits, I know Rennik is not a cold-blooded murderer and I know Ramsi Lier is an unfit substitute for a Master Warden. I am enraged, I am bewildered, and I am humiliated. That is all I have to say. Rennik, I am yours to command. I have nothing to return to on the other side of the river. I have nothing to my name except the oath that I swore and shall uphold."

"You're a rare bird," Ulrig said. "Never heard of a Master Warden willingly becoming a Wilderman."

"I'm not a Master Warden," Yulin said bitterly. "I have nothing but the shirt on my back."

"I am glad for you to join us." Ulrig smiled cheekily and tipped his cup to Yulin's, who glowered at him in return.

There was a slew of curses that flew at him from the unkempt crowd and he retaliated by skirting a dark look about the cave. "Mark my words, Wildermen, I did not come just on my own behalf. I came to warn you of what will come. With Ceitra ruling the roost you will all be outcast for the rest of your lives. She will not grant you pardons. Not ever. Mark my words."

"What say you?" Jorn asked from his seat by the fire.

"I said you're damn fools if you think Ceitra will grant any more pardons. There will be none, not unless the Lord somehow miraculously awakes and returns to his old self."

"But that can't be done," Lorik, the red-bearded father said. "Crowbill says his sleep is enchanted."

"Here, here. I have something to say about that." Ulrig swallowed the rest of his drink and then banged his cup on the table to gather everyone's attention. The Far Reach Wildermen all swung their heads and swiveled in their seats towards him, falling silent as they waited for Ulrig to speak.

"I ask you now my outcast Wilder-whelps to join me in taking this girl on a pilgrimage to the Highpeaks."

A cry of protests arose, questions were shouted, voices were raised. Ulrig raised his hands for silence and then lifted his voice in the airs of a storyteller.

"I have taught you all that I know of the Old Stories. I have taught you of the Old Spirits born from the humors of our hearts. You have all seen for yourselves the Folka beasts you hunt for your pardons and you all believe they are creatures of the Dark Spirits."

The men murmured their agreement. Yulin sat back in his chair and crossed his arms as he listened raptly, a curious look of hungry interest on his face.

"…There is a dark spirit whom we all fear," Ulrig continued. "We have called her the Strix, for she is faceless and ageless and we have known her since the beginning of the Old Stories. She has left the forest to do her evil work in the world of men. Tearing families apart, stealing happiness and eating our hate that comes from it. She has left the forest in the form of a woman. A beautiful, red-haired woman…. And we now know her as the Lady Ceitra, a cunning and beguiling disguise for a wicked spirit.

"This girl you see before you, she is no ordinary person. For her father is an Incarnate of a Good Spirit and she is his Virtue. She is a symbol, whether she likes it or not, in which we must believe to guide us through these dark times. We must follow her to Morinvere where she will find the spirits of the Good Humors that have been driven away by the Folka beasts. We must protect her and keep her safe. You must put your hope and your beliefs in her, for she has a promise to give you. The Dark Spirits will have no power over us if we lend her our thoughts and our prayers." Ulrig gazed around the room at the stunned faces. Yulin's eyes dropped to Paiva, whose cheeks grew hot and red.

"Hold on," Jerrik piped up. "What do we get out of all of this?"

"Salvation," Ulrig answered.

The man scratched his head thoughtfully, then spat into the fire. "I don't need salvation," he answered.

"A pardon then," Ulrig said impatiently.

"How can that be if the Lord's asleep and Ceitra won't grant anymore pardons?"

Ulrig sighed impatiently and rubbed a hand over his face. "By my beard," he muttered. "If we bring this girl to Morinvere and she raises the Old Spirits, they will drive Ceitra back into the woods."

Paiva looked around at the empty eyes of the men. Yulin rose then and cleared his throat. "You lot have been thrown into the woods because nobody gives a damn about you or your families. And you know why that is? Because you're all damned selfish cowards. Show some spine, rise and do something good. Be men, be honorable and redeem yourselves."

"Honor means nothing to damned men," Ennig's deep voice called out. The others seemed to agree. "We don't want honor. We want a pardon. None of us will find our pardons in Morinvere. We will find only our deaths." The other Wildermen agreed.

Paiva looked to Renn helplessly. He shrugged and stuck his pipe in his mouth, for he had nothing else to offer. Paiva's mind raced with possible solutions, wondering how she could convince these men to take her to the Vale of the Spirits. She felt tears whelm in her eyes, knowing she could not face the odds of this journey alone.

"Please," she said to them, "I need your help." But her voice was drowned out by arguments that broke out amongst the men. Yulin sat down, his nose turned up in disgust. Ulrig looked to Renn beseechingly.

"No, old man," Renn muttered.

"Please Renn," Ulrig urged. "Set these men straight."

Paiva looked to him anxiously, her eyes wide with pleading. He returned her stare with a blank look, and she could not coax any support from him.

"No one goes into the Vale," the red-bearded man said, his son quivering beside him, "for no man ever returns from beyond the Highpeaks. It is the dark spirit Varloga himself who guards the valley. He is the dark conjurer."

"I don't trust her," another one said, pointing at Paiva. "How we sure she ain't some malicious being here to enchant us? Spirits take many forms. How are we even sure she's who you say she is?"

"No one can kill Varloga. He's as old as time, I've heard what he can do to men. He steals souls, I'd like to keep mine, however worthless it is," Gartri protested.

"No, not going. You're on your own."

Ulrig looked to Paiva apologetically and sat down again.

"I'm going," she said.

Yulin shook his head and gave her a stern look. "You're as good as dead on your own."

"I can't very well live out the rest of my life hiding in a cave. I have nowhere else to go." She rose from her seat briskly and plowed her way through the smoky air of the cave. She slunk out the crooked door to escape into the fresh air of the night.

"I'll take her myself if you won't," Ulrig said looking to Renn dismally.

Renn sighed miserably. "There must be a safe place somewhere she can go. The rest of the world can go to hell for all I care."

"Her mother's in the Quarry," Ulrig spat. "Her father's been spirited away by the Folka. Where else does she have to go? She'd have better chances of finding answers in Morinvere than facing persecution in the lowlands."

"Jekka found a safe place," Renn said levelly, eyeing the old man coldly, "without anyone's help."

Ulrig's temper flared violently at the slight. "You cannot even dare compare the two," Ulrig snarled. "Two different circumstances."

"Not entirely," Renn mused. "Perhaps Jekka would have an idea of what to do. She must know a safe place."

"You will not involve my daughter in this. I don't want her dabbling in the affairs of spirits. I want her to be safe from this. There is no other solution — the girl must not lose everything she loves, for then she will be ruined. As Jekka was."

"As you wish."

"Go see to that girl," Ulrig spat. "Fie on your soul if you dare let her heart be broken. You protect her and you keep her from harm, if it's the last thing you do. I don't care if you disagree or if you don't believe. Every moment she spends in anguish is a triumph for the Strix."

Renn rose stiffly, his eyes clouded over with indifference. "As you wish, Ulrig," he repeated, "but perhaps you should send Yulin. I am not one for consoling delicate things."

"Just go," Ulrig flared. "Out of my sight."

As Renn made his way towards the door Ulrig called out to him again.

"You know," he said, "your mother would be ashamed of you. Even if the whole world damned her, she would never damn the world."

Renn's eyes landed on Ulrig and froze, but Ulrig looked away, suddenly feeling ashamed himself. Renn strode out of the cavern and disappeared without a word.

Yulin looked to Ulrig and sighed.

"So, old friend," Yulin said. "It seems you still harbor the forbidden love that outcast you so many moons ago."

Ulrig scowled. "Love, no matter how great or small, should ever be forgotten."

"Of course it should," Yulin sighed. "Think of the life you could have had if it hadn't been for your heart leading you astray."

Ulrig smiled cunningly and sat back in his chair, crossing his arms squarely across his chest and setting his speckled eyes on Yulin with a stern look of sympathy. "Funny," he said, "how you should say that. For you're the very man who never gave his heart away, and look how we both now sit together. Both outcasts on the far side of the river."

Yulin smiled, his face resigned. "You always were a wit, weren't you?"

Ulrig nodded sagely. "It is funny. I was the Lord's left hand and you were his right. Here we both sit, without him."

Yulin leaned over and mockingly toasted his cup to Ulrig's. "To our follies, then. You threw your life away out of a blinding love and I threw mine away out of blinding hate."

"To us, then." Ulrig suddenly laughed. "To our many, many follies. To love and loyalty…"

— «» —

Renn found Paiva sitting on a ledge off the path down to the Berg horses' corral, her feet swung over and dangling in the open air. Her head was tilted back, allowing her to stare at the sweep of stars spangled out over the hills. She didn't look at him as he came to stand beside her. She was too angry to face him.

"I'm going," she said. "With or without anyone's help."

"It isn't wise," he said. He found a seat on a mossy boulder.

"I have no choice. What else is there...? Please, tell me."

"You could hide here — a few months, a year — until people forget you. Then you could cross back to the lowlands and run south. Find a new town, a new family."

"Is that what you would have done if it was you? Abandon your family? Give up hope on them?"

"I am not you," he said. "I am stronger, more capable."

"I am strong," she said and swung her head to him. Even in the dark he could feel her eyes burning into him. "I have my will."

"Out here you are prey, Paiva. No matter how much you will yourself through this forest, there are predators, of men, animals, and spirits. Not to mention the exposure, the starvation, your own fear."

"Then you take me."

"I have taken you as far as I can," he said. "Any farther and I fear I could not hold true to my promise to keep you safe. The farther north we go, the more savage the Wildermen become. What if I failed you? What if I couldn't protect you from violation, from torture? Whatever light you have left in you, take it and run from here. Your father would not want this of you, nor your mother. They would want you to be safe, to be whole."

She shook her head vehemently. "I started all of this," she said. "How could I doom my family, how could I abandon them, when all of this is my fault? I took my mask off on Mummers-eve, I followed Varloga up to the altar. Because of me, you were almost sentenced to death."

"Paiva," he sighed. "I doomed your family by stepping foot inside your household that night. It is my fault, not yours. Don't ever think it is."

"My father begged you to stay."

"And I should have left."

"But you kept us safe. My father should have never written of it, it should have been forgotten. Wherever he is, I am certain he regrets it. He probably thinks he caused your death. We have to find him." This time when Paiva looked at him her gaze was soft, pleading. "Somewhere out there in the forest he is all alone, fighting against the monsters we have created from our fear. Not only is he my father, whom I love and adore for all the world, but he is the last of his kind."

"No, Paiva."

"Do it for your own father, then. To lift his madness."

"No."

"Do it to avenge your brother."

"No."

"Why?" she asked sadly.

"It's too late," he said bitterly. "The Strix has won."

"She has won because you have given up. I won't."

"I won't let you go," he repeated. "I promised your mother I would keep you safe."

"My mother will die in the Quarry. Your father will be lost in madness, and Ceitra will rule the lowlands. How can you let the world stand like this?"

He sighed wearily, shaking his head in dismay.

"The Old Ones need their believers. I need you, and I believe in you," she said. "It couldn't have been chance that brought us together. I have seen your strength, your abilities, and I am in awe of you."

"Don't you dare put your faith in me."

"It is too late," she said. "Even if you chose to stay your hand, I could never accuse you of anything but being a good man."

For the first time in a long time, he felt a burst of pride. He remembered the first time he had seen her. A wraith of a girl standing in a slanted moonbeam, her face shattered with fear as she gazed into the eyes of the malevolent Varloga. The Ibbies were good people and turning away from Paiva now would cause more harm than could ever be undone. Her family would be lost, the spirit he saw soaring inside of her would be broken, and to him that was unforgivable. He could die a damned man without a pardon; he could find peace in that. He would have no rest for this error, and surely it would haunt him for the rest of his days.

He let loose another of his weary sighs and rose.

"Come along then," he said. She swung her head to him in question, then bounded off her rock and followed him back up to the cave.

— «» —

"Wildermen," he said, his voice deep and low. It radiated out into the cave. They fell silent again and turned their heads to listen. "The idea is that if we find this Morinvere, and we set the good spirits free, they will drive out all spirits of the dark humors. They will drive out the Folka and leave Grimenna in peace."

"And then how are we supposed to be granted a pardon? The Lord won't grant a pardon for a stuffed elk head," Jerrik argued.

"There will be no more pardons regardless. The tower has been burned, the Lord has succumbed to madness, and Ceitra rules the Keep," Renn said. "We are all trapped out here. Killing a Folka is worthless. There is only one way to end this, for all of us. We must take Varloga's head."

"Varloga's head," Lorik spluttered. "Might as well go jump off Far Fall instead."

"You're a fool, Renn," Ennig said. "This girl has brought you a false hope."

"It's the only hope I have," Renn mused, "and it is the only thing I believe."

"I believe it," Jerrik said. His nose was scrunched up and he was nodding his head thoughtfully. "I believe I'd get a pardon for that. I believe we'd all get a pardon for that. Find Morinvere, let this Virtue set the banished spirits free, cut off Varloga's bloody head. Sounds simple. Except for the fact that it's guarded by hundreds of Folka."

"That's why we're going to Maggra's," Renn said. The men grew quiet then. There was a tremor of excitement mixed with outrage.

Jerrik's jaw slacked open in shock. "I'll go to Morinvere but I'm not going to Maggra's, by my beard," he said. "They're all mad badgers up there. Every last one of them."

"They kill Folka and eat them, they don't bother using them for Pardons. That's why they're so mad," Ginver interjected. Renn's face grew hard as stone as he listened to their protests.

"Listen to me, for what it's worth," he exclaimed, silencing them again. "You are all as cursed as I now. Do anyone of you truly believe that if you were to bring a Folka head back now you would be pardoned? Do you think that Ceitra would be the one to forgive you? You will hunt in vain, for there will be no pardons for any one of you. You will be sent back here until you are dead; she would not let you have your happiness back. You will never see your families again, you will never have homes again."

"Neither if we go to the Vale," Ennig spat.

"You don't know that," Renn said, and then he looked to Paiva. "I will not let the world stand like this."

He said it simply and plainly, but his words carried a firmness that struck into the men's hearts. They looked to Renn in obvious disbelief.

"What say you?" Ennig asked for them all.

"There is no hope for any of us," Renn said. "Not here. It is in Morinvere. I go to take Varloga's head, and the lot of you can take it from my bloody hands and have your pardons."

Renn seemed to hold sway over them. His eyes were hard as steel as he swung them around the room and looked at each man, willing them the confidence he felt at his decision. Paiva realized he was a force to be reckoned with. He had spoken hardly more than a handful of words but they carried more intent and meaning then Ulrig's, Yulin's, or hers because they had come from him. It made her wonder who he really was, aside from a Virtue, a Wilderman, or an outcast Lord. Who truly was the stern man standing there beneath those tattered rags whose presence had such influence over the others? She realized in that moment he was more than what she had at first discerned. He had earned his own respect in these woods; he was an unassuming leader. Ulrig knew this, and she watched Yulin's face for the recognition of his qualities that soon came. She saw a flash of dreamlike hope that passed over Yulin's eyes and she knew he was thinking of the possibilities of what it would be like to have Renn restored to the Lowlands as a true lord. She saw it herself for a brief moment, before the image was collapsed by the Wildermen's arguing.

"It's an empty promise," Ennig said.

"You are being a Vex," Ulrig spluttered. "It is a true promise. The only thing empty is your future if you do not listen to me. The Forest will plunge into darkness if we do nothing. Winters will be starving as you have never known, the Folka will drive the game out as they have done so in the past. They will come in the long nights, they will swallow us and drive us mad with terror. And when they are done with us, how long do you think before they will cross the river? How long do you think it will take them to reach the lowlands, and swallow it up like they did all the settlements here? We did not listen! We did not listen to the old people who remembered these things, we did not heed their warnings! So listen to me now! Listen that this girl has the blood of myth in her and she is the daughter of Hope. He will not fail us." Ulrig struck his fist angrily into the table, sending his mug of Cures All flying. Paiva remembered how Ceitra had said her light would cast long shadows — that the Good Spirits had made the mistake of using fear to keep men from straying into darkness. Ulrig spoke of terrible fears, and it was not fear that she wanted to use to propel these men towards Morinvere.

"I am tired of being hated," a melodious voice spoke out and Paiva turned her eyes to Ginver. He was looking at the brand in his palm, studying it in the low light as if it had a message to decipher. "I am tired of being afraid," he said. He looked up to Paiva. "I am with you. The world needs to change."

"I am as well," the red bearded Lorik said, looking to his son. "I would break the world for my child. I'll not damn my son because I was too afraid to rise up." One by one the Wilderman conceded and Ulrig sat back down in relief. He looked to Ennig for his say.

"Oh, I'm a-coming with you. For no other reason than that I want to see this slip of a girl convince Maggra to help us," Ennig smiled dully. The men began to talk amongst each other in hushed tones as Renn took his seat. Paiva watched him, trying to discern the thoughts beneath his dark brow. She felt a tightness in her chest, a flutter of wings that beat against her ribs with a strange warm happiness. The feeling washed over her, lifting her soul and making her smile. It was Hope.

Chapter 14

Paiva had found her usual spot to sleep before the fire. Yulin and Renn both lay alongside her to separate her from the rest of the slumbering men. At first she had felt very uncomfortable and out of place amongst them, but she eased herself into sleep by imagining she was sleeping amongst her flock of sheep and not a gang of outcast criminals. Indeed some of the bodily noises that escaped them were remarkably beastly.

They were up the next morning at the crack of dawn as a cold high wind swept down from the north. Jorn, who was unable to go with them much to his contempt, stormed about the cave in a vengeance.

"I'm coming with you, Renn!" he howled angrily as he prepared his meagre belongings for the journey.

"No, Jorn, you stay put. You're lame. You know as well as I you have little chance of making it as far as Maggra's in your health."

"I'm coming, Renn."

"You should have taken the head of the beast that lamed you. You would have been pardoned and out of my hair," Renn snapped in exasperation.

"I wouldn't take another man's pardon, you know that. I said myself that I'd help to fix this. I am coming."

"Stay here," Ulrig urged. "Keep the camp safe. When we return you will claim a part of the pardon."

"And what if you should not return?"

"It's not a choice, Jorn, we will not have you with us. You're lame."

"I'm still able."

"However able you are, use it to keep the camp from being raided. If we fail then we will still need a safe place to return to."

Jorn argued and blundered about the cave like a raging bull until Renn neatly went and knocked the crutch from under his arm. Without it he staggered and fell heavily into the wall for support, whilst snapping his teeth at Renn for the insult.

"If you can make it out of this cave and atop your horse without this crutch, or any help, you can come," Renn said, tossing the wooden implement aside. Jorn's rage was quieted as he reached and grasped his leg, pain taking the place of pride.

"Damn you," he muttered.

"You will still claim a part of the pardon, either way," Renn said. "At least if you stay here you will have a chance to claim it. You won't cause your own death or the death of any others trying to help you."

"Agh," he grunted and then hopped on one leg to a chair where he sat in his formidable shape before the dying embers of the hearth and grumbled to himself. Renn left to attend to the others while Ulrig hurried after him. It was Paiva who retrieved the crutch and returned it to Jorn.

"I want you to stay here," she said. "I want you to be able to see your family again one day. I want you to be able to hitch King and plow your fields."

He looked up at her sharply before a sad smile pulled at his mouth. "You remember," he said.

She smiled at him and then turned to make her way to the others down by the horses.

"May all the shining stars light your way little shepherdess," he said. "My prayers are with you." He bent his head back to stare at the ash streaks in the hearth.

— «»‹› —

Ulrig sat atop Felder and behind him he towed a Berg laden high with the bundles of furs, leathers, and the sweet wine he was hoping to seduce Maggra with. The other men followed behind on their own horses, each armed to the teeth with bows, rusted swords, wooden lances, stone daggers and the like. Paiva sat astride Jakbur wrapped in Crowbill's fur while Renn and Runa led them onwards. Ulrig gave her a pitted iron dagger she hung at her hip, which Ennig said would be better suited to picking teeth. Yulin followed up behind on his own wily Berg he kept arguing with while Ulrig took the lead and headed them down the mountain.

Ennig took up the rear, chewing a grass stalk and twirling it between his yellow teeth. The air about him seemed to ripple with malice. Paiva could feel his eyes raking over her and it sent goosebumps puckering across her skin. She looked back up to the cave and found Jorn standing atop it, leaning on his crutch. She thought he truly did have the heart of a bear, thinking of him returning to his loved ones gave her the extra gumption she needed to swallow the last of her doubts. He waved them off, then disappeared.

It was different from travelling with the score of rangers from Birchloam. The Bergs were constantly biting and kicking at each other, which issued curses from the Wildermen who struggled to keep their seats. They had to avoid being rubbed against trees, or have their legs thrown in the way of a backwards kick. The Bergs didn't care if they were halfway down a slope when suddenly prompted to lunge at their neighbors with bared teeth and pinned back ears, forgetting their riders that grappled for hold of their manes to keep from plunging off. There was much cursing, readjusting of bodies and laughing when someone did slide down their horse's neck. The men jeered and jested at each other, unlike the rangers who had been grave in their silence.

When the Bergs finally settled and they had descended into the valley north of Far Reach Camp, Ginver began singing and was soon joined in by the others.

'I am a Wilderman,
I've been outcast to the woods,
A brand burnt in my hand,
To keep me from trading goods.

A man is made of what he owns
A man is only worth his name
But a cursed brand upon his hand
takes from him everything but shame

The only way to be set free
Is to be good and dead
Unless he brings the Lord
A Folka's filthy head.'

— «» —

They travelled hard their first day, making it to the
bottom of the Far Reach valley by nightfall where they set up
camp in a copse of red oak. Paiva again found a sleeping spot
separate from the others and Yulin and Renn both lay down
on either side of her. Paiva felt danger lurking all around
her. Wolves howled eerily in the distance, things moved
and crashed through the trees in the shadows. Ennig's eyes
trailed over her and lingered. She could find no true comfort
for she felt naked and exposed and terribly afraid. Every
sound made her flinch, every pop and hiss of the fire made
her envision the snarling face of Varloga.

Renn leaned back into the moss beside her, keeping her
between him and the width of a tree. He pulled his oilskin
over himself and crossed his arms, then tilted his head back
and peered at the stars that soaked through the canopy of
branches above him. There was a heavy silence that hung
through the camp, the men made no noise except to scratch
at themselves and sharpen their knives.

"Ginver," Ulrig called out. "In the song about the Hidden
Rock, is it that the Wilderman shoots a hawk from the sky or
a heron?"

"I can't remember…" Ginver said, so he put down his
knife he was sharpening and cleared his throat and began to
sing about a man who was cast away to the woods to become
a Wilderman. His wife, unable to be parted from him, went
in search of him. When they found each other after her great
long searching, the other Wilderman tried to steal her away.
He found a rock cave to hide her in while he went away
hunting for their food. It was so well hidden that her husband
could not find her on his return, and he wandered about in
search of her while she remained hidden and waiting.

The song spoke of this woman praying for her husband
to remember the meadow from which he had braided her a

wreath of lilies, then from there to remember the hawk he had shot from the sky that flew above the mountains shaped like her tears. They found each other eventually, and kept their love hidden under the hidden rock.

Ulrig knew that in all Wildermen songs the hawk always flew west, the heron east, the crow north, and the geese south. He simply wanted to hear Ginver sing, and they all felt better as the timbre of his melodious voice resonated through the creeping shadows.

— «·» —

The next morning they headed west into a valley that continued to gradually slope downwards. Within a few hours of trekking, the cool air of the woods suddenly became hot and damp. There came the strong, sulphurous smell of swamp and soon the ground beneath their feet began to soften and grow thick with bracken and webs of moss. They came to a marsh where it seemed all the water that ran from the hills collected in a dead pool that drowned the trees and rotted the earth. Great skeletal trees reached into the sky, bleached gray by the sun and by death, their branches snapped from their bodies. Some were fallen over, their roots lifted from the earth and half-submerged in the black water of the marsh. These great masses of broken roots made Paiva think of giant bird's nest that had fallen from the sky. Despite the dead trees and the dead looking black water, the swamp teemed with life. There were masses of flowering lily pads upon which insects hummed and frogs perched. Rushes filled with darting, peeping birds tending to nests in their stalks. There were grasses and snaking vines that grew from the dead stumps of trees and in the hollows of chalky roots. The swamp was narrow but not crossable. It seemed to stretch on forever, and Ulrig found a game trail to follow along its perimeter to guide them around it.

At one point they dismounted their horses and led them by hand, for the ground was wet and the path narrow. She removed her fur and stowed it atop Jakbur, then tied her skirt up above her knees to make it easier to move. She did not have a hard time keeping up for they moved slow as they battled their way through clouds of rushes and snagging deadwood. The underbrush was flowing with plants and flowers she did not recognize and she could not help but to pluck at pretty flowers as they made their way. She absently thought to keep them for her father, thinking he would marvel at them and find a place in his books for them. But she remembered his books were burned, her home was taken from her, and her father was still unfound. Realizing this, and that the flowers would be safer in the swamp then coming with her, she let them be. The ones she had already taken were knotted into a spray and tied into her hair, for the simple sake that they smelled better than she did. She had noticed the Wildermen used a plant called horsemint to disguise their odors as well. They chewed on it after they ate and rubbed the oils from the leaves on themselves and their horses. At first it had been too pungent for her to find pleasant, but it had grown familiar to her and she began to find comfort in it.

They were making headway along the swamp when a stinging began in her legs. She looked down to inspect them. Her skin was beginning to redden and at first she dismissed it and continued on, but it was not long before the stinging became painful. She cried out to Ulrig in complaint. Bluish veins began rising in her ankles and an angry rash began to break out, burning her like a red-hot iron. Ulrig left Felder to crop at the greenery and came to inspect.

"What's this now?" he muttered as he bent to look at her shins. "By my beard! Spiteweed!" He doubled back to Felder hurriedly and began tearing into his saddlebags.

"Renn!" he exclaimed. "Water!" A second later Renn materialized at her side, glanced at the rash, then scooped Paiva up in his arms and dashed towards the water.

"I'm alright!" she cried out at his urgent reaction. Renn ignored her and carried her waist deep into the black water, his steps sinking deep into the muck and slime of the bottom. She recoiled in disgust of the weeds and filth about her, thankful to be held aloft until he plunged her lower half in. The water was surprisingly cool and soothed her burning skin. A moment later Ulrig was hurriedly splashing in after them, a small leather pouch in hand. When he reached her he grabbed a fistful of its contents, a white powder that she thought might have been some of his tanning salt, and began to scour her legs mercilessly. She clung to Renn and tried to keep from crying out as the pain intensified and she began to think Ulrig was skinning her.

"I know it hurts," he muttered, "but much less than if I didn't."

"What is Spiteweed?" she asked worriedly as she looked up to the other Wildermen who gathered to watch amusedly at the edge of the water.

"A mean little shrub that grows anywhere wet. It causes very bad burns, can even make a man blind if he gets it in his eyes the first time he touches it. Don't worry — as long as we wash the oils off before they set you will be fine. The next time you run into Spiteweed it might not even bother you again."

When Ulrig was content with his scrubbing, Renn carried Paiva back to the bank where he set her down swiftly and began plucking at leeches that had latched onto his cloak and boots. She inspected her legs again and though they were painfully red and raw, it was not worse than could be tolerated.

"Thank you Ulrig," she said as he waded back to them. He sat down with a huff and pulled his boots off to tug at leeches between his toes. Realizing they were hungrily latched on, he sprinkled a small amount of the salt over them and waited for them to shrivel up before plucking them off and throwing them into the grasses. He then tipped his boots to drain them of water.

"No fret, my lady," he said. "We've all had our run-ins with Spiteweed. It only spites you once, like Crowbill swill. You develop a tolerance after some time. Lucky it was that and not Bruisewort."

"What is Bruisewort?" she asked naively.

"Stains your skin blue like a bruise, and if it gets into your blood you'd be delirious for days. Feed a man Bruisewort berries and his guts will bleed out. It used to happen to cows and horses in the lowlands before they eradicated the weed altogether. Has not found its way back across the river yet."

"Grand," she mused as she casually stepped out of the way of a frantically wriggling leech that was making an attempt to return back to the water. "What else is there out here?" she asked.

"Oh, there's lots," Ulrig said as he stuffed his feet back into his boots. "There's Foxbells, a pretty flower which when crushed beneath a man's fingertips can cause his heart to stop. Crampwort, which will colic him to death. Blisterberry, Weepwort, Strixbane…. A great number of botanicals a wanderer of the Wilderlands must be cautious of. Ironically, as deadly as these plants may be they also have the capacity to be used as medicines, if prepared by the right hands."

"Like Jekka's."

"Indeed." He smiled and got to his feet. She saw a gleam of pride flash through his eyes before he turned back for his horse. "It can be that Crampwort can act as a vermifuge if its oils are mixed with a binding compound like clay. Foxbells can make a faltering heart beat stronger if the poison is boiled out of it first. There's no reason to be afraid of nature, for it is not evil. You simply must understand it."

He finished with warning her to untie her dress and keep her legs protected from the underbrush, then led the procession on after securing Felder's saddlebags. He stopped a ways up to point out Spiteweed to her, but did not seemed concerned for her legs. They burned and bothered her but she did not complain, mostly because Renn followed closely behind her and she had an urgent desire to prove her strong will to him. She wanted more than anything to earn his respect and not to feel like the blundering fool she was. Her dress chafed at her legs but she ignored it and gritted her teeth, stepping tenderly while she coaxed Jakbur behind her.

When they stopped to rest at midday she collapsed wearily on a fallen log and poured her waterskin over her legs to cool the lingering burning sensation. She was already exhausted and the small meal that Renn brought her did little to strengthen her.

"I hate to sound like a whiny Wilder-whelp," she said as he sat down to eat next to her. "But how long do you think it's going to take us to get to the Vale?"

He smiled, and though it wasn't much of a smile it was the most reassuring thing she'd seen all day. "I can't say," he mused. "If it were a straight march to the Highpeaks we'd be lucky enough to make it in five days. However it is not a straight march; there are mountains and valleys and other obstacles in the way. We'll be lucky if we make it out of the bog by nightfall."

"The bog?" she asked, wondering if that was what they called the treacherous Spiteweed-filled swamp.

"The marshlands run from the bog, but it's a little tricky because the bog floats, or so Ulrig says. It always changes, never stays in one spot. He says if the bog's hungry, it will make it harder for us to pass, but he also thinks the Stones walk around at night."

"They do," Ulrig said in passing as he trampled down a spot for himself to sit in the bracken across from them. "When I first came to the woods there was a big rock in the Far Fall valley that had a little birch tree growing from it. Thirty years later that same rock sits on top of the Snowy Crags and has a great big birch tree growing from it."

"There are lots of rocks that have trees growing on them," Renn reminded him.

"There are no birch trees in the Crags," Ulrig said smartly and stuffed his mouth with a handful of dried berries.

"Do all the stones move?" she asked curiously.

"No," Ulrig replied. "Only the enchanted ones."

"Is the bog enchanted?"

"I don't really think so," he said. "I think it is more of a living thing then an enchanted thing. But don't worry, the Bergs will guide us through it. They were called Bog Horses before it got shortened to Berg."

"Why were they called Bog Horses?" Paiva asked as Renn rolled his eyes at another of her endless questions.

"Because when you try to catch a wild Berg they run into a bog and hide. Was a very clever Wilderman who caught the first one."

— «» —

They were back on their feet again shortly after, leading the horses by hand up the last length of the swamp. Mervig was sent up ahead to scout and look for signs of this infamous bog, but they went a good ways before Ulrig muttered that the bog must have had a good meal and he hoped it was of Folka and not of Wildermen. They were making good ground when of a sudden Mervig's horse threw its head and whinnied, stamping its feet firmly into the ground and looking about the thick trees in alarm. Its nostrils flared and its mane bristled. Every Wilderman in the party reached for their weapons and took a guarded stance, peering cautiously into the trees and listening for any noise. Yulin and Renn were instantly by Paiva's side.

Mervig looked back to Ulrig and shrugged.

"I see naught," he said, and took one step forward before disappearing into the earth. A black curse flew out of Ulrig's mouth as Mervig's horse reared and threw itself backwards. Ulrig went for the horse while Yulin and Renn bolted to the spot where Mervig had disappeared. The ground looked deceptively firm, but they both stuck their hands into it like it was no more than soup. Beneath the dead leaves and calmly growing ferns was nothing but a soft, brown clay. Their hands grasped at nothing and Yulin was the first to lay on his belly and plunge his whole upper body down into it while Renn held fast to his belt. In seconds the other Wildermen had swarmed them and by the time Yulin began kicking his feet there were four men to help pull him back. There was an immense amount of suction. Yulin's head broke the surface with a sickening slurp. Mervig emerged a second later, his hands clinging tightly to Yulin's.

They were both pulled safely to firmer ground where they collapsed in shock and panted lungful's of burning fresh air. Yulin was covered in mud to his waist while Mervig was entirely covered. He spat filth from his mouth and scooped mud from his eyes, blinking frantically and choking.

"Warden," he choked when he made out his rescuer. "The Warden saved me."

"I did what I could," Yulin sniffed. Mervig extended his hand to Yulin in thanks, the branded hand clasping the one that had branded it. Ulrig, who had managed to subdue Mervig's horse, bent and patted him on the shoulder.

"Best we listen to our Bergs," he said. "Another wrong step and who knows how deep you'll sink."

Despite the incident they pressed on in relative good humor. Ginver struck up a tune and the other men exchanged dry jokes. Paiva found herself admiring them, for when faced with treachery the Wildermen seemed to adopt an airy nonchalance, as if being swallowed by a bog were no more than a part of daily routine. Renn returned and threw her up on Jakbur and they pressed on atop their horses, who seemed to have a sixth sense instilled in them as to where to put their feet. Felder took the lead, and as Ulrig was the wisest of the Wildermen, Felder seemed to be the wisest and most trusted of the Bergs. Renn towed Jakbur behind him and sat atop Runa like he was made of stone. Paiva on the other hand grappled with arm and leg to keep her seat as the horses lurched, jumped, and shimmied themselves between trees. She fell once, sliding down Jakbur's neck with a helpless yell before plummeting to the ground where she sunk up to her waist. Renn pulled her out before she had time to blink.

She wearily hauled herself back atop Jakbur and tried to scrape the mud from her dress. Renn looked defeated and at a loss of what to do with her so she proclaimed aloud that the bog mud soothed her Spiteweed burns. The mud didn't help her to keep her seat, though, and Jakbur became all the more slippery. This caused her to slow their progress and eventually a chorus of muffled curses began being directed at her.

Even Renn grew impatient when she lost her seat again and he drew her up onto Runa behind him. At a loss for what to do she wrapped her arms about his waist and held fast. Only then did she manage to travail the bog without mishap. She pressed herself into the hard lines of his back and felt the strain of his muscles that kept them both anchored in their seats.

She found herself imagining a different scenario, one wherein he was neither a Lord's son nor a Wilderman but a simple village boy. She wondered what he would have been like, who he would have been if shaped by a different life.

Would he know that love could exist within a family, that fathers were not always disappointed in their sons; that friendship could be true and not forced? She thought of how horribly alone and afraid she would be without him, and how horrible it must have been for him to face these woods by himself.

She gripped him tighter. "Thank you," she said.

Renn said nothing, but she felt his calloused hand close over hers looped about his waist. Then it moved away, pulling at Jakbur's lead line to keep from falling behind as they struggled through the bog.

— «» —

They made it through the bog by late afternoon and decided to make camp early, for the whole party was bone-weary. Ulrig led them to a creek where they washed themselves, their horses and gear. He then started a roaring fire and staked most of his clothing out over it on a hooked branch to dry, then muttered around the camp bare foot in a scrappy pair of jerkins sorting through their wares to make supper. Paiva went into the creek fully clothed and washed the caked mud and grime from herself out of sight of the Wildermen. She returned to the fire and stood before it in her soaked attire to dry, watching curiously as the Wildermen came back from their baths and hung their clothes up in tree limbs. She was quite used to field boys and farm workers who under the heat of the summer sun worked without shirts and their pant cuffs rolled up, but standing amidst a gang of half-bared Wildermen was disconcerting. She found their appearances to be almost alien, for without their great bulk of furs and tattered leathers they looked less like animals and more like men — except Mervig, who was quite as hairy as an animal and who probably didn't need to wear clothes at all to keep himself warm in the cool woods.

She realized how Ennig had earned his name, for across his massive back were whipping scars. In a small way it made her sympathetic towards him for she had seen good horses ruined and turned wicked under the hands of a cruel master. She did not believe men were born wicked, but she did believe some men could not come back from wickedness. She suspected Ennig was one of those. Whoever had broken him had done their job well and he bore the marks to prove it.

Renn sat across the fire from her shirtless and barefoot, and it pained her to look at him as well. He was far too lean. Every muscle and cord of sinew showed in his taut frame. Again she wished she had the means to make him whole. Ginver, who she had by now learned had in fact been a minstrel before being branded, still had a softness to his physique that bespoke of an easy life. He had probably spent most of it in taverns and halls eating and drinking his fill in exchange for his talents. He made up some lyrics and a lively tune about the bog, which swallowed men and spat them out naked. It caused a few chuckles from the others before Mervig clouted him over the head.

"I'd rather Paiva fell into the bog and it took her clothes than mine," Mervig jeered. He winked at her, but she was not entirely sure how harmless a joke it was.

"If that ever did happen, Mervig, I could spin myself a yard of wool from the hair on your chest and make myself a pretty frock," she retorted.

Mervig's eyes bulged and for a second she thought he was going to clout her as well before all at once the entire gang burst into choking laughter.

"It would itch worse than Spiteweed," Ulrig wheezed, slapping his knee. Mervig protectively caressed his chest hair.

"No one's going to turn my gleaming mane into a lady's dress."

"Probably could, there's enough of it," Ginver sniggered. "Mervig Hairy Shirt, wears his beard like a skirt."

"That name better not stick," Mervig hissed. He uttered a slew of curses at Ginver and swung his arm to clout him again, but Ginver was far too quick and rolled out of the way, holding his ribs with laughter.

"You could always call him Bog Mouth," Ulrig noted at the colorful language that erupted from the enraged Wilderman.

"Bog Beard!" Ginver cried. It was readily agreed by the whole party he would from this day forever be called Bog Beard Mervig, and Ginver promised to spread his story far and wide into Grimenna with gales of laughter at how his name had been earned.

Chapter 15

The next day they headed into a rocky pass that lead up to Next Mountain. Paiva, of all people, spotted a figure hunched on a ledge above them. She whirled to Renn and pointed to it in alarm.

"Good eyes," he murmured, then called up to Ulrig. She was momentarily pleased with herself and thought to inform Renn her good eyes were on account of years of watchful shepherding, when she saw the look on Ulrig's face that filled her with unease. He squinted up to the ledge and waved hello. The figure watched them for a moment, then rose from the ledge and disappeared.

"Who was that?" she asked Renn. "Is it Maggra's gang?"

"No," he replied, scanning the trees. "We call him the Spook."

"The Spook?"

"No one knows his name."

"Is he dangerous?"

"He is self-serving. At times that can be dangerous. But never mind, he has no quarrels with us."

They made it halfway up the mountain by nightfall and camped in the thick trees that grew there. The men were unusually quiet as they sat around the fire and Paiva couldn't help but feel like they were being watched.

It was Ulrig who lifted his head to the shadows and called out: "You can come to the fire."

A moment later a shape materialized, silent as a wraith. A tall man garbed in tattered clothes, he stepped into the firelight and gazed about the camp with colorless eyes. He found a lone rock to perch on and sat across from them, dropping his eyes into the fire and spreading his hands to warm them. He was young enough, strangely beardless as Renn was, his hair an ash-colored blond jutting about his face in sharp strands. His clothes were strange for a Wilderman, for instead of wearing furs and leathers he wore wool and cotton. He looked like a woodsman, not a Wilderman, who had somehow gotten lost on his way home from cutting timber.

Ulrig offered him a bowl of hot broth and some ash cake which he took silently.

"We are just passing through," Urlig said. "We're headed to Maggra's."

The Spook nodded and sniffed at the bowl of broth, his eyes lifting to land directly on Paiva with an intensity that sent a chill through her. Everything about him was gray and washed out, and she was sure if she blinked he would disappear into the smoke, which seemed to her the very substance of his being.

"We're going to Morinvere," Ulrig said into the silence of the stranger. The Spook lowered his bowl and looked to Ulrig. Paiva could make out no questioning in his face, but Ulrig seemed to understand him like he did the Stones. Slowly, the Spook shook his head, then looked beyond into the woods, sweeping his gaze through the dark trees.

The Spook's faded eyes grew somber as he looked back to the Wildermen. His eyes were like gravestones, cold and lifeless. "They are coming," he said. Suddenly the fire crackled, spitting sparks into the air with a loud crack that startled them all.

When the smoke cleared the Spook was vanished, his meal lying untouched at the foot of the stone he had been sitting on. Paiva looked anxiously to Renn for an explanation.

"What was that? Who is coming?'

"I don't know," he said and looked across to Ulrig, whose eyes were lost in the fire.

"Who is he?" Paiva asked again.

"A ghost," Renn shrugged. "No one knows. We think he lives in the old vanished village beyond the pass. He comes and he goes, never stays long. He's been here forever, never changed, never aged. No one knows if he is even a Wilderman."

"If he is," Yulin sniffed, "it was not I who branded him."

"Who is coming? What did he mean?" she asked worriedly.

"The Folka," Ulrig answered as the fire crackled its light across his quiet face. He sighed and lay down, huddling beneath his furs to turn in for the night. Paiva stared across the way at the bowl of broth and the ash cake. She shivered as Renn rose and emptied them into the fire, as if they had truly been touched by the unliving.

"Don't worry," Renn said. "That is why we call him the Spook. No one knows if he comes to warn or to scare."

"Some stories say he was cursed by the Strix many, many moons ago; that he is from the Old Settlers' time," Ginver added. "No one knows why. Only that we don't go into the ruins of the vanished villages because of ghosts like him."

"I thought he was a Wilderman who died out here. He never got his pardon so his soul could never rest," Mervig said.

"Leave him be," Renn said. "Ghosts can't hurt the living. They can only haunt."

"My father says that ghosts are souls that could not leave this world because their loved ones would not let them go," Paiva said. It seemed every time she opened her mouth she said something bothersome, for they all turned to look at her in grave silence.

"What do you mean?" Ginver asked.

"The same as how our prayers birthed spirits into this world. When someone we love dies and we cannot accept it, we do more harm to their soul by wishing them back into this world than letting them go. They remain trapped here, unable to move on. The living bring them back." She felt a sudden chill sweep over her and she looked into the trees, somehow sure the Spook was still listening.

The men quietly turned in for the night after that and she found it hard to lie down and find her own rest. Though her body was sore and weary, her mind wandered out into vast spaces. Her father said that all of life was a circle, that all living bodies took their nourishment from the earth and when their bodies failed they were returned to the earth. He said it was the same for the soul, but he himself was too humble to say he knew what souls were truly made of and where they returned. He simply said they were eternal, as life was eternal, and existence was just a means through which it acted. A ghost was neither here nor there.

As she closed her eyes to sleep she sent her prayers out, wishing the Spook to find his peace if that was what he truly was. A ghost, a soul, trapped between the netherworld and here.

— «» —

By nightfall the next day they had reached the top of the mountain without any hindrances. They made a quick camp and collapsed into sleep.

The next morning, by the light of the early dawn, as the Wildermen roused themselves and wiped the soot of the campfire from their eyes, Paiva ventured out to face the northern sky wherein the Highpeaks rose. The valley floor below was deceptively small, looking more like a lush green blanket than a treacherous forest. She had awoken with an empty feeling and rolled over to find Renn was already awake and gone to tend to the horses; the moss alongside her still warm and imprinted from where he had lain. She closed her eyes and recalled the sound of her mother's voice, the smell of bread baking in their small kitchen, and the rich mixture of flowers that grew in the meadows above their little house. Only then did she find the strength to rise and face the mountains that loomed ahead.

Renn came to find her and stood beside her whilst she stared at their formidable shapes.

"I'm sorry," she said. "I am weary."

"It will be easier now," he replied softly. "We have not far to go now before we reach Maggra's."

"What if what the Spook said was true? What if the Folka are coming?"

"That's why they call him the Spook, Paiva, don't let him get to you. I do not doubt we have been watched by the Folka since we left. If they wanted us dead, it would have happened already."

He came to stand next to her, reassuring her with his presence, and followed her gaze out to the mountains.

"Do you suppose on the other side of the river under different circumstances… do you suppose we would have befriended each other in some other way?"

"No," he responded shortly.

"Why not?" she asked.

He shrugged. "Lords do not become friends with kitchen maids or sheep herder's daughters. And if they do they are not sincere."

She was quiet, saddened by his response. "If we return to the world again do you suppose we could try to be true friends? Not this, whatever this is, where you are bound to me because of guilty promises."

Paiva could feel his eyes studying her, could feel him shift his weight. "Surely," he nodded. He made to head back to the others then, but stopped of a sudden and turned back to her thoughtfully. "The person I was before, I am glad he died in that gully. And I would let him die a hundred times again if that is what it would take to make this ragged person I am today. I might be ugly and sullied now, but at least I am sincere. I am bound to you Paiva, but not by guilt. By belief."

She turned her head to him and found his eyes were bright on hers.

"You're not ugly," she said. For a moment she wondered if she could still breathe as a growing tension seemed to mount between them. He blinked uneasily, then stepped away, turning back to the others to make ready for the day.

— «》 —

Hidden Rock, which would lead northwards straight to Maggra's camp, was unlike the rest, for it was painted in swirling blue dye. Paiva studied it curiously, discerning the woman from Ginver's song lying in swirls of flowers as she looked up to a hawk that appeared to be falling above her pierced by an arrow. It was a beautiful and haunting image, primitive in its execution yet clearly depicting the song.

They stopped at the rock to rest the horses and eat a small ration of dried meat and berries. Ulrig went to sit atop it and spread his palms flat against its surface, staring out and into the trees with his strange wide eyes.

"What is he doing?" Yulin asked Renn who was bent over Runa's hoof inspecting it for bruises. He cast a sideways glance to Ulrig and chuckled, dropping Runa's foot and patting her neck.

"Talking to the stones," he answered.

"He's a strange man," Yulin said, watching Ulrig mutter to himself. The rest of the Wildermen took no notice of him and went about their business of tending to the horses and eating their meat.

"I hope they don't have anything bad to say today," Renn noted.

Ulrig snapped out of his reverie and rose, descending back to his horse with a grave face. He muttered to the men around him and Renn watched as their hands darted guardedly for their weapons. Renn stiffened and looked to Yulin.

"That's trouble," Renn said.

"Trouble?" Yulin echoed. "What sort of trouble?"

"Folka."

Yulin's eyes darted into the trees warily. Renn came to help Paiva up onto her horse and then swung up on his, leading them back in line with the others as they headed onwards. Yulin followed up their rear, his hand never straying far from the hilt of his sword. They had not headed out far when Ulrig looked back at Renn and through some small signal Renn fell back, halting his horse to let the others pass him by.

Paiva whirled her head around to give him a questioning look, but he motioned for her to keep going. She turned her questioning eyes on Yulin instead.

"Scouting," Yulin nodded to her as another Wilderman ahead broke away from the procession and cantered up the trail ahead of them. Yulin pressed his horse closer to Paiva and swung his gaze through the trees. They went forwards in silence, moving through the trees in a snaking line. She looked back to Renn nervously, but he had already disappeared.

By the time they made camp that evening, only the forward scout had returned, bringing no ill tidings with him. Paiva helped Ulrig to boil water and waited anxiously for Renn, her mind spinning with possible altercations he had encountered. The air was heavy with unease as the men began to settle in for the night. They bristled together and darted their eyes through the trees in apprehension, but nothing unusual appeared.

Like the Spook Renn returned, riding his horse into camp and tethering it with the others before joining Ulrig by the fire. Yulin and Ulrig both watched him settle down impassively. Only Paiva breathed a sigh of relief at his safe return.

"And?" Ulrig asked as he handed Renn a bowl of hot broth and ash cake.

"They're gathering behind us," he said ominously and sucked on his meal. Paiva looked to Ulrig in alarm, but he was calm.

"We're almost in the Northwoods. I'll call for them in the morning. If any are about they may come."

Paiva gathered he spoke of the Northwoods Wildermen.

"Anything up front?" Renn asked.

"The way is clear," he mused. "So far. How many behind us?"

Renn lifted his eyes up and searched the trees he had come from. Paiva felt the hair on her neck stand on end at his chilling gaze. His face flickered with firelight, his body coiled with tension.

"Too many," he said.

"How close?"

"Too close." He dropped his eyes back into the fire pensively. "They're stalking us, but they don't seem hungry."

"So we do not trespass unnoticed," Ulrig sighed. "Of course not. Let's pray they keep their distance until morning light at least."

— «» —

Paiva could find no sleep as she lay down. Ulrig dozed alongside the blazing fire and Yulin slept propped against a tree. Two Wildermen remained on guard at either end of the camp, and Renn sat up by the fire whittling at a stick. She lay awake for hours, staring into the fire too afraid to close her eyes, jumping at the slightest sound.

At some point in the night Renn rose silently and went to Yulin, who came awake before Renn bent to rouse him. Wordlessly they exchanged watch. Yulin rose and sat by the fire where he began to clean the dirt from beneath his nails with his knife, his eyes bleary and strained. Renn padded along the perimeter of the camp, searching the trees. The other Wildermen on guard were also relieved by their comrades, and Paiva's heart surged with relief to know that half the night was already over.

Renn crept back to their fire and threw more wood on it, then stepped over Paiva and lay down along her back. He instantly filled the drafty void, her exposed backside suddenly warmed by his presence, blocking her from the woods. She heard him rustle with his oilskin cloak, closing himself into it like a bat would its leathery wings. When she looked over her shoulder she found his eyes were wide awake, staring into the ceiling of stars through the branches above. His face was awash with weariness and he closed his eyes in resignation.

"Go to sleep," he murmured and rolled to his side to face the creeping shadows. She took another glance through the trees uneasily and laid her head back down, finding that the air was growing chilled and dewy. The sky above remained black; there was no sign of morning blush. Her own weariness made her bones ache and her eyes feel like they were filled with sand. Unhappily she closed them, but she found no sleep waiting for her there. She shivered miserably with cold and her aching fear, and still she found no rest. When she opened her eyes again Yulin sat hunched over the fire, his hands on his knees, staring at the glow of flames with empty eyes as if he were in a trance. He looked empty, far away in another realm where there were no nightmares watching. Slowly she closed her eyes and sought to find some rest.

She bolted upright when Yulin tossed another scrap of wood on the fire, the noise startling her. Yulin did not notice her alarm. He was staring into the woods with his haggard eyes and she swung her gaze to where he looked. There was nothing but creeping shadows — and then, to her alarm, a flash of eyes that appeared momentarily. They blinked, reflecting the firelight back at her, then dissolved into dark and disappeared.

"Renn," she whispered and nudged him. "Renn, there's something in the trees."

"Go to sleep," he murmured, unmoving. The eyes appeared again, flashing at her before they passed through the slash.

"Renn..." she hissed and reached out to grab his shoulder. As she shook him she felt cold seep up her hand. Hastily she drew away from him, looking to Yulin who still stared vacantly into the trees.

"Renn...?" she said again. He sat up silently and swiveled his head to her, and she gasped when she saw his face. He was ghostly pale, his knotted hair stark white, and his eyes an empty black.

"Go to sleep," he said, and smiled.

— «» —

She realized she was dreaming. No sooner had she begun to scream than the vision vanished and her eyes shot open into darkness. Her scream was muffled about her ears, trapped under the fur she slept in. She tore at it and struggled to rise, grappling in the dark to regain her senses.

The camp site spun into view. Yulin was on his feet with his knife in hand and there were hands on her shoulders.

"Paiva, Paiva!" She heard her name and found Renn's face inches from hers. He appeared normal, whole, and as he should. His eyes were fiercely bright staring into hers as he willed her to come to her senses.

"You're alright," he said gently. "You're alright. Hush."

"What is wrong with her?" Yulin asked nervously.

"She was dreaming, that is all," Renn replied. The others lifted their heads to see what the commotion was about, but Yulin was already sitting back down to resume his watch. The others took his gesture to dismiss any further worry. They soon settled back down and resumed their weary slumber.

"It's alright," Renn said as Paiva looked back to him. "It was only a dream."

"You were him," she trembled. "You looked back to me with a white face and black eyes."

Renn withdrew his hold of her and looked to Ulrig, whose speckled eyes were watching sagely from his sleeping spot.

"He is the Lord of Nightmares," Renn said. "Tomorrow I will find you some mountain sage and burn it in the fire. It will keep him from your dreams."

"But you were him."

"I am Renn. Don't let him trick you."

"What do you mean? Is he here? Is he watching?" Paiva exclaimed in horror. Again Renn looked to Ulrig who imperceptibly shook his head. There was much that could be relayed amongst Wildermen with only the slightest of gestures. "No," he said to her. "But you cannot be afraid. You give him power over you when you are afraid."

"But I am afraid," she hissed fiercely. He watched as her wild eyes roved through the trees in panic.

"He's not here," he said again, and laid his strong hands on her arms. "I am here, and I will keep you safe."

His eyes were steady on hers, filled with firelight and promise.

"Alright," she said, swallowing her heart, for it had leapt into her throat. "Alright." She sidled back down into the moss and stared at the stars as her pulse slowly calmed.

He followed suit, resuming his former position curled with his back against her.

"Renn," she whispered.

"Yes?"

"You were right. I would never be able to do this alone."

— «» —

When she woke in the morning the air was freezing, the moss around her covered in heavy drops. Yet somehow, she was warm. There was a spitting rain falling through the trees — more of a mist than an actual rain. She was surprised, for the sky had been so clear last she had glimpsed of it. There was birdsong filling the trees, along with the gentle snores of the sleeping men. All was hushed, peaceful and undisturbed.

She closed her eyes again to savor it, and realized why she was warm. Renn had rolled over in the night and thrown his oilskin over her to share and to keep her from the damp. His arms were crossed and his chin tucked into his chest, and though he did not touch her she became intensely aware of how close he was. She turned her head to study him and found that in sleep his face became soft and vulnerable, its battered edges smoothed with peace, becoming almost boyish again. She could smell the horsemint he chewed in his long breaths and his strange bodily scent of earth and leather. She found herself wondering intensely who he had been before he had come to the woods — what sort of character he had possessed, what he would have been like had his life not been thrown away. She thought sadly to herself, that he would have been too beautiful.

Suddenly the softness of his face hardened and she knew he was surfacing from his faraway dreams. She did not have time to look away before his eyes opened into the morning light and found hers. It was for a breathless moment he stared back at her and the world around her grew even more hushed.

He rolled away to rise and pulled with him his sheltering cloak. She huddled down into her own fur, trying to preserve the last of his warmth, unable to look up and meet the expression she might find on his face. He moved away without a word, moving off to waken the others.

— «» —

Later that morning, Ulrig stood atop the Stone and bellowed on his horn, calling in long winding blasts that echoed through the hills. He waited for long moments, listening for a return call, but nothing came. With a long face he hopped back down from the rock and found his horse, leading the gang off in silence.

By late afternoon they passed a painted fir tree. Its trunk was covered in swirling blue patterns. She looked to Renn for answers.

"We're entering Maggra's woods now," he muttered darkly. Ulrig stopped again to blow on his horn and wait for a return call, but nothing came. There was only the silence of the hills. They moved on, trespassing into the Northwoods.

— ⟨⟩ —

It was by dusk the creature appeared. A shadow flitted through the trees and spooked the horses, causing the men to shout out in alarm and draw their weapons to the ready. Yulin brandished his sword and tried to keep from losing his seat on his horse. Renn had an arrow notched and aimed into the trees before Paiva could blink. A shriek echoed from the trees, a spine-chilling sound, like a woman would make if she had been stabbed through the heart. It sounded again, closer, louder. The horses began to prance. Jakbur lifted his head and snapped the tether that connected him to Runa. Paiva lunged for his reins and his mane, trying to keep him still and herself from being thrown. Yulin pressed his horse forward and she remained trapped in-between him and Renn, guarded from both sides.

Then a shape appeared before Ulrig at the lead of the group. A shadow that lifted from the trees — a twisted, bearded face with a maw that opened wide and uttered a low, pained moan. It stared at them with gaping, sightless eyes and in them was the shadow of every primal evil known to man. It pulled back its lips in a rictus snarl, its furred body coiling as it drew itself into a crouch.

"It's wounded," Ulrig called, and Paiva saw broken arrow shafts protruding from its back. "Turn back, it's not after us."

An arrow hissed out of the trees, thudding into the creature's back before anyone could react. Then the trees were moving and horses were thundering towards the Wildermen, arrows and spears were flying through the air. Ulrig was knocked off his horse as the Folka lunged passed him, fleeing for escape from the slicing arrows. Renn let loose his own arrow, hearing the satisfying sound of it piercing hide.

Riders flew out of the woods, swarming the Wildermen. Yulin looked around in shock and grabbed hold of Jakbur's broken tether to keep the horse from bolting under the onslaught of commotion. Renn had another arrow notched and aimed; the others of the gang were in a similar struggle of trying to keep their horses reined and their weapons drawn.

The Folka fell, crashing into the trees, so filled with arrows and broken spears there was no more room to stick any. The riders halted their horses and circled the dying beast, then a man dressed in painted animal skins hopped from his horse and wielded a stone axe which he used to sever the creatures head. When the kill was done and the creature's body twitched with dying nerves, the man in the painted furs strode towards them. As he came closer Paiva saw his skin was also painted in swirling, intricate patterns of a dark blue dye. His face was haggard and heavily scarred, an upper lip half torn away revealing part of a row of hooked teeth. He was hairless, his scalp bald and his face beardless, as all the others around him were. He came to a halt before them and leaned on the handle of his bloodied stone axe. There was at least a score of riders dressed similar to this man, closing in around the group of defensive, bristling Far Reach Wildermen.

She thought this man most definitely was the Mad Maggra that they had to surpass and swallowed an icy lump of fear. He did not look like a man that could be easily pleased, nor did he look like he would barter.

Ulrig came forwards then, hands upraised in a signal of peace, giving the man a quick nodding bow. Paiva could see the painted man's eyes snap over Ulrig, assessing him, judging him.

"We're here to speak with Maggra," Ulrig said. "I have brought gifts."

"What do you want from Maggra?" the painted man asked in a deep voice. Paiva was surprised that this man was not in fact the infamous leader. The man's eyes snapped up to the packhorse laden with Ulrig's gifts, then over the rest of the gang and stopped on her. His eyes were unreadable, the same dark blue of the ink swirling across his cheeks and nose.

"Have you come to trade her?" he asked. She could not tell from the hardness of his voice if he was angry or contented.

"No, no," Ulrig spluttered. "Not exactly. It is important. It is most urgent I speak with Maggra. We are on a pilgrimage."

The painted man's piercing eyes did not leave Paiva. Only when Renn urged his horse forward to block his view did he return his attention to Ulrig.

"A pilgrimage?" the man smiled, his mouth twisting grotesquely. "Follow closely."

Ulrig ran back to his horse and ordered for the gang to lay down their weapons. With some residual resentment, they all did as they were asked.

"Mad badgers," she heard Jerrik mutter as the painted riders made quick work of cleaving apart the Folka creature. They pulled it apart like ants would a dead insect. The painted man grabbed the head by a tusked tooth and swung up on his horse. Holding the head in his hand as it dripped blood down his leg and his horse's belly, he trotted ahead of the Far Reach Wilderman and led the way through the woods without a word.

Paiva watched with a mixture of disgust and awe as the other riders picked up their own respective pieces of the kill and followed the painted man into the trees. Ulrig started the procession after them, casting a pale glance over his shoulder to his men. Even Ennig looked taken aback, his eyes unsettled and nervous. Ginver was shaking uncontrollably and looked as if he was about to be sick, and Jerrik threw hateful, mistrustful glances at the painted riders. Yulin held a mixture of disgust and disbelief in his own eyes, and though his sword was sheathed he kept his hand over its pommel in a tight grip.

She heard Renn sigh dejectedly and she turned to look at him. He gave her a withering stare.

"I am really not going to enjoy this at all," he said.

— «» —

They travelled well into the dark before they reached the Northwoods camp. Flickering lights appeared through the trees and Paiva caught the smell of woodsmoke and roasting meats. As they drew nearer she saw figures move through the lights, heard muffled voices. She noticed the trees were painted, their trunks swirling with intricate designs. In their branches were hung bones and antlers that rattled together when the limbs moved.

They followed the painted man into the camp which consisted of wattle huts woven into the trees. There were fires smoldering before almost every hut, men hunched over them with dark faces in the smoke, eating the meat off of dripping bones and sucking the marrow from them. There was a fowl stench masked beneath the woodsmoke of bodily decay and waste. The tableau reminded Paiva vaguely of Mummers-eve, for the men appeared deformed under their painted, naked faces with their bodies covered in furs.

The painted riders drew their horses to a halt in front of a hut and Paiva gaped at it, for it was woven more of bones and antlers than wood. The painted man slipped off his horse and pushed aside a flap of stitched leather that served to protect the doorway. It, too, was stained with the peculiar, swirling patterns. He disappeared inside the hut with his Folka head while the Far Reach gang dismounted and peered cautiously about the camp. It had fallen silent, predatory eyes watched them through smoky fires.

The painted man reappeared again, his hands glistening darkly from the Folka blood.

"Bring the girl," he said to Ulrig, then returned inside the hut. Paiva looked fearfully towards Ulrig who motioned for her to come forwards. Renn lifted his hood over his eyes and followed her without invitation.

The hut was lit with the low light of small lamps burning fat that smelled strongly of something animal. A fire burned low in a crude stone hearth. There were animal skins covering the floor in a carpet, while carved bones and antlers and dried bird wings hung from the ceiling and wall. There were chairs and a bed like a bird's nest, a round frame woven from saplings and filled with furs. Her eyes snapped up to a figure standing over a wooden table on which bled the freshly killed Folka head. The painted man stood off in a shadowy corner and she felt his eyes burn into her.

The figure at the table wore a crown of spiked antlers, its shoulders covered in a thick fur pelt. When it raised its head to peer at them Paiva blinked. She looked up to meet the eyes that stared at her from a hairless face obscured with spirals and intricate patterns. It was a woman.

She was perhaps Paiva's mother's age, her face wide and deep with strength. Her dark eyes dropped from Paiva's stare down to the Folka head, and she reached out a thick hand riddled with sinew and veins to touch it. Gently, she pressed her hands over its eyes and closed them.

"Maggra," Ulrig said. "Good... good to see you again."

She said nothing and raised her eyes to him, then they raked over Renn and landed again on Paiva. Paiva could not quite understand her look. Her eyes were sunk deep in her head above vaulted cheekbones, and the feeling they gave her was raw and cold. There was a ruthlessness in them, a subdued savagery, a hidden, dangerous rage.

"What do you want, Tinker?" she asked, her voice deep and earthy.

"We are on a strange pilgrimage. We come to ask your permission to cross your lands into the Vale of the Spirits, and to ask for your help."

"The Vale? It is across the Highpeaks, it is beyond the reach of men."

"That is only a fable," Ulrig waved dismissively. "The Vale can be crossed, of course it can."

"And how should you return?" she asked decisively, her eyes skirting back to Paiva. A tendril of oily smoke curled past Maggra's face as she stared at Paiva and for a minute it appeared her inked skin was more a part of the air than her body.

"You are no pilgrim," she smiled with yellow teeth, and Paiva knew she was being coy. "There are only two reasons to be mad enough to cross into the Vale. The first is that you are a pilgrim, but there have been no pilgrimages to Morinvere since the Wildermen were thrown out here. The second is that you are after the pilgrims' treasures, left there long ago. But you do not have the air of greed about you. I feel your desperation, but it is not greed that has brought you here."

Ulrig looked from Maggra to Paiva nervously and realized he and Renn were not of obvious interest to her. Ulrig looked about to intercede, but a look from Maggra's painted man silenced him.

"I am not a pilgrim, nor have I ever heard of pilgrim treasure," Paiva said quietly.

"Who are you then? What madness has brought you out here? Why do the Folka gather behind you?" Maggra asked, stepping closer.

Renn stepped closer to Paiva; she could feel him bristling.

"My father has been driven into the Vale by the Folka," Paiva said firmly. "I want to bring him back. Along with the others."

"The others?" Maggra's eyes widened almost imperceptibly. "Who is this man you call a father?" she asked, her voice deepening.

"The Wolf," Ulrig said.

Maggra blinked. Renn stiffened. Ulrig picked at his beard.

"Hope," she breathed, and then Paiva saw a glimmer of savage anger well deep in her eyes. "Where have you been?"

Paiva blinked up at her, not understanding.

"My mother spoke of you. She said Hope would save us from here. Have Hope, keep Hope, hold it fast. But you never came for us, you never saved us, and I became... this. I was as beautiful as you once, I was just as pure." A tremor ran through her jaw. A look of self-disgust entered those deep eyes and mixed with her anger.

"I'm... I'm sorry," Paiva said helplessly.

Maggra's lips trembled with rage, her eyes burning with self-hate. Her hand suddenly flew out and the Folka head went flying into the fire where it hissed and bubbled in the heat.

"Where have you been?!" Maggra roared. "You are too late!" She stormed towards Paiva, pinning her with her fiery gaze.

Renn quickly stepped in front of Paiva and Maggra came to a grinding halt inches from his face. Her nostrils flared and she breathed hard.

"You dare stand in my way?" she breathed. "Let me see her, or I shall maim you beyond repair."

Paiva touched Renn's arm, imploring him to obey. He stood fast, so Paiva crept around and stood before him, shielding him with her small body and facing Maggra who stared at her with her deep, tortured eyes.

Paiva could think of nothing else to do but to reach and close her hand over those eyes, to block out what she saw as if she could somehow diminish it. Just like Maggra had done to the Folka head. She could feel the tremors of anger beneath her hand still and gently she pushed her eyes closed.

"I'm sorry," Paiva said. "I am here now."

Ulrig and Renn watched the exchange with wide eyes, hardly daring to breathe. From beneath Paiva's little hand Maggra's tears spilled, hot as the anger that ate at her soul.

"My father is trapped in the Vale of the spirits," Paiva said. "Trapped there by Folka. I need to set him free."

Paiva lowered her hands and stared into this woman's face. For a long moment she was quiet, her eyes remaining closed, her nostrils flaring. Then Paiva saw the intricate designs appear on her face as she smiled. Paiva touched a finger to a wolf where it was drawn, its shape folded into the swirls and contours of ink lines on Maggra's cheek. Maggra's eyes opened and returned her gaze. She reached and ran a strand of Paiva's hair between her dyed fingertips.

"There is no greater treasure," she whispered, "than a pure heart and a clean conscience."

"Please let me cross," Paiva said. "I need to find my father."

She nodded her head sagely. "Can they forgive a creature like me? Can they truly banish pain? Can they return to me the name my Mother gave me?"

"The good spirits? I hope so. I hope they can right all wrongs."

"Then I shall help you." Her eyes turned from the fire and bore into Paiva's. "I shall cut off Varloga's head myself."

— «» —

Maggra led Paiva to an empty hut wherein she found one of those rounded, bird's nest beds filled with furs. Renn followed, as the painted man followed Maggra. Maggra set a small lamp from the ceiling to cast light about the hut, then she peered warily at Renn.

"Are you her guardian?" she asked.

"Yes," Paiva said before Renn could answer. She did not want to be left alone in this camp.

"Rest then. In the morning we shall talk, for you must be weary and frightened."

"Thank you Maggra."

When Maggra and her painted man left, Paiva sat heavily on the bed and breathed out a deep sigh of relief.

"That was very, very frightening," she said. Renn said nothing, but she heard him also release a low breath. The rest of the gang were sleeping out with the horses in the trees, rather happy to keep their distance from Maggra's men.

"I don't understand," she said. "How is there a woman leading a gang of Wildermen?"

"I think she might be more of an animal than a woman," Renn said. "I told you once how there were some Wildermen who steal women away to the mountains. The story I know is that Maggra's mother was one of those women. Maggra grew up in the wild of Grimenna. She became stronger, crueler, and smarter than the men around her and therefore their leader. They learned not to touch her, because she could invoke curses on their heads."

"It's sad, her eyes are so... sad."

"They call her the queen of the damned," Renn almost whispered. "She's not sad, she's mad. She is rage, she is anger, wrapped in painted skin and fur."

"Anger is a dark humor," Paiva whispered back. "She knows you. You two are familiar, aren't you?"

"Ah," he sighed. "I am a murderer after all. I flitted through here some years ago trying to find a place for myself in the woods. Maggra offered me sanctuary and for a while I stayed. She would not paint me, so I left."

"Why?" she asked.

"Because when you come to Maggra it is because you know you will never be pardoned and you surrender your cause of ever returning to the lowlands. When she paints you it is a symbol of just that, a symbol that you are truly damned and belong to the woods forever." She saw him thumb his scar unconsciously, his eyes growing stern at the thought.

"She wouldn't paint you?" Paiva asked. "She wouldn't damn you?"

This caused him to sigh. "No, she sent me away."

"Why?"

"Well," he said. "It seems even the worst wretches believe in something good. This is where the darkest, most unloved, most hated men gather in the woods and still... the Old Stories are remembered. Maggra, of all people, believes in you. And she must have believed in me as well." He began to rummage through the furs, his face hard and angular in the low light.

"What if I'm making a horrible mistake? What if I'm leading you all to your deaths?" She looked to a patch of stars from a small window that blew in the night air and the smell of smoke.

"All men die, Paiva," he said. "Whether it's now or later. All these men lead damned lives, lives not even worth living. But you have given them something worth dying for."

"But I couldn't bear the guilt, I couldn't."

"You don't have to. It's not you who promised them Varloga's head. I did. You were simply..." he waved his hand dismissively. "The inspiration."

"Renn, that's not true. I convinced you. You can't forever carry all the world's blame on your shoulders."

"Let me rephrase. It's not that you gave them something worth dying for; you gave them something to live for. You are just trying to do something good, and if we should perish it is because I chose to believe that. You cannot be blamed."

He found a fur and threw it down at the door, then peered about the camp. The Far Reach gang gathered in trees across from the hut, warming themselves over a smoky fire and tending to the horses.

"I don't want you to die," she echoed, feeling her chest grow tight.

"I don't want you to die either," he returned insolently.

She laughed, a broken little laugh that stung her eyes with tears. She lay back into the nest with exhaustion and stared out to the little patch of stars while he slumped down to the ground wearily, guarding the door. Her mind spun to her life before all of this had started, to her quiet little village with friendly faces where everything had been safe and familiar. She remembered when the worst feeling in the world had been when she had discovered that Ramsi Lier, who turned out to be all pride and bluster, had no real interest in her.

She had said Ramsi was the most beautiful man she had ever seen. What did she know of beauty then? She had not known the true majesty of the Forest, or that a Wilderman could have more honor then a ranger, or that shadows were made from light. Even in the darkest part of the woods the unforgivable and the unloved still sought to keep light in a world that had thrown them away.

She realized in that moment that what the Strix had said of how it was light that shaped shadows, the opposite was also true. Renn had been thrown into the shadows, and beneath the grime and dirt of shame and guilt, a bright and steady light had been forged.

Renn rummaged with his sleeping arrangements then strode back to her, fumbling with the lamp above their heads.

"Renn," she said. He lowered the lamp, his face softened in its glow. "You are a beautiful soul." She meant it. He blinked at her in surprise, his eyes searching hers. He frowned, opened his mouth as if to say something, then blew out the lamp and vanished into shadow.

Chapter 16

Maggra sat astride a painted Berg horse the next day and led the full numbers of her gang and Paiva's up the mountain. Scores of painted bodies flanked them through the trees and Paiva felt a surge of confidence that they might have a chance to withstand the Folka. There were other women in Maggra's camp, wives or mothers of her Wildermen who were as lethal and dangerous as their male counterparts. She noticed that there were many men who did not carry brands, and she learned that many were born in the forest as Maggra was. Maggra allowed many transparencies within her gang, but she did not allow for women to be stolen. The women that were there came willingly, some rescued from the pit, some the great, great granddaughters of the first people who had not been swallowed by the forest when the Folka rose.

Some joined them in their march towards the Highpeaks, others that were unable to stayed behind to pray. Maggra was resolute and firm with her men, forcing them onwards and upwards for days and for nights until they stood at the top of the Highpeaks on their tired horses and were looking into the valley below.

Ulrig, alongside Paiva, Renn, and Yulin, stared across the expanse with weepy eyes. "It is beautiful," he said, and noted the gleam of streams meandering through the rich green valley floor below. "How could men have forgotten it? How could men have turned away from such beauty? How could he forget how small his life was?"

Yulin seemed in awe of its enormity, and Renn was quiet, his silver eyes gleaming fiercely as they took in the breadth of the view.

"Where is it?" Paiva asked anxiously, "Where is the Vale of the Spirits?"

"We follow the streams to their source, that is where the Vale lies," Maggra answered in her deep tones. "But we cross into another realm now, one that men were driven from long ago. Men may die now."

"I'm sorry," she said. "I don't want anyone to die."

"If it is as you say, to free the beings born of our Good Humors — beings that can bring us peace, and love, and happiness; beings that could have saved lives like mine — it is worth every sacrifice. The world cannot stand the way it does. I will not allow it. I will find my peace down there."

Then she turned away and joined her men in preparing for the coming night. Paiva returned to the Far Reach men who were stirring up a fire and setting down blankets and furs to sleep on. The sun was dipping below the horizon on the west, bleeding the sky red.

They ate from their rations as the stars soaked through the sky and the waning, crescent moon began its celestial rise through the heavens. All about the men were hushed and quiet, staring down into the valley below with the feeling men get when they are staring into the uncertainty of their own fate.

— 《 》 —

Paiva rose then and went to find Renn on his ledge, where he sat whittling a stick with his knife. He did not notice her intrusion; he did not lift his head to her as she came and sat next to him and curled her legs to her chin. She swept her eyes out over the twilit valley and her fear returned, knotting her stomach with dread. Almost instinctively she reached for him, looping her hand through his arm.

He started at her touch and drew his arm away as if she had scalded him. "I'm sorry," she said, startled. He resumed whittling silently as the sun began to sink behind the mountain. She studied him for a long moment, more interested at his concealed thoughts then the mysteries of the valley below.

"Is there someone waiting for you on the other side?" she asked suddenly, her mind racing to Jekka. If there was a woman on earth that could have somehow won Renn's affections surely it would have been her. Tall and quietly beautiful, and a wayward wanderer as Ulrig had said, who had frequented Far Reach over the years. Perhaps she was waiting for him. Perhaps there was an unspoken love between them he secreted away like everything else.

"On the other side of the Panderbank?" he asked. "No, there is no one."

"Why are you so guarded with me then?"

"You're a woman, Paiva. Forgive me if I'm a little unused to your sentimentality."

"It's not just that," she said. He sighed wearily.

"Everything I touch turns to ash," he said and threw his whittling over the ledge.

"Renn. My life, both our lives, have already turned to ash. Right now you are the only thing keeping me from blowing away."

"I am a felon," he said. "I hurt people. I am a murderer of brothers, of Folka, of fellow Wildermen. Black as my dirty hands, my dirty hair, and my dirty heart." He opened his palm upwards to reveal the scarring that marked him so.

"I would wear it for you if I could," she said. "I can't imagine the weight of it, or the seven years it has stolen from you."

His lips twitched at a smile.

"I'd never let you," he said. There was a tenderness in his voice that made her dare to reach out again. Gently she pressed her fingertips to the brand, tracing its deformity. She felt somehow this was the most personal of gestures, that touching this hateful mark was somehow touching his guarded heart. It made her own heart skip and she looked up to find his ghostly eyes on hers. They looked at her almost helplessly, plying her for distance and yet somehow drawing her in. She realized what it was then.

"You're afraid," she said in revelation.

"Terrified," he whispered. Then his eyes dropped to her mouth and his face came unbearably close to hers. She could feel the heat rising between them, mingling on their breaths.

"Renn," a voice from above the ledge shouted. Hastily he sobered and drew away, looking to find Ulrig peering down at them.

"Renn, they found tracks."

"I'm coming," he said. Ulrig frowned at them, then hobbled away.

"I'm sorry," Renn said and stared out over the darkening valley.

"It's too strong, whatever this is," she said. He nodded and looked away.

"That is what I was afraid of."

—— «» ——

"They're here," Ulrig said as he stared into the dark trees, lifting a torch higher into the air to cast flickering light into them. At his feet were a myriad of tracks in the loam, trailing the edges of their camp, littering the mountain top. Maggra stood off to one side with her painted man, watching Ulrig, Renn, and Paiva. Her face was a mask, her eyes calculating. Renn studied the tracks, following them out into the trees, his bow in hand.

"What do you think?" Maggra called. Renn lifted his eyes and peered into the trees, and for a long moment all the world was silent. Suddenly a set of eyes reflected back at him, blinking into existence. They watched him for a moment as the hair on Paiva's nape rose.

Renn cocked his head curiously, trying to make out the form the eyes belonged to. Then in an instant he had an arrow notched and he fired it into the trees in one swift motion.

The eyes vanished without a sound. Maggra chuckled darkly.

"They're herding us," Renn said.

"Yes," Maggra answered.

"What does that mean?" Ulrig swung his head to Maggra, and for the first time Paiva noted fear glowing in his speckled eyes.

"It means we will all be culled if we turn back," she said. "It means they want us to go to the Vale."

"They anticipate us..." Ulrig said. "That means Varloga is expecting us. What do you make of that?"

"It means we've made a mistake," Renn replied, and his eyes turned to Paiva worriedly. "It means we've fallen into his trap. Perhaps we've made things far easier for him than we expected. Perhaps this is what he wanted all along."

Paiva felt her stomach knot with dread and with guilt. Ulrig looked to Maggra again who smiled coldly.

"I told you," she said. "No man returns from the Highpeaks."

"Best we continue forwards then, and hope for a miracle in the Vale," Ulrig muttered. Renn had another arrow notched and was aiming it into the trees. He picked out a shadow and let his arrow fly. It connected with something, for an eldritch shriek rang out and branches snapped. Then there was a steady silence wherein both Renn and the painted man reached for their blades. Nothing materialized out of the woods, nothing moved.

"We go to the Vale," Maggra said, "and hope our Virtue can summon the good spirits to save us." Then she turned her back on the woods and went back to the camp, her painted man silently following. Renn looked back to Ulrig questioningly, who nodded his agreement.

"I'm so sorry," Paiva whispered. Ulrig lowered his torch and looked at her, reaching out a boney hand to clasp to her shoulder.

"Don't give up yet," he said. "We could not have hoped to get through these woods without being noticed. My only true hope is that the Old Ones are waiting for us still, waiting for us to bring them back to the world."

"What if they're not?" Renn asked. "What if there are only ghosts down there?"

"Spirits are eternal," Ulrig muttered. "They do not cease to exist just because we have shunned them. They are waiting, they are not vanished. They could be awakened by one small believer." His voice was so strong with belief that it sent waves of comfort through Paiva. He smiled at her kindly, then pinched her cheek.

"Come, back to the warmth of our fire. In the morning we shall find your father and right this mess."

— «» —

The Far Reach gang slept in a close circle about their fire, keeping a safe distance from the Painted men. Renn lay as usual — by her side staring up at the twinkling stars, his eyes far away and lost in the heavens. Paiva followed his gaze into the wide scope of the sky and for long moments the rest of the world was blotted out, swallowed by the quiet moment they shared. She began to feel the sense of being lost again. Her presence and her purpose drifting away and fraying, becoming meaningless.

"What do you see up there?" he murmured.

"Maps... fate... time. You?"

"I wonder if the stars are watching us back," he answered. "You know the phrase — 'by all the shining stars.' We use it as if they were responsible for us somehow. As if we call on them to be our witness. Can stars avenge a broken oath?"

"I suppose they can. If they are the weavers of fate, the givers of direction and time. Who better to judge us and avenge us than them up there on their perfect perches?"

Perhaps Renn felt the same, for he reached down and curled his fingers over hers. "By all the shining stars," he murmured. "I will not let you blow away."

The warmth of him seeped into her. Tethered together, they both stared up into the gaping heavens until she could not bear the unknown depths into which she gazed any longer. She found comfort in Renn instead, who pulled her into the warmth of his chest and sheltered her from the cold stare of the stars.

— «» —

Maggra lead them into the valley, her painted man at her side, both wielding stone axes and wooden shields. The procession of men that followed her was quiet and subdued, their eyes darting nervously into the greenery about them. For hours they had pressed hard, following the streams until they narrowed into little burbling veins, bleeding from one mysterious source. That was when Maggra stopped and looked back to Paiva.

"This is the beginning of the Vale," she said. "This is where men do not dare to go."

Paiva nodded and swallowed her fear.

The woods were astoundingly peaceful, too serene, too beautiful to contain any nightmares. But she was not deceived. No sooner had the troop begun its procession up the stream than the trees began to stir and noises rose in low howls and blood-curdling shrieks. Shadows swarmed towards them, thickening into the shapes of dark beasts. Black, sightless eyes filled with nightmares gaped at them from beneath the bend of branch and root.

Maggra set her jaw and readied her axe. They came from behind and they came from the front, surrounding the party on all sides.

"We break through," Maggra said. "We cleave our way." She summoned all her rage then, as though it was all the rage and the hurt she had ever known in her life, and roared into the trees.

Her horse leapt into the midst of the shadow creatures, met with the snapping and tearing of maws filled with tusks and fangs. She appeared undaunted, for she had drank from the blood and eaten the very flesh of nightmares and in turn echoed their own horror back to them. She pressed forwards until the disfigured creatures gathered and formed so thick a wall in front of her they were not passable. They stared at her with their unblinking eyes, making Paiva's heart shrink with fear.

Maggra was not daunted. She rallied her men with another cry and raised her axe, her cry so deep and loud with rage it sent chills through Paiva's already trembling body. They rushed the creatures, charging them with their horses and weapons, attempting to clear a path through. Renn, Yulin, and Ulrig formed a circle around Paiva as they moved forward from behind. Paiva trembled at the sounds of men's screams as they were torn from their horses. Blood sprayed the air; riderless horses bolted away from the battle. Folka howled and writhed as they were struck with arrows and lances and cleaved with axes and swords. Ennig flew into the fray and disappeared with a roar while the others of the gang stayed close to Ulrig.

Suddenly the creatures broke through Maggra's men and fell on the Far Reach gang. Ginver was struck down from his horse and his melodious voice broke into a horrified shriek before he landed on the ground and disappeared beneath a mass of swarming bodies. Ulrig, Yulin, Renn were all moving about her. Swords ripped through flesh and shattering claws. She was flung from her horse and landed hard on the ground, the wind nearly knocked from her chest. As she lifted her head, she came eye-level with a black face with disfigured, twisted features — half-man and half-beast. She could not help but to look up into its eyes wherein she saw all her fears reflected back at her. She gasped, but the creature did not approach her. It emitted a rattling growl from deep within its chest, then moved away, onto the next man.

She glimpsed Renn charging after her but a Folka beast intercepted him, knocking him to the ground beneath its weight. She screamed as she saw him fall, calling out his name.

"Stop!" she roared, realization suddenly dawning on her. Her voice was drowned out in the melee. She staggered to her feet and felt the bristling spines of a Folka brush past her as it lunged towards another man. He made one swipe with a spear before he disappeared with a gurgling cry beneath the creature.

"STOP!" she screamed. Renn reappeared, struggling towards her. Ulrig somehow surfaced behind him, staring at her with horror filled eyes.

"Renn! Stop! Relent! They will let me pass!" Paiva screamed to him as hot tears burned down her face. Renn slashed into a beast's face that snapped close to his. He met her eye and took a step back, seeing that she was surrounded by Folka yet none dared touch her.

"Stop, Renn! They will let me pass. You needn't fight them!" she screamed to him as the Folka began to circle her like crows, blotting him out from her vision. Renn lowered his blade tensely and stepped back, Ulrig bellowed the order at the top of his lungs.

"Stand down!" he roared. "Stand down!"

Soon the sound of battle quieted. The Wildermen gathered together and bristled their weapons towards the Folka that circled them guardedly. Paiva looked to Renn one last time.

"I'm sorry," she said. "I should not have brought you all here."

"Go!" Ulrig shouted. "Find Morinvere. Find your father, wake the old ones! Go now! Before it is too late."

Paiva looked to Renn over the swarming bodies between them, his face twisted with panic. His eyes on hers were filled with desperation.

She nodded and turned away without a word. He started after her, but a Folka stepped towards him and drove him back with a rippling snarl. She disappeared from his sight in seconds, heading into the trees, herded by the Folka.

— «» —

"This isn't right," Renn hissed to Ulrig. "We're going to lose her."

"Have hope," Ulrig muttered desperately.

"Don't be a fool," Renn snarled. "They are driving her there just as they drove Viviel. She won't come back."

"Don't," Ulrig warned as he saw Renn's grip tighten on his sword. "Even you can't cut through them."

"She won't come back," Renn said with conviction. "I won't stand to lose her." He lunged into the black bodies before him, ripping and cleaving his way. He ducked and leapt and thwarted them with daring agility as Ulrig cried out after him. He broke into a run and plowed through them.

Ulrig roared in warning, but it was too late — a Folka leapt upon him and tumbled him to the ground where he disappeared beneath the slithering bodies.

"RENNIK!" Ulrig screamed, but all he saw was black.

Chapter 17

Babbling through the mossy roots woven across the forest floor were the seams of water that flowed from a crumbling shape shadowed beneath the twisted branches of trees. There was a tower, its ramparts rotten and decayed with its battle against time and the elements. Crumbling walls with foundations undermined by the upheaval of roots stood unsteadily, surrendering their might to the trees that invaded them. It was nothing more than ruins, standing as a tomblike testament to man's struggles in the Forest.

Paiva felt a deep sense of foreboding as she gazed on it. It was Morinvere, swallowed by the Forest.

Unable to look away, she stepped towards it, the Folka slithering and hissing at her heels, urging her forward — herding her, driving her. The image of her father's face burst into her mind and she broke into a run, calling out his name in a panic. All other thoughts fled from her; the only one that remained was to find her father — the spirit, the Incarnate, that could repair the damage she had done.

She staggered into the ruins through a crumbled arch, tripping on the mass of roots and flowering thickets that grew abundantly over the floor. The Folka watched her enter with their deep, malevolent gazes and then turned away and flitted into the trees where they disappeared.

Paiva found herself inside the structure and peered around. The tower loomed above her, its stones shifted and cracked from the invasion of vines and time. Four crumbling walls contained only a wild garden of vegetation. It must have been a shrine or a church of some kind, for there were carved stone pillars that rose up from the ground and stood, bearing only the weight of the open sky. All was strangled with snaking vines, some pillars fallen and cracked into shards from which grew all things green and flowering.

In the middle of this enclosure, glimmering like a mirror, was a pool into which sprays of roots and flowers were growing. From the pool bled the rivulets of water Paiva had followed, and above it, on a fallen pillar, sat a figure. His clothes were dirty rags, his beard mossy and tangled with leaves and flowers.

He sat watching her quietly, his face empty of emotion except for the intensity of his eyes — which were golden.

"Father?' Paiva breathed.

He stared at her for a long, hard moment before his eyes clouded over with tears. He dropped his face into his hands and wept.

She ran to him and threw her arms around his neck, holding him close to her heart. "Thank the stars I've found you."

He murmured something and she pulled away, taking a step back to peer into his face. It seemed strange to her now, almost unfamiliar. His eyes had a haunted look. She had never before seen him so distraught. "Father," she shook him gently. "Father, are you well?"

Tears whelmed in his eyes again and he blinked them away. "I was wrong," he said, his voice hoarse. "There are no good spirits left in the world."

Paiva swallowed hard. "What?"

Again the tears came and he dropped his head towards the pool. "This is the Conjuring Pool," he said. "This is why Morinvere was built. It is only filled with water, but water is the lifeblood of the Forest. Look into it and tell me what you see."

Paiva peered over the edge and through the reflection held in perfect stillness she saw that the water was a clear turquoise. There was no bottom; it disappeared into a deep chasm that seemed to run to the depths of the earth. Peering into it made her feel afraid. It made her feel as if she were looking into the eye of a strange god, a strange creator.

"It's deep," she said with a chill.

"It is a womb."

She looked back to him, and he stared down into its depths like there was another world beyond it. "This is where spirits are born," he said, "and this is where they come to die."

"What do you mean? Spirits are eternal, like a man's soul!" she exclaimed.

"The water is strange here. Nothing floats in it. If a man were to fall in he would sink to the bottom of the earth — as a spirit would when it wants to die, when it wants to leave this world because it has lost its purpose." He picked a blossoming flower and held it in the water. When he released it, it spun and sank as if it were a stone. She watched it fade away and disappear, spiraling downwards into darkness.

"Only dreams float in these waters. Dreams and prayers and thoughts," her father said. "I was born here. Risen from the bottom of creation, conjured by the dreams of men, as all the others were. My soul bled from these waters and took shape in the moss and root. I believed I would find the others here waiting. I believed I could have found a way to bring them back to the world of men, but I found instead that this place was empty. The spirits must have starved, they must have tried to drink the dreams of these waters and drowned. I cannot believe they would willingly leave... I cannot."

Paiva drew in a sharp breath and stared into the pool with horror. She felt the beginnings of a great and terrible despair begin to wash over her, registering a horrible thought. She had walked into a trap; her hope had led her astray. Somewhere on the other side of those trees were the Wildermen, some wounded and dead, and others that would wait for her. The Folka would not let her return.

Renn was on the other side, and she would never see him again.

"The good spirits are gone?" she whispered. Viviel nodded despairingly, tired and weak and worn. She realized he was grieving, and she felt his sadness like it was her own. It was a soul-breaking, anguishing sadness. She did not know how she could undo it.

"They are gone forever. There is no way to bring them back," he whispered.

"What is at the bottom of it?" she asked.

"The flux of life itself. The longer I stare into it the more I want to return to it, to the deep of life, where I can be absorbed back into the great mother and maybe be given life anew as something else. I do not know. But I do know when I look into these waters I see only peace. There is no pain down there, no hurt, no happiness, no hunger; only peace."

"Don't go. You can't go. You can't leave me. I have come all this way. I have brought death on the heads of many men to find you. Do something, please. Father... please."

He smiled so warmly it brought tears to her eyes.

"Nobody believes in me anymore," he said. "Even I don't."

"I believe in you."

"I can't fight them, those creatures out there. Those nightmares.... I haven't the strength. Not on my own. There are too many."

"Please... there must be a way. For me, for Mother..."

He shook his head and tears spilled anew down his haggard face.

"I give up," he whispered. "I have lost myself."

"But listen," she begged. "Out there in the trees are men being bloodied by nightmares. They each came here with prayers in their hearts, with hope in their hearts. Surely you can hear them calling for you?"

He shook his head again. "I don't want to hear them," he sobbed. "I don't want to hear their souls break when they realize I have failed them."

A noise made her lift her head and she gasped as a dark shape came stumbling into the wild garden. Viviel lifted his head in turn, his eyes shining with the sadness of all the world.

"Renn?!" she cried as he staggered in. His clothes were ripped to shreds and there was blood seeping from his chest, his arms, sprayed across his face. The sword he held was dripping darkly. His eyes flicked up to her and he sagged in relief.

She ran to him and clasped his face between her hands, staring wildly into his haunted eyes. He closed them and shook his head, dispelling the shadows from them. When he opened them again his eyes calmed and searched hers, assessing her, wondering at the sadness that welled in her face.

"You're safe," he said.

"You shouldn't have come," Paiva said, her voice breaking.

"Probably not," he said wincingly, and folded his own hand over hers where it clasped his face. "What is wrong?" he asked. "What can I do?"

She pulled away from him, and looked towards the pool. Her father watched them for a moment, then dropped his eyes again to the mirror shined waters, to the barren womb.

"I was wrong," she said. "I am so... sorry."

"What do you mean?"

"There are no spirits here," she breathed. "There is no one to save us. I've led you to your doom." Then a sickening knot formed in her stomach and tears spilled from her eyes.

Renn looked about the garden, to Viviel, and then back to Paiva. "Where did they all go?" he asked.

She told him of the pool, unable to keep the anguish from her voice.

"I'm sorry," she said. "You will die here, and you will die if you try to leave. Forgive me."

For some reason, he laughed. She looked up to him with wide, bewildered eyes.

"I already knew that coming here," he replied and curled his hand about her neck, he bent his forehead to hers. "There is nothing to forgive."

All she could do was to whimper his name again, her heart breaking as she realized what he said. He had not ever meant to come back from Morinvere; he had not ever meant to find a pardon. Now he never would. He had followed her for something other than her pointless hope.

"Why did you come with me then?" she sobbed. "Why would you follow me?"

"To keep you safe."

— «» —

Suddenly a shadow fell over them. Renn lifted his head upwards and saw two shapes descend from the heavens, gliding through the trees on the spans of pale wings. Viviel rose in alarm, watching with a stricken face as the shapes landed in the garden with a rustle of feathers and leaves. Renn pushed Paiva behind him and readied his bloodied sword.

There was a white shape and a red shape, changing and morphing, feathers sliding and molting, features twisting and untwisting. Paiva recognized the white shape as its wings folded back and took a more human form. A face appeared, ghoulish and imperfectly human. His white hair tumbled in feathery curls, his eyes black and empty. *Varloga.*

Beside him the red shape parted her wings, and her face changed from something birdlike and grotesque to that of something fair and beautiful. Red hair streamed from her head, pearls glittering in the slanted shafts of moted light. Ceitra stood before them, half-woman, half-bird. Her feathers molted into silk and skin, her claws shrinking into long, delicate fingers. Her eyes, black as death, raked across Paiva and Renn. Then she turned her eyes on Viviel as a smile uncurled on her full red lips.

Paiva stepped away from Renn towards her father, but he raised a hand to halt her. Ceitra laughed, her voice floating through the air like silken feathers. "See what you are?" Ceitra said to Viviel. "I have revealed you at last. You are a naive Hope, you are a false Hope, and an empty promise. For here before me stand your believers who have come to your aid, strung along by the Hope you have promised them, and you cannot save them."

Viviel's golden eyes dimmed.

"You are a murderer," he whispered. "You are beyond saving now."

"I am far from needing salvation," she said. "For every time you fail I gain more believers. Every thought that strays from you I claim."

"You have murdered the sacred. What have you become … please, you do not know what you have done," Viviel said.

"It is you who has done this," she sneered. "I remember

a time when it was I who was driven away into the woods, hidden from men and forgotten while you and the good kind did their work in the world. But then you began to fail them, and then they began to forget you. Their thoughts rang out, and their fear and their hate gave me power and drew me back into the world. I evolved. I grew as I tasted their hate — hate which is so easily stirred in the hearts of men. This is my forest now, Viviel. This is my world."

"I will remain," Viviel said adamantly.

"I will banish you at last, Viviel," she said. "It is not you I need. It is the pain of your defiled Virtue that I need, and how wonderful it tastes."

Suddenly Varloga had wings again. He was swooping towards Paiva before she had a chance to even take a step back. His talons outstretched and cinched about her, throwing her into the ground where she gasped with the pain of cracking ribs. Viviel's face went pale with horror.

"Don't," he whispered hoarsely. "Please."

Ceitra dropped her accusing hand and tilted her head back in triumph. "Sink into the pool, Viviel! Be banished forever, or watch your Virtue die."

"Do not harm her!"

"That is up to you to decide. Fie on you for making yourself so weak, for creating something that could destroy you. How long I have been waiting for such a crutch! Go now, Viviel."

"You might be rid of me this way you old harpy — you might think this will undo her and you can harvest the grief from her little soul — but I know she will never be yours." He looked to Paiva, his eyes burning into her. "I know she will not forget the love she was born from."

"Father," Paiva croaked, unable to sound the words to make him stay.

"Hold fast to yourself," he said as he took a step towards the water. "You are my last hope."

Paiva screamed as her father took a stumbling step towards the water. From his golden eyes fell golden tears, staining his cheeks and mossy beard. Her screams only drove him further and he stepped a foot into the silky, green waters. The mirror-shined surface broke into shivering ripples.

"Go on," Ceitra smiled.

"Let my memory be the hope that guides you," he said to his daughter. "Remember me. Don't let the dark humors have you, no matter what she does to you."

In the split moment when Varloga canted his head away to watch Viviel's descent, Renn stepped forward, drawing his blade back to strike. Varloga swung his head towards him and in an instant his face morphed, his features changed. The face that appeared stopped Renn in his tracks.

Odrik blinked at him with black eyes. The heaviness of Renn's sword seemed to drag his arm down. He appeared stricken with horror and guilt, as though it were crushing the inner workings of his heart. Ceitra laughed, her hair blooming red with the force of Renn's terror, with Paiva and Viviel's despair.

"Yes," she said. "Be afraid. For the shadow of the fear you have lived in all these years has been a sweet nectar. I remember the taste of Odrik's fear, I remember the flavor of his own self-hate. How I grieved for it when it was gone."

Odrik smiled, feathers rustling down his winged arms. His face was pale and ghostly and summoned the memory of Renn's brother's lifeless body broken on the earth. Renn was stricken, unable even to breathe.

"Odrik?" he choked.

"No, Renn! It's not Ordik!" Paiva cried to him and then gasped as Varloga's talons clenched her tighter. Ceitra laughed again as Renn struggled within himself.

"Oh, Rennik," she cried in delight, breathing in the rippling current of fear that radiated from him. "You have always been a thorn in my side. I remember the day Varloga possessed your brother in the same way. Muting his memories, binding him with the dark humors. But he died a Virtue. He overcame the shadows in his last moments and ended his life so he could spare yours. I will never forgive you for that. Hate does not ruin men. Love does."

"Renn!" Paiva screamed. Varloga held Renn's gaze and as they stared into each other's souls, Paiva saw the change occur in Renn's eyes. They grew wide and filled with shadows, turning bleak with emptiness. Varloga stepped away from Paiva, releasing her from his clutches as he became transfixed on binding Renn with fear. Paiva rolled away, wincing with the pain of bruised bones.

"Renn..." she sobbed as he fell to his knees, his body collapsing. Varloga's face changed, from Odrik back to the ghoulish creature's. His mouth split open in a glitter of fangs. Renn was blind to him; all he saw was every horrible image of every horrible thing he had done in his life. He saw himself throw his brother with his own hands; he saw Paiva trampled lifeless by the Folka. He saw his fellow Wildermen slain in the greenery. All of it was because of him.

"I've found it," Varloga hissed to his mistress. "I have found the fear to undo him at last."

"Tell me," she begged.

"Helplessness. He fears to be helpless, to be unable to stop wretched things. It was there beneath the cold armor of indifference, all this time."

"Break him," Ceitra purred. "Ruin him or kill him. Be over with it."

"Yesss…" Varloga's smile grew wider as he stepped closer, relishing the unravelling of the soul before him.

Paiva lurched to her feet and threw herself between them, collapsing on Renn with her broken body. She held his head to her heart to blind him from Varloga's dark gaze while the white spirit began to snarl in fury behind her.

Before Varloga could approach her, a shaggy shape leapt into him, knocking him to the ground in a flurry of white feathers. Varloga reared up and snapped his maws at the shape, tearing fur from its neck.

Paiva swung her head back to the pool and found her father missing. Her heart lurched, for the shape attacking Varloga was half-man, half-wolf. A tattered homespun shirt clung to him in shreds, a long tail sweeping behind him. His arms and his legs were elongated, clawed, and covered in fine brown fur. The face atop his wide shoulders was her father's, changed somehow into something feral and strong.

His lips pulled back in a rictus snarl as he lunged at the white spirit. They tore at each other with claws and teeth, feathers ripped, hide and skin severed. Varloga dealt him a sickening blow and he spun away, hitting the ground hard. Paiva stared, wide-eyed, as her father struggled, his head tilting up where she found his bright, golden eyes staring at her desperately. Then he was on his feet again, dodging, lunging, tearing.

Suddenly Paiva felt claws in her hair as Ceitra came up behind her and grabbed a fistful of it and began to pull her towards the pool. She was dragged away from Renn, who remained on his knees staring at her vacantly. She remembered the Spook they had met in the pass, his eyes colorless, cold and lifeless as stone.

"Viviel!" Ceitra shrieked, her face contorting in her rage, trying to draw his attention from mauling Varloga. Viviel hesitated as he heard Paiva's screams. In that moment Varloga struck him down. With a powerful wrench Ceitra hurled Paiva into the pool, holding her from sinking by the length of her hair. Paiva choked on the water that splashed down her throat, sweet and warm and pure. She thrashed and found a braided vine of flowers at the edge of the pool to grasp onto, though she could do little to free herself from Ceitra's grip.

"Viviel," Ceitra hissed and gave Paiva's head a violent shake. "I banish you."

As Paiva struggled, her eyes fell on Renn again. She called out to him, her voice broken.

"Renn..." she choked. "Hold fast to yourself. Remember who you are, remember me." She willed him with all her might to see through the shadows cast upon him. The water spilled from the pool with her thrashing, bleeding into the forest floor.

Renn blinked, her voice breaking through the spell. His eyes cleared, gleaming silver like the reflection of the pool. They settled on Paiva and then slowly trailed up to Ceitra.

Ceitra's dark eyes flashed as she realized too late Renn was upon her, springing up from the ground like a startled bird and diving towards her. He threw his whole body forward before she had time to blink, then she was falling backwards into the pool with Renn on top of her.

Paiva clung to the vine as Ceitra's claws ripped through her hair and only just managed to hold fast and keep from being pulled along. She looked down into the waters, unable to see for the ripples that obscured the surface.

A broken cry rose from her throat as her heart surged with panic. "Renn!" she cried. But he was already disappearing into the void beneath her, sinking into the oblivion below. Paiva watched helplessly as he sank. She realized there were not enough prayers in all the world to save him now.

— «» —

Renn pushed Ceitra away from him and watched her panic through the blur of the water. She thrashed, her red hair streaming like silken ribbons about her horrified face. She fought to swim, clawing madly for the surface, but the water did not support her. Bubbles erupted from her mouth in a drowned scream, but even the bubbles sank with her. She fell still, her eyes opening wide as she became listless, surrendering to her demise. He watched as the red flooded from her hair, watched as the black of her eyes became empty except for the green of the waters about her. It was a slow, painful descent to watch.

He looked beyond her into the womb.

He did not even try to fight the pull of the water, for he knew it was futile. Instead he let his body drift, opening his arms wide to the darkness that would swallow him. As he looked into it, he felt only peace. He would find his absolution; he would find his forgiveness in its immeasurable depth.

He closed his eyes and tasted the sweetness of its waters. In his ears was the sound of his own heart beating. As his thoughts scattered, the only one that remained was how it was a shame he was dirtying this peaceful place.

Suddenly something caught his cloak and held him fast. His descent came to a jarring halt. Petals and feathers brushed past his face as they fell. Ceitra disappeared below, yet he did not follow. His head was forced to look up where, in the blurred halo of light from the surface, he saw a girl clinging to a braided vine of flowers. Her pale hair floated out about her head in shining streams.

He could not at first make sense of her, and a pang of anger flared in him at this person who would take him from his peace. He was wrenched upwards, he felt an arm about his neck, tendrils of hair floating against his face. She struggled to haul him to the surface, fighting the pull of the chasm. He heard her thoughts echo out through the water, felt her anxious hope that the vines would hold fast and she would make it to the surface before she lost her breath.

"Heavy," he heard her voice, "too heavy. Renn, help me, by all the stars help me. I can't do this."

Paiva. Her name jolted him from his daze. He felt the burn in his chest from lack of air and he sprung back to life in a panic. He clambered for hold on the vine, pulling Paiva into his chest where she clung about his neck as he hauled them upwards.

Her thoughts echoed out and floated about him in the dream waters and he wondered if she could hear his own. "I will not let you go," he heard; "I will not lose you." She wrapped her arms tighter about his neck and pressed her face against the wall of his chest. Seconds later his hands broke the surface with a muted splash and he surged up and into the air where he gasped in burning breaths.

Paiva choked and coughed, her body spasming violently. Renn held her to him, cradling her within the bend of his arm. They clung to each other as they caught their breaths, the waters spilling into the forest. A thousand heartbeats were shared between them before he looked about for Varloga.

He found the creature tearing into Viviel, crushing the beautiful flowers beneath them.

"Save him," he heard Paiva whisper. "Please save him."

He pulled them from the pool, setting Paiva aside to wilt

into the flowers. In one fluid motion he retrieved his pitted sword and swung it back.

Everything seemed to slow in that moment. Varloga lifted his snarling head from Viviel and turned it to Renn. Its features changed. Odrik reappeared, but Renn's sword was already swinging.

There was a spray of black blood, a flutter of white feathers. The force of the swing sent Renn rolling into the ground. For a long moment he rested, unable to lift his head to witness the damage he had done. White feathers fluttered to the ground around him, crushed flowers bleeding their scent into the air.

When he raised his head, time returned to its normal flow.

Viviel lay stricken on the ground, staring at the headless winged body above him. Blood dripped onto his chest and into his face. The body twitched, the wings jerked, then it staggered away as if looking for its missing head. Viviel surged to his feet and pushed it hard, toppling the twitching body into the Conjuring pool. He watched it thrash, then sink, rippling the surface and disappearing into the deep.

With that, its evil sank back into the creation from which it was born.

Viviel touched his forehead in the familiar gesture of warding off bad luck, then turned back to Renn. Renn stared at him in disbelief. He felt a great flood of emotion, a cleansing and a banishing of pain and hurt. He choked on a sob.

Lying in the trampled greenery was the head. Odrik's face stared at him, his jaw clacking open and shut, his black eyes staring coldly into Renn's soul. Slowly the shadows departed, diminishing until they were empty of every accusing fear and hurt. The face changed and there remained only a ghoulish monster in its stead. Renn shuddered a sigh and closed his eyes.

"Renn," he heard. Then Paiva was beside him, pulling him to his knees and cradling his face in her hands.

"Renn, you did it," she said. "Renn you are... you are a hero!"

"You *are* a hero," Viviel laughed. "Claim Varloga's head. Rise and you shall be followed."

"But I can't... I..." he floundered, his throat suddenly too dry to voice sound. "But the Spirits... they're gone. Who will save us now? Who will save man from himself?"

He found Viviel's golden eyes on him, emanating such kindness he felt it warm into his bones. "Man will have to save himself," Viviel smiled, dried tears staining his wolfish face. "Man will have to remember that there is great goodness in his heart and it is he and he alone who has the power to use it. Come. Rise."

"I can't," he begged.

"Are you afraid?" Paiva asked, and he looked up into her smiling eyes. Viviel's laugh echoed out into the garden, then the Incarnate turned and began to walk away. His fur seemed to melt from him, his shape receding back into that of a man. He stepped out of the crumbled ruins and into the woods, peering about into the lush greenery.

"Where are you going?" Paiva called.

"Let us return to the world of men," he said. "For we have our work to do, my beautiful Virtue."

— «» —

Maggra stared in disbelief as the Folka snarling at her, keeping her from crossing the threshold into the Vale, suddenly shrank back into the shadows of the trees. She blinked, trying to comprehend what had happened. Ulrig limped up beside her, his head bleeding into his white beard and staining it red. He peered into the trees and a smile broke over his face, then a laugh burst forth from his chest and echoed out into the forest.

A shape appeared from the woods, tall and dark with silver eyes. In his hand was the bloodied white head of Varloga, its maws slacked open dragging a snaked tongue in a grim tableau of death. The Folka backed away from him as he came, crouching low and hissing.

Renn raised the head to them, his heart hammering in his chest.

"I have slain your creator, your conjurer and master," he bellowed to the wisps of Folka. "You are nothing but shadows, bound to this earth through our fear. I banish you."

Renn watched as the Folka bowed their heads and slithered into the trees, dissolving like the shadows they were.

— «» —

Renn dropped his arm, feeling the weight of the dead thing drain the last of his strength. His head spun dizzyingly, his breaths came short. He looked down at his ruined body and wondered how much longer he'd be able to keep standing.

From behind him came Viviel and Paiva, walking through the trees together looking like they were more a part of the forest than human beings. Paiva's eyes shone green and gold as she smiled to Renn. Life sprang beneath every one of Viviel's footsteps and he left a trail of blossoming flowers in his wake.

Maggra felt the blood drain from her body. It left her knees weak. There was a claw tear in her chest, over her heart, from which she waited for the last of her life's blood to drain. She fell to her knees, her head bowed before this golden-eyed man that came forwards from the depths of the Forest.

"Wolf Father," she whispered. He stopped before her and looked into her struggling eyes. "I will die now," she said. "But can you help me? I want to remember the name my Mother gave me."

"You could stay," he said gently, touching at her cheek with his fingertips. Flowers spiraled up her legs and grew their roots into her wounds. She shook her head as tears fell from her eyes.

"No," she whispered. "Look at me. I am not worth saving."

He placed his hand over the top of her head.

"Every life is precious," he said. "Every life matters." He looked around at the others, the painted faces and the bearded faces, bleeding ones and ones in awe.

"Thank you," he said to them all. Maggra gasped as flowers and vines snaked up from the forest floor, winding around her body and closing over her wounds. In moments she completely disappeared beneath the flowery mass and everyone turned to stare in wonder. The flowers budded and bloomed, opening their petals to the sun, then one by one they wilted and their petals fell away like snow. Viviel bent his head and whispered to her, "Only you can remember your name. Only you can choose to heal."

For a long moment nothing happened, then the flowers began to wilt as if a sudden autumn had come. Petals fell away and within the cocoon of greenery Maggra rose, her wounds healed, her lifeblood restored. She gaped at herself, looking at the hands she spread before her, smoothed and erased of her painted pain.

Paiva gaped at her, for Maggra appeared renewed and beautiful. From her dark eyes she wept the last of her hurts and fell to Viviel's feet. "Thank you," she whispered both to him and the Forest, clutching handfuls of earth. Flowers and tender shoots bloomed about him as he went to every man and touched him, their wounds healing, their hearts filling with awe. The bodies of the dead were swept over with flowers, disappearing into the earth from which new life sprang.

Renn tossed the head amidst the Wildermen and watched as flowers blossomed about it from the ground. Then he sagged to his knees and drew in deep breaths, his body succumbing to its injuries. Paiva crouched beside him and took his hand as flowers swallowed them. His bones sang and vibrated with energies of the forest, the very magic he was a part of. When the flowers wilted Paiva swept them from his face, and he found his pains were gone. He drew in breaths of sweet air and ached with the beauty all around him, the beauty shining through Paiva's wide eyes into his.

"Thank you," she said to him.

"Where are the others Good Spirits?" Ulrig asked then.

"They are returned to the magic that made them," Viviel said. "They are a part of the Forest again."

"Then we must not forget them," Ulrig said and bowed his head. "We must not forget their stories."

Chapter 18

Yulin sat beside Lord Pratermora on his bedside. Gently he reached out and placed his hand on the Lord's shoulder and shook it. The old man shrunk under the touch, muttered something and turned his head away.

"My Lord," Yulin whispered low.

"Go away," Pratermora murmured. "No more medicines."

"No more medicines," Yulin promised. "Rennik is back from the woods."

"Rennik?" the Lord moaned, then he tossed his head and his face contorted into a pained frown. "Odrik," the Lord whimpered, and then was still.

Yulin sighed wearily and turned to look helplessly at a figure standing across the room. Viviel blinked his golden eyes at the Warden, then strode forward to take his place by the bedside. Yulin anxiously paced to the back of the chamber, clutching his hands behind his back as he was often given to doing when he was sufficiently worried.

Viviel reached out his wide, calloused hand and placed it over the Lord's chest. Pratermora drew in his breath quickly and tossed his head again, then his body spasmed and tensed, curling and coiling as if Viviel's hand was a hot iron. Then he was still again, a long, shattered breath expelled. Yulin watched anxiously.

Slowly Pratermora's eyes blinked open and shone blue. They were clear and without fog, they spun around the room and landed on Viviel. He blinked again, transfixed by Viviel's eyes.

"Your son has returned from the woods," Viviel said in deep, gentle tones.

"Rennik?" the Lord choked. Tears flooded his eyes and spilled down the lines in his cheeks. Viviel moved his hand to the Lord's brow, clasping it tenderly beneath his gentle warmth.

"What have I done?" The Lord gaped as memory flew back to him, "What have I done?"

— ‹› —

It had been nearly a week that the Wildermen had returned from the woods and news spread quickly throughout the Keep of what had come to pass in the deep of Grimenna. Bards, minstrels and heralds were dispatched to the villages and towns where they spread the news through stories and songs. People were taken aback in disbelief, others outrage. They cursed Ceitra's name and her dark spirits, rejoicing with hope for a brighter future with her gone.

Ramsi was sent from the Keep as sorry as a dog. His proud, good name was ruined, his red cloak stripped from him for life. Yulin resumed his station as Master Warden and the first thing he did, aside from hurrying to the kitchens to gorge himself on Bessil's cooking, was to give Viviel his double brand of Pardon. There was no ceremony, though the Lord signed his ledger and sent a troop of rangers to Quarrytown on the fastest horses in his stables to free Kess from the work pit.

Paiva would never forget the long wait. She and Aunt Bess sat on the steps of the entrance to the Keep watching Viviel pace the bailey square. The scorched tower watched over them from above and for hours they sat there, not wanting to miss the moment when Kess should arrive.

At last a horse cart came trotting into the bailey through the gates surrounded by rangers on dusty, tired mounts. In the back of the cart sat her mother, dressed in disheveled rags with a haggard, gaunt face. When her eyes alighted on Viviel, she threw herself from the cart and raced through the bailey, tears streaming from her eyes as she threw herself into her husband's arms. Paiva laughed and felt her own eyes whelm with tears. She ran up to her parents where she received a shower of love and joy. She could not recollect a single moment in her life that had ever been so happy.

Bess lurched to her feet and came round, where she received a warm, tearful embrace from her sister. After that Bess ushered them inside the Keep where they were given their own chambers and fresh clothes and servants to attend to their every need. Her mother chased the servants away after they had filled a tub with hot water and her father had helped her to undress from her soiled clothing. Paiva glimpsed reddened marks and welts in her mother's back, saw mangled, healing flesh on her legs and turned away with a sickened stomach. She remembered how Kess had drawn the hounds away in the qaurry; her legs were indication of how it must have ended.

Viviel touched his gentle hands to her hurts and her mother wept, then he bathed her in the tub. Paiva left them alone then, her heart hurting from the sobs her mother tried to stifle as her pain and hurts were washed away.

They slept together on a straw pallet by the fire that night, Kess with her arms over Viviel's great chest, her head against his heart. Paiva lay alongside her mother and played with her hair while they told her the story of what had come to pass. It was a long story and Paiva fell asleep with her face nestled in her mother's hair to the sound of her father's snores and the crackle of the fire.

She slept deep and with peace, waking in the morning to the sounds of horns blaring. Her father rose sleepily and went to look out the slanted window with a smile. The horns trumpeted over the Keep, ringing out into the surrounding farms announcing the Pardoning ceremony.

— «» —

The Great Hall was filled with every last soul in the Keep. People spilled out into the streets and gathered in thick droves. Their voices rang up, deafening the air with noise. Paiva sat beside her parents at a rough table dressed in the finest gown she had ever worn in her life.

A kindly group of maids had arrived that morning under direction of Yulin with armfuls of clothes. Her mother had helped her to pick out a gown, then helped her into it and fussed tenderly over her all morning, brushing her hair and plaiting it with flowers plucked from the Keep's own garden.

The dress was of a sage-colored silk, so soft and fine she felt like she was wearing a spider web. Her mother had chosen a dark green gown stitched with intricate designs and Paiva in return had helped to arrange her hair and weave it with small purple flowers.

Her father himself was dressed in newly cut brown breeches, a crisp fresh shirt with a patterned vest, and over his shoulders was cast a brown wool cloak with a wooden brooch. On his head he wore a wool cap with a long striped feather poked through it. Her mother had muttered about how she had not remembered the last time he had looked so handsome, for he had groomed his beard and washed the dirt from beneath his fingernails. He sat as fine and as handsome as a nobleman would, his golden eyes glittering beneath the dark curls on his forehead.

Bessil had put on a magnificent feast and spared no expense. The tables were laden with breads and roasted meats, sugared nuts and glazed fruits and every last fine wine and ale that she had ever stowed away in her cellar. She rushed around ordering her maids, blushing under Yulin's warm gaze that followed her wherever she went.

The Great Hall fell hushed as the Lord descended from his chambers. Paiva had not seen him since their return from the woods, but as she gazed at him now, she saw that a great change had passed over him. He wore his deep purple robes, the silver and gold chains draped across the sigil on his chest. His face was still gaunt and pale, but his fierce blue eyes shone with life. In them was every happiness of the world returned.

Varloga's head was presented to everyone. It sat impaled on a pike in the middle of the hall for all to admire. Yulin approached the high table and bowed low to his Lord. He wore a fine red cloak, and it was fastened over his chest by his silver star-shaped brooch of a Master Warden.

"My Great Lord of Grimenna, there are Wildermen here today whom are due for their pardons."

He straightened and looked to Pratermora, who raised his hand. "Bring them forth, Yulin. Let me see who it is who has come to claim this most worthy pardon."

Paiva watched as the crowd parted under Yulin's gaze towards the great hearth before which the dirty, ragged ensemble of the Far Reach gang sat. Renn rose from his seat and stepped forward as whispering voices floated about him. He lifted his head towards his father and stood resolute and still. Paiva's heart beat madly in her chest as she gazed at him.

"Come forward, Wilderman, like the Wildermen of old before you, so you may ask for your pardon," the Lord Pratermora said with a stern face. Paiva felt her heart leap into her throat as Renn stepped forward again. She did not know if Pratermora carried any residual resentment towards Renn. His voice was hard and empty, as though there was no joy for the return of a lost son.

She looked to Yulin who stood calm with a contented gleam in his eyes. He did not clasp his hands nervously behind his back.

"Come forward, boy, tell me your name," Pratermora commanded.

"They call me Black Renn," he said, his voice muted. Paiva did not take her eyes from him.

"And the name you wish restored to you?" the Lord asked slowly, his voice softening.

"Rennik... Pratermora," Renn said and held his father's gaze.

The room was hushed as Pratermora stared at him. His face was impassive, stern as stone. He reached for a silk napkin and wetted it in a bowl of water, then rose from his seat and came to stand before Renn. His blue eyes bore into Renn's silver ones, and his face became awash with sadness. Gently he lifted the wetted silk and wiped the dirt from Renn's face.

Renn closed his eyes against his father's touch, and Paiva saw him purse his lips as if to keep them from trembling. When he was done the Lord let the silk drop to the ground, and for a long moment he stared at the revelation before him.

"Rennik Pratermora," the Lord said softly, "I cannot grant you a pardon."

Paiva saw the surprise that started on Renn's face as his eyes flew open, his lips breaking apart as if he were about to protest. But then he shut his mouth and dropped his head, his eyes burning into the floor at his father's feet.

"I cannot grant you a Pardon until I am Pardoned first," the Lord said with emotion delved deep from his heart. "I ask you to forgive me, as a man and as your father. I have wronged you, and blamed you undeservingly. For that I am sorry, so gravely sorry. I can hardly find the strength to even ask for your pardon. I am so ashamed of myself to have fallen under the powers of... my own dark humors." Then he reached out and laid a hand on Renn's shoulders. Paiva saw a silver tear glimmer and fall through the air. Renn lifted his head to his father and smiled, his eyes liquid with silvery tears.

"Of course I forgive you," Renn whispered. Pratermora's mouth trembled, his eyes shining. He lifted his hand and clasped Renn's face.

"Thank you," he murmured, and bent his forehead to Renn's. When he drew away, his eyes were aglow with happiness.

"Yulin," he barked. "Cast the brand in the fire." The crowd murmured in excitement as Yulin shoved the long metal rod into the heart of coals. He returned with it when the end glowed hot and red, handing it to his Lord with a graceful flourish. Pratermora seized it and laid out his other hand in which Renn put his. He looked deep into his son's eyes and nodded his head.

"You are pardoned, for you have proved your valor and firmness in the dark of the woods. Welcome back, my most deserving son, Rennik Pratermora."

The crowd cheered as the brand sizzled into the meat of Renn's hand. He hardly flinched, and when the hot iron was drawn away, he stared at his burning mark of freedom and forgiveness. Viviel, Paiva, and Kess all watched proudly from their seats and raised their wine in a toast.

"To Rennik Pratermora, bravest man in all Grimenna," Yulin cried. Every last person in the room found a cup and raised it, spilling wine and ale down their arms as they cheered. Paiva raised her cup and thumped her eating knife atop the table, yelling as loud as she could in cheer. Renn cowered under the assault of noise, but his eyes glowed with happiness and his lips parted in a joyous smile. Pratermora drew him into his arms and clutched him to his heart.

"I remember you," he whispered to his son. "And I love you. As you are, no more or less."

Then Pratermora drew him to the high table where he was given a seat beside his father and served a platter of the choicest meats and breads. He sat there in his ragged, dirty attire looking like a wild crow beside an elegant swan. The Lord turned his attentions to other Wildermen then, each one coming forth to be thanked and have a pardoning brand scorched into their palms.

"Bear Jorn," Yulin called, and Jorn arose from the back of the hall to limp forward on his stooped crutch. He opened his palm to the warden and as the brand sizzled into his hand tears flowed from his eyes.

"You are pardoned," Yulin smiled, and clapped him firmly on the shoulder.

No sooner had his ledger been sealed and he had turned around to face the hall then he stopped short, frozen in his tracks. Paiva rose out of her seat to see who he stared at and found a group of people who had come forward from the crowd. There was a young girl with dark hair, clinging to a woman's arm who stared at Jorn like she was looking at a ghost. Behind her stood two young men, each one with tears glistening in their eyes.

"Sarsha," Jorn breathed, his face crumpling as he stared back at the woman. Slowly she smiled and tears poured down her cheeks. The young girl was the first to step forward, her face pensive as she took in the Wilderman before her.

"Father?" she asked.

"Yes, love," he replied hoarsely and then fell to his knee and opened his arms wide to her as she ran to him and threw her arms about his neck. It brought tears to Paiva's eyes to see Jorn's face break with such tenderness and love.

"You've come back," his wife wept and went to touch at his face and kiss his cheeks.

"Sarsha," Jorn choked. His two sons came forward as well. The crowd cheered for them and raised their goblets as Jorn leaned on one of his son's strong shoulders and was helped back to the fire.

When it was over and every man was accounted for, his ledger signed and sealed, and his name restored, the feast began.

Voices clouded the air. Minstrels struck up their songs and sang the brave young Lord's tale. Renn seemed to shrink back in his chair, overwhelmed by the magnitude of people gladly opening their hearts and pinning their newfound hope on him. His eyes wheeled around the room with a mild look of panic, until in the midst of the crowd they landed on Paiva. She returned his gaze and offered him a warm smile, and only then did he seem to relax and let go his breath.

The Lord raised his goblet of wine to the crowd and in a deep, reverent voice said, "Let us give thanks, to the Spirits of Old who have guided us. Let us give thanks to the forest Grimenna, our mother and provider."

Paiva saw her father's eyes shine as people raised their voices in thanks and in prayer. Viviel smiled contentedly and her mother reached out to grasp his hand.

"Let us give thanks," said Kess.

Soon the air became hot and stuffy with smoke and the mingling of bodies. In the midst of it all, Paiva saw Renn rise and slink away from the hall. He wandered away from the crowd, disappearing up into the tower.

Pratermora watched him go, then he lowered his drink and rose to follow.

— ‹› —

Renn skirted down the tall corridors, stopping when his shape reflected back at him in a window. He stepped closer, staring at the strange face that revealed itself to him. He felt the hairs rise on the nape of his neck as he studied himself, then reached up and touched the glass as if to somehow change or erase the mirrored image.

How he had changed. The last time he had stopped to look at himself he had been but a boy. No wonder his father had refused to recognize him. His face had filled in with hard lines and coldness, a face he did not want to belong to him. He turned hurriedly away from the revelation and climbed the tower, stopping to look out over the ramparts from which his brother had fallen all those long years before.

He stared down to the ground where visions of Odrik's death assailed him. He turned away with an acid taste in his mouth and continued upwards to the top of the tower where he stopped at the charred ruins of the trophy room. Slowly he stepped inside and found the roof to be completely burned away, some of the walls crumbled and split. A wind blew through and ruffled his hair, scattering ashes out over the sweep of land below. There was no trace of any Folka heads. They were burnt and turned to dust.

"Rennik?" a voice called out behind him. He gave a start and turned around in surprise.

"Father." His voice was raw, the word unfamiliar on his tongue.

"What is wrong?" he asked, coming to stand next to him and stare out over the sweep of land below.

"I can't stay here." Renn bent to scoop up a handful of ash. He rubbed it between his fingers thoughtfully and then opened his palm to the wind and let the ash blow away, hoping it would take with it his feeling of overwhelming panic. He stared at his hand, empty but for the swelling brand. He closed his fingers over it, and drew his hand away.

"I understand," Pratermora said. Renn smiled grimly, his eyes shining silver with the setting sun.

"Seven years I lived in the woods and was hated by all those people down there. Seven years I carried blame and a heart filled with bitter memories," Renn said.

"You are loved again," Pratermora confirmed.

"Just like that?" he asked. "You do not even know who I am. I am not the boy you knew."

"Stay with me, let me discover who you are," his father breathed. "I can't face this world alone. I have become old and feeble. I need you to guide me."

"That was Odrik's place," Renn said, flinching as he said the name aloud. Quickly he looked to his father to ascertain he had not upset him. "I am still a Wilderman in my heart. The Forest became my home. I did not want a pardon to come back here. I only wanted you to stop hating me."

"Go then," Pratermora said and lifted his hand to his son's shoulder. "I release you. Go find what it is you need to make you happy. I will wait for you to find it. And I will wait for you to open your heart to me so I can try to be a father again. I have learned, at long last, that is the only legacy I wish to leave behind."

He turned away from his son then and headed down towards the Great Hall. But he stopped short, a happy thought making him laugh out loud. Renn turned to him curiously, cherishing the sound of his father's long absent laughter.

"Did you hear?" he asked. "Yulin is going to marry my cook."

Chapter 19

When the Ibbies returned to Birchloam they found their homestead to be derelict. The house was hauntingly empty and lifeless, the eaves filled with birds' nests, the windows clouded over with dust. Kess cried out at her garden tangled with weeds and when she walked into the house she cried out even louder at the absence of their belongings.

Their flock of sheep had been auctioned off by Warden Lier along with many other implements from their home, but no sooner had they arrived safely back than the villagers began appearing at their door stoop to return what had been taken, giving it freely without reimbursement for the money they had spent to obtain them. Soon the pasture was dotted with sheep again, pots and plates returned to their places in the cupboards. Tools found their way back into the barn and books back to the bookshelf.

Not only did they regain their property but they were showered with gifts. Rorna and her father the miller appeared with a sack of flour and crushed oats and corn. Mrs. Switch arrived in their yard with a barrel of ale on her shoulder. She set it down quietly and looked at Viviel, then touched her forehead with a gnarled finger and smiled to him knowingly. The most kindest of gestures that left Paiva nearly in tears was when Jekka arrived with a brown dog on a tether. She had been helping Viviel in the barn when she heard the excited yelps and came outside to find the two standing in the yard.

Viviel's laugh boomed out as Jekka released Elki and the dog hurtled himself towards them, so overjoyed to be reunited with his master and home that he could do nothing but bark and run around in circles while occasionally stopping to lick their hands and faces.

"He's a good dog," Jekka said simply, her speckled eyes shining at them though her face was expressionless. "Guarded your flock until Ranger Lier tried to shoot him down. Then he skulked through the village looking for scraps until I took him in."

Paiva smiled happily to her and bent to scruff Elki's ears. When she looked up again Jekka was gone. Paiva hurried out of the yard after her, finding her already headed down the lane way.

Elki skipped happily beside her as she ran up to Jekka who stopped to look at her questioningly. "Jekka," Paiva breathed. "Thank you."

"You're welcome." A small smile crept over her lips shyly. She was tall, and upon looking at her with a fresh set of eyes Paiva could see she was truly Ulrig's daughter. She had his vaulted cheekbones and strange green eyes. She had a strange earthy beauty and serene manner, a sinewy, lean build with feet that turned slightly inwards as Ulrig's did. Her hair was darkly coiled and flew about her face. Her eyes were not as dark as Ulrig's, speckled as they were with flecks of rust. Their inner depths seemed to contain something brighter, more alive.

"I did not know your story," Paiva said. "I did not know your father was a Wilderman."

"The thing about secrets," Jekka said, "is that that the less you tell them the safer they are."

"You crossed the Panderbank, all by yourself," Paiva continued. "I want to know everything, if you'll tell me. I can't imagine how alone you have truly been all this time."

"That is kind of you," she smiled. "If you want to know my story just ask the Stones." She turned then and made to continue on her way, but Paiva followed.

"Jekka," she began again as she fell into step alongside her. "What about Renn?"

"What about him?"

Paiva blinked at her uncertainly, but Jekka's gaze did not waver.

"You must understand," Jekka said. "It was the same for my father when he was pardoned. He came back and found the clamor and busy flow of society too much. He was overwhelmed after spending so long in the slow pace of the forest being his own master. He might have stayed, if I had been more loving towards him. Instead I shunned him, and he crept back into the sanctuary of the woods."

"But you followed him."

"Once I realized the only reason he came back was for me."

"But Renn hasn't come back. He didn't even say goodbye."

"Patience." Jekka's eyes sparkled and she turned away. "Patience is also a Virtue. He may be the Virtue of Courage, but he is very afraid of this world."

Then she was gone, darting down the lane to leave Paiva staring after her.

— «» —

Paiva was patient. She spent long days in the pastures waiting for some sign of him or for news to reach her from the Keep of his return. It never did, and she grew anxious and irritated, wondering if she should not go into the woods herself to find him.

Her father came up to the fields to bring her lunch one day and he sat next to her on her favorite perch. "He'll come back," he said as he rooted through the basket and pulled out bread and a chunk of cheese.

"No he won't," Paiva answered bitterly. "He told me once, when we were at the top of Far Fall. He said he would never leave the forest."

Her father squinted into the distance at a flock of birds scattering over the treetops.

"Set a bird free and if they return they are yours," he said, offering her food.

"What do you think he's doing out there?" she asked.

"According to Yulin and Bess, there has been an uprising amongst the Wildermen. I don't know what Renn is doing, but I imagine he is out there with his fellows he left behind. Whether or not he likes it, he is probably the only man in all of Grimenna the Wildermen will respect — an ambassador of sorts, between the lowlands and the Wilderlands. Yulin has begun to call him the River Lord."

"How can they send men to the woods now? How can they earn pardons if there are no Folka to hunt?"

"Oh, there are still Folka, but they are not as terrible as they were. One by one they will be killed and then the Wildermen will have to find a new way to earn a pardon. Yulin is talking of implementing a new system. Instead of culling Folka they would be building, learning trades, hunting and gathering and learning to read, bettering them as men over all. We shall see what happens. The double brand of pardon may soon mean not that you have earned your freedom through killing a nightmare, but from becoming a better man."

"Wasn't killing a Folka meant to prove that?"

"Yes," he chuckled. "But killing is a ruthless and wicked act. Forgiveness should not be earned in such a way."

"What of the women in the work pit?"

"They will be treated better. Along with cutting stone they will learn other things. Word has it the Lord is rebuilding his tower, not as a trophy room but as a library. He has enlisted the Goddish monks to begin making him books with the help of the women from the pit. They will be scribes, not sculptors of stone. A much better way to rule the land, through knowledge and confidence rather than fear."

"And what of Maggra? What has become of her?"

"Yulin has informed me she abides in Morinvere now. Word has it Yulin plans on turning the outcasts into a work force to rebuild the old temple. Maggra has already begun. There may be a time when pilgrimages are made again."

She followed his gaze out over the hills and wondered what was transpiring amongst the Wildermen.

"He didn't even say goodbye," Paiva said.

"He didn't know how," Viviel returned. "They smothered him." She remembered all the bright colors and noises and people pressing in on him at the Keep.

"Did you know what he was, that night of Mummers-eve? Is that why you made him stay with us?" she asked suddenly.

"Yes."

"And how did Ramsi get your books?"

"After you left for the Keep, rumors began. I think they were started by Ramsi himself. His pride was wounded by us. The rumors called me a spirit summoner, alleged that I invoked dark things through my worship of the Forest. They started as whispers, then accusations began, until finally Ramsi had enough suspicion amongst the village to muster a warrant. He was looking for something to hurt us. You should have seen the contentment on his face when he procured my books." The Liers were disappeared from Birchloam now, having been shamefully disgraced. There was not a trace of them. Even the red curtains in the Warden's Quarters had vanished with them. Word had spread that they were headed to the Southlands, fearing they would be branded themselves if they stayed.

"Why did I never know who I was?" she said. "Why didn't you ever tell me your secret?"

"It was too difficult to tell you," he said. "It was too hard. I have never grown old, but I will with your mother. I have never had a child, I never bore new life into this world. You changed it all for me. I learned how to be human. And human is how I intend to stay. It is a good life. I knew my kind were fading and I wanted to die as a man, not as a myth. I learned I didn't need the worship of a thousand believers to be revered, and that is not what made life worthwhile in the end. It took me a long time to learn that all that matters is one true love, for it can build a whole world. I have you and your mother, that is more than I could ever ask for. That is all that matters in the end."

She leant her head against his strong shoulder and smiled, feeling blessed to know she was so loved.

— «» —

How many hours she sat at the top of her pasture waiting! She stared at the trees until they began to move and dance on their own. Her hope that Renn would one day appear drove her to worry. What if he had met some harm in the woods and was not able to return?

A chilled wind blew down from the hills, carrying with it the fresh scent of a dying summer. She rose from her perch atop her usual rock and looked out over the forest. It was changing, for the autumn season was beginning, and she feared that winter would lock the hills with snow and trap him across the river.

With nothing else she could do, she went up to the altar and fell to her knees.

"Grimenna," she whispered as she bent her head and touched the stones. "Great Mother, bring him back to me." Tears spilt down her face as her heart filled with longing.

"Make him come back to me," she prayed.

— «» —

Far off on the other side of the forest, Ulrig looked up from skinning a rabbit. He looked about the smoky cave, listening hard. Beneath his feet the stones were resonating, making his bones ache with longing. He ambled outside and stood atop Far Reach, looking out over the hills and turned his face into the wind, still listening.

"Renn," he called. A moment later Renn appeared from the horses below, wrapped warmly in his cloak against the chilled wind.

"Ulrig," he shook his head in mild humor. "You should see yourself, you look like a madman up there."

"Renn, it is time for you to leave here."

Renn frowned and looked at him hard, at his speckled eyes wide and staring over the trees.

"The Stones are whispering to me," Ulrig said. "They say you must go."

"Why?" Renn asked. "What is wrong?"

"Can't you hear her?" Ulrig cocked his head. "Can't you hear her calling you?"

Renn followed his gaze out to the winding river in the distance, his face softening.

"Always," he murmured.

— «» —

Winter was moving in on the hills before Paiva knew it. Soon the river would be frozen over and become uncrossable. Despite pestering her father constantly for news from the Keep, the only thing he could impart to her was that Yulin was busily cleaving together a new plan for the Wildermen who had threatened to swarm the river. In a missive he posted to them he said it was true that the one person the Wildermen truly respected was Renn, the great beheader of Varloga, who had quieted the uprise. Renn had requested rations and supplies from the Keep to see the different camps through the winter but Yulin had no clue as to Renn's future plans and stated only that he hoped Renn would come to his senses and realize he was pardoned and that there was no need to live in a cave and ride a filthy Berg any longer.

As the frost crept in, Paiva worried constantly over Renn, over what he was doing and why he had never said goodbye. She relived every moment they had shared and she could not understand what it was she had done to deserve being so cruelly forgotten. Just one word, that was all she longed for. She had the thought that maybe Renn would follow in Ulrig's footsteps, turning his back on the world of men altogether and becoming a hermit until the end of his days. To Ulrig the Forest was a woman, and Paiva wondered whether Renn felt the same.

The worst part about her pining was that she saw him everywhere she went. She would catch a glimpse of a dark figure out of the corner of her eye while she walked through the village and turn to find it to be someone else. She'd sit in her pasture and feel him watching her, but when she scoured the trees for him she found them empty save for the wind blowing through them. She had hoped the coming cold would drive him back to her, but he remained distant.

It was on a chilled evening when she sat on her favorite perch that his likeness appeared in the trees. She was so used to imagining him she almost turned away, but her unbearable longing made her stop and stare. Slowly his shape materialized, and despite furious blinking it did not go away.

"Renn?" she called timidly.

"Paiva," his call returned to her and confirmed his reality. Her heart beat so hard in her chest she had to grab hold of the rock to keep from falling off. She gaped at him, not knowing what to say or if she should dare to truly believe he was there. She leapt to her feet and ran towards him, coming to stop a healthy distance away where she continued to stare at him, wishing to somehow conjure the magic words that would keep him there.

"Renn!" was all she managed. "You know you are pardoned now, you can come out of the woods."

"It feels strange," he said, taking a step into the frosted meadow as if he were still trespassing. She stared at him, taking him in, and found that he had changed. He had acquired himself new clothes, which were already fatigued from wear. He wore a similar oilskin cloak she was used to him wearing, only it was not shredded and ripped about the hem. His hair was groomed, shining black like polished crow feathers and no longer as wild and knotted as a Berg's mane. His frame was still lean, but he was broader in the shoulder and his face had lost its gauntness. His nose was still bent, his brow still scarred, but his face was swept clean of dirt and weariness. It struck her then, that he was a truly handsome man. There was nothing boyish or un-grown about him.

"You never said goodbye," she said sadly as his pale eyes found hers.

"I have come at last to tell you—"

"You can't say goodbye!" she cut him off angrily. Her heart plummeted and she felt as if the earth would split and swallow her whole. "You said that if we ever returned to the world we would learn to be friends," she spat.

A sad smile crept over his face. "I also said I would never leave the woods," he replied as she glared at him. "I only wanted my father's forgiveness."

"You can't say goodbye," she keened.

He sighed, his eyes growing as cold as the frost as a sadness washed over them. "The Forest is empty for me now," he murmured.

"Are you going back to the Keep then?"

"No," he shook his head sharply. "Never there."

"Renn. I know this world has trampled you, but just stay long enough to let me show you there is kindness here. There is happiness and warmth. I will keep you safe as you kept me safe in the Forest," she said.

She wiped away her tears and looked at him sternly, watching as he tentatively took a few steps farther from the trees towards her. He looked back at the woods, as if it were a skin he had shed and was afraid to leave. When he looked back to Paiva his eyes implored her for acceptance and understanding, as if he were afraid she would send him back.

"I am in love with you," she said. "Renn, you are allowed to be loved."

His eyes swam with tears and he swallowed hard, unable to reply. "Birchloam does need a Warden," he replied softly when he found his voice.

Tears burst from her eyes then and she gasped a sigh of relief.

"Promise me you'll dance with me next Mummers-eve," she said.

He nodded. "I promise I will dance with you every Mummers-eve," he replied.

Her heart seemed to shatter into a million pieces then. She stepped forward and leapt into his arms, molding into his chest where the world suddenly took shape and made sense again. His arms folded around her and held her tightly against him as he buried his face in her hair and breathed her in. She clung to him, afraid to let go. His arms pressed against her back, drawing her in and upwards so that their faces met.

After a suspended breath, he took her mouth with a searing kiss.

She could feel the force of it, like the frost that burnt the ground with cold and cracked the Stones and mountains. It made her ache. She felt the breaking of the pain that had kept her waiting for him. Tears rose both from her happiness and her undoing as his lips moved across her skin and into her hair and whispered over and over how much he had loved her all along.

For long quiet moments after they simply held each other, listening to the rush of wind in the trees, reveling in each other's warmth. When Paiva finally convinced herself this was not all a dream, she began to laugh.

He drew his head back and looked down at her with a curious frown.

"Oh Renn," she smiled. "I always did fancy a man in a red cloak."

— «» —

About the Author:

Natasha K. Blazevic was born in Montreal and currently lives in St André D'Argenteuil, Quebec, where she has become a passionate beekeeper. She studied art for a year in college but she could not nurture her talent or interest there. She was much more interested in being outdoors. She fled to the countryside of the Quebec Laurentians where she apprenticed for a stone mason and cultivated her love of art and animals. She considers herself a student of life with a keen interest in the natural world. She hopes her book Grimenna can not only entertain and enchant readers, but can help to promote a green renaissance.